G. B. STERN

(1890–1973) was christened Gladys Bertha (she later adopted 'Bronwyn' as her second name), the second daughter of Albert and Elizabeth Stern. The family lived in Holland Park until the Vaal River diamond smash in which they lost their money. From the age of fourteen to twenty five, G. B. Stern lived in a series of hotels, boarding houses and furnished flats. She attended Notting Hill High School until at sixteen, she travelled with her parents to Germany and Switzerland and attended schools there. She then spent two years at the Academcy of Dramatic Art. G. B. Stern wrote her first play at the age of seven and her first novel *Pantomime* was published in 1914. Five years later she married a New Zealander, Geoffrey Lisle Holdsworth, but they soon divorced.

The appearance of *Twos and Threes* in 1916 brought G. B. Stern critical attention, but her most substantial and popular achievement was the series of novels based on her own family circle. The first of these, *Tents of Israel* (1924, published by Virago as *The Matriarch*), was followed by *A Deputy Was King* (1926), *Mosaic* (1930), *Shining and Free* (1935) and *The Young Matriarch* (1942). In 1929 Mrs Patrick Campbell starred as 'the Matriarch' in the stage version, co-written with Frank Vosper, and in 1932 the first three volumes were published as *The Rakonitz Chronicles*.

G. B. Stern's friends – who called her 'Peter' – included Noel Coward (with whom she selected the songs for *Cavalcade*), John van Druten, Rebecca West, Somerset Maugham and Sheila Kaye-Smith (with whom she wrote two books about Jane Austen). She continued to travel throughout her life: she spent five years in Italy and lived in New York, Hollywood, France, as well as Cornwall and London (where her home was bombed during the Second World War). In 1947 G. B. Stern converted to Catholicism, and wrote of this in *All in Good Time* (1954). She died at the age of eighty-three.

G. B. Stern's other work includes over forty novels, several plays, volumes of short stories, and a book about Robert Lo~~~ ~~~venson, in addition to five discursive and semi-~~~ ~~~ works. Virago will publish A *Deputy Wa*~~~ ~~~ ~~~ ~~~ming years.

THE
MATRIARCH

A CHRONICLE

G. B. STERN

With a New Introduction by
JULIA   NEUBERGER

PENGUIN BOOKS – VIRAGO PRESS

PENGUIN BOOKS
Viking Penguin Inc., 40 West 23rd Street,
New York, New York 10010, U.S.A.
Penguin Books Ltd, Harmondsworth,
Middlesex, England
Penguin Books Australia Ltd, Ringwood,
Victoria, Australia
Penguin Books Canada Limited, 2801 John Street,
Markham, Ontario, Canada L3R 1B4
Penguin Books (N.Z.) Ltd, 182–190 Wairau Road,
Auckland 10, New Zealand

First published in Great Britain as *Tents of Israel, A Chronicle*
by Chapman & Hall, 1924
First published in the United States of America as *The Matriarch*
by Alfred A. Knopf, Inc. 1925
This edition first published in Great Britain
by Virago Press Limited, 1987
Published in Penguin Books, 1987

Printed in Great Britain
by Cox and Wyman Ltd., Reading, Berks.

To

JOHN GALSWORTHY

PREFACE

SOME people are fascinated by a genealogical table; and I, myself, like to study the intricate relationships of a large family. But some are bored and bewildered by it. So to the latter I would mention that it need not upset their understanding of this story, in the very slightest, if they cannot follow the who-is-who of the first chapter. The only individual characters who are going to be important are those printed in capital letters for that very reason: the Matriarch, who is Anastasia, and her children and grandchildren . . . "the oldest of the oldest of the oldest of the oldest," as Toni described them.

I introduced an enormous amount of aunts and cousins and great-uncles and so forth, in that long first chapter, because I wanted to show Anastasia, and later on, Toni, against a crowded background, and not descended along a single thread. But Toni herself, and Val, and Maxine, the "younger ones," never bothered to know exactly *how* their relations were related. They just called them, in a lump, "the family"; or else classified them, casually, as "the Paris lot" or "the Vienna lot."

For this is partly a true chronicle.

G. B. STERN.

I am young, and ye are very old . . .
Great men are not always wise:
neither do the aged understand judgment.

THE BOOK OF JOB.

INTRODUCTION

G. B. Stern wrote five novels based on the colourful and picturesque Rakonitz and Czelovar families – and the odd Czelovar appears quite out of the blue in several of her other books too. She regarded the saga as something of a "Forsyte" chronicle: indeed she dedicated the first of them to John Galsworthy. At the same time the five novels are totally independent, and unlike the "Forsyte Saga", or indeed more modern chronicles such as Anthony Powell's *Dance to the Music of Time*, the family tree and the relationships change slightly from novel to novel, to the serious reader's intense irritation.

The whole is loosely based on G. B. Stern's own family, also called Rakonitz, who were not atypical of the period. For they were comfortably off Jews with interests in the city and in the jewel business, who came from varied places, including Hungary, Poland, Russia and Austria. Strange as it sounds now, in the days of the Austro-Hungarian Empire, those Jews who emerged from the tiny villages of Galicia and Bosnia gradually centred on the wealthy and cosmopolitan Vienna, retaining links and trading with other members of their families elsewhere in Europe.

This was the familar scenario for the Jews who had come to England in the middle of the nineteenth century, as G. B. Stern's family had. Their relationship with their families throughout Europe became of paramount importance: all the men travelled on business; they stayed in each other's houses; and they sent their sons to each other to learn foreign languages, or the skills of another business, or the custom of another country. The women travelled too, to seek husbands for their daughters, or to pay social calls on other members of the family. And it is this lost world which is recaptured so successfully by G. B. Stern in her "Rakonitz Chronicles".

Gladys Bronwyn Stern was born into this cosmopolitan
Jewish family in London in 1890. It was idiosyncratic, to say
the least. The character Anastasia, the Matriarch, was based
on her great-aunt on the Rakonitz side, whom she referred to
as the "Matriarch" in real life. But some of her own mother
comes out in the descriptions of her, particularly the extravagance and disregard for money. In a volume of belles lettres,
G. B. Stern tells how there were terrible rows in their house
when the Whiteley's bills came in. Her father would bellow
(men did, as she described it), and her mother would be
tearful. But the next month it would be exactly the same. Little
different from the Matriarch in that regard. The Matriarch,
and all the Rakonitz women, are obsessed with food – as were
G. B. Stern's own relatives – and particular dishes have to be
made for special occasions. The classic example of this in the
novel is a pudding of meringue and choux pastry cakes called
"Crême-Düten", which Anastasia continues to make well into
old age. On an ordinary Sunday, in the early years before the
crash, when the family comes to lunch, the main dishes are
made by the Matriarch herself, the recipes handed on to her
eldest daughter, and from her on to hers. It is a very Jewish
custom to treat recipes, and food, in this way. The fact that the
dishes are different from the chicken soup and bagels associated
with Jewish cookery in the United States merely indicates a
difference of back-ground and country of origin. The classic
Rakonitz menus are risotto with chicken-livers and raisins,
cooked in goose fat, or Hungarian goulash with paprika; or
open fruit tart, crisped up round the edges, with hot plums and
thin pastry filled with crème patissière.

But G. B. Stern's mother had not been like that. The other
women could make apfel-strudel: "Mother was the only one in
the family who could not cook at all." The others could make
clothes for their children – even though they did not need to –
and could go round to the butcher's to choose a joint. ("The
way Aunt Elsa bewitched her butcher was nobody's business!")
These were the women of G. B. Stern's background who, with
their efficiency and ability to cope with anything, people the
pages of the "Rakonitz Chronicles".

The Matriarch

Meanwhile, men seem shadowy figures, there only to pro-
vide for their women. When that is no longer possible – after
the Nong-Khan mine crash disaster – they either die or
commit suicide. In any case, three of them do not survive. But
the one who is left, Louis, sits and meditates in his study,
thinking he would rather be dead:

Suddenly it seemed to Louis' aching eyes as though the room were
full of shadowy women in black—Anastasia and Elsa; Susan and
Wanda; Eugène's widow; Gustava and Berthe . . . In a gust of
irritable fury he demanded of them where were their men? Why
could they not keep their men alive, and leave him alone? He wanted
to be left *alone* . . . They trailed past him in a procession. They
paused in front of him. They surrounded him. Rakonitz women . . .
No, he could not get away.

In G. B. Stern's own life, that same shadowy quality of the
men is observable. She married Geoffrey Holdsworth in 1919,
whom Rebecca West described as "her beautiful Geoffrey"
(letter to Sylvia Lynd), but the divorce followed fairly soon
after; and he was constantly depressed. Again according to
Rebecca West, "her husband has been greatly improved by
psycho-analysis" (letter to Henry James Forman 1923), but this
improvement did not last long. Those who were G. B. Stern's
close associates in later years described him as rather a pathetic
figure, whom G. B. Stern tried to avoid meeting or contacting
in any way. Some of them made their dislike quite obvious –
Rebecca West wrote of the couple: "I was very fond of G. B.
Stern, but I was not at all fond of her husband" (draft letter to
Gordon Ray, early 1970s).

Her closest male friends for much of her life were the
playwright John van Druten, and his friend Jack Cohen. They
used to spend summers together in the South of France in the
1920s and 30s. Rebecca West might be there as well, or
Pamela Frankau, or both. At that time Rebecca West called
G. B. Stern "Tynx", and later "Peter", the name by which she
became generally known. Her long friendship with Rebecca
was often difficult, for, in a vicious mood, Rebecca could be
appallingly wounding to the sensitive "Peter". According to
Freda Bromhead, G. B. Stern's secretary, she would often take

to her bed after receiving Rebecca West's letters. With her broken marriage, her desire to be thin (she talked of thin women with long cool necks), and her overwhelming need to be taken seriously as a writer – like Rebecca West – she was an easy target for sarcasm and anger. G. B. Stern was always surrounded by a group of supportive women, including her secretary of the moment. Many secretaries found her demands too great and left after a year, but Freda Bromhead survived the pressure for an astonishing five years, becoming a valued companion. (In 1939 she was called back in extremis, as G. B. Stern, who was in a nursing home, was too ill to correct book proofs herself.)

Veronica Poingdestre was also a good friend. She became the model for Diana in *Debonair*, whilst the character Judith, an "older woman", is based on G. B. Stern herself. Veronica's mother disapproved of their friendship, as does her fictional counterpart. In the novel the disapproval is marked by Mrs Poingdestre's actual expression, "We can remain perfectly good friends but need never meet again." In turn G. B. Stern did not approve of Veronica's marriage – and never saw her again. Such scenes were typical of the way G. B. Stern lived. For it was like that in her world, both in her childhood, with family quarrels interspersed with a gaiety of her mother's making, and in later life when her friends and close companions lived with high drama in the air.

It is this real experience of a dramatic, heightened sensibility which makes the "Rakonitz Chronicles" so believable. Many of the "Rakonitz" characters were alive when the Chronicles were first published. The "Matriarch" herself, the great aunt, was reputed to be "looking for Gladys with a gun", but softened as the book became a bestseller. Freda Bromhead recalls seeing the aunt sitting at the first night of the dramatised version at the Royalty Theatre in 1929, watching herself played by Mrs Patrick Campbell – and enjoying it. That G. B. Stern was not particularly fond of the "Matriarch" shows in the portrait of her in the Chronicles and in *Monogram*, her semi-autobiographical work, she is described as "too despotic".

Despotic Anastasia undoubtedly is, and the house, both

before and after the crash, revolves round her. She conveys part of that strength of character to her granddaughter Toni, who equally can stand up against the odds, because, in some indefinable way, there are more important things in life, such as "the family".

The Matriarch has no qualms about spoiling things for Toni when it seems appropriate to do so. Toni describes just how formidable and impossible Anastasia can be when she tells Danny how she scared off a would-be suitor of hers:

Look you, Danny—here was a handsome and eligible young man, of good family; a Goy, certainly, but that can be overlooked; and here was I, an eldest granddaughter, and a maiden of Israel. Here were things just in that promising stage when good intention should solidify; when, in short, the young man should be "approached" . . . Well, Grandmère heard hints here and there; you can't help hints getting through, and she formally sent for this man of mine. She granted him an interview! . . . She asked my man his intentions; she asked him what he was going to settle on me; she made enquiries about his honourable family, and told him a great deal more than was necessary about our honourable family . . . I gather that she was quite regal and magnificent, with about seven generations of Rakonitz forming up behind her, and the ghosts of the Uncles looming about the room.

This is typical of the Matriarch's extreme eccentricity – which she cannot judge – as is the assembling of the seven generations of Rakonitzes, for she is not to be trifled with by some non-Jew whose family claim absurd English antiquity! The Rakonitzes mock the "Englishness" of Raoul Czelovar, who marries a clergyman's daughter, and brings up his children in a cool, airy, English nursery way, but produces a third child, Helen, who looks more Jewish than any of the other children of her generation.

These characters reflect the views of their era. There was no embarrassment about being Jewish; it was something to be proud of, even if one did not practise the religion, and the family and all its ramifications were a source of great joy. These deeply European Jews, rich and secure in the late nineteenth and early twentieth century, were completely

different from the later immigrants of Jews from Russia and
Poland of 1880 to 1905, who were profoundly religious, and
had experienced an endemic anti-semitism which made them
far more sensitive to possible slights.

   With these Jews, the Matriarch and her friends have little
sympathy. They are "different" from them, and not "known".
Nevertheless an occasional one of that type creeps into the
family; Otto Solomonson for instance, who marries Henrietta
Czelovar, is nice, charming and acceptable as an individual,
but never part of the "clan" in the same way as the others. This
betrays a great deal about G. B. Stern's own background. She
freely confessed to hating the word "Jew" and was unwilling to
use it in the title of any "Rakonitz Chronicle". The first
volume was originally published in England as *Tents of Israel*.
She described herself as having friends who were all "Goyem"
(a curious mis-spelling of the Hebrew word Goyim, meaning
non-Jews), who had no "anti-Israelite prejudices", and
described Israelite as being a word of pride, for "a Jew can
cringe, an Israelite never".

   Yet to Danny, those "Israelites" are all wrong. They are
cosmo-politan, certainly, but they have no wanderlust as he
has. They are full of responsibilities, debts to be paid, meals to
be cooked, festivities and sad occasions to be observed as a
family. And Danny is no part of it, though he has lived with
them and been supported by them for twenty years and more.
In his need for freedom Danny pulls together the strands of G.
B. Stern's own ambivalence about her family. Did she herself
not break away? No Rakonitz had hitherto lived in the Albany,
or had a cottage in the country. That was not Rakonitz style.
But G. B. Stern did not share the bravery, even the foolhardi-
ness, of the character she created in Danny. She needed to be
settled, whereas he, and his father, Oliver Maitland, can not
keep still. They are un-Jewish in that regard. Unwittingly
perhaps, G. B. Stern put her finger on a characteristic of
central European Jews. Though experienced in travelling
through historical necessity, they did not like it. They settled
all too easily when they could. Such Jews put down roots, even
though they must have felt, subconsciously at least, that they

might have to pull them up again. They liked their houses in Hampstead and Bayswater, Ealing in poorer times, and Maida Vale. To them, the magic of travel for its own sake would have had no appeal. For a moment, the lovely Toni, granddaughter of the first Matriarch and with many similarities, is swept off her feet. But reality prevails. There are higher standards, more important things. She is, in the end, no wanderer.

Through her own practicality, her own Matriarch quality, Toni loses her love and her lover. In her attempt to keep him, she claims her English background. "I'm not a bit like Grandmère; not a Rakonitz at all. My mother was English, Susan Lake, and Hannah Lake, and George Lake, my grandfather. I'm like them – I'm a Lake – I'm not like anybody . . . You can't prove it" – Toni becomes terrified, betraying more than she knows or means in those few panic-stricken words. For she cannot escape. Her family, often unpleasant, difficult and demanding, has her in its grasp. She can never be free of it and is, though diluted and born in England, a central European Jew with the values of that now dead community.

Toni becomes the successful businesswoman, fulfilling in her way, in her generation, the role that the Matriarch had filled in hers. There is skilful writing in the parallels and differences between the two key Rakonitz women – and Toni is not yet a fully developed character. That remains for the next two volumes. But G. B. Stern saw family resemblances and knew the love that often exists between grandparents and their grandchildren. In a book that often lacks fully developed characterisation, the relationship between Anastasia the Matriarch, and Toni the young Matriarch, is delicately etched. It is never overdefined. It reads as if of G. B. Stern's own experience.

So much of this work is personal. How much of it is historical it is hard to ascertain. Many aspects of it are undeniably true. Still more are impressions of a childhood spent amongst very powerful people. Resentments remained – against the continental quality of it all, the loudness, the insistence on family duty, and on the superior treatment accorded to males. "Truda was one of those rare beings whom injustice made just, and she could never forget what she and Sophie had suffered long ago from Anastasia's overwhelming partiality for her sons . . . In [her own] home, it's the girls, and not always the boys and the boys and the boys, who are to be considered first." Is this the note of G. B. Stern's early experience? She had a sister, but no brothers. Or is it rather the reflection of an intelligent woman on the main social mores of her day? That we shall never know. Suffice it to say that *The Matriarch* is filled with personal and family recollections, of quite amazing detail, though the writing itself is occasionally clumsy, and the characterisation, particularly of men, leaves something to be desired. *The Matriarch* takes us into another world, long forgotten. It is not the world of Jewish memory that has become fashionable in American literature, nor is it. the world of Russia and Poland, the Pale of Settlement and extreme poverty – the world of Isaac Bashevis Singer and Chaim Potok. This is altogether different. There is wealth here, and gaiety. There is middle European style, and food in abundance. It is very un-English, and enormously attractive. But G. B. Stern, all the way through, retains her ambivalence. It was not where she wanted to be, but, like Toni in the book, she was honest enough to know that she could never escape completely.

Julia Neuberger, London, 1986

CHAPTER I

I

SINCE memory itself is but a picture-book, we can, if we turn back among the chronicles of the Rakonitz family, catch and loop into a frame, that sudden vision of Babette at fifteen, walking demurely with two of Napoleon's officers on her right, and three on her left. For when, in 1805, Napoleon came to Pressburg, he found no one in all the town who could interpret between the troops and the natives, until he heard of the young girl, Babette Weinberg, and her marvellous gift of languages, and gave orders she was to come to the camp, morning and evening. Imagine the horror of Babette's mother; the indignation of her father! Napoleon's messages became more respectful; he quite understood the objections, and would send, as invariable escort, five officers; the child should not go through the streets of Pressburg without protection. Strangely enough, Babette's parents saw safety in five officers, and so we get our picture again—Babette, very much envied of her friends, who, to be sure, began to see some use in the study of languages, after all; pretty Babette in a broad-brimmed hat tied under her firm little chin; straight, high-waisted bodice and wide skirt—I think it must have been green—black shoes strapped quaintly over her white stockings, and just that dangle of the scarf over the back in a half-moon from the elbows. It would be pleasant to know whether she kept her eyes primly downcast, or whether she chattered gaily to her escort; and by what caprice she selected the arm on which she leant. Five of them, a straight row of ten white trouser-legs, grotesquely long and tight, broken only by Babette's green gown. She found the red and yellow coats very dashing, no doubt, and boasted of them afterwards to her friends, Carlotta, and Minna, and Lili.

1

I cannot clearly see Babette at the camp among the raw-tongued troops; only afterwards, in the evening, in her comfortable home, being questioned anxiously by her mother : " And I hope you have remembered, my little girl, that you are promised to Simon Rakonitz, the son of your father's old friend; and that, though it is an honour to be chosen for what you are doing, yet the French army will move on and go away; and that—and that—" she has not yet asked what is truly troubling her mind, and Babette's blue eyes are still hidden under their lids. It is so queer that she should have been given blue eyes, and a straight, almost impertinent, nose. No one would have guessed her race if it were not for the address in the ghetto, and the surname so recently purchased— Weinberg, " wine on a hill "—Babette's father was a wine-merchant growing his own vines.

When old Ladislas Weinberg died, a year or two later, and his wife stoutly went on with the business—and, good fellow, how anoyed he would have been to know that she was so very much more competent than he !—she kept open house, as she could well afford; so that when the peasants came to Pressburg for the fairs, and to sell produce and grapes for her, she commanded mattresses to be spread on the floor of her great hall, where they could sleep, to save them the expense of going to an inn; and she gave them a good dinner, over which she presided, a large hospitable figure, with spreading flounces of silk, and an elaborate cap on her modish arrangement of flat curls. This is the moment to catch sight of her, carelessly spilling a glassful of wine in a red stain across the cloth, so that her guests may not feel uncomfortable if they should clumsily stain the cloth afterwards. A very great hostess, this mother of Babette; and Anastasia Rakonitz, who stands midway between the old family and the new, granddaughter of Babette, and grandmother of to-day's Toni, she too has been famous, all her life long, for hospitality, unchecked by every sensational rise or fall of her fortunes.

For Babette is married now; Babette and Simon Rakonitz—already they sound like ancestors; already we can see them, as hereafter Derek and Maxine and Iris

saw them, during their three meals a day; a comely old
lady and a genial old gentleman, in heavy gold frames,
hanging on the dining-room wall. But Babette could
not have felt very solidly an ancestor, as a frightened
child of seventeen, waiting in a state of ridiculous
innocence for Sigismund to be born; and her thirteen-
year-old sister, lent to her for company, was so very
much more innocent, that she rushed to the window and
shouted: 'fire.' . . . and thus, fantastically, the young
gentleman was born with firemen in attendance. I wish
we knew what costume firemen wore in Pressburg in the
early years of the nineteenth century, for then we could
have visualized them being indignantly shooed from the
room by Babette's mother or Babette's old nurse, who
must surely have arrived by then to take charge; and, indeed, I cannot think where Simon, her husband, could have
been—tending his grapes, perhaps? (he, too, was in the
wine business)—yet one could have understood better
his absence at the birth of Rachel, the fourteenth of his
children, than of Sigismund, the first. One of the firemen, himself a father, threw a kindly look back at the
girl in the great canopied bed, under the big pillow eider-
down. . . . Everybody was scolding, and little sister was
weeping because she had made such a silly mistake, and
Babette's blue eyes were frightened, and the doctor
said " Na, na, na ! " . . .

II

Sigismund, Ludovic, Daniel, Andreas, Eugène, Lena
. . . and then the Rakonitz family moved up the Danube,
from Pressburg to Vienna. There is a tribal feeling
about the manner of their travellings, and of their
settlings. . . . The history of the Israelites was just at
that time shaping and hardening in Hungary and Austria;
and it was Simon who had first won for the ghetto folk
the right to vote in Pressburg, and had founded their
first good school. But even then, Pressburg was just
beyond the outer gates of Vienna; the gates of Vienna
itself were still closed to the Jews; and only under pre-

fence of being attached to and in the service of some Austrian nobility high in favour, were the Chosen People allowed to dwell within the town. It is easy to imagine, however, that when the careless young Austrians wanted money they were ready enough to announce almost any eligible family as in their service. So the Jews came up the Danube from the east, lingering for awhile in the small Hungarian villages, and there picking up and proudly bearing their first surnames, a privilege only recently awarded. In this fashion had Simon's father chosen to be known as Rakonitz. Indeed, it must have been awkward, if picturesque, to have been accosted for so many generations as 'Simon, the son of Nathan, the son of Abraham, the son of Simon.' . . .

The words 'tribe' and 'Jew' and 'ghetto' carry an inevitable significance of greasy ringlets, hooked noses, and ancient fur-trimmed gaberdines; of a dark archway opening on to a huddle of dark houses; and of swarming dark children, complete with business instincts of how to get the better of the Gentile. But it is to have been misled from the start, to form such an idea of the Rakonitz personality. The distinctive feature which has slipped down from generation to generation of the family is a pair of bright blue eyes under a queer haughty twist of eyebrow, a straight delicate nose, and a mouth which is lifted at the corners into a crescent, so that it seems to smile even when it is unsmilingly in repose. The Rakonitzes do not live in a huddle; in fact, there is no record that they have ever been housed otherwise than spaciously. And as for their business instincts, there are no good careless fools like the Rakonitz men have been; fools, absolute fools!—generous and extravagant on the swooping up-curve of their fortunes; plausible optimists on their heavy dramatic plunges down. Nor is there much inherited melancholy about them; heavens, how Babette could laugh! And how Anastasia, Sigismund's eldest daughter, could make the room brilliant with her wit, her diverting anecdotes with herself figuring as buffoon! And Haidée of the next generation, and Toni of the next, their instincts flew straight to pleasure, as

the arrow hums towards the gold—that special lightness
and brightness of pleasure which old Vienna created best
of all the cities of the world. They did not bother to sit
and brood over their persecuted race, nor to mourn for
so much longer than was necessary the subjection to
Pharaoh or the betrayal of Esau. The Rakonitzes were a
gay family, with waltz tunes in their blood.

III

. . Sigismund, Ludovic, Daniel, Andreas, Eugène,
Lena, Albrecht, Grethe, Isidore, Rachel. . . . And then
Babette, still mourning for the four who had died, feeling
that the faces of ten children round her table were still
too few, adopted the two orphans, Karl and Léon, of
Simon's late partner, Konrad Czelovar.

And now, at Paul's birth in 1832, here is Babette, a
grandmother! How much more often we talk of Babette
than of Simon; how much more often we shall talk of
Anastasia than of her husband Paul; of Toni than of her
brother Gerald. And yet, in a typical chronicle of the
Israelites, it would be taken for granted that the girls
did not count at all; they are not recognised; they do
not have their places in the synagogue, nor are they seen
at funerals; officially they receive no names; if they give
birth to a boy who will grow into a man, they have ful-
filled their destiny in the only possible way. But later
on, when you have heard more about the adventure of
being a Rakonitz, or, indeed, a Czelovar or a Bettelheim,
whose names intertwine so confusedly with the Rakonitz
genealogical tree, you will recognise why I have called
them the very topsy-turvydom of Jews. It was a family
of women bucaneers. They were thrown forward, and
the men receded a very little bit into dependence.
Matriarchy—and Anastasia was to be the Matriarch of
all the family. It is time that Anastasia, Sigismund's
daughter, was looped into a picture. . . . For she was
born in 1835. And six months later she was suddenly
missing.

For two days her parents were frantic about her, and

sought her everywhere. It seemed incredible that a child of that age, with her nurse and her perambulator, could be so completely lost; still more incredible that she should have eventually been found where one expects to find the family prodigal after he has come of age and wasted his substance on riotous living. . . . Yes, peacefully, drunkenly asleep at an inn on the road that led out of Vienna towards Semmering.

. . . "Anastasia's nurse had abundant hair, and dressed it beautifully "—Truda, telling the story, in after years, to Toni and Val and her own Maxine, always put in that little bit about the hair, in just this place. " But she was very wicked to have taken the baby to the inn, and to make her drunk so that she should keep quiet, and after-wards to abandon her !" And yet, glancing at the future of Anastasia, one cannot help feeling that she knew what she was about, and that her fantastic, rollicking, arrogant career was even then in her system, groping its way towards a first assertion of self. If her mother had watched her very carefully while she gurgled and crowed with other Viennese babies during the few days following her spree, it is quite likely that she would have seen Anastasia boasting, slapping herself metaphorically on the chest as a three-bottle baby.

She grew up a great favourite with her grandmamma Babette; even after other grandchildren, Simone, Felix, Dietrich and Maximilian, were born in that tall, old house looking on the Danube, Anastasia still continued the favourite. Simon and Babette lived, as a matter of course, in the same house as their eldest son Sigismund and his wife, who had been Olga Bettleheim; one of the tough Bettelheims, bringing their special quality of long life to strengthen the Rakonitz fibre. The Bettel-heims were so unreceptive of death as to appear almost uncanny to their more vulnerable contemporaries, as they swung merrily along for ten and fifteen and twenty years beyond their three-score-and-ten, and gave no sign of weakening. True, Olga died early, but she was killed in a carriage accident. Her sisters, Hermina and Gisela, reached their hundreds.

Sigismund's younger brothers, Andréas and Eugène, were soon to be spreading away from Vienna towards other capitals, Madrid, Cairo, Paris and Constantinople, like spokes from the hub. But Ludovic, the only Rakonitz who was not a nomad, faithfully married a real Viennese little lady, Wili Taliman, and vowed that nothing would ever make him move away from where he could see the spire of his beloved Stefanskirche. They had all contrived, however, to be still in Vienna for Daniel's wedding, the first in that family; and for Sigismund's, three years later. Then must have been great festivities; any casual disposal of such occasions was contrary to their tenaciously clannish instincts and love of merry-making. Much laughter, united with great doings in the kitchen; gallantry, and kissing of ladies' hands, and luscious tears of sentiment. Grandfather Bettelheim travelled up from Constantinople, where he sold amber. And large cinnamon cakes were baked, and a Pflaumen-torte as big as an island.

IV

Ludovic and Wili took a summer-house at the Semmering one year, and all the brothers and their wives, and, of course, Simon and Babette and their still unmarried daughters, Lena and Rachel, were invited to come too; and they lived on different floors, and ran up and down to see each other. It would have been unheard-of, in the earlier chronicles of the Rakonitz tribe, if friends had been invited, and relations ignored. Maybe relations agreed more felicitously then, than now; at any rate, there were peals of laughter and clear, high voices in that house on the Semmerung. Eugène was the special butt of their amusement—Eugène, the gay bachelor brother, who used to come home every night very late, but always swore that he came home early, and that they were already in bed. . . . Now it happened that Wili, Ludovic's wife, had been ordered by her doctor to suck raw eggs, pricking them at each end; and one night, when the young dandy stealthily let himself in and stealthily walked upstairs, crack—crack—crack— All the doors opened at the sound, and a lively, pretty, young sister-in-law was standing at each, dark curls and mischievous sleepy eyes and a candle held high : " Eugène, Eugène, do you know that it is two o'clock? " . . . Broken egg-shells all up the stairs, and spread around the feet of the hero of too many revels, as he leant, somewhat dazed, against the balustrade, feeling rather foolish, too, at being thus caught out in his escapade; not far from anger, and perhaps a little too far from sobriety; and yet, being a Viennese (and he must have looked a true son of the Biedemeyer period, in his long, tight pantaloons, his cambric frills and double-breasted white silk waistcoat) he cannot but have blended with his annoyance, a whimsical appreciation of the charming picture they made —Olga and Wili and Lisa—disarrayed and triumphant.

And yet again Eugène, in Constantinople now, some-what wiser, but still a scapegrace, boasting to a white-haired old Greek, of some transaction in mother-o'-pearl which he had just completed; but the old man shook his head, and said slowly : " Young man, you are in too much of a hurry. You should take to smoking cigarettes of your own making; and if you are offered a parcel of precious stones, take out your tobacco-box and then your cigarette papers, tear one off and put some tobacco in and roll it and re-roll it and then stick it down; get out your matches without any hurry, young man, without any hurry, and light the cigarette and take three puffs—and by then give your answer . . . and you will find the merchandise will be cheaper." Thus Eugène was made free of the East . . . and settled there, and married Chryse Stefanopoulos, and did not come back—no, not even for Grethe's wedding, nor for Lena's, to the con-sternation of his mother. And no more was heard of Eugène . . . till forty years later, when Neil and Sylvia Czelovar, leaning from the window of their London nursery, saw a pale, shabby little old woman in black ringing at the front door bell; and saw her go away an hour later, most astonishingly, with a bottle of wine under each arm; and were told by their mother that it was

9

their Tante Eugène from Athens, and that they were not
to ask silly questions. Neil was rather surprised that she
did not look more like the statue of Pallas Athene on the
Acropolis, of which he had seen pictures.

Andreas also slipped into legend, and took no more part
at Rakonitz weddings, nor at Rakonitz funerals, nor at
those supreme affairs when a Rakonitz or a Czelovar or a
Bettelheim reached the age of seventy and was not yet
dead. Indeed, most of the women would have thought it
shame to be dead at seventy—a slur on their vitality.
The men died earlier. It is a fact, in natural history,
that the female spider attains to the closest of all possible
unions with her mate, by gradually absorbing and
swallowing him; about the Rakonitz happy marriages,
was the same effect of complete oneness. When they did
not marry each other, or a Czelovar, or a Bettelheim,
thus ravelling relations into a tighter and more intricate
tangle, then the tribe of whoever was not a Czelovar nor
a Bettelheim, dropped out and ceased to count; and the
intruder himself, when he spoke of "the family," meant
that unwieldy bulk of Rakonitz. "The family" to Wili,
for instance, never meant the Talimans. Never.

Andreas went to Spain; and his only touch with the
Rakonitz children of a future generation, was when Val
got hold of a story, less tragic and more grotesque than
the swift tableau of Tante Eugène and her bottles, that
a nephew-in-law of Andreas, Pinto Panja, was exhibiting,
in his capacity as professional showman, an idyll of
connubial domesticity from Burmah: "King Theebaw's
Hairy Family." Val was immensely delighted at the
thought of the unique connection between herself and
the Hairy Family, and she drew a series of spirited
sketches for the benefit of Danny and Toni, showing how
the various members of Rakonitz would behave on
welcoming the Hairy Ones to London; especially Uncle
Maximilian, whose nickname was le Grand Seigneur, and
who was so tall and aristocratic, and had such a straight
and delicate nose. You know, the family *were* proud of
that nose. . . .

But Babette—and we are back again in a room of the tall old house by the Danube, where Simon smoked the meerschaum with the amber mouthpiece, of which Grandpapa Bettelheim had sold so many, and his wife knitted in the other armchair by the big black stove—Babette mourned heartily over the defection of Andreas and Eugène; and told Anastasia, sitting dutifully beside her, long tales of their good looks, and their talents, and that gifted quality about their pranks which made them different from all other boys' pranks. She did not own to her grandchild what she knew well enough herself, that Andreas and Eugène were of weaker material than her daughters Grethe and Lena and Rachel, and of weaker material than herself. She did not say it, partly because Simon was sitting there too, and it was her duty to uphold the prestige of man, whatever she was secretly aware of to the contrary; and partly because she had never quite forgiven Grethe and Lena and Rachel for being girls; and also she thought it unnecessary that 'Stasia, aged twelve, should learn to exalt her aunts above her uncles. Anastasia marvelled that Grandmamma should be so persistent in mourning. She could not see ahead, of course, to a little oval picture of the future, slipped in, by accident, among these miniatures of the Rakonitz past. . . . Anastasia herself, looking startlingly like Babette, and with the same obstinate upcurving lips and deep-set blue eyes, imperiously ordering off young Danny Maitland, her grandson, Sophie's boy, to South America on a wild-goose chase after his errant uncle Ludovic, who had not been heard of for at least six years, but who, of all Anastasia's children, happened to be the one most indispensable to her happiness. . . .

During the day-time, Sigismund's children loved their home on the Danube; they could run about and pick up tiny shreds of amber and opal; and, without telling their parents, sell them to passers-by for a few kreutzer, and buy plums. But at night the high rooms were gloomy, menaced from the corners by tall iron stoves; the chairs

and windows heavily upholstered in plush; every chair
antimacassared; every bed a cave. It was curious from
what solid, sombre, settings glittered those jewels the
Viennese held most precious : wit and elegance and lightness of heart. The long double windows were seldom
open; and mostly looked out on courtyards which were
in themselves rooms without a ceiling; but the curtains
remained nearly always a formidable barrier between
inside and outside. Babette and Simon had reached the
age where they talked a lot of warm sentimentalities about
comfort and peace, and their grandchildren around their
knees. Unfortunately for them, the end of their long
string of children was still lively; Isidore and Rachel,
their two youngest, had by no means consented to quiet
obedience; in fact, Isidore's reluctance ever to go to bed
at all before dawn, might have been a premonition of
what next year would bring, of sleep and sleep and eternal
sleep for him. How the Viennese, of all people, must
have hated to die, when there were balls at the Hofburg;
and riding down six straight miles of Prater; supper
after the opera at Sacher; and when, every first of
May, the beautiful Empress drove round the Ring-
strasse wearing a white dress as a sign that Spring was
there and that it was time to wear white ! . . . But
Simon and Babette sat in front of the stove, with
Anastasia between them, winding her grandmother's
wool; and they wondered why young people could not
be content.

Came a ring at the door, and loud knocking; and
Babette laid down her work and said : " Du lieber Gott !
but who can this be at such a time of night? " and
Simon, who was a little deaf, said that he had heard
nothing and that she was full of fancies. " I have heard
a lot of moving about for the last hour or two," said
Anastasia, " bumping and bustling—there goes Friedel
to the door." The old man-servant, in slippers, shuffled
down the stairs, and along the stone hall, and a minute
later threw open the doors—

. . . And the truth was that Isidore and Rachel had
sent out invitations for a surprise ball for that very

night, and here were the first of the guests, Ottilie and Adèle, two such pretty girls, delicately holding their lacy handkerchiefs by the middle, letting the corners drop from a bent wrist, smilingly conscious of their blue and white brocade party-dresses, full skirts and short puffed sleeves, their hair festively arranged, with fringes of grass that hung down each side.

The grandparents, caught in their homely employments, rise in consternation, chairs pushed back, mouth and eyes open, full of welcome and hospitality—yes, but—but—these dresses? Ottilie, who was a little the older, apologises charmingly, shyly—they had not worn their very best silks because Isidore and Rachel had given them such short notice. . . . More ringing at the door, more and more guests! Anastasia, who unwittingly had assisted the conspirators, by keeping Grandmamma entertained and at her stories while the ballroom and buffet were being prepared, was now sent in a hurry, pirouetting and skipping with joy, to fetch Sigismund and Olga, Ludovic and Wili, and the culprits, Lena, Isidore, and Rachel. But it was unfair to blame Lena; she had disapproved; she told Babette so at once, whereat the old lady replied tartly that her brother Isidore was perfectly entitled to give parties whenever he wanted to, and that she liked plenty of young people in the house. And here were the musicians on the doorstep, in mufflers and mittens, carrying their heavy cases; here was the wine being carried up from the cellar. Isidore had seen to it all. More than thirty couples already swaying to the magic of Schubert and Strauss— that Johann of the 'Blue Danube.' And Babette, suddenly young again, and secretly rejoicing, being scuffled into her black moiré with the lace fichu, fastened grandly by a brooch large enough to clasp pieces of hair belonging to Sigismund, Ludovic, Daniel, Andreas, Eugène, Lena, Albrecht, Grethe, Isidore, and Rachel, and of those four who had died. . . . A most overwhelming brooch, more treasured by her than even the signet ring which Napoleon had left her in recognition of those daily promenades with the five officers of his camp!

VI

Four years later, and little Anastasia, who had twirled
gaily with the rest, in her short skirts, curls flying, eyes
a brilliant blue under that peculiar Rakonitz twist of
eyebrow, was demanding her father's consent to her
marriage.

"You are too young," thundered Sigismund, but
without very much conviction, for the semi-Oriental idea
still prevailed, that a maiden in her first bloom was a
maiden ripe for marriage. Twenty-two and twenty-
three were anxious ages; a daughter of twenty-four unmarried, and the parents became feverishly uneasy;
twenty-five, and she was done for—on the shelf—without hope. But what really disturbed Sigismund, was
that Anastasia should have dared to choose, instead of
waiting until he should choose for her. And then, to
face him herself! It was unheard of. Where were all
the slow and formal preliminaries? Where was the
young man's father, with courteous approach, and
careful enquiries as to settlements? Where, in fact, was
the young man? *Who*, in fact, was the young man?

Then a shock awaited Sigismund. The young man's
father was playing dominoes at the coffee-house round
the corner; it was his own brother Daniel. Anastasia and
young Paul, first cousins, had fallen headlong in love.

Sigismund was a sensible man, but with a fierce and
autocratic manner. His sense foresaw disaster in such
a marriage, his autocratic manner forbade it, without
deeming it necessary to give the reason. Anastasia, his
eldest daughter, who at sixteen was confident, as she
still would be at sixty, that she could manage her father,
her grandparents, her uncle Daniel, the whole household, the whole clan, all the Czelovars and the Bettelheims, and Maria the cook into the bargain, Anastasia
defied him. She was going to marry young Paul, even
though he was her first cousin, whom she had only met
once since he had been grown-up! . . . The girl was on
her hands and knees, a blue cloth bound tightly round
her head, polishing the parquet floor; the young man in

his heavy travelling coat, just back from his counting-house in Egypt, stood in the doorway, his feet very much in the way of her brisk movements, hopelessly infatuated at first sight; suddenly she looked up; the two pairs of eyes are ridiculously alike, as they meet; and the two long obstinate chins; they might have been brother and sister. . . .

"How funny!" mused Toni, coming across photographs, in the old family album, of Paul and Antasasia at about this stage, "to fall in love with somebody so awfully the same as oneself!" . . .

Anastasia carried it through. It took her a year; and each scene she had with her father was like a crisis in Greek tragedy, so fierce and eloquent were the speeches, and so universally comprehending the past and the future of Rakonitz, reaching back three and four and five generations, and pointing warningly forward to Anastasia's problematical grandchildren and great-grandchildren. Councils of the entire family were called; or, at least, of those branches still in Vienna. Anastasia's mother should have raised her voice dramatically at these councils, but she had died two years ago; so that Sigismund might have pleaded with his daughter, had he not been too proud, that there was no one, if she went, to look after his household, and to look after his other children, Felix, Simone, Dietrich and Maximilian. Little Maximilian was a delicate child and always weeping, but I doubt if Anastasia would have stayed in her course for that; though when, seven years afterwards in Paris, Paul wanted to celebrate a stroke of financial luck by giving her a pearl necklace, she asked instead that Maximilian, as a present, should be allowed to come and live with them, at her expense, and be trained to enter Paul's business; a proof that there was nothing hard and cold about Anastasia, nor anything lacking in sentimental devotion to her family. Nevertheless, she went her way, and nothing stopped her, not even disaster. So, to the wailing of her aunts, Gisela and Hermina Bettelheim, who had married Czelovars, uncle and nephew, she lengthened her skirts, rolled up

her heavy dark mane into a sagging net between her
shoulders, and announced her engagement.

In a year she was still Anastasia Rakonitz, but she was
Paul's wife, and so entitled to wear, at seventeen, a
bonnet that would cover her back hair, and that was
to be bought in Paris.

But, hearing that her beloved Anastasia was going to
live in Paris, Babette decided, for Simon and herself,
that they would give up their rooms in Sigismund's
house in Vienna, and go to Paris too, where Babette's
daughter Lena was already established, with her husband,
Jules Dupont, and two children, Berthe and Rosalie.
Except Albrecht, all Babette's children were married
by now, and zig-zagging about the world; Grethe, long
ago, to Enrico Salsoni, of San Remo; Rachel, the
youngest, had made a brilliant conquest on the very night
of the surprise ball, and was now the Countess
Yanoshaza, and had gone back down the Danube again,
past Pressburg, where her father had been born, to the
Castle Yanoshaza outside Buda-Pesth.

Simon was a simple, kind, good-tempered man, with a
broad, jolly face, and as much ever-present admiration
for his wife, Babette, as all five officers of her youthful
romance could have had if compressed into one. He was
looking forward, as eagerly as a child, to their residence
in a different city, in a different country; though quite
willing that Babette should travel ahead with old Maria,
to meet Anastasia and Paul, and find a flat.

Cholera broke out in Vienna, and Simon was one of
the victims.

VII

Sigismund was now left alone in the house by the
Danube, with his four remaining children. He was
lonely, and all his relations said to him encouragingly:
"Now, Sigi, you must look for another wife, who will
be clever at managing those wild children of yours; who
will look after little Max's chest, and reprove Felix for
pertness, and, above all things, keep prudent watch on
Simone with the young men, for there will be a pro-

cession of husbands for her to choose from in three or four years from now." And then Sigismund remembered how, when Olga had still been alive, he had gone on a business trip to Trieste and Venice, and how the glass-manufacurer, Antonio Civrian, had taken him to dine at his little palazzo just above the Rialto, and had introduced him to his five lovely daughters. . . . He had thought even then, with a pang of regret, how exciting it would have been to have paid court to one of these; to have gone to his wedding in a gondola; and then to have brought her proudly home, and shown her to all the Rakonitz tribe in Vienna. But Olga had to be remembered; Olga was a worthy wife—the Bettelheims were all worthy wives. Sigismund shrugged his shoulders and went home. Now, urged to re-marry, he wondered whether, by a stroke of good luck, any of the Civrian daughters were still single and in their father's house. He was not particular which daughter; he never thought of them apart, only as five, dark and shy and lovely; living where the water rose and fell on the doorstep with every tide from the Adriatic. He went back to Venice, and found only Clementina left, who was neither the youngest nor the eldest, but perhaps the most timid. She was quite ready to fall in love with this splendid autocratic Sigismund Rakonitz. His forty-five years were nothing to her, and she was delighted when she saw the four good-looking children, Felix, Simone, Dietrich and Maximilian. But it was not long before she herself became the child of the house, petted and bashful, and very much submerged by the Rakonitz will, which was like an overbearing torrent. Her own baby son, Louis, took after Sigismund as well, though with something of his quiet little mother's sweetness. Her step-children were not sullen and rebellious, as is usual in tradition, just as she was by no means the cruel stepmother who tries to exalt her own child at the expense of the others. They used to tease her, and recall lively anecdotes about her absentmindedness; their favourite story told how she went out one Saturday evening with her husband to the Graben; he very tall and upright and protective, and she a little dark thing with hesitating step, cuddled close against his arm. She could never get quite used to traffic that rattled on firm cobbles instead of gliding soundlessly along canals. He left her outside a tobacconist's shop while he went in to make a purchase; presently he came out again; she tucked her hand beneath his elbow and trotted happily off beside him. Presently she said, wonderingly: "But, Sigi, why don't you talk to me?" . . . and there the adventure might fittingly have begun, of the little Venetian lady and the quite unknown gallant, tall as Sigismund, who had happened to be the first to come out of the tobacconist's. But when Clementina suddenly realised with a gasp that she had paid a strange man the compliment of taking a walk with him, instead of with Sigismund, she dropped his arm and fled. "But what did he *answer*, Mamma, to make you notice that he wasn't Papa? That is what you never tell us. Is it too dreadful to tell us? Felix, look, she is blushing!" You can imagine Simone, her vivid face one flash of mischief, pursuing poor Clementina endlessly with this question. "*I* should have waited to see if he was elegant and amusing!" Simone would assuredly have waited. At sixteen, and seventeen, and eighteen, she was the most beautiful coquette in Vienna; so spoilt as to be heedless of blame. When she sat in a chair and imperiously commanded her little cousin, Laura Czelovar, to brush out her red-gold hair, Laura would have to step back further and further, till she stood at the very end of the room. It was the hair of a princess of fairy-tale—the great shining wave and fall of it, touching the floor when Simone stood up, though she was tall and carried her head high. Romance follows red-gold hair; and at her first Industriellenball, when the Emperor and the Royal Family walked once in solemn procession through the rooms and then retire, she achieved the triumph of dancing with the Emperor's younger brother, who lingered behind with the populace. . . . If this sounds incredibly the pretty-pretty story of the merchant's daughter who married the prince, remember that in three ways it wandered from tradition:

for Simone was not modest as such heroines almost
always are; how could she be modest, when the very
coachmen of those smart little fiacres that drove at such
a careless pace through Vienna, used to beg her to give
them the honour of driving her, for nothing, wherever
she wanted to go? What courtiers even the coachmen
were, of this fatal foolish nation of Austrians! There
was style and finish and delicate compliment in the way
they handed her in: "Küss die Hand, gnädiges
Fräulein"—then an agile spring on to the box, a flourish
of the whip, a look of merry scorn directed towards the
other fiacre drivers who had been too late with their
offer, and away went the two horses, with ' the beautiful
Simone Rakonitz ' sitting behind, certainly more insolent
and more arrogant than either Cinderella or Beauty or
the Goose-Girl, whom her career might otherwise have
resembled. But again a difference; Simone danced once
with the Emperor's younger brother, but he did not
send round his herald in the morning; nor did he marry
her. He merely succeeded, as her father said, in
stuffing her head with silly ideas, so that she refused
suitor after suitor, convinced that they were not good
enough. When she was twenty-one and twenty-two, they
began to get fewer; and at twenty-three the crowd had
thinned so visibly that her aunts began to warn her that
she might leave it too late, until there was no choice at
all. But still Simone laughed, and looked contemptuous,
and mocked the good men who, unlike the Emperor's
brother, were eager to marry her. At twenty-four and
twenty-five she began to be secretly alarmed, although
her red-gold hair was as wonderful as ever; and at
twenty-seven, an old maid, and on the shelf, she suddenly
grew impatient of waiting for the peerless parti; and with
outward thankfulness, but sick with disappointment, she
accepted, as her betrothed, Karl Czelovar, of the same
generation as her father, and a very worthy man, with
wrinkles; and all the aunts chattered in relief: " God
be praised, I thought she had left it too late!" . . .
And this is not quite the end of the story of the beautiful Simone Rakonitz, whose red-gold hair touched the

ground when she stood; for six years later, she lay dying
of fever in her great canopied bed; the big specialist was
called in; he said that nothing could be done, listened for
a moment to her imperial ravings, and then he added
simply : " But she is quite right; with that shining mantle,
she *is* an Empress ! " From which we can guess what
had been running on and on, always, in the dreaming part
of Simone's brain. She died . . . and there is a moral to
all this, but we can leave it to her daughter, Haidée, and
her grand-daughter Val, to discover; and, if they wish it,
to apply. I believe Haidée, also, left it too long; and as
for Val, she did not bother whether she left it or not.
They were neither of them as beautiful as Simone, but
Iris, who was Anastasia's youngest grandchild, was said,
by crossways inheritance, to have the same red-gold hair.

VIII

In the year 1868, in Paris, Babette was sitting down,
fair and square, eyes bright with curiosity, to her first
meal of ham.

And this, though it came near the end of a series of
adventures which began with five of Napoleon's officers
to the escort of one maiden, was no less adventure to
Babette Rakonitz. At seventy-eight, the relish for
romance and experience still oozed from her, young and
fresh as resin from the pine in Spring! Anastasia and
Paul, Lena, and Lena's two daughters, Berthe and
Rosalie, stood around her in solemn expectation, for this
was an occasion. Babette had been, all her life, dutiful
in religious observance. She had not been able to keep
her children to it, and her grandchildren still less, but she
herself had punctually gone to synagogue; had kept the
Jewish feast-days; above all, she had never, never eaten
food that had not been kosher killed and kosher prepared.
Since they had come to Paris, and after the death of old
Maria, the shopping had been entrusted to Françoise, who
had now been in their service for nearly fourteen years;
but it happened that Babette and Anastasia wanted
suddenly to countermand an order, and had followed

Françoise to market; unseen, they had watched her
bargaining at the stalls; listened, and realised with horror
that for nearly fourteen years she must have been bringing home and cooking for them unkosher food, putting
the difference in price in her own pocket.

Babette took the blow with typical fortitude; she was
damned, that was certain; she had broken the Law; she
did not belong any more to those chosen and set apart.
"Well, well," said Babette, philosophically, "at least I
might as well try now the taste of this ham that you have
all told me so much about!"

Babette ate a large plateful of ham, and pronounced
it excellent.

She lived to enjoy ham for another year. If she had
lived until 1870, she would have seen the Franco-Prussian
War and the Siege of Paris, and, after that, London.
One feels strongly that Babette and London would have
liked each other. All the Rakonitz women were happiest
in Cosmopolis. Imagination cannot easily picture them
in a setting of brown ploughed field on a whipped grey
morning after storm. Instead, spacious drawing-rooms,
with parquet floor throwing back the glitter from the
Venetian crystal candelabra, brocade hangings, and a
polished grand-piano—these were more natural than
nature to Babette and her descendants. They scattered
from Vienna, certainly, but always to other big cities,
capitals of the world; Paris, Budapest, Constantinople,
Venice, London—Anastasia was the first Rakonitz in
London. The doctor had told Paul that the siege would
mean no milk for the five children, of whom Sophie was
still a baby, and three of the other four, very delicate.
Very delicate; highly-strung, and weak in morals. . . .
Sigismund, who was still in Vienna, was the only person
who might have frequently said; "I told you so" to that
self-willed daughter who had insisted on marrying her
first cousin. But even then, Anastasia was incapable of
admitting it, even silently. What she did was right, and
what went wrong with it was accident. Moreover, she
was one of those lucky beings who did not fritter energy
on regret or self-reproach or any futile form of might-

have-been. Those were little twigs that catch some at
the skirt and hamper the feet, but she swept them on with
irresistible force.

Maximilian, whom Anastasia had more or less adopted,
remained behind in Paris with Paul. Felix, Sigismund's
eldest son, joined them in business; and, a little later,
Dietrich. Paul Rakonitz was a dealer in precious stones.
The Rakonitz tribe was instinctively attracted to the
trading of gems, if trade they must, though they would
have preferred to collect them, in a dilettante spirit.
Eugène and his mother-o'-pearl; Grandpapa Bettelheim
and his amber; even the children of Sigismund, bartering
their specks of opal, picked up on the shores of the
Danube, all had a natural feeling and quick eye for the
good and bad points of a jewel still unpolished and in
the matrix. Paul did very well. He did still better,
with the help of his young partner, Maximilian. They
specialized in Burmese and Siamese rubies. This was
before the Burma Ruby Company was formed in 1889;
and many queer persons, natives, and soldiers of fortune,
came to the firm of Rakonitz, to sell, or to have their
treasure valued.

Once again, and for the second time, a fever for change
broke out in the family; Sigismund wrote from Vienna
to say that he and Clementina, with their children, Louis
and Wanda, had also decided to move tribally on to
London. There was news, in his letter, which caused
Anastasia to break into little cries of ecstasy and
surprise : actually, her Uncle Albrecht, nearly fifty years
old, was to be married, and to her little cousin, Elsa
Czelovar !

"You remember Elsa, don't you, Paul? Such a
coquette even as a baby ! She had a dimple just under
her left eye, and because she was always smiling, it
always showed. I don't envy Albrecht, if she is still the
same coquette. And more than thirty years younger than
he ! You will see, that means trouble ! And Papa says
they may settle in London, too ! That would be fine.
You and Albrecht might unite, when you are able to
move your business over there. Do you remember, Paul,

when they wrote to us about that famous carnival ball, where Elsa climbed out of her room to go with the artist, Fritz Roya? And when she sent that conceited old fool, Llandini, a lock of horsehair, and said it was hers, and that she was dying of love for him, but that she must not give her name because she was royal! I shall be glad to have Elsa in London. And Papa too, of course," she added, much more doubtfully.

Their flight from Paris was by the last train, in cattle-trucks, and the Prussians shot at them as they passed. Anastasia collected all the refugees around her; they drew comfort and reassurance from her witticisms, her merry contempt of the enemy. Soon they had all told her their life-stories; and were, in turn, made free of the best Rakonitz anecdotes, illustrating the family daring, their comical absent-mindedness, and the abnormal length and thickness of their hair. She told them how to manage their babies and their futures; and they helped her with her own brood of five. Such viands as could be gathered on the train were brought to her to dispense, and in her own inimitable way, she transformed the journey into a gracious reception and " at home."

Because they did not know where to go in a strange city, a business friends of Paul's had given them the key of his bachelor house at Hammersmith; so, of all the emigrés who were pouring into London to escape the siege, Anastasia and her family were the only ones who knew where to go on arrival; and their cab was followed by a long procession of other cabs, whose drivers had all been blankly told "Amèresmit" by the French families, echoing Anastasia. And that is how colonies begin in West Kensington!

IX

The story of the next twenty-four years cannot be told in little pictures. Nor why, down a street of tall grey houses by the sea, a woman was blown, staggered and tousled by the high wind, one arm roughly gripping on to a baby, while with the other she supported herself

from lamp-post to wall. Clouds were tossed across the
moon, torn apart for a few seconds, spilling enough
light for the wayfarer to discover that she was clinging
for a moment's rest to the very house where Sophie
Rakonitz lived in Plymouth, after she had married Oliver
Maitland. The front-door bell pealed so loudly as the
woman from outside tugged and frenziedly tugged at it,
that it could have been heard from several yards up and
down the black deserted street. The baby began to cry;
he was only a fortnight old, and he disliked the rain which
slanted maliciously into their very shelter under the
porch, while they waited. . . .

CHAPTER II

I

SOPHIE's pathetic longing to impress her mother, dated from when she was quite a little girl, and realised that Anastasia's pride was all for Bertrand, Ludovic and Blaise; it reached its climax in Blaise. Sophie was in the house, like something unconsidered, which had been dropped and never picked up again. She was a morbid child, with sick, cross ways that might have alarmed Anastasia had not her attention been so fixed on Blaise. Sophie soon gave up hungering for love; her dreams took an odd turn; if only she could impress her mother! She watched Anastasia and studied her till she realised the one way in which she could be impressed; not by anything personal that a daughter did; the boy, the son, the male, was all that mattered. If Sophie were the first of her children to have a son, surely then her mother would admire her, spoil her even a little, too; talk to her as though she were present. Sophie pictured herself standing with the fierce, hot rays of her mother's vivid realisation beating upon her, till it was a shock whenever she was drawn back into the reality of neglect. . . .

"What! Sophie with a little boy?" So she imagined the news brought to her mother; "*Sophie*? But that is splendid! I must go to her at once. No, Blaise, I have no time for you. Sophie will need me. To think that the youngest of you all should give me my first grandson" . . . And then, suddenly conjured into Sophie's presence: "But we must take the greatest care of you, my darling. To have brought a boy into the world, yes, that was worth doing. Now, tell me exactly all you feel about him. We'll make plans together, you and I. I have told the boys that they need not expect me home,

24

not for months "—Sophie's dreams always allowed her
limitless time with her mother, she who now was never
granted more than a few irritated moments when she
was ill, or if her new frock did not fit her. She had
queer little wisdoms of her own, this Sophie, moulded
out of queer little experiences. She was quite sure, for
instance, that it would be no good, and a mere waste of
time, making futile attempts to divert Anastasia's
favouritism away from Bertrand, Ludovic and Blaise,
and focus it on herself, before she had this baby son to
show for justification. She was sure of this, without
trying. Another child might have plucked persistently
at the vagueness which was not aware of her; might
have carried things and fetched things with ostentatious
readiness; traded on sickliness; thrown arms around a
reluctant neck; or produced samples of diligent needlework; but this shy, unwanted Israelite child did not
squander energy on delusions. The only possible fulfilment for her was fixed in her mind . . . till it almost
lay faintly outlined in her cradling arms. She did not
read much, nor play games, nor romp with her brothers.
Truda was the housewife of the two sisters; and thus
gained a certain amount of Anastasia's critical com-
panionship while baking a cinnamon cake, or polishing
to a glitter the heavy embossed silver for a dinner-party.
Down in the unnoticed twilight, Sophie crept about, and
longed and longed for her son. It was dreadful to be
only a girl if Anastasia Rakonitz were your mother;
she would hate to inflict girlhood on any infant of hers.
A boy . . . a boy . . .

II

Perhaps from sheer ardent desire, or perhaps because
of the Oriental heritage which causes girls of her race
to ripen early, Sophie at sixteen glided into sudden
beauty, with the rich tender promise of an exotic flower
that, grown in a too shadowy corner, has lost its colour
but kept its velvet. Yet Anastasia continued perversely
blind to anything that concerned Sophie. She would

rather that either Blaise should have been her youngest,
which is next best in position to the eldest, or that her
line had gone on and on after Sophie's birth; four more
splendid boys, perhaps. Truda was indispensable for
domesticity's sake; but where was the sense, so
Anastasia's checked instincts argued, in Sophie and no
more after Sophie? Truda was strong and good-
looking; Sophie was plain and weakly; that was all the
difference she beheld. So, indulging the boys, planning
for them, building up her house and her entertainments
and her friendships so that all should ultimately benefit
the boys, Anastasia missed seeing the sudden help which
nature had lent Sophie to fulfil her stubborn purpose.
From sixteen to seventeen, for just one year, Sophie,
brushed with soft flame, might have reflected glory on
her mother. And with dark eyes steadily fixed on the
swiftest way to make up for her cheated childhood,
Sophie accepted the very first man who offered himself.
There was something really sinister about this mournful
intensity of hers; her ironic smile declared that she knew
exactly what she was about. A dash of inconsistency,
of youthful caprice, would have been so refreshing in
Sophie; had she been vainer, even, of the amazing spell
that she, from sixteen to seventeen, cast over Oliver
Maitland and the other suitors who trooped up behind him,
too late! But she took the first, steadily impatient to get
on and on to the baby boy, Anastasia's first grandchild.
Why, supposing Bertrand should marry first, or Truda!
Sophie was only grateful that men were so easily
attracted by her look of warmth and glow half-lost in
duskiness; such glimmering specks of gold as remain on
a coppery vineyard in Autumn, when the afternoon light
has lain across it, and left it, mysteriously quenched,
yet mysteriously burning. . . .

If she did not bear a son who was also Anastasia's
first grandchild, she determined to kill herself; it would
be no good going on! No, Sophie was not a normal girl;
indeed, Anastasia should not have married her first
cousin. . . .

And Oliver Maitland, of all men, for Sophie's husband.

Not only a stranger, and a Gentile, but, from the point of view of Rakonitz, such a ludicrous stranger! The only person, so far, whom they had failed to knit into the closely woven Rakonitz web; who raised unmagnetic substance to Anastasia's magnetism. An Englishman, and what was known as a profligate, without any sense cf family or any power of attaching himself permanently; an artist by temperament, although not overmuch by virtue of work and creation; but carrying all the suspicious attributes of an artist as they were in the late nineteenth century. It seemed to him that he *had* to own Sophie, could not deny himself this luxury, because for one incredible year she was so beautiful.

It was very soon over. It was over before any baby son was born . . . and during eight years Sohpie slowly lost hope; hope dripped away with a melancholy plangent sound of water from the eaves. During eight years Sophie saw herself losing her beauty, losing Oliver. . . . At the end of that time she sat with a lost dream, and knew she was barren, a last blessing from Anastasia's happy marriage.

Her mother apparently did not notice that Sophie was not having children. After all, Sophie lived at Plymouth, and Anastasia in London, and this was the period of the Rakonitz high prosperity. She forgot, even, to let Sophie know when her brother Bertrand married Susie Lake. They all forgot to let Sohpie know; she had so very much dropped out, and as she had never been very deeply in, this was easy. Truda corresponded with her for a year or two after her marriage, but as Anastasia entertained more and more lavishly, there was less and less time to spare from making cinnamon cake, gulas, and spiced risotto, and those special Crême-Düten, of which old Maria had handed down the secret recipe to Anastasia, in their kitchen in Vienna.

The Matriarch first began to assert itself in Anastasia, when she insisted that her eldest son and her eldest son's wife—poor, pretty little Susie Lake, who had so longed for a home of her own—should, as a matter of course, dwell with her in the same house, sharing her table and controlled by her wishes.

Bertrand was usually called ' Bertie,' for this branch of the family, rapidly anglicizing, had assimilated with their usual ease the slang and habits which Ludovic and Blaise brought in from their English school. He was a large, loose-limbed person, genial as his great-grand-father, Simon; inheriting, too, a dash of his Great-Uncle Eugène, that dandy of the Biedemeyer period. How easily a man of fashion leads us up and down the ladder of the periods! At one moment we know him as a "beau"; at another as a "toff" or a "masher" or a "nut" . . . Bertrand Rakonitz was, undoubtedly, a swell. So had been Eugène; and Leopold Josef, in Vienna, Anastasia's cousin, a hero with whom Simone had danced and Elsa had flirted; so was his son Franz, last of the Rakonitz dandies to wear Imperial Austria's uniform of the 12th Hussars, light blue jacket, white shako, and silver buttons; so was Raoul Czelovar, of the same generation, in Budapest; yes, and his sister Haidée, too; both Simone's children were dandies. And now the superlative dandy and grand seigneur of them all, was Maximilian, that little snivelling, weak-chested lad whom Anastasia had adopted because she knew that he so irritated their father, Sigismund.

Bertie Rakonitz was too lazy to compete seriously with Maximilian; though it is possible that this personality of his was assumed, because his sub-conscious instinct knew that, even as a strong man, he could not stand up to his mother, and therefore it was better to have the reputation of giving in because you were too indolent for combat, than because you were worsted in combat.

But to Susie, brought from the outer world of a pleasant English suburb into the very Rakonitz stronghold itself, into the house of the Matriarch, life was a tragedy and a bewilderment. Susie had anticipated, with shrewd philosophy, how existence ought to have shaped itself after marriage : husbands had their rights, and were sometimes irritable, but still you loved them, and your friends had to put up with the same burdens. And then, of course, you could not expect the tradesmen's books to fit exactly into the household allowance, not at first, anyhow; still, you would learn how to manage, and there was always Mother to consult. And you had to be tactful with your husband's relations, who, naturally, would come to see you fairly often, perhaps even as much as once a week. Mothers-in-law—Susie had heard of difficult mothers-in-law, but never of a mother-in-law in the least like Anastasia Rakonitz ! A home and children and Bertie, and a few normal troubles—she looked back, now, to these visions, with absolute wonderment at their simplicity. Instead, she was given a large room, heavily furnished by more exotic and profuse taste than her own, on the top floor of a house resembling some foreign palace within, with its antiques used as though they were commonplace; heirlooms thickly clustered about with anecdotes less conventionally romantic than broadly ludicrous; treasures brought from distant cities, not *via* the medium of shops, but by real people—real relations; dark, heavy furniture, and chandeliers that were a thousand dropping crystals that swayed and reflected light; portraits of ancestors. . . . No wonder Susie marvelled how such a fantastic caravanserai could still manage, from the outside, to look almost like every house in Granville Terrace. Susie was not mistress of this house, though she was often told, and especially on arrival, that she was as welcome as though she had lived there all her life, and that she must look on it as hers, and not mind if an old woman who liked to be with her children still kept in it some relics and a few bits of furniture. This was Rakonitz hospitality, well dashed with sentiment. The " old woman " was Anastasia, at the age of sixty, in full blossom, at the very height of her mental and physical powers, brilliant, tireless,

despotic, at the apex of the family triangle, drawing up
for consultation and management all the family affairs,
big and little, as they stretched outwards to a broader
base. Two of her brothers and her half-brother, Felix,
Maximilian and Louis, were making fortunes in rubies
and sapphires; and none of them were married. Their
profound admiration for Anastasia led them into asking
her to be hostess whenever they entertained, which was
on a grand scale. She also figured as hostess at their
sybaritic house-parties; and their business friends usually
went away considerably impressed by Madame Rakonitz,
her gracious manner, her edifices of diverting talk, for
she built up talk like a clever craftsman. Anastasia could
still get drunk, as on the road from Vienna, fifty-nine
years ago; but now it was with the sheer exhilaration of
hospitality. If she could not have entertained, she might
as well have died. To Susie, used to a few friends to
tea, or a modest dinner-party of four neighbours and the
vicar and his wife, living in the Matriarch's house was
like living in the midst of an eastern bazaar and a dog-
fight—the dog-fight represented by that tribe of Rakonitz,
Czelovar and Bettelheim, who either lived affectionately
in the same road, or round the corner, or in Paris,
Vienna and Constantinople; from all these places using
the Matriarch's house as headquarters, where their
quarrels were brought and decided; where births, deaths,
marriages, engagements, bankruptcies, artistic triumphs,
and—yes, herein lies the amazement!—and Christmas,
were still celebrated with the same rollicking fervour and
clatter of tongues as in the old days under Babette's
supervision. Susie thought the family was boundless in
its members; even if one of them cleared a temporary
space by dying, it was quickly crowded up again by at
least three new babies, and the arrival of an entire family
who had been forgotten somewhere in Central Europe
until now, but who were cousins by marriage two
generations removed, related over again on the Bettelheim side. Their store of reminiscences and messages
and greeting, made them heartily dear to the Matriarch.
She liked further opportunities for exercise of power;

and further reassurances that the family was strong, that the family prospered, and that they continued to recognise her as the eldest daughter of the eldest son of Simon and Babette.

Susie had a brisk, determined little mind of her own; she was no frightened fool; but she could not stand up to Anastasia. Instead, she begged and begged Bertie to take her to a home of her own, however small, a home which was not full of people she did not know, talking about other people she did not know, in a variety of foreign accents. To Susie and her type, the Rakonitz fluency in languages was an added horror. She could have sympathised with poor forlorn foreigners, and been a perfect darling to their helplessness; but when the poor foreigners talked English just a little quicker than herself, and she had heard them talking French and German at the same rate, and perhaps Italian, and Viennese and Parisian argots, with occasionally a word of Yiddisher slang or solemn Hebrew benediction, they loomed in her eyes as rather superhuman.

"*Can't* we move, Bertie? You promised we should, the night before last."

Bertrand laughed, and stretched his long sprawling limbs, and petted her.

"Yes, but Bertie, your mother " . . .

"Oh, mother's all right so long as she has her own way," quoth Bertrand, easily. "All girls find it difficult to get on with their mothers-in-law."

"It isn't a question of getting on or not getting on," Susie replied shrewdly. "*She* gets on!"

"Why, you are quite comfortable, aren't you?"

Susie sought round for some definite cause for complaint, however small. ' She gives so many parties," at last.

"My dear little girl, I thought you liked parties. Why, we met at a party!"

"That's different. And nothing in the house is mine."

"Except your husband!" Bertrand broke into cheery laughter.

She might have replied :"Not even that," and with truth.

"Besides, mother lets you fuss about with the furniture and things, doesn't she? Dust the china and arrange the cushions and—I told her that you would naturally want to have a fair say in all that, if we shared the house."

"We are *not* sharing the house," cried Susie, desperately. "It's her house, and we are allowed to live in it."

Bertrand screwed in his monocle and began to look irritable. Deep down in his heart he knew that Susie was right, but he preferred to keep up the illusion of "women bickering" in the same way that he kept up the "easy good-nature" idea about himself. And what rubbish was Susie saying now? "—She likes to have us here, I know that, but it isn't because she loves us; it's because if the house weren't full of us, there'd be no one for her to order about. Truda feels just the same, I know; I believe she'd marry anybody to get out of it. And then there's Zillah Korishelski living here, though nobody knows why, except your mother; and your brothers live here, of course; and the uncles give their parties here, and Aunt Elsa and Uncle Albrecht live next door, which is almost as bad as in the house. And Wanda living with Aunt Elsa and the Marcuses just up the road. Sometimes, I am sure," added Susie, ending up a long speech, as people so often do, by saying the one unpardonable thing "your father must be glad he's dead and out of all the clatter." And, indeed, Paul Rakonitz, who had died of business worry, followed by a cold which he had caught at Sigismund's funeral some eleven years ago, was reported, by those who had visited the death-chamber, to have been stamped with a look of extraordinary peace.

"Look here, Susie," Bertrand brought the discussion to an end, or so he hoped, "Can't you see that it's just because my father's dead, that I think it my duty—our duty, if you prefer it— "

"It isn't mine," interrupted Susie, who saw what was coming.

"—to go on living here, and look after my poor old mother? A man in the house— "

Susie would have been wiser to have let this image

pass, of the Matriarch as a pale, grief-stricken widow, needing the constant prop and consolation of her eldest son; but Susie was still young, and believed that an argument ought to go on until the opponent, as in the game of Nuts-and-May, was pulled over the handkerchief; so she offered tentatively Bertrand's brothers, Ludovic and Blaise, as twin props for their mother's support.

"Oh, they will soon be marrying," said Bertrand, looking more and more injured, because Susie would so persistently not allow him to be good-humoured and jolly.

"I expect *their* wives will have homes of their own."

"Why are you so anxious for a home of your own, little girl? Put on your prettiest frock and let's dine out somewhere and go on to 'The Geisha' afterwards, and forget all about Mother. You will be getting on together like a house on fire to-morrow morning again."

Susie sighed. She felt that her husband was dismissing what was really her cry of a thousand tiny torments, as mere nagging. She did not want to be a nagging wife; and she knew quite well that she need not have nagged if she had been started fairly and without complications, in the sort of daily life, like a neat, bright pattern in chintz, which was her due. She would never have nagged at Bertie for smoking in the sitting-room, for instance; nor for stopping out late; nor for dropping his lighted cigarette on that lovely carpet which had been a wedding present; nor for flirting a little with her friend, Polly Baxter; nor for being ill-humoured because the servant had left without warning, and Susie had not had time to change into an evening blouse before he came home. All these items were duly set down in her mind's "Book of the Young Wife; What She May Expect." But in this conventional list of trials, the Matriarch had not figured. . . .

"We can't go to the theatre to-night," said Susie, after a long pause, "Mother's expecting us."

"Oh, Heavens!" groaned Bertrand, "All that way?"

"She never comes here because she doesn't get on with

your mother. I like to see her sometimes, and you can't blame me. As for ' all that way,' why, it's not so far as from here to the West End when we go to a theatre."

" That's different," said Bertrand, in her words of a few minutes back. " You know we always take a hansom."

" I know you are the most extravagant family I have ever met. Money rushes through this house like water. I have never seen anything like your mother for spending money; your money and her money and the Uncle's money. . . . There'll be a smash one of these days; that's one reason why I'd like to be living by ourselves. And you're as bad as she is, and we must think of——"Susie stopped. These were days when a young woman of Susie's age always stopped before mentioning, even to her husband, the possibility, or, as now, the certainty, of a child to come. The women of the Rakonitz family shocked Susie unspeakably by the frank gusto of their conversation on birth and the human body (but these were, very conspicuously, the wives and not the maidens of the tribe). After some pretty hesitation, Susie whispered to Bertrand, and he whispered back, and was very lover-like all that evening, and no one could be a more charming lover than Bertrand if he were not being nagged at. And she put on her prettiest frock, and they went to the theatre in a hansom. If the play were not " The Geisha," it must have been " Dorothy," or " Les Cloches de Corneville," one of those light-hearted operettas that were so agreeable to the Rakonitz temperament. And he took Susie out to supper at Gatti's afterwards, and they came home again in a hansom. But "home" was still with Anastasia; and she and Susie did not get on together, the next morning, like a house on fire.

Toni was born under the Matriarch's roof.

CHAPTER III

I

Three mornings after Toni was born, the Matriarch had a letter from Sophie. She delayed opening it, because her first grandchild was an event to fill her with such excitement, that nothing Sophie could do could possibly make an impression. It was Truda who first saw the letter lying unopened on the dressing-table, and, with the Matriarch's careless permission, read it aloud.

"Why, Mamma! Sophie has a little boy! Fancy, and we never knew before, or we might have . . ."

Truda stopped. She was not quite sure what they might have done, except that it seemed queer and wrong that a Rakonitz—for Sophie was a Rakonitz, for all that she had married Oliver Maitland—should have been born without all the usual atmosphere of concentrated fuss and importance and singing of the Messiah—" For unto us a child is born; for unto us a Son is given! "

" A *boy*, Mamma, just think! Sophie says he weighed eight pounds at birth, and we always thought her so delicate. She doesn't say if Oliver is pleased. I don't think that Oliver will make a good father. It is best to marry a Jew. Mamma, listen! Sophie says . . . " But by this time the Matriarch, half her dark hair lying thickly down her back, and the other half gathered up into elaborate curls, the tortoiseshell comb already surmounting it, had gathered that the letter was not one that an unmarried Truda could be suffered to browse upon. Truda was not of much account, except to be useful, but the most valuable thing about her was her state of innocence; so the letter was taken away from her; and the Matriarch, really pleased and proud over

her accumulating grand-children, might have read it with
tears, as Sophie had so hoped; might have put on her
mantle and bonnet, and sent for a hansom, and rushed
impetuously down to the fishing-village in Devonshire,
to see the little child who had already managed to live
to the age of six weeks without the authoritative voice of
Anastasia telling the nurse how babies of the Rakonitz
family had been reared in Pressburg, Vienna and Paris,
and should undoubtedly have been reared in Devonshire.
. . . Yes, Sophie might have had her hour with her
mother all to herself; her mother bending over little
Danny, crooning over his strength and lustiness, praising
Sophie for having achieved this miracle, the one miracle
in which a Jewish maiden can score over a Jewish man.
. . . But just then Bertrand came to the door, very
perturbed, with a message that the doctor wanted to
see Madame Rakonitz; that little Antoinette had developed sudden alarming symptoms; and that Mrs. Lake,
Susie's mother, a mother of no importance, had arrived,
and was giving contradictory orders to Anastasia's faith-
ful Minna. The Matriarch rushed upstairs to the top
floor, which was supposed to be the private and unvio-
lated property of her son and his family, where she had
promised, on his marriage, she would only enter as a
visitor—or hadn't she promised? Bertrand told Susie
that she had, but then Bertrand was an easy-going man,
and took the line of least resistance. It did not sound
like the sort of vow any Rakonitz was likely to make;
a son, even an eldest son, being maternal property, and
his wife no less a property, and his wife's mother—not a
property, but an insult! Mrs. Lake, indeed! The
Matriarch was royally indignant. A rival grandmother
to have any say in the treatment of Antoinette Rakonitz,
aged three days!
. . . Susie never forgot the Matriarch's kindness
during the time of crisis for her and the baby, which
followed the battle in which Mrs. Lake, routed by the
sheer weight of Anastasia's temperament, was driven
forth. Susie never forgot the tireless nights when her
mother-in-law sat up with her, and nursed Toni, and

managed Bertrand, and scolded Truda, and energetically
directed the household, and wove for her patient's entertainment, between-whiles, a tapestry of the Rakonitz past
and present, which, to Susie's fevered hearing, seemed a
very part of fever itself. . . . A tapestry through which
was drawn the bright thread of Simone's red-gold hair;
and a special recipe for gulas; and difficult words to
spell, like " meerschaum " and " Constantinople "; and
crowding figures, thousands of them; and a young girl
waltzing, in a stiff white muslin dress, spreading skirts,
and twisted coral for a wreath :—" Papa gave me ten
gulden, and I had to make that do! There was not
enough of the ten gulden left over for the gloves, and
what do you think? Papa said : ' You may have mine;
they have just been to the cleaners, and no one will
notice that they are too large if you keep your fists
closed . . . ' " Susie was ill for a long time, and she
never forgot the Matriarch's kindness, and she never
forgot that she could not have her own mother, her plain,
dumpy, sensible mother to look after her, because this
was not her own house. .

II

And Sophie's letter remained half read, and wholly
unanswered, except by her elder sister Truda, who sent
her several pages of simple pleasure at the tidings, saying
how delighted Mamma had been to hear about Daniel,
especially as he had been called after poor Papa's father;
and how Mamma would write very soon, but of course
she was so busy looking after Susie and the baby, Bertrand's baby—" and you know, Sophie, what Mamma
is like when it is anything to do with one of the boys ! "
Mamma had thought it wonderful of Sophie to have had
a baby who weighed eight pounds at birth, and why had
Sophie waited six weeks before she told them anything?
And Truda went on to tell her little sister about a black
velvet, tight fitting bodice with red buttons, and red
trimming, and big sleeves gathered into a long, tight

wrist-band, which their cousin, Berthe Czelovar, had just brought her from Paris. Such a pretty bodice, she wished Sophie could see it! How did Sophie manage for clothes, buried away in the country? And was Oliver kind to her? And she, Truda, was tired of being a nobody at home, and though she did not want to marry without love, she and Wanda had agreed that anything was better than home where one's brothers were so spoilt—

"It's just as hard for Wanda as for me, you know, Sophie, because she has Felix, and Maximilian, and sometimes Louis when he isn't abroad, who say that everybody she wants to marry isn't good enough, which I think is such a pity, because Edward Dunbar was a nice man, and I think she loved him, though he wanted to take her out to Australia, and, of course, that would have been dreadful, and not very suitable, but at least she would have had her own home and perhaps children; although Mamma says I ought not to talk about having children, but it is very difficult not to, with Toni just born in the house; and, of course, I have to do most of the cooking, though Aunt Elsa comes in every day, and tries to tell me what to do, as though she had not her own Mélanie and Freda and Gisela to bully, but you know what Aunt Elsa is! or don't you ever think about the family now? Sometimes I wish we had no family . . ." and then Truda gossipped, in her fine pointed handwriting, about her aunts, and her cousins, and ended up her long letter by repeating once more: "Mamma sends her love and was so delighted to hear about Danny." She was a dear, this Truda; she could not bear to give pain; but if she had been only a little cleverer, she would have invented some actual exclamations, cries of joy and gratification, tender broodings about the welfare of Sophie herself, which the news had brought forth from the Matriarch. This would have been some comfort to Sophie; Sophie would want it; needed it; had staked for it, on this son of sons. She had spent hours composing the letter, wondering how to make it sound genuine. Once, in perplexity, she had laid down her pen and gone into the village, and visited a

young mother. . . . Faltering a little, had asked her
questions, a great many questions, and then had hurried
home, and finished her letter to Anastasia. . . .

And it had not mattered much, after all, that the description was what Lizzy Huxtable went through, and
what the doctor had said to Lizzy Huxtable. . . . It did
not matter whether the pangs were Sophie's own or not,
because the Matriarch did not get as far in reading the
letter, and Truda skipped that part, from innate modesty,
not because she knew she ought to.

III

Anastasia's son had a daughter, and Anastasia's
daughter had a son. And Bertrand won, and Sophie was
forgotten.

She lived on at Cotsford by herself, for Oliver was one
of those people who can throw away a wife as easily and
carelessly as one throws away a worn-out boot; and he
was sick of Sophie, especially since she had had that
crazy passion for adopting poor Nell's brat. Though
whatever Nell wanted to take it to Sophie for . . .
Oliver shrugged his shoulders . . . Women! But Sophie
had driven a bargain with him that night of a high wind
in Plymouth, when the shape of a woman carrying a
bundle had staggered down the street of dark houses . . .
and had stood pealing the bell. . . .

Oliver came home a couple of hours later, to find his
wife, not a shrill fury, a-quiver with jealousy corrobor-
ated, but in a glow of strange happiness, with tears in her
eyes, and mouth set into determination. And she was
carrying a baby as though instinct had taught her how to
hold it.

"I don't care what you do, Oliver, and I don't care
where you go, and I am not going to be angry over this,
although I suppose most wives would cry and scream
and behave dreadfully, but you have got to let me keep
him and call him mine, do you hear? Mine. We can
go away from here, where people would know. We can

go down to Cotsford, where we went that first summer
. . . do you remember? "

"I remember," said Oliver. "Awful hole!"

He looked at Sophie standing there with Danny in
her arms, and his lips shaped to a soft whistle. His
wife and his son—it sounded all right. It sounded completely decorous.

"What do you want him for, Sophie? Charity, is that
it? The little beggar wouldn't have starved, you
know."

He did not mention Nell. Even his impudent treatment
of the facts of life, his utter carelessness, had limits when
it came to speech, though not in deeds. And Sophie and
Nell of those days, wife and woman, mistress of the
house and—mistress, were kept wide apart; might not
meet even in a discussion, still less in the same room, or
the same society.

"I want him," replied Sophie doggedly.

Oliver felt uneasy for a reason he could not visualise.
It was because he, a man of a thousand scattered,
shifting, and inconsistent ideas, was confronted here with
a creature of one idea, a fanatic.

"I want him," repeated Sophie. "He's my son. If
you don't remember that, Oliver, I will tell everybody,
your friends and your relations and my people, and all
Plymouth, what I heard about you to-night. I won't
make things easy for you. But if you let me take the
baby to Cotsford, where nobody knows, and bring him up
as mine—after all, why shouldn't he be mine? He's
mine by right, if he's yours! Then you can do what you
like, without me to plague you with questions."

"Oh, I don't care," quoth Oliver Maitland, airily.
"Only I'm not domestic by nature, Sophie, my girl; so
long as you're not expecting me to do pretty pictures with
you and the brat, and a cat, and a dog, and a kettle, and a
vase of pink roses—"

. . . Sophie's dark, smooth head bent lower over the
baby, so cosily drowsing in her arms. Suddenly she
smiled, and began to croon an old rhyme she had heard
her mother singing to Blaise :

> " Schlaf, kindchen, Schlaf . . .
> Dein' Vater ist ein Graf,
> Dein' Mutter ist ein Edelfrau. . . ."

Oliver saw that he was not wanted. He went to South America, and did not write often. He was really very tired of Sophie, who was a bore, and in delicate health, and whom he deemed not quite right in the head. He found it difficult to remember why he had married her, except that her beauty had made him ache for her as he had ached for Plymouth Nell, and Margaret, and Chloe, and many others.

He sent her money now and then; presently, for a while, he had none to send; and by the time he had some again, it seemed a pity to bother her with fitful remittances, as she was sure to be drawing a regular allowance from her relations—the Rakonitzes were rich. So Oliver called a Spanish girl to his table, in the picturesque, tropical street where he lounged and drank and smoked, and through the smoke we see him dimly and more dimly, and now he has vanished. . . .

IV

As soon as Danny was old enough, before he was old enough, Sophie began to sow his ancestors in his mind, with the anxiety of a gardener who is not quite sure of the soil. She did not tell these stories well; not so well as Truda, who had absorbed the family into her being, and took them for granted, and saw no more romance, and no less, in the chips of opal and amber that Anastasia and Felix and Simone used to pick up outside their house on the banks of the Danube, than in the exact quality and price of the sausages that her grandpapa Daniel had eaten when he was a little boy, because he was tired of eating Kosher—" But when he took his first bite, Toni, there was a terrible clap of thunder, and he thought God was angry with him. He was very good-looking, with a straight nose, like Uncle Maximilian. All the Rakonitz family have noses like that, and thick, lovely hair, though none

of them like your great-aunt Simone's " . . . and then
came the story of the tall beauty who had danced with
the Emperor's brother, and who was such a tease, and
hid her sister Anastasia's love-letters—" That was Grandmère, you know, Toni; but she did not get many, because
not long after her first ball, her cousin Paul came home
from Egypt, and saw her polishing the floor." And that
led up to the story of Anastasia's engagement, and how
she sat up all night afterwards lengthening one of her
dresses, because, although she was only sixteen years old,
it was a great shame to have to wear short dresses when
one was betrothed. . . .

"And did I ever tell you how Uncle Konrad, when he
got married, was so absent-minded, that on his wedding-
day he forgot he was married, and went for a stroll.
When he did not come back to his wife, they looked for
him, and found him at his favourite coffee-house. Afterwards he went to Egypt, too, to the Czelovars' bank out
there, where he did a lot to help the Austrians, and was
later rewarded by an Austrian title, and made a big
fortune, and settled in Paris. I expect you will visit
him one day. It was his wife, Aunt Berthe, who sent me
those red buttons you are so fond of playing with. They
were on a black velvet bodice; she had such a lovely voice,
and sang Schubert; it is worn out now, though I have
taken a pattern of it, because I was wearing it when
I first met your Uncle Benno—"

"Tell me," interrupted Toni, in a great hurry, "about
Clementina and the burning books." Her great-grand-
father's second wife was sufficiently remote from her
small self, to be thus familiarly hailed without respectful
prefix. Sufficiently remote, too, to be interesting in a
story. . . . Toni saw Uncle Benno and Aunt Truda
nearly every day, and did not enjoy the chronicle of their
wooing as much as she relished bits from the "further-
back " part; how Clementina, whose Venetian name,
Civrian, sounded so strange and melodious among the
pile of harsh Hungarian and Austrian surnames, was
escaping from a fire at the State Library, on the other
side of the Danube . . . and the pieces of burning books

are flying about—now several other houses are on fire—
" and Clementina called out to her children to get dressed,
and she got ready, putting on several skirts one on top of
another, and taking her jewels in a bag; and they went
to stay the night with Great-uncle Ludovic and Great-
aunt Wili. And when she undressed, she found she had
several skirts on, and when she got back to her house
the next day, she found that she had packed her empty
jewel-cases and thrown her jewellery back into the
drawer. . . ."

Such an absent-minded family!

But Truda, once she had started bringing in Benno,
was like a horse that had sniffed the stables from afar;
except that she did not go quicker; she went slower,
savouring what was not, certainly, the romance of Benno,
a stout, hearty, bearded man, whom she did not love over-
whelmingly, but the glamour of marriage in itself, of
being the heroine of a wedding. Benno was an incidental,
to whom she was grateful for taking her away from
home, and for giving her this crowning day, for which
her dress had been specially discussed and planned and
ordered; and all the family came, not only from London,
but some from the Continent, to stay with other London
relatives, all because of her. It made Truda feel very
gracious and important, for, like Sophie, she had deeply
felt the inferiority of her affairs, at any rate in her
mother's eyes, compared with anything connected with
the boys. But even Bertrand and Ludovic and Blaise
did not count for much, on her wedding day . . . the day
when the synagogue swam in a mist of dusky gold,
through which dimly loomed the shining top-hats firmly
poised upon every male Rakonitz head, and indeed, upon
every other male head, except old Mr. Lake's, Susie's
father, who simply *could not* remember that one did not
take off one's hat in a synagogue, as in a church. And
the canopy of white satin was held over Truda and no
one else—except Benno. And it was in her honour that
the glass was smashed into splinters by Benno's vigorous
foot. And it was she, who in the sight of all, stood with
modestly lowered eyelids, while the Rabbi spoke to her in

a fatherly way, telling her of all the others of her family
whom he had married, and how happy they were, and
how many children they had, mentioning them cosily by
their pre-names, or rolling out the long syllables of their
family name, wishing her the same happiness and fruitfulness. . . .

But all this pageantry of Truda's wedding-day had to be
led up to by avenues of solemn approach. Truda dwelt
lovingly upon every detail of the courtship, till it occupied
such a swelling volume of time and space compared with
the other anecdotes and legends, that Toni's sense of proportion went all awry, and it seemed to her as though
other members of the family were having their histories
crowded up into corners, almost squeezed away out of
sight. But Toni was not a brutal child; and besides,
it was rather fascinating, hearing for the seventh time,
and the seventeenth, about the Exhibition at Olympia,
and the new hat shape, and what Mrs. Ischel had said to
the Matriarch; and then Truda had a quaint trick of
suddenly calling herself " Truda " and not " I," when she
came to the story of her wooing; perhaps because she
felt the difference of her rôle as heroine, and needed to
emphasize it :

" It was the April after you were born, Toni, and Mr.
and Mrs. Ischel were coming to dinner, but Bertie wired
at the last moment that he would not be in town, so
Mamma suggested taking them to Olympia, and Mamma
went up West, and left Truda and Wanda, who was
staying with us, to look after the wash and settle with
the laundress, and shop, and look after the dinner. Truda
had just trimmed a new shape to go to the races with
Uncle Maximilian. The winter shapes were shabby, but
Truda told Wanda : ' I'm blessed if I am going to wear
my new hat to go out with old mother Ischel.'—' What
will you wear?'—' Last year's hat that I wore in San
Remo, when we went to stay with the de Yongs ! '

" Truda inked it, and oiled it, and baked it, and trimmed
it out of the rag-bag. On the way to Olympia, Mrs.
Ischel asked Mamma : ' Where did you get Truda's
charming hat?' Fancy ! and Truda was twenty-eight !

'*I* did not buy it.' 'Do you mean to say that Truda buys hats without your knowledge?' And Wanda poked Truda with her elbow.

"Well, we met Benno Silber that evening, and if Truda had known that she was going to meet her future husband, she would not have thought her new hat too good. It was a case of first sight with him, but she treated the whole matter as a joke at first.

"Things being quite unbearable at home, she had begged and begged to be allowed to go in for millinery, but the Uncles would not allow it, saying that they could not take their money away with them when they died, and Truda would have no need to do anything; but they did not know how unhappy she was. Nothing could be worse than home, and Benno was such a good fellow, and she felt sorry for his loneliness.

"Well, at the Earl's Court Exhibition, Mamma tries to get in with her Civil Service ticket, declaring that it *must* be the right one. When walking in the grounds, she suddenly dragged Truda by the arm into a side walk, having seen Mr. Silber coming along, much to Truda's amazement, who knew that Mamma rather wished for her to marry, being anxious to get rid of her to make more room for Bertie and Susie. . . ."

Truda came to a sudden embarrassed stop here, remembering that her listener was the small daughter of Susie and Bertie. And started afresh, with Benno Silber's visit to the house :

—"Benno noisily dropped a salad-dish, because in answer to Blaise's tactless teasing, Truda declared she was not of a kissing sort and hated it. After supper Truda was sent on a job to the top of the house, while Mamma entertained Benno with old family photos, all of which he dropped when Truda came into the room!"

And then came that bit of drama which, again by some odd trick, the narrator always forgot to include earlier in its right place; so went back for it, and picked it up afterwards, to set like a final diamond in her crown :

"And I forgot to tell you, Toni, that the night we met Benno at the Olympia, for the first time, there was a performance in the grounds, but Benno stared at me, and not at the stage. Going away, I pushed Wanda between us. You know that Wanda and I were the same age, and were friends, and sometimes quarrelled, and loved each other."

"But, Aunt Truda, she's your aunt, just like you are mine—how could she be the same age?" Toni was always puzzled by this.

"I will show you later how that was, Toni. Well, Wanda kept poking me with her elbow, saying: 'It's you he wants to speak to, not me!' but I ignored it. Then we went into the big hall, where an unusually large orchestra was playing, and little marble-topped tables stood about, with a china menu-stand on each. We secured one, and ordered refreshments. Of course, Benno had the place next to me; and all of a sudden there was a loud crash from the band and the vibration caused the menu-stand to hop off the table and fall at Benno's and my feet, and it smashed in ever so many tiny pieces, and fancy, how could she?—Mrs. Ischel said: 'Maseltopf!' quite audibly."

"Why did she say that, Aunt Truda?" Toni always privately thought Mrs. Ischel a very silly woman.

"It means 'Good Luck,' dear. You know Jewish people break china at engagements for luck. We broke a pink cup at your mother's engagement, and I still have a piece of it, though, of course, she wasn't . . ." Again Truda remembered that this was not fit audience for her private convictions that her brother Bertie would have done better to have married a nice Jewish girl.

"Aunt Truda . . ." And, with a start, Truda dragged herself back to the present, from that enormously great hall of the dazzling lights, where the unusually large orchestra had played celestial music, and thousands of marble-topped tables had formed her proud paradise— "Aunt Truda, you promised to show me about you and Aunty Wanda being friends."

So then Truda, whose own little daughter, Maxine, was two years younger than Toni, and far more interested in her baby sister Iris than in the chronicles of Rakonitz,

rummaged out a large sheet of writing-paper, and then
another and another, and stuck them all together at the
back with stamp paper, and even then it was not big
enough for what she wanted, and when she had manu-
factured a shiny white surface large enough for her
intentions, she took a fine quill pen and wrote, right at
the top, in the middle : " Simon Rakonitz," and beside it
" Babette Weinberg," and a little line joining them.
Toni pushed against her arm, trembling with excitement. . . .

" Don't, darling, you'll spoil it. This must be done
very beautifully." And very beautifully Truda did it,
in her slanting, pointed handwriting that betrayed so
clearly her foreign origin. Toni's writing was not in
the least like that. It slanted, certainly, sometimes backwards and sometimes forwards; and sometimes right
away from the restraining lines, down towards the corner
of the page, but the general effect of it was round.

Ludovic came whistling into the room.

" What are you two doing? " And he took up his small
niece and tossed her into the air, with that limited idea
of all uncles that this is a popular treatment.

" I think we ought to have a family tree to show the
children, Ludo," his sister explained conscientiously.
" I like them to take an interest, and sometimes it is so
difficult when cousins come over, and I'm not sure now
just where Berthe and Konrad came in, though she gave
me that black and red bodice of mine that I was so fond
of. And who did Aunt Grethe marry? "

" Klaus Sellabach," replied Ludovic promptly, which,
of course, put them all wrong, because Aunt Grethe did
not marry Sellabach at all! That was Babette, the
daughter of Ludovic and Wili. They were the Vienna
branch, and so he had been named after Toni's great-
great-grandmamma Babette, who was Toni's favourite of
all. Toni had a doll called Babette, in compliment to its
wide green skirt and a little muslin bodice, and hat tied
under the chin with a broad ribbon, just like great-grandmamma, no, great-*great*-grandmamma, must have worn,
when she walked with the five officers.

"It does not help me at all if you make mistakes, Ludo. The Sellabachs are the Vienna branch, and both Babette and Klaus are dead, or else, of course, little Klaus would not have been sent over here to live with Aunt Elsa; though Mamma always says she cannot understand why the other Vienna cousins, Josef and his wife, did not take the boy, now their own Franz is in the Army. But I daresay there has been a quarrel. And we still don't know whom Grethe married."

And they never knew; and the Matriarch, when consulted, could not remember either.

"Aunt Grethe was always a great goose," she said crisply, "and I expect her husband was another goose."

So Truda left it a blank; though she carefully filled in that Grethe had a daughter, Amélie, which gave that branch of the tree, the San Remo branch, a somewhat rakish appearance, quite undeserved.

"Are these *all* my cousins, and my uncles, and my aunts and my grandmothers, Aunty Truda?" asked Toni in an awed voice, as the names spread and scattered over the white paper.

"Look, Toni, this is what you wanted to understand— you see your great-grandfather, he was my grandfather, Sigismund; he held himself so upright when he walked that they called him 'The Officer' here in Hammersmith; well, he had two wives."

Toni's eyes widened.

"One after another?" she asked.

And Ludovic broke into a great roar of laughter.

"Of course, one after the other; it isn't right or good any other way, Toni dear. Well, Grandmère, and she's my mother, do you see?—Anastasia, she was his eldest daughter, and she was already married when her father married for the second time, so that she had a little girl— that was me—and he had a little girl—that was Wanda— in the same year; so that we could be great friends when later on we were brought to London, I from Paris, and she from Vienna."

"Even though she's one line higher than you?" Toni was studying the tree, her eyebrows, with the funny little Rakonitz bend to them, drawn low into a puzzled frown. This was really the most difficult thing which had yet been brought to her notice, though quite the most interesting and fascinating. She gave a gasp of sheer pleasure when on the extreme left of the paper, and perilously near the edge—Truda had only just allowed herself enough room—her own name presently appeared, shedding a glamour on herself which had never before been there.

"Why can't I be in the middle?"

"Because you don't matter enough," Ludovic teased her.

But Truda never teased children, but always strove painstakingly after truth, which sometimes made her almost a bore, because a lie can be flung out daringly, but truth has to be propped up with facts and explanations.

"You needn't believe that, Toni; nobody is much more important than anyone else, except Mummy and Daddy and Grandmère."

—"And your Uncle Ludovic," put in that gentleman. "He ought to be printed in red letters, really!"

"Ought he, Aunty?"

'No, dear," said Truda, with a reproachful look at her brother. "But you see, Toni, you are the eldest daughter of the eldest son of the eldest daughter of the eldest son of your great-great-grandfather, Simon Rakonitz, and so you ought to be specially good."

Toni thought this an anti-climax. She had thrilled right through her little body when the following pen had traced her descent from Sigismund to Anastasia, and from Anastasia to Bertrand; and if Truda had had imagination enough to wind up this demonstration of her position in the direct line of the oldest branch of the Rakonitzes, by saying—"And so you ought to be specially proud"—there was nothing that Toni would not have done for her.

"I'm not going to be good," she cried, prancing wildly round and round the room, and knocking over the chairs as she went. "I'm the oldest of the oldest of the oldest!" improvising a song of war. "And so I shall always do just as I like, and knock down everybody, and everybody will love me best, because I'm the oldest of the oldest of the oldest!"

—Susie came in, and caught the whirl of brandishing arms and legs into a firm embrace, bringing them to a standstill.

"What nonsense have you been telling her, Truda? You know how careful we have to be with Toni, she gets over-excited in no time."

But the family tree was crumpled into Toni's hand, and could not be dislodged. For several days she loved it better than dolls; better than the wonderful little milliner's shop with real tiny hats and tiny veils on their stands, which the Matriarch had brought her from the last visit to Paris. She liked picking out the people she knew on the tree; Aunt Elsa, who lived in the same street; and Uncle Ferdie Marcus, who also lived in the same street, with Deb and Richard. He belonged to Dorotéa —Toni laboriously spelt it out, but even then she did not know who Dorotéa was; Aunty Truda had put a tiny little " d " in brackets next to her name. Toni was especially interested in them, because they came as far over on the right of the paper, as she was on the left, so that if she was the oldest of the oldest of the oldest, they must be the youngest of the youngest of the youngest, especially Richard, who was younger than Deb; only two years old, in fact.

"The youngest of the youngest of the youngest!" chanted Toni triumphantly, till her little brother, hearing something sisister in the reverberations, let his chubby face pucker, heralding howls of anguish.

Toni took her treasure, uncrumpled and folded again, over to the Marcuses, next time she went there to tea. She would have liked to have shown it to Richard, who was as far on the right as she was on the left, but his was not an intelligent age, so it had to be Deb, who was bored with it, and went away and had secrets in the bath-room with her cousin Gisela Rakonitz, the third of Aunt Elsa's four daughters.

"I hate you! I hate you!" pounded Toni, on the wrong side of the bolted door. "Beasts! I hate you!

I've got a secret too; I'm the oldest of the oldest of the oldest— " but it did not help her much at the moment; and when she, in her turn, took that accommodating plumpness, Gisela, into the bath-room, and tried to pass on some of the thrill from the things which Aunt Truda had said—that entrancing little bit, for instance, about Mrs. Ischel crying : " Maseltopf ! " — Gisela said hurriedly : " Yes, I know, but don't let's talk about it; *please* don't let's talk about it ! " Gisela always said that, and thus checked many a promising conversation.

"This is silly; let's have an act," Deb suggested; " act " was their name for an impromptu play.

So they started enthusiastically preparing programmes, and hauling in the promise of an audience, of which the nucleus was Deb's Aunt Stella, and the gallery were Gerald and Richard, who both hated it; Richard because he had to keep still, and didn't know what they were talking about; and Gerald, because he was quite sure that his beloved Toni was being hurt, so that he cried most of the time, and had to be comforted by hasty dashes from the stage, and : " Look, darling, it's all right; sister's all right ! The fairy isn't hurting her really. Look, it's only Pearl, really ! "

Pearl was always the fairy, because she had flaxen hair and fat legs; just as Toni was always the princess, because she could throw a lot of passion and romance into her interpretation, and wear a thin nightgown with plenty of sashes to sustain it. As for Deb, having once acquired a pale blue sateen page's suit, she could obviously never be anything but the principal boy. This happened to be a specially good " act," with Toni looking over the top of a screen, representing a window in the Enchanted Castle of the Seven Chandeliers; and Gerald howled louder than ever, and it was all a huge success. Even Gisela forgot to spoil it by saying in the middle : " Oh, don't let's have it ! Please don't let's have it ! " And Toni was fetched long before they were ready to go, and forgot all about her family tree, and left it at the Marcuses, where it got lost among the bricks and dolls and picture-books in the old toy-cupboard.

CHAPTER IV.

I

Again, as once before, Sophie would have created the sensation she so desired with the Matriarch, had it not been for something which happened three days before, to cheat her of it. In fact, the sensation was actually achieved this time, when a letter reached Anastasia saying that she was to fetch her grandchild away from Cotsford, or else please to make some arrangements, being his grandmother and therefore the right person to do so, no nearer relations being known to Mrs. Mitchell, who was penning these lines, though she had heard that the little boy's father was alive, leastways, she had not heard that he was dead which came to the same thing, but having no address, would Mrs. Rakonitz kindly come and make arrangements, as said already, Mrs. Mitchell having done her best and all that was right and proper for Mrs. Maitland's last illness, but it had happened so sudden that, well, Mrs Mitchell had had hardly time, so to speak, to smoothe the poor lady's pillow, let alone to hunt up addresses, she being unconscious, but the doctor's certificate was quite right and proper as Mrs. Rakonitz should see for herself; syncope, they called it, and hoping that Mrs. Rakonitz was well, what was to be done with the little boy?

Sophie, if she had not died three days before Anastasia read this letter, might at last have been satisfied by its reception. Quite suddenly, excitement took the Matriarch like a wind bellying out her sails. Excitement and haste. Her *grandson*! and she had never seen him. Of course, he must come to live with her. Such and such a room should he have—disregarding whomever was in the room at the moment. His lessons, his clothes, his future, all

52

were planned with much bombast and irrelevant detail, even while with trembling fingers the Matriarch was twisting up the other half of her hair, and scolding Susie, and sending for Truda; blaming Susie for preventing her from going to Cotsford when first the news of Danny's being had reached her; gaily telling Toni and Gerald about the little cousin who was going to play with them; despatching a message to the Uncles, that Danny was to be taken into the business; and arguing with Aunt Elsa, who had just come in on the rumour of a letter from Sophie, about a train which did not leave Paddington at a certain hour, but which manifestly ought to have, if the Matriarch needed it.

Wearing her beautiful sables, and with two bottles of hot milk firmly wedged into a basket of eatables that she carried shamelessly slung over her arm, she hurried off to Paddington, and indignantly insisted on an interview with the station-master; forthwith, she told him the whole story of Sophie's indiscreet marriage with Oliver Maitland, affirming that she personally had never approved of it, but that he, the station-master, being a father himself, would know how difficult girls were. The Matriarch combined with her miraculous inconsequence, an equally miraculous power of universal friendship. Probably because she went so gaily over the hurdles of class, nationality, and convention. In consequence, the station-master became very helpful, and personally put her into her train, with a lot of brotherly advice; and afterwards, at home, spoke well of the lady in sables with a basket of eatables on her arm, who had cried to him over her girl who had died in Devon, and had told him what to do for their own little Ethel's chilblains.

She had not cried very much. It was of Danny that she thought all the way down to Cotsford, and very little of Sophie, even as Danny's mother. She now had six grandchildren, Toni and Gerald, Maxine, Derek and baby Iris, and Danny. She wished that Ludovic and Blaise would marry, so that she could have more and more grandchildren. There was an arrogance of human property in the possession of her children's children, which

was greater even than in the possession of Bertrand and
Truda, Ludovic, Blaise, and Sophie. They were spreading themselves, rooting themselves, or scattering to far
countries; by marriage lassoing outer tribes into the tribe
of Rakonitz. Danny was fresh power in the house;
Danny would one day have children, and they would still,
in a sense, be hers, Anastasia's. She did not wonder if
he would look like a Rakonitz, for the Matriarch was not
speculative by nature, and she had already settled his
looks. Undoubtedly, he must resemble his namesake,
Daniel, her husband's father, who was her uncle as well
as her father-in-law. He had been almost fair, and very
gentle, and absent-minded.

The Matriarch first saw Danny poised to throw the
claw of a dead crab at a gentleman walking along the
beach, whom he afterwards described indifferently as a
foreigner. His adoption into the house of Rakonitz,
seemed retribution out of all proportion for this deed.
He at once contradicted any of his grandmother's
imperious suppositions, by resembling Oliver Maitland;
which did not mean that he was a fair-haired, blue-eyed
Saxon type, in contrast with the swarthy Israelites; but
that, comically enough, he was a good deal darker than
they. A rough little boy, with a tanned skin, mobile
mouth, wide-set impudent brown eyes and gipsy black
hair. Anastasia liked him from the very first, and from
the very first he refused to take the Matriarch seriously.
He was possessed by a spirit of irreverence, that would
not be overawed by Oriental despotism. Where the whole
of Cotsford saw her impressive in sables, he saw her
as humorous, an old basket under her arm, with Bücklinge peeping out, which were herrings smoked by herself
according to old Maria's Viennese recipe; she had
brought them down to Cotsford because it was a fishing
village, and she was interested to find out if they ever
treated their pilchards in the same way. They did not;
so she volunteered to show them; and a group of interested fishermen and their wives clumped round her in
old Huxtable's kitchen that night, learning the secret . . .
till suddenly, some trifling thing she said reminded her of

Sophie, and that Sophie was dead, and that she had
travelled all the way to Cotsford too late to see her;
and the Matriarch wept and mourned aloud, her head on
Lizzy's motherly shoulder, telling them of that time when
Sophie, as a little girl, had been naughty and shut up
in the room where the clean washing had been put, and
how the child, in a fit of temper—it was despair, but
Anastasia had never known this—had thrown out of the
window into the road below, all the snowy washing which
the Matriarch always had done at home because of
the beautiful old lace on the pillowcases; handmade
Valenciennes—one could not trust the London laundries
who did it with machinery; and here all the good Devon
housewives came clamouring in, with their shrill views
on the best methods of washing lace, the best soap to
use, and whether to rinse in cold or lukewarm; and in
the discussion the Matriarch grew happy again, and the
Bücklinge lay unheeded in the raftered, smoky room.

II

Danny and Toni both behaved in the Matriarch's house
as though each were an only child; and as Grandmère
herself also behaved distinctly as though she were an only
child, the result could not have been anything else but
collision and conflict. For they all had the temperament
of an only child, fearless and spoilt, vivid and capricious.
Their quarrels were like flames fanned in a draught.
The other cousins who came in and out of the house, to
tea, or with messages, Maxine and Gisela and Val, looked
on with impatient amusement or else with extreme horror,
according to their separate points of view, on this Trojan
warfare that rarely seemed in abeyance. Down below,
in the drawing-room part of the house, the Matriarch
and Susie were likewise at war. The Matriarch would
tell Susie how Toni ought to be treated for naughtiness;
but she thought Toni was naughty in matters that Susie
did not mind, and benignly allowed things which Susie
would not suffer for a moment. Anyhow, Anastasia
declared Danny should be entirely under own control;

but she would forget him for days at a time, so that Susie, crisp and practical and loving, drew him back into her personal care, until suddenly Anastasia, reminded of his existence, tugged him away again. Toni naturally resented the indulgence which Danny wheedled from the Matriarch, which she might equally successfully have wheedled if Susie had let her, such as stopping up late, or long rides in a hansom to see one of the Uncles, or a really good bout of over-eating; but she flared into jealousy when Danny, neglected and, of course, in mischief, was briskly slapped by Susie . . .

—" You're not to slap him! You're *my* mother! He isn't yours at all. He doesn't count enough to be slapped!" Meanwhile herself battering Danny as hard as she could, with both her clenched fists. Danny, of cooler blood, merely laughed at her. Once, however, just to see what she would do, he allowed himself to become dramatic :

"It's all very well for you," said Danny, very clenched and white, and holding his head high. " You *have* got a mother, so you know you can do what you like and she'll back you. I've no one to back me . . . " It was rather crude, but effective enough for Toni. Metaphorically, she threw herself at Danny's feet—herself and everything she possessed, including her beloved mother, half-a-crown which Uncle Dietrich had given her last Sunday, her complete set of Dickens, and a confession that she had been in the wrong over their last quarrel but one. . . . It was a really generous display. Danny thanked her, took the half-crown—and the confession, for future use when Toni should again attempt to be uppish; went out and bought a box of chocolates, costing two shillings and sixpence, brought them back into the nursery, and gave Toni more than half.

" Here you are, you beastly little hedgehog! "

She groped for traces of the tragic, misunderstood boy who had so fascinated her into humility, half an hour ago. She would have done anything for that Danny. He rolled over on the floor, chuckling; pelted her with chocolates.

" I was pretending ! " he boasted. " I didn't mean a word of it. I like being without a mother. I wish I was without a grandmother too ! "

Toni, with terrific dignity, laid down the chocolates she had picked up, even to one which had already been in the shadow of her mouth.

" Thank you very much, Daniel Maitland, but I don't eat what people I hate give me." She did not mention the original ownership of the half-crown, being a decent child at heart; but this unworthy cousin of hers must be taught that she could not be intimidated with impunity by hypocritical renderings of non-existent pathos; that was not quite the way she put it, however :

" As for a grandmother, you don't deserve one like ours ! "

" Oh, you like her because she gives you raw eggs to suck, because you pretend you are delicate."

This was a hit below the sash. Far from pretending to be delicate, Toni was more ashamed of her brittle health, her body's weak capitulation to colds or fever or infection, than of anything else in the world, and covered it up by every ingenious device she could. To have a tireless spirit and a zest for pleasure, a longing and a tug towards it which is purely Viennese in its origin, and then to be the first to be fetched from a party because : " You know you get over-excited so easily, and then you don't sleep and have to suffer for it the next morning,"— this was tragedy; and a worse agony when Danny began to notice it.

" Mummy, why *should* I be ill ? "

" None of the Rakonitz family, after Grandmère, are strong, darling."

" But why? Anyway, I am going to do as much as though I was strong, always." And gallantly enough, little Toni made a game out of her proneness to be ill, taking risks, daring herself, finding out how long she could keep up the pretence of enjoyment while her head ached or her legs ached, or less polite parts of her; making a drama even out of surrender at the last moment, as though there were two Tonis, and one was robust and broad-shouldered and invulnerable, as she wished to be; and the other, the leader of a losing cause; and these secret games were perhaps the beginning of Toni's relish for a fight with everything against her. But it was mean of Danny to have said that about the raw eggs. Danny never had anything the matter with him.

" It's because you are a nigger !" she spat back, tingling with a desire to say one thing that would really thrust between the joints of his scoffing indifference. " You're brown all over. Niggers have got an extra skin, a brown one, like yours, so they don't feel things, or catch things, or mind things. It's as bad as a rhinoceros. *I* wouldn't be a nigger ! *I* wouldn't be a rhinoceros ! "

She jigged up and down at him, waiting for temper; hoping for it, yet apprehensive. Danny was still rather an unknown quantity.

" I like being a nigger! like being a rhinoceros ! like watching you in a wax ! "

Now Toni knew that there was one thing which she could say to Danny, which would really hurt him as much as, and more than, she wanted to. It was Toni's continual temptation, this one thing. She had not yet yielded to it, because she belonged to the chivalrous sex, and knew that you used nearly the worst weapon of all, but never, under the extremest provocation or goad, nor in self-defence, the final worst. You just didn't. The funny part of it was that Danny did; without a flicker of an eyelid he had said that about her liking being delicate, and pretending to it for the sake of the benefits it brought; and still she could not retort : " Your father went away and left you, and nobody knows where he is, so he can't care a bit about you, not one bit ! " She had heard Aunt Elsa and Grandmother and Truda discussing this heartless Oliver Maitland, and her instinct was sensitively sure that Danny's heart was too sore to be touched on the subject. She was right about the soreness, but it was not Danny's heart, it was his pride.

" I'm going to the pantomime this year," murmured Danny, with a quick roguish flash of his eyes at Toni, to see how she would take it.   She stopped jigging suddenly.

"Oh! you're *not*? who said so?"

"Grandmother—yesterday—to Uncle Max, when he asked how many rows of stalls he should take this year. She said 'Danny and Toni are both old enough.'"

Toni's pale face reddened into sudden rapture.

"But then Aunt Susie said—" continued Danny happily,—"'I am afraid I can't risk it with Toni for a year or two, Uncle Max; you know how wildly excited she gets, especially if it's at night; I should have her ill for weeks afterwards.'"

Toni bit her lip fiercely.

"Then," continued Danny, with the utmost relish, and appreciating her pluck so much that he desired to test it to the very limit of its strength, "Then Uncle Max said: 'Well, if one can't go, then the other had better not. They are the same age, aren't they?' and then your father said—" Danny dragged out his words slowly— "Your—own—father—said—'Toni would hate it if Danny had to go without the pantomime just because she could not have it.'"

Toni was silent; her back was slightly turned to the boy. She was trying hard to play up to this noble presentment of herself hating Danny to go without the pantomime because she was not strong and got overexcited. She admired this Antoinette immensely, and supposed if her father said so, these *must* be her real feelings—but oh! it would have made the disappointment so much less acute if Danny had not been going either, and that was the truth. For Danny was the same age. Besides, it was not only the pantomime—her mother would probably take her one afternoon to a pantomime. It was that this yearly revelry was a family event. A rather splendid affair organised in princely fashion by Uncle Maximilian, quite her favourite uncle. He took the two first rows of the stalls at Drury Lane on the first night. Two whole rows; and all the family was invited; and he provided the carriages as well; and after the pantomime there was a supper in a resturant, some

mysterious glittering place of long tables and lights and
exotic food. It was because of the honour of being
admitted at last to play her part in tradition, it was
because of this, really, and because Toni was a romanti-
cist and worshipped the family, that the invitation to
" Dick Whittington " meant so much more to her than
to Danny. Danny would have enjoyed his evening, as a
materialist enjoys. . . . And then, through her hard
struggle not to betray the ignoble Toni, she heard the
voice of her tormentor, very soft and wheedling :

"Did I tell you, Toni darling, what I said downstairs :
that I wouldn't go without you? "

" Danny ! " she flung herself at him. He floated aloft
into heroism in her sight, as though he were seated on a
winged horse, all glorious and golden.

"I knew jolly well," continued Danny, " that I
shouldn't have to stop at home; not with Grandmère anywhere about. She and Uncle Max talked over Aunt
Susie, and we are both going ! "

CHAPTER V.

I

The family were rich—Danny noticed that at once—especially the Uncles. They used to draw little packets out of their pockets, and shake the contents on to the table, and sometimes invited the Matriarch or Aunt Elsa, or Haidée Power, who was a great favourite of theirs, to choose one. Just imagine it! rubies rolling all over the table, and sometimes they danced like drops of flashing red dew over the edge and on to the carpet, and Danny and Toni would scramble to pick them up.

"Oh, these clever ladies!" Uncle Maximilian mocked the choice that Haidée, perhaps, had made, "they are the ones to wear precious stones, if you please, and when you give them the chance of a magnificent pigeon's-blood ruby,"—he always pronounced it "mannificent," and it was one of his favourite words,—"they select a spinel ruby, because it is the brighter red. No—no—don't blush, Haidée; we are delighted, Felix and I! We were especially anxious to get rid of that one, and I know no jeweller who would have been so obliging as to take it!" But then, good-naturedly, he would present her with the pigeon's-blood ruby, all the same; and, moreover, teach her how to tell the flawless rubies by the faint bluish light that should filter through. The Matriarch seldom made mistakes, when they tested her. Paul had trained her in the old Paris days. She had a sure eye for the male sapphire with a tiny purple speck in it, that spoilt its value; and for the little white blemish just visible in the female sapphire, which was not a pure stone—and she never mixed these up with the priceless, peerless star sapphire; her brothers were very proud of her judgment in their trade.

61

The Uncles all had big houses of their own in the West
End, except Louis, who lived in the country, and had
already retired, which was funny, because he was the
youngest. Val liked Louis the best; but Toni's favourite
was Uncle Maximilian, who was so lordly and splendid;
so that all the head-waiters in whatever restaurant he
went to, came rushing away from their clients, however
important, yes, even from Royalty, Toni believed, and
hung round Uncle Maximilian's chair, consulting with
him about this dish and that dish; and even when he
autocratically contradicted them, they did not seem to
mind, because of the way he did it; and whether he paid
in gold or in notes, he just waved away the change when it
came—not ostentatiously and complacently generous, but
simply, as one who could not be bothered. Women
adored Uncle Maximilian, though he used to tease them,
and never flattered them, and showed them clearly that
he could do without them; and men sought him out too,
because, somehow or other, in mysterious terms of
finance, it " sent up a man's stock " to be seen with him.
He owned a horse which ran second in the Derby, once;
and he had dined with the Prince of Wales; and when
he wore a wine-coloured dressing-gown, and green
brocade slippers embroidered in purple, they had the
effect of being just the right things to wear, because he
was so tall and thin and good-looking. Clothes that were
eccentric on other people, looked austere on him. His
fair hair and moustache had silvered before he was forty;
and his nose—but Truda has told you about the Rakonitz
nose. It was, in a sense, their greatest treasure. You
have to be a Jew to understand what fun it is to have a
nose that is purely Greek in outline. Uncle Maximilian's
presents were always the best; and it was he who inaugu-
rated the pantomime habit; but some of the children
were afraid of him. He liked Toni, because she was
cheeky, and answered him back, and told him she was
coming up to the City to help him dig for rubies. It
was a long time before she realised that the actual manual
work was not done by Uncle Maximilian.

Uncle Dietrich and Uncle Felix were very much alike

—small and baked and genial, and also very thin. They were not quite so lavish as Uncle Maximilian, and did not roll rubies over the table quite so often, saying " Choose !" In fact, Uncle Felix was positively careful over presents. On the other hand, they were not so frightening. One of them had a house in Half Moon Street, and the other in Brook Street. Uncle Felix had snuff-boxes, a wonderful collection, of which the best shut inside its gold lid a tiny trilling bird with jewelled eyes; he also had the first gramophone that Toni ever remembered seeing; a frightfully expensive gramophone, mounted on its own tall stand, instead of just being put on the table. Uncle Louis shut his eyes and suffered when it was turned on in his presence, but his brother remarked irritably that he was hypersensitive. Uncle Felix always rang for his valet to wind the gramophone and change the records, in the same spirit that an old dowager keeps a companion to groom her lapdogs. Uncle Maximilian had a valet, too. As for Uncle Dietrich, nobody quite knew what he had in his house, because for some reason never explained to the children, they were not allowed in it; and they knew that the grown-up ladies of the family never went into it, either, not even the Matriarch; and this was queer, because she was always going to Uncle Felix and to Uncle Maximilian to act as hostess at their parties, and sometimes down to Uncle Louis, who lived on the river. But there was a sort of " Glamis Monster " attitude about what Uncle Dietrich kept in his house. Toni and Danny, and Val Power, and Neil Czelovar, held a council, in imitation of the family councils, and formed a club for the sheer purpose of finding out what it was that Uncle Dietrich kept in his house, that they might not see. It could not have been anything savage, because he emerged into company looking quite amiable and well tended; and it could not have been anything infectious, because, funnily enough, the men of the family went in and out without being any the worse. In fact, and this was valuable data to the club, Danny was allowed to go once with Bertrand, and when Toni had cried: " Me too ! " her Grandmother and her Aunt Truda had both exclaimed in horrified chorus: " Of course not! What are you thinking of, Bertie? " Danny strutted rather on account of this; but he was forced to confess, when cross-examined by Val, that he had not seen anything whatever of the " Glamis Monster," had not even smelt it, though he went down on his hands and knees all over the carpet, sniffing, and Uncle Dietrich had laughed indulgently, thinking he was playing at wild beasts, and had given him half-a-crown.

" Club funds," said Val curtly, and, as treasurer, annexed it.

Danny had meant to impress Toni with the notion that he had solved the mystery of the " Glamis Monster," but that she, being a girl, would not be suffered to know it; but Val was four years older than Danny, and he had not been able to evade her keener questionings.

Uncle Louis stood a little apart from " The Uncles "; " The Uncles " meant three, not four. For one thing, he did not dig for rubies; for another, he did not live in London, in the West End; and finally, as Toni had discovered from the family tree, Louis was only half-brother to Anastasia, just as Wanda was only half-sister. Nevertheless, he looked like a dark-brown version of Uncle Maximilian—" That is because they are both like Papa," Anastasia had said; he also looked like a thin and high-bred pedigree dog. The bridge of his nose was fiercely aquiline, and he wore a monocle, and head-waiters and maîtres-d'hotel rushed to do his bidding too, but with perhaps not quite so deferential a rush as for Uncle Maximilian. Louis was more an elegant patron of the arts, and less a distinguished man of the world. He was a melancholy epicure, slightly cantankerous but not irascible, always ready to assert his own pessimism, his lack of belief in anything good from anywhere, and his cosmic disappointment. As each of the children had claimed a particular Uncle, so Louis was Val's. It was a point of honour not to be afraid of one's own, however much of the others. Truth to tell, all the children were rather afraid of all the Uncles. There was such a fuss about them, and you had to be hastily changed into best clothes when they came, and the mothers were so obviously anxious that you should make a good impression . . . and then they just monocled at you, and asked rather impatiently how lessons were getting on, and the mothers made you recite, or play the piano, or they displayed your embroidery and school prizes, and the Uncles wished they had not asked, and the mothers quickly twitched your hair a different way so that you should look your best, and there was an atmosphere of boredom all round.

Danny had selected Dietrich for his patron saint, for reasons of the " Glamis Monster "; and the little ones, Maxine and Derek Silber, and Gerald, and Richard Marcus, easily wooed by trivialities, preferred Uncle Felix because of the snuff-boxes and the gramophone.

But they all hated Zillah Korischelski.

Zillah had been brought to the Matriarch's notice by the three Uncles, so it would be hard to say which of them loved her, if, indeed, any of them did. She was not a relation, but lived on the overflow of Anastasia's protective bounty. She was a large, fattish, dashing girl, with the name of an adventuress . . . Zillah Korischelski—listen to it! Zillah Korischelski. Her actual parents seemed to be self-effacing people; they existed, but they did not worry Zillah. To all intents and purposes, she was a daughter of the Matriarch, her protegée, her jester, and her crony. Above all, her minstrel; for Zillah had a wonderful contralto voice, and Uncle Maximilian paid for her to have the best lessons. She made such long stays in the house that their bulk, separated only by the two or three days she occasionally went home, made it appear as though she lived there permanently. Anastasia took her everywhere; treated her to everything; and, backed by the Uncles' benevolence, started her in all sorts of pleasing businesses, which, however, flagged and failed after a few months. She was a very definite influence at all the festivals; and even present when the family met in council over some disaster. The Uncles teased her and flirted with her. The children detested her, because she used to say:

" Now, *you* be quiet, Miss ! " and they resented this from one who was not of the blood royal—not a Rakonitz. Zillah and the Matriarch had terrific rows, but never quite terrific enough to send Zillah spinning out of the house. She had rows, too, spasmodically, with Truda or Susan or Aunt Elsa or Haidée or Aunt Gustava, who then went about saying: " I really can't see why Anastasia puts up with Zillah ! "

" I believe she means to marry Felix ! " was a frequent prophecy; or: " I believe she prefers Dietrich ! " And, most apprehensively of all : " I should not be surprised if Maximilian . . . " But Felix and Dietrich and Maximilian never finally succumbed ! They continued to chaff her, to compliment her, to give her presents, and to insist that she should have her share in anything Rakonitz; but none of them married her, and the family were glad. Somehow, they liked to keep the Uncles bachelors; especially Anastasia, who, perversely enough, did not mind her sons marrying; wished, indeed, that Ludovic and Blaise would choose a nice girl apiece, and so fill out the ranks of the grandchildren. But the Uncles were her property; she was very proud of them, and no one was good enough; not even Zillah, who pleased her, however, as a show daughter, which Truda had never been. Zillah was aware of men in every fibre of her being, which was a great asset in entertaining. Anastasia, having a marvellous flair for misfitting people to their jobs, arranged imperiously that Zillah, in her spare moments, should assist in Danny's education.

Danny's education could only be noted as eccentric. For a year before his eventful seventh birthday, he had gone to the village school at Cotsford. Then for two years he was taught variously, in the house of the Matriarch, by his nurse, Susie, or Zillah. Zillah's lessons were languid and exotic; Susie's practical but element- ary; Susie would have been better at teaching her own small daughter, for cooking and needlework were her specialities, if Toni had not hated both. Quite suddenly, Uncle Maximilian discovered that the boy knew nothing at all, and spoke severely to Anastasia about it; and

Danny was sent for two years to a perfectly normal preparatory school in the neighbourhood, where all his rags and tags of education were picked up and kneaded into something like conformity. Blissfully he anticipated public school, and then the University, just like other boys; but he wished he need not have to return from school, every day, to what he called carelessly: "that mess at home."

Danny was about ten when Rakonitz moved from Hammersmith to Holland Terrace. They were suddenly richer than ever, now, through a boom in Burmese rubies, on whose fluctuations most of the family were dependent, either because they were supported by the Uncles, or in business with them, or had made investments according to their advice. Anastasia took a house with an opulent dining-room, a still more opulent ball-room with parquet flooring, and coloured windows; St. George and the Dragon in stained glass most inappropriately presiding over the staircase. The reception-rooms led on to a spacious conservatory, cooled by a fountain that recklessly tossed water, morning, noon, and—usually—night, for the household were far too extravagant to remember to turn it off. King Henry VIII, in stained glass, glowered down upon them while they ate in the great six-windowed dining-room. The drawing-room had a fireplace at each end. It was curious how the Rakonitz style of decoration, the brocades and candelabra that came from Venice and Vienna, the furniture of the First French Empire, the Bokhara rugs, and the Chinese cloisonné ornaments, blended in with the quiet dignity of Georgian architecture. It may be that the best in art cannot quarrel. Anastasia's ancestors had had a selective taste, and when they used the word "elegant," meant it as "perfection." Toni revelled in the deep-coloured bronzes, and the husky umber silk sunblinds that had once been a crude blaze in the dim shadowy canals that wriggled crooked ways between the Rialto and San

Marco. The incrustations of luxury never oppressed her, as they did her mother. Susan never ceased to long for a cosy English interior of chintz and freshness and ordinary new furniture that could be kept clean without votive sacrifice. " Half of us give half a lifetime to this house, and then it's never done," she used to say impatiently. The great orgies of cleaning that the Matriarch insisted upon every spring, with their consequent turning out of garret after garret, drawer after drawer, trunk after trunk, revealed an accumulation of lumber that could not be thrown away as lumber, because the things were mostly too reminiscently precious or too valuable, though beyond use. The house in Holland Terrace was worse even than Hammersmith, from Susie's point of view.

Presently, in true tribal fashion, Aunt Elsa decided to move with all her family to another house in Holland Terrace; and then Truda and Benno came, with Derek, Maxine and baby Iris; and the Marcuses. Four sets of Rakonitz descent were living in Holland Terrace now; it was much more convenient, to find them thus collected, for relations from abroad, who came over with imperative orders not to miss out any of the family, and to dine with all of them in turn. Aunt Henrietta was already living in that neighbourhood; and Aunt Gustava and her children were not far off. Aunt Henrietta was the daughter of Julian Czelovar, who had married Gisela Bettelheim. They must have been related somehow to the Rakonitzes, because all the Bettelheims and Czelovars were. At any rate, the chidren called Henrietta "Aunty"; and thought her a darling, but wished her kisses were not so hard and defiant; and both Elsa and Anastasia claimed her as their special cousin, and were very jealous if she cared for one of them more than for the other. She was rather beautiful, with a serious face, and curly dark hair, and an ivory skin; and perhaps she had married Otto Solomonson because she loved him, but it is difficult to believe, because he was fat and oily, with a little black moustache, and a nose that really was Jewish—a nose that disgraced the entire clan when its aggressive curve was thrust upon their notice. He had plenty of money, and they both liked whist very much, and bridge, after it had ousted the fashion for whist; and when Henrietta and Otto and Anastasia and Felix sat down to a game, Elsa sitting by ready to cut in at the first possible moment, and to give unwanted advice in the intervals, the row was deafening, and the abuse, in several languages, torrential. Toni used to hear it rising and falling, lull and storm, from her bed at the top of the house. . . .

III

When the tribe were gathered for council in Anastasia's drawing-room, it was usually because something untoward had occurred . . . such as the dramatic appearance of a little dark dingy old woman from Constantinople, who had somehow been misdirected to the house of Neil and Sylvia's mother. She announced, in broken French, that she was the wife of Great-uncle Eugène, and that he was dead, and she penniless, and their four children—afterwards discovered to be idiots—were starving, and she had been told, in Paris, to come to this branch of the family. It was a dreadful mistake to have made, because Constance Czelovar, who was the wife of Raoul, who was the son of Simone, was not at all a warm-hearted woman. She had been Constance Wyatt before her marriage, and her father was a Dean who did not like Jews, even though he admitted that Raoul Czelovar was not in the least like a Jew, and began forthwith to talk tactfully of the Rakonitzes and Czelovars as: "a distinguished cosmopolitan family." When Raoul first became engaged to Constance, he was very careful about which of his relations he allowed to trickle through as far as the Dean. He struck his first good impression with Uncle Louis; and kept Uncle Maximilian in reserve for three days, before nonchalantly producing him as an effective climax. The Dean had never really met the whole swarm, except at the wedding; and even then, though he may have thought it rather too—cosmopolitan—to have quite such a multiplicity of relations, he still had to admit that they were not in the least Israelite in its more objectionable form.

Constance was very fair and slim and listless, and it always sounded absurd and not quite natural when she had to call a Rakonitz "Aunt" or "Uncle"—or said "Mama" to Gustava Czelovar, who was Raoul's step-mother. So it was rather a pity that Aunt Eugène should have appealed first of all, helplessly, for spontaneous affection from Raoul's wife. Constance sent down the butler for four bottles of Burgundy, and courteously redirected Aunt Eugène to the house of Uncle Albrecht and Aunt Elsa. It is not on record what she told the butler; and she was certainly annoyed to discover that both her offspring, Neil and Sylvia, had been looking out of the nursery window, and had seen the dingy little old woman in black go down the steps, cuddling her bottles closely, and faltering blessings in some unknown tongue, on her benefactress.

Elsa's house was a warm glowing cavern of welcome, after this rather chilly doorstep: "Wass! In trouble?" One of the family in trouble and in need of help?—it had to be attended to at once. Elsa put on her best black silk coat with the heavy jet trimming, and with her little toque tilted in agitation rather to one side of her head, went round to Anastasia, who was still doing her hair. The affairs of state, whenever they had to be adjusted by Anastasia before one o'clock in the afternoon, had perforce to revolve round her massive toilet-table, and her serene acceptance of these conditions was like that of a king's mistress in eighteenth-century France. Elsa demanded, a little hysterically, a private audience; so that only Susie and Zillah and Toni and the hair-dresser were actually in the room when she poured out the dire story of poor Eugène's wife and her state of distress. Elsa cried a little bit, because, after all, Aunt Eugène was her husband's sister-in-law, though no one knew what her name was before she married. And Anastasia said emphatically how glad she was, yes, glad, that they could show Eugène that his trust in the family loyalty had not been misplaced, and, of course, she would see to it that the Uncles took at least three of the four boys—afterwards discovered to be idiots—into their business. The Uncles would be coming for dinner the next day, which was Sunday, so Elsa and Albrecht had better come too, and Truda and Benno could drop in afterwards, and Henrietta and Otto Solomonson, and Haidée Power if she liked, though she was too flippant and selfish to be of much use, and Ferdie Marcus—" and we really must *not* forget poor Gustava this time, for when we do, she cries so much the next time "—and they would settle what had to be done, and how much each member of the family should subscribe, and who should collect the subscriptions, and with whom Aunt Eugène and her four children —afterwards discovered to be idiots—should live, in London. The Matriarch thought it had better be with Raoul and Constance, because they had a big house. She had a big house herself, but then it already bulged and overflowed with Bertrand and his family, with Ludovic and Blaise, still unmarried, with Danny, and with Zillah Korischelski; Albrecht and Elsa were not too well off, and besides, Wanda was living with them, and little Klaus. Wanda wanted to live with her brother Louis and keep house for him, but the Matriarch had decreed otherwise. She had said Wanda was too young and lively, and that her head was stuffed with feathers instead of solid domestic qualities. Wanda was forty-one by now, and ought to have been married, only she was wilful and had pettishly refused Otto Solomonson's brother, especially imported from Germany for her benefit, and had had a flirtation, instead, with one Edward Dunbar, who had actually wanted to start a ranch in the Colonies somewhere, and to take Wanda with him. This was not good enough, the family decided, and they told Wanda that the Uncles would not hear of it. It is quite possible that the Uncles had literally not heard of it, but at all events, by some atmospheric pressure known only to the Matriarch, Edward Dunbar had been detached from the idea of marrying Wanda Rakonitz. And she lived with Aunt Elsa, whom she did not like, and she was not quite as lively as she had been, though still too lively to be

allowed to rule Louis' household for him. The Matriarch
had given him a white-haired housekeeper, instead.

IV

Imagine the family then, that Sunday after dinner,
sitting in Anastasia's drawing-room in the big house in
Holland Terrace. They had eaten, with epicurean appreciation, but not too robust in their appetites, a meal that
was rich with spices and association; the main dishes
had been cooked by the Matriarch herself, and the recipes
would be handed down to Truda, who would hand them
down to her own eldest daughter, so that they should
not get lost; for her risotto, containing chicken-livers and
raisins, and cooked in goose-fat, Felix's favourite
Bücklinge, their crackly skins smoked to a peculiar red,
the Hungarian gulas with paprika, the enormous
open tart, hot slices of plum, faintly crisped, on
its round bed of delectable pastry—all these were essentially Rakonitz. "Do you remember how old Maria
used to cook these? . . . and these? . . . and these?
. . . and how she made the Crême-Düten? And how she
gave notice every year when the priests came to Vienna
and told her it was wicked to remain in service with the
Jews, and came crying to Mamma a week later, begging
to be taken back? . . ."
The wine they drank had been chosen for the
Matriarch's special use by Uncle Maximilian; he had laid
down a very fair cellar for her; some '84 Port of Cock-
burn's, several dozen of a fine Clos Veugeot, not yet
ready for drinking, Château Yquem 1894, bottled sun-
shine that grew better every year, a '71 Madeira, very
pale, and a few cobwebby bottles of Napoleon brandy. He
added to it from time to time, whenever he pulled off a
big deal in rubies; and Louis, who was a connoisseur of
art, had just brought in a gift of a dozen old Chelsea
wine-glasses, with twisted stems, beautiful things—
Anastasia was very touched and pleased.   The long
mahogany table supported a barbaric pageantry of Crown
Derby china, jostling old Rakonitz silver, richly embossed,

inherited from Simon and Babette; tall Salviati fruit-dishes, clear glass, gold-powdered and blown into dragon-shapes, lifted their luscious pyramids of peaches and nectarines and grapes all down the centre.

The children—Danny and Toni and Gerald—were allowed to come in for dessert; and King Henry VIII, in stained glass, looked down on this incongruous family from his window, and maybe ill-wished them; though Simon and Babette, ancestors now, in ornate gilt frames on the wall, could have countered with a blessing for continued prosperity, optimism, and fruitfulness. . . . Maximilian had just shaken some rubies out of the little packet on to the brilliant white tablecloth, in front of Anastasia, and had said " Choose ! "

The gentlemen were not allowed to smoke in the drawing-room after dinner, but the scent of good cigars still hung faintly about them, when they followed the ladies in. Anastasia and Elsa were talking again about this question of Aunt Eugène; and Aunt Gustava, who was the late Karl Czelovar's second wife, sat apart, looking offendedly as she always did, at the painting which Roya, the Polish artist, had done of Simone, Karl Czelovar's first wife. Aunt Gustava had been Haidèe's governess. She was German, of old-fashioned appearance, and freckled, with her hair cut short behind, and falling in ringlets on either side, and wore a broad black velvet ribbon round her head. Haidèe had been a very naughty spoilt girl, and when her father, several years a widower, had brought her from Budapest to London, and had asked the Matriarch's advice on what were best done for her welfare, the Matriarch had said he had better marry his nice governess. Gustava was always very easily offended, so that when you went to say " How d'you do? " to her, you could never be sure whether she might not look away as though she had not seen you, and pucker her chubby mouth into disdain. But she had a permanent pout for the painting of Simone. It was rather an affected portrait, showing the ruddy hair twisted round with pearls, and flowing down the girl's back, right away out of the frame; one pretty shoulder was slipped from its ruching, and her pretty face simpered a little. Her low dress, what showed of it, was forget-me-not blue brocade, tightly laced down the front. The family were just beginning to say : " I believe Iris is going to be very like Simone ! " . . . Iris was Truda's youngest—she was not yet four years old.

Truda and Wanda and Haidée were whispering together over by the Adam fireplace, and laughing a great deal; and Henrietta Solomonson was laying down the law to Zillah, whom she disliked. Zillah quite simply waited for the men to come in. Later on, when this tiresome affair of Aunt Eugène had been argued to a finish, she would be commanded to sing, and Maximilian would ask for his beloved verses of Heine, set to Schumann's music :

"Ich grolle nicht, and wenn das Herz auch bricht,
　　Ewig verlornes Lieb ! ich grolle nicht . . . "

Susie was busy among the coffee-cups. They were real Sèvres and had been one of the Matriarch's most cherished wedding-presents. But Susie disliked all the Rakonitz possessions, and could never see that they had achieved, in this room, an accidental beauty, smouldering, burnished, fantastic, dwindling into tinier and tinier rooms, brilliant in miniature, locked one within the other, down the pavilions of the many mirrors; mirrors—but no pictures, except the one of Simone. The Uncles did not buy pictures. But they had bought, a magnificent bargain, the two Venetian candelabra which swung from the painted ceiling. Silky Persian rugs blended their faint blues and pinks and fawns on the parquet flooring. The shining Bechstein grand had nothing on it except, thrown over one corner, a heavy Chinese cover Paul had brought from the Paris Exhibition of 1900—deep plum colour interwoven with formal arabesques of rusty gold. The furniture was in the French Second Empire style, with the Egyptian influence—straight gilt legs and backs, that spread into carvings of queer beast faces and god faces. The tall Buhl cabinets showed Sèvres again behind their glass ; and the bureau enshrined a pair of priceless Vernet Martins in its panels. The damask embroideries on the

couch and the chairs were not as vivid as they had been
when Maximilian first gave them to his sister. He and
Louis had quarrelled over the Cloisonné jar which stood
in one corner; Louis had condemned it, but it had
remained there all the same. If Maximilian had been
the one to say " Horrible ! " the Matriarch would have
banished it from favour at once.

It was a room in which the East and the West and
Cosmopolis had poured their very best craftsmanship,
and the result was superb, though worshippers of
austerity would have stalked away in horror. Vienna
and Constantinople were in this room, Egypt and China;
it savoured, too, of Empress Eugénie's Paris. Bokhara
lay on the floor; and the English brothers Adam, with
their huge wigs and twinkling shoe-buckles, had pro-
portioned it, and so done their share. The riot of colour
repeated itself a thousandfold in the flashing crystals that
swung from the candelabra, and danced and pirouetted
from mirror to parquet, and back again, spots of minute
fire in the old paste and rubies of the Matriarch's great
marquise ring. Maximilian, who was the first to enter
from the dining-room, stood for an instant in the doorway, lord of all this opulence. . . . The period of
Rakonitz glory had, like every climax, something vaguely
ominous in it. You might hear it, sounding through the
rich notes of Zillah Korischelski's voice . . . for, tired
of waiting, she was already at the piano :

> " Du hast Diamanten und Perlen,
>   Hast alles was Menschenbegehr . . ."

v

—" And who, I should like to know," demanded Felix
irritably, " was the fool who sent her to Connie and
Raoul ? "

Aunt Gustava began to look offended :

" I am sure Raoul would have been pleased to see her
if he had been at home. Raoul is a dear boy, but of
course he has to think of the butler."

"Why has he to think of the butler? Tell me that!" demanded Maximilian. "Do I think of my butler?"

"No, but I have been thinking about him," cried Anastasia. "You will have to get rid of that man, Max, I have been meaning to tell you about him. Last time I came to your house, it was only a quarter to eleven, and he contradicted me, saying it was past midnight and that you were out, so I could not ask you the time then and there. But my watch is always right now I never set it by the church clock, which everybody knows is wrong, because I remember at Truda's wedding they all insisted by the church clock that it was two before it was twelve."

"Mamma, you know we had to do that. You hadn't started your hair by the time I was ready, all except the veil, and Ludo said the only way to make Mamma in time at the synagogue was to tell her that the church clock . . ."

It was Max who interrupted her. "We all enjoyed your wedding very much, Truda!" in that crushing manner which, according to their temperaments, could utterly subdue Truda, Wanda, and Aunt Elsa's children, but which utterly roused the dormant devil of impudence in Haidée and little Toni. "But for the moment it is of Tante Eugène that we are speaking."

"It was of your butler, dear Uncle Max," put in his niece Haidée, sweetly, while Truda made a mental note that she would put Mamma right over that question of the church clock, after everybody had gone. She could not bear injustice; and it seemed to her as though her anxiety that nothing should go wrong at her wedding, might have been the indirect cause of getting the sack for Uncle Max's butler.

Elsa said: "It was Berthe who sent Tante Eugène to the wrong house. Tante Eugène went to Paris first, and Berthe may have been in a hurry to get rid of her, and told her the first address she could think of. Yes, indeed, I know Berthe; she's a fine woman still—and prefers having that fashionable Comte d'Adhémer in her salon, to her own family."

"Well, but why didn't Uncle Eugène leave any pro-

vision for his wife?" asked Louis wearily—"Anastasia,
I wish you would have that Cloisonné vase taken away.
It spoils the room, I tell you."

Anastasia laughed good-naturedly. "It does not spoil
it for me! You do what you like in your own rooms,
Louis, and don't interfere with me, and I won't interfere
with you, and so we remain good friends."

"What a whopper!" whispered the irrepressible
Haidée to Wanda. "As if any of us did as we liked in
our own rooms, when Aunt 'Stasia comes into them?"

"Sh!" Wanda implored, giggling a little hysterically,
but terrified lest one of the Uncles should hear.

"For goodness' sake, Wanda! When one is talking of
serious matters!" The snub came from Aunt Elsa this
time.

"Perhaps, Louis, you will go to heaven and tell our good
Uncle Eugène your opinion of him. It doesn't take us
very far, does it, just to sit and blame him?"

Albrecht, who was the only person present, of the
late Eugène Rakonitz's own generation, said very simply
and gently : " Eugène did not care what became of anyone
except himself. He made Mamma very unhappy, while
he was still in Vienna, though he was much more fashionable and popular than I; I expect he made his wife
unhappy too. What is to be done for her? Elsa tells
me there is no money at all, and four children."

This was the cue for Anastasia to issue her verdict
that it was the duty of the Uncles to take at least three of
the four children into their own business.

"Thank you, my dear sister," said Dietrich. "That will
be charming. Elsa has discovered that they are all
idiots."

There was a moment's awkward silence, as the family
were thus directly confronted by the luxuriance of Tante
Eugène's tragedy, in having not one imbecile among her
offspring, as might any ordinary person, but four. Presently the Rakonitz temperament found vent, as it always
did, in a burst of renewed irascibility all round . . . all
the more aggressive, in that it hid a pitiful anger at the
visitations of Jehovah; and more anger that Eugène had

most certainly deserved this visitation, and then had slipped through and away in his irresponsible fashion, leaving them to deal with it.

" The best thing you can all do," exclaimed Maximilian, furiously, "is to stop jabbering and let us have some more music. Go on, Zillah, I would rather hear your voice than any other, for the moment."

" But how about Tante Eugène?" cried Elsa, dismayed at this collapse of the council.

Maximilian glared at her haughtily. " What is that to do with you?" Privately he had determined that the entire keep of Tante Eugène and her four children was to be his affair. Terrified, therefore, least Elsa's bright twinkling eyes should instantly discover this generous impulse in him, he snapped out further : " Haven't you four idiots of your own to look after?"

All the mother in Elsa flew up, as he had meant it to do, at this undeserved taunt at Mélanie, Freda, Gisela, and Pearl, whom she asserted were the best girls in the world, the most industrious, the most thoughtful for others. " You shall see, Max, the cloth they are working for me for my birthday next week. Three yards long, and all hand-made lace."

" Spare me ! " laughed Max, relieved at having diverted the conversation. " I do not want to see your cloth . . . Heaven forbid. Three miles long, did you say? Then my nieces are all Pearls, not one of them, but all. Felix, did you hear Elsa reminding us that it is her birthday next week?"

Elsa shrieked in dismay—he was a brute ! She had not meant . . . she did not want . . . little flutterings, ashamed wrigglings of the shoulder, dabs in Maximilian's direction . . . a naughty dimple that came and went in the cheek close under her left eye. Elsa was very, very pretty still, and a born coquette. . . . Uncle Felix called out to her to come and sit beside him, and he would tell her a good story he had lately heard. . . . They all liked telling Elsa a well-spiced story, knowing that she would pretend to be mightily shocked; knowing, too, that she loved it, and that whisperings pleased her, and secrets, and the irrepressible badness of handsome men. . . . A very typical little Viennese lady was Elsa, witty as a rule, with paprika at her tongue's end, but well aware that one must not be too witty when it was a question of a present·from Uncle Felix. He pinched her ear, and she shrieked; and he promised her some ear-rings; and she shrieked again in ecstasy, and told him that he must not —indeed no!

"I have already decided," said Anastasia, "that Tante Eugène shall have a suite of rooms with Raoul and Constance. It will give Constance something to think about, and they already have two nurses for Neil and Sylvia, so they will not have to get any more for Eugène's four babies."

"Five minutes ago, my dear 'Stasia, you had put them into our business. Now they are to be allowed to crawl about on the floor, with bibs round their necks. Does anyone know, perhaps, if Constance has agreed to this?"

"Constance? Constance has nothing to say!"

Haidée began softly to whistle. She knew her sister-in-law; and she was aware of Raoul's firm intention of presenting to the world at large, the picture of rather a cold, aloof English gentleman, with a fair, well-bred wife, and two aristocratic children who rode in the Row every morning. She did not quite see Tante Eugène in the picture. . . .

Albrecht said that he would not allow his brother Eugène's widow, and his brother Eugène's children, to go and live in any house where they were not welcome.

"My dear Albrecht, who said they would not be welcome? She is probably a charming woman, and she could help Neil with his Greek; it will be a great advantage, for that reason, for Constance and Raoul to have her in the house." And Anastasia looked imperiously at Albrecht, challenging him to produce an objection to this unanswerable fact. She did not greatly like Albrecht. He had once said, very quietly and in rather a melancholy voice, to Benno Silber and to Ferdie Marcus, that Anastasia was a stupid goose, yes, a goose!—and they had nodded a great many times, not daring to affirm this heresy in speech; but it comforted them sometimes, when they had got very much the worst of it in family debate, just to look over towards Albrecht, with his long grizzled fawn whiskers, and his long upper lip and drooping eyelids; and to remember, with an inward chuckle of disloyalty, what he had said. The Matriarch felt his secret opinion of her, without actually knowing it, and it disturbed her. Therefore, she did not like her father's brother.

He repeated now, obstinately: " Neil can learn his Greek at school. I do not wish my brother Eugène's wife to make her home where she is not welcome. We will have them to live with us."

And then Haidée, speaking with the voice of a younger generation, suggested: " Why should they live with anyone at all? Why do all you people have all your relations to live with all of you?"—And Aunt Gustava, who had already been offended in turn with Simone's picture, and with Zillah Korischelski for elbowing her from the right-hand corner of the sofa where she was entitled to sit, now prepared to be whole-heartedly offended with Haidée for thus thoughtlessly affirming in public that it was a trial to have her stepmother living with her—as indeed it was. But heedless of this gathering darkness in the background, Haidée went on :"Why not take two or three comfortable rooms somewhere for poor Tante Eugène, where there is a nice landlady; and hire some kind, practical woman to help her with the idiots; and let her be on her own. I'm sure she would prefer it."

" I'm sure she would prefer it," echoed Susie, in a low but heartfelt voice.

The Matriarch did not hear, but Haidée did, and flashed her a look of understanding.

CHAPTER VI.

I

WHEN the Matriarch told Danny that she had arranged
for him to leave his school, and to go abroad to stay
with either the Rakonitz relations in Vienna, or the de
Yongs in San Remo, and go to school with foreign boys
and learn languages, he suddenly knew that he hated her.
He had always suspected it. He was *happy* at his jolly,
ordinary boys' preparatory school in West Kensington.
What business was it of hers, to say where he should or
should not go? She had never been to a boys' school, so
knew nothing about them. She could not get inside him,
and experience his feelings about cricket and football and
Thurston Minor. He was even getting healthily interested in the Greeks and Romans. Now all that would
be broken up and wasted. It seemed to Danny, in his
rebellious kick against circumstances, that he was always
starting again. He supposed moodily that as soon as he
had begun to feel at home abroad, which was not in the
least likely, his grandmother would probably haul him
back again. If only he had people, like other boys'
people. He could not recollect one single boy whose
family were in the least like the Rakonitzes. Danny
longed for a conventional background, as others, differently placed, may have longed for excitement and
originality. A snivelling little idiot of a kid at St.
Christopher's, with eyes too big for his face, who read
poetry for fun, had once said to him : " D'you know,
Maitland, I think your family is most awfully
picturesque ! " Picturesque ! Danny had promptly kicked
him. Danny's one consolation was that he did not have
to lug about Rakonitz as a name. It was bad form to
have a " z " in one's name. " Maitland " was all right.

He could put up with " Maitland "—lucky that you took
your name not from your mother, but from your father.
. . . And here came that pang of hurt pride which struck
at what Danny did not yet call his " soul," whenever he
thought of his father. Apparently " Maitland " did not
want him, as he wanted " Maitland." It was no good
pretending—except to Toni! His father had forgotten
him, did not care what became of him, left him lying
around for Rakonitz to pick up. Danny was alternately
apathetic and fiercely haughty about embraces from
Grandmère or Toni, or any of his aunts, except Susan,
from whom he suffered them; but when he thought of his
reprehensibly absent-minded father, then that perverse
abstraction which Danny did not call his " soul," sank
a little, ached a little. . . . And yet, crumbs! how his
father had let him down! leaving him to this! leaving
him to people who knew so little how boys felt, that they
could drag them away from a fairly decent school
to send them abroad! To study and learn languages—
languages! Danny appealed to Uncle Max, who once
before had rescued him from the ignominy of lessons
with Zillah. He wrote as follows:

" Dear Uncle Max,

I hate to bother you, but I wish you would just
step down and speak to Grandmère. She wants to
take me away from school and send me abroad. I am
not saying anything against abroad, because I know
you come from there, but the Second XI at St. Christopher's rather depends on me. You see how it is,
don't you?"

He pondered for a while whether he should add anything
to this concise statement of facts; then with that sudden
wheel towards drama which neither he nor Toni could
ever resist, he added:—

" I have only you in all the world, Uncle Max, who
cares if I live or die or get my colours or not. Please
don't just send me a tip and think that'll do because
it won't."

But the trouble about this was, that it might too
effectually and forever stem Uncle Maximilian's habitual

generosity. And a tip would do very well indeed, as well
as talking to Grandmère about school, though not instead
of it. Danny's literary subtlety gave out, in the effort
to make this clear, and he brought his problem to Toni.

" I don't want him to kid himself that everything can
be settled with a sov. The Uncles do, you know. But
if I've got to go abroad anyhow, I'm better off with a
pocketful than without. See?"

But Toni was no opportunist. "You must risk all
that, and not mention tips at all," she declared, scratching
out all of the letter from "colours or not." And, with a
slight grimace at her point of view, which he considered
tinged with silliness, Danny signed himself : " Yours
truly, Sir, Daniel Maitland (née Rakonitz)."

"What's the bit in brackets?" asked Toni, over his
shoulder.

" 'Née' means born," briefly. "It's his name, too, so it'll
remind him of his duty to a relation. I heard Uncle
Ferdie say once that Uncle Max had an over-rated sense
of duty to his relations. So it might as well be over-
rated now when it's some use to me !"

" But you were never born a Rakonitz. Otherwise
I'd be ' née' 'Lake,' and I'm sure I'm not. One's 'née'
is nothing to do with one's mother, I tell you, Danny;
it's one's father's name before one's married and then
only when one's a girl."

A consultation with Aunt Truda proved Toni's rather
cryptic summing-up to be right. Danny was annoyed.
Each time Toni was right was a brick in the edifice of
her Castle Vanity.

Maximilian's moustache twitched a little when he read
the letter and the imperfectly erased alterations, and he
showed it to Louis, who happened to be in the office,
but they were both decent enough not to pass it on any
further.

" You must obey your grandmother for a few years
longer, my boy !" was the only satisfaction Danny got.
"Remember, she's a very wonderful woman."

II

The Uncles always said that, but Danny could not see it; and when Toni, who was partly rebellious and partly under the spell, tried to make him see where and how Anastasia was wonderful, Danny brought up that old stale taunt about the raw eggs. To him, the Matriarch was someone who interfered, and gave orders, and exulted in power like some wicked old Roman emperor. He could not see that impetuous benevolence which would urge her at all times to do anything for anybody; not only for the family, but for any stray, of any class, any nation, any religion, who just needed help. Anastasia had once canvassed tirelessly for weeks, up to late hours of night, to obtain the votes for the son of a servant of an old friend, who had been left destitute, and wanted her child admitted to a Masonic school. If anyone were ill, Anastasia would not rest until the right doctors, the right food, and the right treatment had been provided; and she would give of her own cheerful company lavishly, however crowded her social life might be.

When she appeared to make herself ridiculous in her sudden exploitations of this or that protégé, it was with the fervent desire that young artists should have their chances, that young workers should be encouraged and stimulated; and disappointments left her still an optimist. Emergency could successfully call on her to play nurse, cook, midwife; her resourcefulness was boundless, and her belief in her own resourcefulness still more boundless.

Her instincts for hospitality were such that whatever house she reigned over might have been an inn, so genial was her welcome to visitors by day or night, whether they wanted wine and cooked meats at two o'clock in the morning, or whether they begged to be allowed to stay with her for a year. There could be no coldness in entertainments where Anastasia was hostess. She was simply incredulous of shyness or formality, or of people who stiffly refused to get on with each other; and by her very incredulity, bewitched it all away. "And she looks like a duchess, too!" Maximilian or Louis would murmur proudly, watching her move about among their guests, in a dress that Blaise had given her for her seventieth birthday. . . .

The dress was of stiff black satin, embroidered with little white silk flowers, and finished off by some very fine old lace. The heavy train and the full skirt, weighted with jet trimmings, would have overwhelmed a slighter woman, but the Matriarch's height carried them regally. On her left arm she wore a bracelet in which a very fine pale ruby was surrounded by diamonds; on her right arm, another bracelet was set with rubies and diamonds alternately. Her pendant was an enamel portrait of an angel's head, surrounded by rubies; and the brooch clasped into her lace was a bird set with diamonds, in a circle of diamonds, with a large pigeon-blood ruby drop on either side. In her hair, still black, though with a frosty gleam along the left side, was set a tall comb studded with tiny brilliants. She held a fan of black Chantilly lace, with occasional diamonds sewn on it, the handle and sticks of dark grey mother-o'-pearl, inset with a design of brilliants and rubies.

. . . Do not mind looking with interest at Anastasia Rakonitz, sitting in that dress, at the head of her brothers' table, at their dinner-party. For you will not see her attired in it again. She had worn it but this once, when a young singer of her passing acquaintance, in great distress and practically starving, was offered a part with the Carl Rosa Company. One of the conditions was that she should supply a handsome black evening-dress for herself. She had sold all her things during her long period of enforced " resting," and was nearly desperate, when Anastasia, who happened to hear of it, impetuously came to the rescue with the gift of her own beautiful black satin frock. . . .

She went to one of the Carl Rosa performances at the Coronet Theatre, and was heartily glad to see what gradeur it conferred on her new protégé.

Anastasia was eternally gay, as she was eternally bountiful. And there was no rust of snobbery in her heart. She did not care who her friends were, nor how

she picked them up. She had beaten a man with her
costly enamel umbrella until it broke, because she had
seen him ill-treating a horse that dragged a too-heavy
van up the steep slope of Camden Hill; and her subsequent encounter with the policeman to whom the
injured vanman had appealed, eventually led to her going
to tea, the following Sunday, with his wife, and the
vanman too, in a state of grudging repentance, and
thrilling the whole party with her spirited account of the
thirty-one Libyan horses which were kept in the Spanish
riding-school for the sole use of the Hapsburg Royal
Family in Vienna. "And what do you think?" cried
Anastasia, leaping like a chamois from story to story,
"Vienna was so dirty when I was a young girl, that when
I went to my first ball, my white muslin dress was soiled
by the mud in the cab, so that I could not show myself
when we arrived, and I had to take it off and wait while
the maid washed it and ironed it, and all my impatient
partners came and clamoured at the dressing-room door
and cried : 'Na, 'Stasia, what are you doing so long in
there? They are playing our favourite waltz; you will
miss the "Blue Danube"!' . . . You know the dear
'Blue Danube'?" And then and there she sat down at
the wheezy little harmonium in the constable's best
parlour, and played the witching old melodies of Johann
Strauss, till the three children were all holding out their
skirts and dancing, and the vanman danced with the
constable's wife, and they all enjoyed themselves hugely.

III

Danny would have been first amazed and then a scoffer
if anyone had told him that his twelve-year-old horror of
being expelled abroad would be as nothing to his fifteen-
year-old sorrow and rage at being hauled back again.
He adored Vienna, he revelled in the Italian Riviera, he
was crazy about Paris. He could have dispensed, certainly, with the eternal family that he found lying like
patchwork over the Continent; nearly all with some trait
of the Rakonitz face, or the face complete, to remind

him unwillingly of home and Grandmère; but the strangeness of the places themselves, the twisting facets that
every day brought round to him, were a perpetual joy to
Danny, whose temperament proved to be adaptable, and
his curiosity eternal. And then there was Franz—Uncle
Franz, he supposed it ought to have been, but Franz
himself had declared wearily that "uncle" was a grizzly
word, and if it were applied to him too often he would
lose all his reputation as a witty rake, and settle down
instead into middle age and become worthy.

"I am exactly thirty-nine," remarked Franz, raising
his left brow to screw in the monocle which made him
so absurdly resemble Uncle Louis. "Have you ever
heard them speak of forty as 'l'âge dangereux,' Danny?"

Franz was the grandson of Sigismund's brother,
Ludovic, who had married Wili Taliman. His father,
Leopold Josef, had been their only son. Franz, too, like
Leopold Josef, was a typically Viennese Rakonitz, in
the famous Wein-Weib-und-Gesang style; England only
knew that style, witty and gallant, wearing incredible
white and silver and light blue uniforms, in musical
rendering, as, later on, Fall and Lehar and Oskar Strauss
were to present them to us. But they actually did exist,
and Franz Rakonitz was one of them. Franz wore his
clothes better than any other man in Vienna; could
play the piano, by ear, as well as any other man in
Vienna; flirted as well as he danced; and could shoot as
well as he flirted; he had shrewd ironical eyes; did everything as though he were bored; mocked eternally at himself and his reputation and the family. . . .

Danny was just beginning to talk Viennese argot a good
deal more fluently than the scholarly German of Goethe
and Schiller, when the summons came that he was to
return to England. The Matriarch wrote that she had
discovered a genius, a marvellous man, a most gifted and
unfortunate mortal, with brilliant ideas for a new method
of teaching, and absolutely no school to teach it in; so she
had found the small capital necessary for the premises—
and here, unwritten but large between the lines, the words
"the Uncles" winked up at Danny! She had canvassed

vigorously, on behalf of this rarity among school-masters, for pupils, of whom she had managed to assemble a nucleus of twenty-one, and one more promised seven years after his birth, unless he turned out to be a girl; and Danny, of course, had been dedicated to Signor Warrington's experiment from the very beginning.

"Why the devil should she call him ' Signor '?" reflected the victim, impatiently.

The Matriarch promised Danny abundant joy in his new school, and he was not to waste a minute, as term started three days before the Matriarch wrote and she desired him to be there from the very first day. . . .

—" Gently, my son !" said Franz, coming into the room and hearing Danny's oaths. "Don't use them all up in your early youth. What has upset your calm?"

"My Grandmother !" Danny handed over the letter.

"She's a wonderful woman," pronounced Franz, after reading it.

"Oh, stow it ! That's what the Uncles say !"

" The Uncles are right. I like her devastating insouciance ! I'm afraid you will have to go, Danny. You are still a minor, you see; otherwise, of course, we would defy her, and then she would come to Vienna to fetch you, and we would introduce her to the keeper of the Spanish horses, and she would be too busy telling him that their diet has been all wrong and that he ought to mix anchovy with their bran-mash, to bother any more about you. Do you care about the Opera to-night, or shall we drive out to the Rockenbauer and sing songs with the students?"

Danny tore himself away from Vienna, with every fibre of his emotions torn and aching.

When he arrived in Holland Terrace, rumpled and wrathful and loudly denouncing all masters of freak schools, it was to find that it had been Toni, of all people, who had helped to recall him; who had skilfully cajoled the Matriarch into financing Mr. Warrington's new school, for the secret purpose of having Danny in it.

" Well ! Of all the interfering little idiots ! " He stood speechless in the middle of the nursery, glaring at her.

"You hated going abroad," said Toni. "You made me promise to do whatever I could to get her to send for you back again."

"Hated it? I loved it! I never hated it."

"You did, before you went. You wanted to stop in London."

But now Toni found herself confronted with a curious blankness in Danny. He simply could not, or would not, remember his former state of mind. He just coolly denied the self which had been furious at leaving London, and denied, too, that that self could have had anything to do with Toni's loyal behaviour in encouraging a whole new school into existence, in order that Daniel Maitland might not be left to languish among foreigners. Danny was to go through life cutting all his day-before-yester-days, as though he had never met them before; and this was Toni's first definite collision with his ingratitude. Toni was not a meek child, and she wrestled with Danny instead of giving in to him. They had always quarrelled, but from this moment began a long warfare with very rare truces, a juvenile version of "The Taming of the Shrew." If Toni had had thin lank hair scraped back from her forehead, and toes that awkwardly turned in, she might have been submissive to Danny's dictum that he had never minded leaving London; but, unfortunately for his lordliness, Toni at fifteen was very pretty; a wild-petal prettiness, with thick tumbled hair veiling her shoulders, a dainty way of wearing her clothes, and a thoroughly annoying way of tilting her chin and saying: "People always do things for me!" Toni had read a great many books about the little-princess girl, or the little mem-sahib, in which devoted black servants swarmed about and adored, or devoted school-girls laid offerings of india-rubbers and service at the bronze-shod feet of the "favourite." Sometimes she beheld herself as the little queen of the shack, beloved of all the rude cowboys, or as a disdainful little marquise in an old French garden, accepting delicious compliments from the gardener's infatuated son—"or sons," put in Danny when she had got thus far in her plans for the future. "Don't

stop at one! I've noticed that whenever you work out
your future, it always includes about a dozen people
who wait upon you. What you want, young Toni, is a
dash of adversity to teach you to wait on yourself."

"Oh! I can't be bothered with adversity and that sort
of thing!" quoth Toni flippantly—and thus challenged
the fates.

It was very bad for Toni, exasperatingly bad, Danny
thought, that she happened to be the type whom servants
actually did adore, and who was waited upon by less vivid
and less comely maidens of her own age. The secret of her
popularity was that she still so intensely enjoyed things;
parties, and people, and music. There were no limits to
her resilience, just as there were no limits to her wildly
affectionate impulses. Toni had that little extra zest
added to every one of her five senses, which always seems
to be the lot of those who are not strong, and who thus
have a perpetual threat hanging over them whenever they
see, hear, touch, smell or taste too keenly.

She took care, however, that Danny should realise her
supremacy in the house, and perhaps it was a misjudg-
ment to have used the words "my imperial sway," even
in joke.

"Imperial grandmother!" retorted Danny, but without
reference to the Matriarch. "You are only a conceited
ass!"

Toni tossed her head, and smiled provokingly. "I can
make even Grandmère do as I want," she said.

"Next time you had better want something a bit less
silly than that ass Warrington's school. Running it 'on
Greek lines,' indeed! A lot of mildewy piffle! Throwing
javelins instead of a decent game of rugger."

"You wouldn't carry my satchel upstairs this morning,
because you're afraid of me."

"That would make me carry it up, wouldn't it? I like
your logic!"

"You were afraid that if you did it once you would
be in my power, and you would have to go on doing it."

"You haven't got any power for me to be in!"

"I have!"

" Who says so?"

" Everybody. I heard Uncle Benno telling Father—"

" Yes, you are the sort of girl who listens at doors hoping to hear something nice about themselves, and if they don't you make it up."

" It's time you came back from abroad and learnt English," said Toni. " You made me sound like seven girls, just then!"

" You behave like seven girls."

" You would prefer it, darling Danny, wouldn't you, if I behaved like a quarter of a girl?"

Danny looked at her, grinning. He wished that she really had a face more like a pudding. He was afraid that if she went on improving at the rate of the last three years—mere surface improvement, of course—that more and more people would run about and carry satchels for her, strengthening her belief that she was one of those precious few at whose " open sesame " doors respond eagerly. Derek Silber, for instance, was very much his cousin Toni's slave during the holidays, and her own brother, Gerald, was simply a fool about her. Danny was quite weighed down at the responsibility thus developing on him alone, of teaching Toni that she was a child of absolutely no importance. Maxine had told him that at their Christmas party, one of those four-thirty to nine-thirty affairs, which are such an improvement on the infantile three to seven, Toni had had four partners for the supper-dance, and had said—" Tossing her head, I bet!" Danny growled—that she could sit with all four of them. As a matter of fact, Danny had not heard the rest of that story in which Toni, swiftly realising before anyone else, even the grown-ups, that three rather shy awkward girls were left with no partners at all, and were too diffident to say so, had simulated a sudden " imperial " friendship for these same girls, whom she did not care about at all, and had dragged them, her arms about their necks, into the supper-room, wilfully ignoring her own four partners, who, following her to the same table, had given the three an appearance, at least, of a perfectly good male partner each, and one over for Toni.

Their pride had never known that Toni nor anyone else had guessed their plight. . . .

"What time do you go to bed now?" asked Danny. "And don't throw your curls about and say 'whenever I choose,' because I'm not going to believe it."

"Nine o'clock," in an offhand way.

"With your delicate constitution, it ought to be a quarter to seven," he teased.

"Oh, I'm not a bit delicate any more. I'm going to be a dancer, you know." Toni's family had not heard about this, yet.

"In Vienna," said Danny, "and in France, kids never seem to go to bed at all. They are always up."

"Oh, Danny. Do tell me about our old house in Vienna. What's it like?"

"What old house?"

"The one on the Danube, where Grandmère was born, and Aunt Simone, and all of them; where our ancestors lived."

But Danny had not been to see it.

"How could you not go!" cried Toni, amazed.

"I wasn't interested. There were tons of other things to see."

And Toni, whose romantic imagination had lived in every room of that house; had sat, in fancy, beside Great-great-grandmother Babette and wound her wool for her; had picked up specks of amber and opal beside the yellow river, so falsely blue by the legend; Toni, who had throbbed with Simone's own pride, at an echo of a fiacre drawn up smartly outside the house, the driver inviting her to step in for the sake of her beauty. . . . Toni simply looked at Danny as though he were an imbecile.

"But they belong to us! We belong to them! All over Europe there are people with our faces, and who trade in our name. All over Europe are houses that we have lived in. It's all joined together, back and back, through that house which you didn't go and see, and down the Danube to other little towns. . . . Oh, I'd like to simply follow and follow and follow our family wherever it twisted, to hundreds of years ago. Danny, doesn't it thrill you?"

She was so on fire with her speech that for once he did not chaff her, but answered, startlingly enough: "No, it doesn't.   It bores me.   It's tiresome.   It's like travelling with an awful lot of luggage when you could do with none; or dragging about weights, or living in an untidy room which you never cleared out.   What *would* thrill me, would be to belong to nobody, to begin everything from the very beginning, even a family, only I shouldn't have any family, not much!   The only Rakonitz I care tuppence about is Franz, and then it's not because he's a Rakonitz, because he might just as well be anyone else, only he happens to be quite the rippingest chap I know."

And then, a teller of tales in his turn, and, when he chose, a much more potent one than Truda, he built up for Toni the Vienna which Franz had shown him: the gallant and swaggering Vienna, without burdensome grandmères or cousins or uncles; without one generation forever sitting on the other's back, or memories kicking at the heel of the glorious present, but simply a light-hearted city of pleasure and wit and waltzing . . . Till Toni's eyes shone with excitement, and she promised herself that all her life long she would never worry about anything, and never be heavy, and never do her duty, but just live as buoyantly as the Viennese, and flirt with men like Franz who knew it was all a graceful game; and substitute, for sorrow, a flippant irony; and dance, and be gay and attractive, and go where there were lights and little tables and wine with golden bubbles that shot to the surface of her glass. . . . All this was Toni's inheritance, and had she but known it, was enchanted into the one word " Stimmung." . . .

" I say, Toni, what on earth has happened to Uncle Ludo?"

" Don't you know?"   Toni was partly elated that the incomparable Danny should have been left out of a secret, and partly ashamed that in the telling she had to tarnish the silvery edifice of family glory, which Danny, anyway, was so impishly fond of demolishing for her whenever with battlements and pinnacles she had built it up afresh.

"They may have told me," Danny lied, knowing full well that he lied. "'I was very busy in Vienna and San Remo, and perhaps I didn't read all the letters quite through. Aunt Truda's, for instance; she goes on for pages about things that happened a hundred years ago. Why, when I was in Paris, she scribbled me a long story all about when *she* went to Paris, when she was quite a girl, and went to the theatre ' with three gentlemen '—"

" I know," Toni cried, an authority on family history. " Aunt Wanda was there, too, and Aunt Rosalie Dupont, and they wore pale blue silk blouses with enormous balloon sleeves, so that if you wanted to talk to anybody next to you, you couldn't. Blouses like that were just coming into fashion. Grandmère allowed them to go unchaperoned with Franz, because he was a cousin, but as he was very handsome and a rake, *that* didn't make it any better, especially as two of his bachelor friends joined them in the box. . ."

Danny, who had picked up a book and begun to read it with absorption, indifferent to Toni's tale, now put it down again and listened; a story which enshrined Franz could not be wholly boring, even though some of the family came in, too.

" The three tall girls in their pale blue silk blouses were fairly innocent, as young girls were, then," Toni continued, amused from her superior standpoint of 1909 at the mere idea of an 1880 upbringing, " but they all understood French, and could not help knowing that the play was rather awful and that they shouldn't have been there. . . . And when the prince began to marry the princess *on* the stage, they couldn't stand it any longer, because all the gentlemen in the theatre were turning opera-glasses on them. So Aunt Truda said she was very tired and please might they go home." . . . She had related the incident almost in Truda's own words. " I expect Franz was glad," she added, in conclusion.

"I bet he was. What's this about Uncle Ludo, though?"

Toni tiptoed to the door and closed it, after making sure that there was no one on the landing.

"Oh! do stop being important!" groaned her cousin.

"It's a secret. I'm not even sure if I ought to tell you."

"If you're not going to tell me, there's not much sense in closing the door, is there? You had better open it again."

Toni perceived that he was really curious. Softly she hummed a tune, rocking herself to and fro astride of Gerald's old wooden Dobbin.

"You and Camille de Yong about take the cake for airs and graces! If she hadn't been so gloriously beautiful," continued Danny, getting some of his own back, "I wouldn't have stood hers; but there's no excuse for you, young Toni."

Toni continued to hum. . . . She jealously wanted to hear about her cousin in San Remo.

"Fair or dark? Fair or dark?" she wove into her tune.

"Golden," replied Danny fervently, his voice one throb of admiration. And then, after a pause, in his old insinuating way which Toni found so difficult to resist: "Do you know, Toni, I believe I should like curly brown hair much better than smooth golden . . . if only I knew where Uncle Ludo was." And he put out his hand to stop the rocking of her palfrey.

Toni, appeased, bent down towards him.

"Nicaragua!" she whispered.

Danny looked puzzled. "Where's that?"

"Oh, it's somewhere on the other side of the Equator," Toni replied carelessly.

Danny lugged out a map. To him it was much more important to find Nicaragua, than to discover purely local information as to why Ludovic should suddenly have disappeared from Holland Terrace and be obliterated from family discussion.

"It isn't on the other side of the Equator. You're

a perfect ass, Toni. You'll get into trouble one day for giving false information. Suppose you were teaching in a school?"

Toni refused to worry about such an unromantic possibility. She did not see herself teaching in a school. She came and looked over Danny's shoulder.

"It's on the bit that joins the two Americas. There's a big lake in it—oh! and a cape called Gracias-a-Dios—that means 'Goodness-gracious-me,' Toni. Oh, and Toni, just listen to the exports : rosewood, tortoise-shell, indigo, hides, and gold chains."

They exchanged glowing looks over the great atlas, friends for a moment. . . .

"Uncle Ludo has all the luck," and Danny drew a long breath.

"He didn't want to go a bit. Danny—he must have done something wrong. Grandmère cried, and the Uncles came every evening, and Aunt Elsa was here all the time, and I could tell by the way they closed doors, or spoke German or French when I was about, that something was wrong; and I understood bits, too. They were all frightfully angry with Uncle Ludo, and he whistled a lot up and down stairs. You remember how he whistled? only he did it more than ever now. And quite soon afterwards he went away; early, before any of us were up. Grandmère didn't get up at all, that day, and Aunt Gustava and Aunt Henrietta and Aunt Elsa all came and sat with her, and when I asked where Uncle Ludo was, they told me he had been called away on business, but that I was not to ask in front of people. There has been one letter from him; I saw the writing. And they gave Gerald the stamp, and it was Nicaragua. But all that was nearly a year ago, and I don't think he has written since. Danny, what do you think he did?"

"Nothing," said Danny. "He wanted a change and he went. The family kick up such a fuss about everything. I shall go, too, as soon as I am old enough to get away."

But Toni persisted that there was something wrong. . . .

CHAPTER VII.

I

FROM the year 1909 to 1910 Danny remained at his crank school in Hampstead, where he was likened to Alcibiades, more than once, by his master, that ass Warrington.

During that year were the usual amount of Rakonitz festivals and Rakonitz rows, and also one or two funerals; Blaise, for instance, Anastasia's darling, whose petted childhood Sophie had so bitterly envied, just died, rather slowly and petulantly, for no apparent reason except, as the doctor said, that he had no stamina. Had he been a girl of the eighteenth century they would have called his illness a " decline." In ten years' time it would have been called primarily a "nervous breakdown." They got nearer to the right word in the old days, when we "declined" to live; when, quite simply, we turned our faces from laughter and pleasure and battle. Blaise, on the surface, had had all the plausible charm, the generosity, the touch of arrogant lordliness which belonged to one generation after another of the Rakonitz men. He had their weakness, too; he dared not be—not generous, lest anyone should think him mean; he dared not be—not charming, lest anyone should ever dislike him. He had been given what he wanted, by his mother, until he wanted nothing more that she could give him, and because of that, and because she had married her first cousin, and because he had no stamina, he died. And the two haggard lines which were ploughed down either side of the Matriarch's mouth, in times of trouble, from now onwards, remained permanent; and her abundant hair was iron-grey, from now onwards; and she was rather more picturesque than ever in her disregard of the clock's effect upon the world's movement.

97

One other Rakonitz, Felix, died that year in London; and a Czelovar in Paris, Konrad, the husband of Berthe Dupont, who was the daughter of Lena, who was the daughter of Simon and Babette. No woman of the family had died for a long time.

And Dietrich produced his " Glamis Monster."

Quite suddenly the children were allowed to visit him at his house; and a serene, plump, homely little French woman appeared at the head of his table, whom they were told to call Aunt Annette, and who apparently had been there all the time, and was not in the least sinister or like a monster, nor indeed like that other word beginning with " m " which the grown-ups of the family had called her in whispers . . . until Uncle Dietrich, very crossly, and on a sudden, quite inexplicable impulse, had marched her off to the Registrar one morning. And after this, Danny lost all interest in Dietrich, who hitherto had been his patron uncle. There were still three, when you spoke about the Uncles; only now that Felix was dead, Louis was called in to discuss and adjudicate, as well as Dietrich and Maximilian. He came very reluctantly, and, usually from sheerly perverse motives, took the opposite side from authority, as represented by Dietrich, Maximilian, and Anastasia, and thus delayed judgment considerably, though he could not ultimately dictate it.

Haidée had declared that she was going to leave her husband, and could give no better reason than that she was not happy with him. She had secret allies in Truda and in Susan Lake, but that generation lay crushingly sandwiched between the overwhelming generation of Anastasia, and the imperious claims, pushing upwards, of the younger lot, Val, Danny, Toni and Gerald, Maxine, Derek and Iris, Neil and Sylvia. Haidée shrugged her shoulders, gave in, and continued to sit at the head of Francis Power's solid mahogany dining-room table, to regulate his mid-Victorian household according to his mid-Victorian ideas, and dutifully to kiss his white walrus moustache every night and every morning. He really did not make any demands on her, except her constant presence in the house. That satisfied him. If, while in his house, her little toe ached, he would lavish on it all the tender care, consideration and expense that his £10,000 a year could procure; but if she had gone away, independently of his wishes, for so much as a solitary week-end, and then he had heard that she was suffering from mortal illness, he would have pursed obstinate lips together and replied that the matter did not concern him. A queer love, that of Francis Power for his wife. He disapproved of her flippancy. He tried to crush down mischief in her. He said that she was extravagant, and that she talked too freely and lightly to his friends; but at the same time, he was very proud of her popularity which flowered from this soil of which he disapproved. The family liked him; in many ways he was the English version of what they were themselves in cosmopolitan edition; but they were far from being as solid in temperament. They respected his lack of brilliance, his carefulness with money, his uneccentricity; he added prestige to the family gatherings, and always he assisted them to uphold convention and to subjugate the young. So they could not understand why Haidée should want to leave him— "Especially," as Elsa gossiped to Anastasia, "as there is no lover."

"Me you can teach nothing," replied Anastasia, with her invariable slogan. "Does a pretty woman want to go and live alone for no harm? For no man? Does she mean to live alone, always? Believe me, Elsa, she has gone to fry some other fish!"

"And what will become of Val?" exclaimed Elsa. "She is already, between ourselves, 'Stasia, in some things, a most terrible girl."

Val Power, now aged nineteen, was the bitterest drop in Aunt Elsa's cup of holy trials. Clamorously she disapproved of her all day long, and most of the night. She persecuted her, she scandalised about her—but she could not forget her. Actually, Val was her favourite niece, albeit three generations removed. Val was the sort of audacious dandy whom Aunt Elsa would most dearly have loved for a daughter; for it was the tragedy of Vienna's sauciest coquette, that her own four daughters, Mélanie, Freda, Gisela and Pearl—well, perhaps they could best be summed up by Danny's triumphant rhyme :

" Mélanie, Freda, Gisela and Pearl,
  Make me thank Heaven that I'm not a girl ! "

It was not that they were bad girls, but that they were good girls, industrious, pliable, considerate, and domestic. It is not that they were ugly, no, they were neatly, cheerfully pretty, but they waged a perpetual warfare against their own prettiness and femininity, so that men should not notice them, even as they never noticed men. When a man came into the room in which one of them, or all four were sitting, smooth coils of fawn hair bent over their needlework, he did not go near them; he either went and sat next to some other girls, or if there were no other girls, he left the room. They had a great many friends, all girls; they were very much liked; they were helpful, wholesome, and useful. They were four queer little nuns for whom sex did not exist. Four little nuns of varying sizes, who would say reprovingly to Val or Toni—" Oh, don't let's talk of that, it's not very nice," when the other cousins shocked them with light talk of kisses and conquests. Four little nuns—as punishment for Vienna's most irresistible coquette. And oh! how bravely Elsa boasted of her good girls, and their industry and thrift; and how proud she would have been of a daughter who was impertinent, a daughter who was lazy and extravagant and rebellious, to whom men came, straight as an arrow from a bow, when they entered the room. How she would have exulted in such a daughter, and how warmly, closely akin she would have felt to her ! She would have appreciated exactly what each glance meant, in the game of light flirtation; each trick, each advance and retirement. And if she had scolded such a daughter—and she would have scolded her, far more often than Mélanie, Freda, Gisela and Pearl required to be scolded—but it would have been fun, scolding her; not the dreary duty that she now found it.

So when Elsa gallantly, loyally, boasted of her four

good girls to other mothers of the family, the mother of
Toni, the mother of Val, the mother of Maxine, they
did not bother to swagger back; and they did not envy
Elsa, for they preferred their less, their much less good
girls, who could attract men. Mothers are like that!
. . . Elsa had no boys, whom she would have adored,
as Anastasia had adored hers; but Val, Haidée's
daughter, was very like a boy, while remaining also a
scornfully attractive girl, when she nonchalantly dug her
hands in her pockets, and cheeked Aunt Elsa, of whom
she was not in the least afraid. So Elsa scratched and
scandalised, and there was bitterness in the scratches.

Mélanie, Freda, Gisela and Pearl considered Val rather
awful, and thought she had a bad influence over Toni.
Freda tried to supplant her as an influence where Toni
was concerned. Toni accepted Freda's presents, listened
to her gentle sermons, but said she could not be bothered
to take up botany. Botany for Toni! when there were
kisses, and dancing feet on shining parquet! Then she
hugged Freda and called her a darling, but continued to
admire Val and copied her whenever possible.

Haidée remained with Francis Power, not being young
enough to carry solitary rebellion through opposition to
fulfilment. It was easier to remain with dear old Francis,
to be flippant, and rather sarcastic. Her mother Simone
had remained with dear old Karl Czelovar until she had
died, raving that she was an Empress. . . .

Val went to study painting in Paris and in Munich; she
also travelled down into Italy. Every time she journeyed
on from one country to another, there was a fresh out-
burst of family councils and family rows, because she
would not accept family decrees as to which relations
she was to stay with, and preferred to make her own
dangerous artistic friends. . . .

"You should insist, Haidée," cried Anastasia. "Val
is only nineteen, she can't possibly distinguish yet who
are nice people!"

Haidée shrugged her shoulders—her usual response.

Of family festivities there were two that year—Aunt
Gustava's seventieth birthday, and the wedding of
Camille de Yong, the eldest daughter of Amélie, who
was the daughter of Grethe, whose husband had been
left out of Truda's rendering of the family tree
because nobody could remember his name. It is
perhaps hardly fair to speak of the wedding as
entirely Camille's, from the family point of view, for she
was marrying Etienne Czelovar, her second cousin, the
son of Berthe, who had married Konrad Czelovar; and
Berthe was the daughter of Lena, wife of Jules Dupont;
and thus the Paris and San Remo branches of Rakonitz
were twisted together again, for the second time; Berthe
and Konrad, too, had been connected. Because Paris
was nearer than San Remo, the wedding took place at
the Czelovars' apartment in the Hôtel Drucot. Quite a
number of the London family were over for the event :
Uncle Maximilian and Anastasia, with Zillah Korischelski in attendance, Truda and Benno, Otto Solomonson and his wife Henrietta, who was the daughter of
Great-Aunt Gisela, wife of Julian Czelovar. Elsa went,
but not Albrecht, because he was getting too old and
feeble, so she took Pearl instead; and Pearl was fille
d'honneur, and thus in a position to have strutted her
advantage arrogantly in front of Toni and Maxine on
her return, if Pearl had had any strut in her, which she
had not, and so the advantage was wasted.

Aunt Berthe, the mother of the bridegroom, was
indignant from the very start of the festivities, as she
resented the presence of Zillah, and thought it indiscreet
of the Matriarch to have brought her protégée along;
Zillah took her welcome as a matter of course. Zillah
always did. She had discovered that it eased her passage
through society. Berthe and Zillah were both large fine
women with large fine voices, and probably more for the
latter reason than for the former, both great favourites
with the Uncles. A crisis occurred when Uncle Felix
asked Berthe if she still sang—" Sing? My dee-urr, I
sing more vonderful zan effer ! " . . .

Zillah sniggered. . . . And after bed-time that same evening, the two ladies, in dressing-gowns, with heavily powdered faces, regrettably called each other " Espèce d'animal ! " one of them leaning with threatening gestures over the staircase balustrade, the other glaring upwards from the landing below. . . .

But Berthe, who was very much the nicer of the two, so naïf in her tremendous vanity that it became laughable and lovable, Berthe scored when her brother-in-law, Anatol Czelovar, begged her, within earshot of at least three of the family, including Uncle Felix, not to put him near that too terrible Korischelski at the wedding-breakfast.

Anatol was Konrad's younger brother, whom English boys would have called " La-di-da " at that time, on account of his pale lavender gloves and his exquisite boots, and the thinness on his crown, which was obviously the result of a merry and misspent career, and not the pressure of industry and responsibility.

It was not long since Etienne's father had died, so that the bridegroom, who was both fluent and sentimental, referred many times to the tears that were in his heart because his sainted papa could not see him in his present delirious felicity. . . . " Moi, j'ai les larmes au coeur " was, indeed, the catch-phrase of this rollicking wedding. And the two supreme figures were Aunts Hermina and Gisela, both over ninety, and full of good cheer and conceit. A tough pair ! Toni would have enjoyed hearing them reprove Henrietta for giddiness, and Anastasia for the extravagance of her sables; lecturing Maximilian, le " Grand Seigneur," for giving her these same sables instead of putting the money carefully away; for Aunts Hermina and Gisela were of the Bettelheim, not of the Rakonitz, family, and the main characteristics of the Bettelheims were toughness and thrift. They both cackled derisively on hearing that their brother-in-law Albrecht, the last surviving male Rakonitz of Sigismund's generation, had not been brisk enough to appear at the wedding of his great-niece with his great-nephew. And they offended Elsa mightily by remarking that she might have chosen her present more carefully, which was unfair, because Elsa, besides having all the trouble of choosing her own present for any member of the family who married, was also for some reason of self-appointment, the deputy who went round to every other member of the family directly the date of a wedding was announced, to discuss what each would give, so that the bride should start with neither gaps nor duplicates in her household equipment.

"But *liebe* Elsa," with that appalling frankness which seems to be the prerogative of centenarians, particularly Bettelheim centenarians, "to bring a dinner-service from London all the way, with two plates smashed, and to have paid *that* price for it, which neither Gisela nor I believe you did, but still, we will not argue, when you might have so much better arranged for Franz to have bought a dinner-service in Vienna that was more fit for our Camille to display to visitors, while you and Albrecht surely, together with Anastasia, could have presented all the cutlery, which they tell me is better in England than anywhere else."

Elsa lost her temper, and great care had to be exercised during the few days of festivities that she was not placed anywhere near her mother or her Aunt Gisela at table. And the more tactful relations, when viewing the presents, remarked several times, whenever Elsa was within earshot : "But what a beautiful dinner-service ! How fortunate is Camille ! Whoever gave this must indeed have had both taste and generosity ! "

"What did the Uncles give? " was the question most frequently asked of Camille's mother; asked with awe, as though whoever sought information were anticipating an answer that would take their breath away. The Uncles had given a cheque. It would pay for the honeymoon, furnish a modest apartment, and buy Etienne the partnership he desired in the antique-furnishing business. "The Uncles are never mean," said Truda; "they would have bought Benno for me, but there was no need, of course, because he was in love."

Jeanne-Marie, Camille's little sister, a charming golden-

haired child of nine, with a flavour of sophistication and
the Casino already in her speech, and an imitation of the
fashionable Riviera in the way her sash was tied, was
fille d'honneur with Aunt Elsa's Pearl. Her flirtation
with Anatol, aged fifty-one, was an affair with the highest
polish on it; and Pearl, had she been less shocked, might
have learnt a thousand lessons, trivial but exquisite, from
Jeanne-Marie.

Aunt Gustava's seventieth birthday was mainly remark-
able for the fact that the family sentiment had to be
redoubled in heartiness, in case Aunt Gustava should
suddenly remember that she was not by birth a member
of the family, or suspect someone else of remembering.
Val, too, the eldest step-grandchild, from whom a little
tact and consideration might really have been expected,
and who, besought feverishly by Haidée's letters, had
returned from Vienna especially not to miss the occasion,
had a really tempestuous quarrel with the old lady about
five days before the birthday. Val was quite ready to
make it up the day afterwards, but Aunt Gustava, not
having Val's indolently humorous outlook, remained
offended up to the very eve of the important day, and
then only was reconciled with drama and tears. Val's
offence had been as follows : she had actually managed
to smuggle through, as a birthday offering, a bottle of
Imperial Tokay. Aunt Gustava had been very pleased
indeed, and had punctured the air with little cries and
chortles of anticipation. The talk had naturally turned
on wines, and Neil, the eldest step-grandson, who, at
eighteen, was beginning rather to fancy himself as a
gourmet and an epicure, produced a wine-list and invited
Val to help him select an ideal cellar.

"The list might be a description of the different
members of the family," murmured Val. "Listen, Neil,
isn't this one like Aunt Anastasia?—'Grand bouquet,
great character, magnificent Burgundy, probably un-
equalled of this growth'; or this one, Chambolle Musigny,
this might be Uncle Maximilian : 'Very smooth and
refined, beautiful bouquet, most elegant, rich and
velvety !'"

Haidée chuckled and joined them over the wine-list.
"And who does this remind you of?" she asked.
"'Classic bouquet, great breed, good body.'"

"Me!" promptly replied Val. "And here's Aunt Elsa
—'fine style, brisk, fresh and delicate.' What jolly words
they use—'velvety,' 'grapey,' 'fruity,' 'mellow.' 'Magnificent old Tawny, very old, nutty, brown'—that was
great-great-grandmother Babette. Uncle Anatol is 'very
choice old Amaroso, deep golden, full, dry, nutty'—and
all the Rakonitzes have a 'beautiful bouquet.'"

Gustava began to bridle; she thought Val was hinting
that she was not one of the Rakonitz family, and therefore not entitled to a bouquet.

"What wine would you say was like me?" she
demanded shrilly.

Val hastily ran her eye down the list. Truth to tell,
Gustava did not remind her of any wine at all, but at
random she selected one, and read aloud "full-bodied, old
bottled, generous and very soft—old brown Solera—1834
vintage."

"*Thank* you, Val! Full-bodied! *Thank* you very
much indeed!" She was quivering from head to foot.

"Touchée!" whispered Haidée into her daughter's
ear. "She's been following a diet for six months now,
and hopes it has really reduced her figure."

"Full-bodied!" repeated Gustava. "And old-
fashioned! And very soft! *Thank* you, Val. But you
need not have come all the way from Vienna to insult
an old woman who has never wished you anything but
good." Her eyes and mouth puckered like a baby's for
weeping, and Val fled.

III

The Matriarch's extravagance began now to wave into
eccentricity. She gave several balls, for Toni's sake,
although Toni was not allowed to go to them, being too
young—"But it will do her good in the future," the
Matriarch explained firmly to Maximilian, who defrayed
the costs of her lavish entertaining. When she gave

colossal dinner-parties, it was for Gerald's sake, and
Derek's, that they might find influential friends waiting
for them when they were of an age to push into the
world. Nobody quite knew for whose sake it was that
she set up Zillah expensively as a corsetière in Bond
Street. Anyhow, Zillah did not remain a corsetière for
long, because a fashion in West End palmists and exotic
seers began to rage, and Zillah, possibly by her address,
possibly by the ' z ' in her name, began by mistake to
attract people to her premises who wanted the future,
not corsets. Zillah Korischelski was an opportunist, and
did not see why her supply should not meet the popular
demand; so the corsets gradually sank out of sight, and
all the most wonderful Eastern draperies accumulated
by the Rakonitz travels were required to drape Zillah's
parlours of mystery. Anastasia laughed heartily at this
departure from intention; her credulity being purely on
the material plane, she would believe it if told that Zillah
were starving, and rush to the rescue, or send Maximilian
rushing to the rescue; but when Zillah began to assume
airs about her powers of divination, Anastasia's joyous
chuckling could be heard all down Bond Street.

Burmese rubies and sapphires were to Anastasia like
the flash of lamps beckoning into wilder and ever wilder
extravagance. The wealth that poured from the precious
blue and red was hers, so she imagined; and indeed, there
was an atmosphere of the generous Oriental indulging
a beloved mistress, in the way those three Rakonitz
brothers gratified their sister's most bizarre caprices,
spoiled and humoured her, listened to her with deference,
admired her, and yet resolutely refused to tell her anything definite about their business or their expenditure—
such things were not for the women of the family.

So Anastasia went on spending, unchecked. Her
treasures accumulated—furs and jewels, objets d'art,
silken hangings, bronzes, shawls and dresses and brocade
shoes, old paste buttons, carven combs, enamel boxes and
painted fans, ostrich feathers. Her carriage, the carriage
they had given her for her seventieth birthday, she had
ordered to be freshly upholstered every few months.

At one time it was rich violet; then some specialist, she said, had forbidden her to look upon violet, had said it would be disastrous for the delicate retina, and so dim grey cushions took the place of violet; and the Matriarch, satisfied, proceeded to embroider further details into her richly woven narrative of what this specialist, and that, had said to her, ordered her, and forbidden her. Special massage, special cures abroad, special wines, and out-of-season delicacies *might* preserve her life, they said; but hers was a most original and highly-specialized case, they said; with unique symptoms, they said. She never took anybody with her when she consulted a doctor, for it made her nervous; and it was difficult for even Susan, who of all the household distrusted her host, to find out where truth ended and invention began; or how much, if it were all invented, the Matriarch herself believed to be true. She was not at all a tiresome or a plaintive invalid, and her accounts of her interviews with Harley Street were full of character and animation, though certainly startling in diagnosis, and full of whimsical contradictions. Anastasia spent money on her illnesses with extreme gusto. Money—there was always plenty of money. The Uncles were wealthy, and recently they had acquired almost complete control and owner-ship of shares in the Nong-Khan sapphire mine in Lower Siam. A few wonderfully pure stones, of good size and of a velvety "corn-flower" blue, had suddenly been found there, in a district rather remote from the mines which had hitherto been worked and exploited, and it was believed, among those who were in the know, that in a few years' time, the new mine would repay a thousand per cent. whatever money was invested in it. Acting on the Uncles' advice, as they always did, and particularly Maximilian's advice, the men of the family, except Raoul Czelovar, had staked nearly all they pos-sessed in the Nong-Khan. Besides Dietrich and Maxi-milian, Albrecht was a nominal partner in the Uncles' business; and Louis, though he had withdrawn from active partnership, had also left his money there. Bertrand had recently been made a partner, and Ludovic would have been, had not mystery suddenly called him to Nicaragua. Rather against their will, but at the Matriarch's pleading, they had just admitted Blaise into the concern, about a year or two before he died. Francis Power, Benno Silber, and Otto Solomonson had all invested in Nong-Khan sapphires. The Rakonitz fortunes were like a great ship, with innumerable cargoes in the hold, and at the helm an extravagant, domineering woman, who laughed because she saw that the wind was hard and fair, and would not take in a single reef.

But Raoul Czelovar did not trust his money in any pie, to alter the metaphor, where the Matriarch's finger was deeply inserted. Raoul, for some reason or other known only to himself, and perhaps to his wife Constance, preferred to keep aloof both personally and financially. A sort of invisible paling prevented the family from interfering too much, even in the way Constance managed her servants, or about how Sylvia's hair was done. There is no doubt that the Raoul Czelovars were rather supercilious; they were also quite unbearably pseudo-English. Val once declared, irreverently, that her young cousins were brought up in exact imitation of the Royal children at Osborne. They wore plain dark blue sailor suits, and ate mutton and rice pudding, and rode in the Row every morning. They were not allowed to go to tea very often with their cousins Toni and Gerald, or with Maxine, Derek and Iris; and Raoul actually told Anastasia that he considered sending Danny abroad to school a " very silly mistake." Few people told Anastasia that she made " very silly mistakes "; and when, in Raoul's stuffiest and most condescending accents, it pierced her understanding, she informed him heartily that until he had Sylvia's adenoids attended to, as they should have been long ago, he had no right to speak about the education of other people's children. Raoul hated his little daughter's winsome and high-bred delicacy of throat to be spoken of as " adenoids," as though she were a charwoman's child, nor was he pleased when Anastasia's cussedness wrote " Pimlico " on letters addressed to him, instead of " Eaton Square." A coolness blew between them.

It may be that destiny resented Raoul Czelovar's disloyalty towards his race, for a terrible vengeance was
preparing for him, in the shape of his baby daughter,
Helen, born a year before; or rather, in the shape of
Helen's nose. Raoul and Constance had trusted too
heavily in fair play from the Graeco-Etonian gods. . . .
Anastasia and Haidée and Val, Aunt Elsa and Uncle
Albrecht, watching with a fearful bated joy, saw Helen,
the child of Constance, the Dean's daughter, the child
of the imperturbable and irreproachable man of the
world, Raoul Czelovar, developing into "the most complete little Jewess I have ever set eyes on," as Haidée
reported to Val, after her first visit to inspect the new
baby, and she allowed her stifled mirth to break out
into peals of mocking laughter—"Good heavens, Val,
she's worse than Jewish, she's *Yiddish*!"

Thus judgment fell upon Raoul and Constance for dis-
owning the traditions of their nation and of their house.
Little Helen's hair grew blacker and fuzzier, and little
Helen's skin grew swarthier, and her nose curved into
the bland hook, which, to be perfectly Israelite, must take
its bend half-way down the nose; for otherwise, if it
should come too high up at the bridge, it is aquiline
instead. And Helen lisped directly she could speak, and
her adenoids were worse than Sylvia's, and her lips were
too mobile and her eyes too expressive—in fact, if you
had put her behind a barrow in Whitechapel Road on a
Saturday evening, she would have looked more at home
than in her mother's arrangement of cool and thoroughly·
Anglo-Saxon nurseries. Val and Toni, who were not
generous in their enjoyment of Helen's reversion to type,
made up a happy story between them, in which Raoul
and Constance, tempted beyond their endurance, stole out
at night with a bag, and dropped the bag into the river
Thames, and took a hansom home, and said casually that
they had been dining at St James' Palace and that Helen
must have been stolen by a gipsy. . . .

But something curious was happening. Deep down in
Raoul's anti-Semitic heart a love for Helen grew up, far
exceeding his love for his other two handsome children

with straight noses. It was ridiculous, of course; but on the other hand, it was the most true and natural thing that had ever happened to Raoul Czelovar, whose life hitherto had been one of careful severity, and the respectful worship of good form. Swarthy little Helen, with her fuzz of black hair and her un-English lisp, became his spoilt and petted darling. He would not hear a word against her. Nevertheless, he knew well that she was a little Yiddisher girl, this daughter of his heart. It was most upsetting to his preconceived notions to be so helplessly fond of her. His sister Haidée told him that he was becoming almost preposterously human . . . and Raoul did not wish to become preposterously human. Yet, because of little Helen, he ceased to look pained and surprised, as of yore, at any haphazard mention of a Jew; and even allowed himself to be seen, without wincing, in the company of Otto Solomonson. A rumour circulated round the family that he had himself told a good " Jew story " in the vernacular, for the entertainment of several of his Christian friends, faithfully mimicking the accent, and thereby proving himself to belong to the despised race.

Uncle Otto Solomonson had a daughter by a previous marriage, before he met Henrietta Czelovar. Emma Solomonson was a beady-eyed little person who had married a vacuous young Jew called Leslie Moss. A queer unaccountable rivalry had sprung up between Constance Czelovar and Emma Moss. They grew their children one against the other, as gardeners might try to outstrip each other in the growth of choice blossoms. For some inexplicable reason, the Moss children had " gone Irish " in what were—by courtesy—their Christian names. Eileen, Bridget and Moya were they called, to the ironic delight of their cousin Val, who promptly nicknamed them " the Colleens." Neil and Sylvia were certainly more distinguished children in looks and bearing than either Eileen or Bridget, and Constance had scored, too, over Emma, by having a boy for her eldest; but Helen—again to quote Val—" would need a lot of getting over "; and Moya Moss, who was born at about the same

time, was perverse enough to prove quite the prettiest of
" the Colleens." No babies ever had such a devoted
grandmother as Henrietta, who actually was only their
step-grandmother, and not a blood-relation at all. Had
she adored children less, she would not have been so
hard and terrifying in her kisses to Danny and Gerald and
Derek when they were little. How were they to understand how this shy handsome Aunt had hungered to
possess them, instead of merely being lent them by
tolerant mothers. Her " Well, do you want to go home
now? Shall I give you half-a-crown? Do you know
where the big cake is kept? " sounded like three distinct
threats, so fierce and bullying was her tone; and Derek,
who cried easily, usually arrived home with his face all
stained and woebegone from a Sunday morning visit to
Aunt Henrietta; and Truda used to say: " Benno, I
wonder what Aunt Henry does to upset Derek every time
he goes? "

Henrietta was glad when her husband's daughter
married, simply for the sake of the boy babies Emma
might have. Eileen was to disappoint Emma and Leslie
profoundly for being only a girl. They were still more
disappointed over Bridget, and absolutely exasperated at
Moyas; but Henrietta, who was proud, could not bear
anyone to know what she was feeling, and always main-
tained stoutly that she was *glad* it was a girl, she had
wanted another grand-daughter, she preferred girls. Perhaps only Wanda glimpsed a little of the disillusion that
lay behind Aunt Henrietta's ivory mask and stoic mouth;
Wanda's glimpse had been at the time when she so badly
wanted to marry young Edward Dunbar, years ago; and
when the family, having disposed of him, had tried to
thrust upon her, instead, Otto Solomonson's rich and
somewhat repulsive brother. Quite suddenly, in the
midst of the conclave, Aunt Henrietta had burst forth,
to the astonishment of everybody:

" You marry a nice man, Wanda, who is young, and
whom you love, and I will give you a beautiful wedding-
present. . . . Let him be young, Wanda, and love him.
. . . You see? " The colour of her own vehemence had

rushed like a flame over her face. How Anastasia and Elsa had stared !

And that was all; Wanda did not marry the nice man whom she could love, nor did she marry the brother of Uncle Otto Solomonson. But ever since then, a subtle bond had linked her with this stern, scornful aunt, though she had never dared pull forth their single thread of alliance into visibility. Later on she told Val about it.

Val said : " I always rather suspected Aunt Henry of being a V.C. at heart. But whenever I felt romantic about her I used to hear her calling Uncle Otto names over the bridge table, and so I just lumped her in with the others."

" Romantic people aren't romantic all the time "; Wanda remembered Edward Dunbar's temporary boil on the neck.

" No. What a shame, though, that she didn't make a stand for herself when it was a question of marrying that oily baboon. . . . I suppose the family pushed her into it, just like they did with Mother, and . . ." Val ran her eye mentally along the line of her mother's contemporaries. Husbands all so much older than themselves—fourteen, fifteen, twenty years older was deemed nothing in the arrangement of these suitable marriages. Sigismund with Clementina, Simone with Karl Czelovar, Truda with Benno Silber, Haidée with Francis Power, Elsa with Albrecht, Aunt Henrietta. . . . And here was Wanda, who had rebelled, left on the shelf. Only Anastasia had pleased herself in her choice of a husband.

IV

Toni was swinging along home from school, in very high spirits. She had just been at a rehearsal of " King Lear" at the Dramatic Club. She herself was playing Lear in that most appropriate of all plays to be performed by maidens in their teens, and several of her disciples had nearly come to blows as to which of them should play Cordelia, her favourite daughter. Toni had acted the mad scene in the storm with probably even more dramatic power in her rendering than Shakespeare himself had intended. She then had balanced the claims of her various rival adorers, and "managed" Miss Hamilton, the dramatic mistress, so that the final choice of a Cordelia was subconsciously guided by Toni's decision. Toni went home thrilling alternately to the drama of the play, and the drama which lay in the exercise of power. Her excited imagination began to run riot, and staged scene after scene in which she, with imperial ease, coped with disaster, crime, ruin, and death, and overthrew them, and buoyantly went on to fresh mastery of the world. . . .

Her abundant thoughts carried her along quickly, unseeingly, to the doorstep of home. The front-door stood open and she ran in, banging her satchel about. . . .

Then, from upstairs, she heard the noise of wailing.

It was Zillah Korischelski who told her. From Zillah, whom she hated, Toni heard that Uncle Maximilian was ruined, and had died of heart failure that morning; that Uncle Albrecht, too old to rally from shock, had had a stroke and was not expected to live; and that Toni's own father—

Toni had wanted tragedy. It had come down and over the family like a tidal wave, like the displeasure of the gods. The Nong-Khan mine had been cleverly "salted"; actually only spinel sapphires, of practically no value, were to be found in it; the Rakonitz prosperity was over; the gambler had crashed, and in his crash brought down his brothers, his nephews, all his relations in blood and in law, who had so eagerly followed his luck. Maximilian was dead, and Albrecht was dying. Dietrich and Louis would be poor now; and Anastasia would be very poor, and so would Elsa and her four daughters. Benno Silber and Francis Power would be poorer now than before, much poorer; and Wanda, who was supported by Louis; and Aunt Eugène, who ever since her arrival had been kept in luxury by Uncle Maximilian and by no one else, because each of the family had believed that the others were contributing, and did not bother further. And the

Solomonsons would be poorer, and Aunt Gustava, who had also lived on Uncle Maximilian's bounty; and Toni and Gerald and their mother would be poorest of all, because Bertrand, who in all his easy-going, selfish existence had cared deeply for one person, Maximilian, had thrown himself under a train; Bertrand was dead, and Maximilian was dead, and Albrecht, the oldest Rakonitz, died late that night.

Toni, who had wanted tragedy on a giant scale because she thought pettier troubles were unworthy of her mettle, heard Anastasia wailing and lamenting as she came into the house in Holland Terrace, and she found Susan lying in a dead faint, and Aunt Truda too overcome with crying to revive her; and for once the family did not arrive in great comforting batches to sit with the one member of the family who had been stricken, as they usually did, for they had all been stricken alike; they had all gone crashing down with Maximilian.

CHAPTER VIII.

Louis Rakonitz sank into the deep chair in his smoking-room. He was tired. There had been a great deal to do.

He had loved very few people; only one or two, in fact, perhaps only one. And Maximilian was dead.

Albrecht was dead, and Bertrand was dead; Dietrich had asserted, hysterically, that he was going to live henceforth in Rome. Dietrich was no good.

A little wearily Louis shrugged his shoulders. He had never cared much for Dietrich; let him go to Rome!

That meant only himself left, only his shoulders for the burden. The Rakonitz family was almost a family of women, now. Anastasia, Elsa, Susan, Wanda . . . Louis, in a sudden panic, gripped the arms of his chair. He wanted to run away. His mind hunted uneasily among the remaining men of the family : Silber? Marcus? Solomonson? Power?—yes, but none of these were Rakonitz men. Ludovic had been no good, and Blaise had been no good, and Bertrand had failed at a crisis, as he had always known Bertrand would fail. Raoul Czelovar? For a few seconds his mind dwelt with hope on Raoul—then tossed the thought of him aside. He remembered hearing Raoul say something perilously like " I told you so " when the news of Maximilian's disaster was brought to him. Raoul would keep aloof. Raoul was no good.

If even old Albrecht had lived, Louis would not have felt quite so desolate, with the knowledge of him there, representing Rakonitz, figure-head of a once powerful galleon.

But Albrecht was dead, and Felix was dead, and Dietrich was no good. Sigismund, Louis' father, was dead. And where was Paul—Paul Rakonitz, who had married Anastasia? Dead.

116

. . . Suddenly it seemed to Louis' aching eyes as
though the room were full of shadowy women in black—
Anastasia and Elsa; Susan and Wanda; Eugène's widow;
Gustava and Berthe. . . . In a gust of irritable fury he
demanded of them where were their men? Why could
they not keep their men alive, and leave him alone? He
wanted to be left *alone* . . . They trailed past him in a
procession. They paused in front of him. They surrounded him. Rakonitz women . . . No, he could not
get away. Here was Babette, Babette Rakonitz, the wife
of Simon, shrewdly smiling down at him, as she did from
the portrait in the gold frame on Anastasia's dining-room
wall. . . . And Olga Bettelheim, Anastasia's mother . . .
all here, in the room with him, stifling him. . . . Only
not his own mother, the pretty timid Venetian girl,
Clementina Civrian. . . .

Babette and Olga, Elsa and Wanda and Eugène's
widow . . . Anastasia. . . . And now they all had
Anastasia's face. . . . She was looking for Maximilian,
but Maximilian was dead. . . . Never mind, Louis would
do, instead!

Maximilian was dead. From the very bottom of his
soul Louis envied him.

CHAPTER IX.

I

Followed days which were a bewilderment of quarrels, and shrill voices, and the sound of crying in every house. All the family being measured for mourning; all the family wearing black; the arrival of black-bordered letters of condolence and distress from all the family in different parts of Europe; letters that were read, and passed round, and read afresh, with more tears and cerebral sighs. All the family giving up their houses, packing and sorting their belongings; moving on. Lawyers calling, and house-agents calling. A great tribal shifting and rearrangement and tearing-up of tents.

Dietrich had gone to live in Rome, asserting up to the very last moment that nothing could prevent him from going to live in Rome, that he had made up his mind even before the crash, to live in Rome; Annette, Annette did not like London, was not well in London. . . . He shoved the " Glamis Monster " in front of him, for protection against insinuations of rats and sinking ships.

Nobody could quite tell yet what walls were standing, when so many had tumbled into ruin. There were piles of papers to go through; financiers, and accountants, and former clients of the firm never ceased from pestering Louis with questions. There had been three solemn funerals; Albrecht Rakonitz, and Maximilian Rakonitz, and Bertrand Rakonitz put under the allotted space of earth which Sigismund Rakonitz had already broken for them. Blaise was buried there too, and Felix. No women, as yet. No women. Three wills were reverently read; complicated documents of no value, for hardly any of the money so carefully testamented existed any more. Everywhere debts and everywhere grief—but everywhere

118

movement. Rakonitz widows to be supported, Rakonitz children to be educated. Illness too, but this was not the time for illness. If either Elsa or Susie had singly lost their husbands, their claims would have been indisputable to all the luscious sympathy and luscious attention of the family, but a single loss did not show in the turmoil of losses.

Who was going to live with whom? Members of the Rakonitz family did not live alone; it never occurred to them that one might live alone. Aunts and cousins and grandmothers and brothers-in-law belonged together; they were settled by authority in suitable clumps. Authority was usually Anastasia, with the Uncles to back her, the Uncles as a final court of appeal; but the Uncles were now only Louis. . . . " Go to Louis; ask Louis. Louis will tell you. Louis knows. Louis will settle it." And after Louis' name, Toni's was heard most often during the dazed sodden days that followed the smash.

For Toni had dared to carry through her own way, and she and her brother and her mother were not going to live with the Matriarch any more.

II

Susan's one terrible fear, now that Bertrand was dead, had been that she would have to live with the Matriarch for ever, without deliverance. She had always hoped that one day Bertrand might have come home, looking rather mysterious, and saying : " Put on your hat and jacket, little woman, and just come out with me. I've got something to show you." And then he would have shown her, in a row of red brick houses, that small but inviting red brick house which was to be all her own. A small garden of her own in which to plant the pansies and the sweet williams that she loved. A kitchen range of her own on which affectionately to cook wholesome English bread-and-butter-pudding and apple-pudding, instead of idly standing by while the Matriarch taught the eternally new cook how to make Zwetshken-Knödel. A nursery of her own, with plenty of fresh air and white wood furniture, but not too much of it, where she could treat her children as she liked, without silly indulgences or fitful harsh economies. A pretty little sitting-room of her own, arranged to her own taste, and with no elaborate Venetian glass candelabra on which to clean away youth and happiness. And thither she would invite her own friends, and they would see that she was mistress in her own house, instead of going through the humiliation of watching them acquisitively welcomed by her mother-in-law. And her own mother would be honoured in her own home.

At the bottom of her heart, Susan must have known this was a dream that could never come true. Bertrand would have done nothing without consulting the Matriarch. He simply could not be bothered with the rows afterwards. Years and years ago, in Vienna, Sigismund Rakonitz and his wife Olga had lived as a matter of course in the same house as his parents, Simon and Babette. But still, Susan had hoped. . . . The huge house in Holland Terrace, even more than the one at Hammersmith, had seemed to her a sort of nightmare palace from which she and Bertrand might one day escape. But now Bertrand had slipped away from out of life, and had left her to the nightmare.

The Matriarch was giving up the house in Holland Terrace; it was too large and sumptuous and costly for her change in fortune; and Louis had insisted, with all the irritable dominating energy which had not yet begun to be worn away, on the necessity for making a move quickly. It occurred to him, too, that it would give her something active to think about; an alternative from brooding over the deaths of her brother and of her son.

"You can do this to help me," Louis had said; and because he was one of those men who somehow appear more boyish when they are looking very worried, his appeal did not fail. So the Matriarch began to pack and unpack, to turn the contents of one great trunk into another, to gather together the treasures from rooms downstairs, and pile them in rooms upstairs, to strew

the ottomans and armchairs, and to litter the beds, so
that there was no place on which to lie prone and cry
suddenly. The house-agents were legion, who now heard
from her the entire story of the rise and fall of the house
of Rakonitz. But in her final selection of a house, she
showed unexpected commonsense. It was at Ealing—
a comfortable red brick house in a row of red brick
houses. . . .

"It is larger than it looks," said the Matriarch, showing it to Susan. "You and Antoinette will share this
room; and Danny and Gerald this little one; and I will
have this room; and this one will do for Ludovic when
he comes back. I was wondering if we could find room
for Truda and Benno and their children?"

Susan began to sob. This was the very house, materi-
alized, in which she and Bertrand ought to have lived . . .
only now she was going to live here with the Matriarch,
and perhaps Truda and Benno and their children, and
perhaps Zillah Korischelski, and a room for Ludovic
when he came back—"Until he comes, Wanda might
have this room," suggested Anastasia. "Louis was
wondering where Wanda should live, now that poor Elsa
must move out of her house, into quite a tiny flat. Then
when Ludo comes back, the poor boy will naturally want
to be in his home with his own mother; Wanda can't
possibly expect to occupy his room, then," the Matriarch
argued indignantly; "she can go on a visit to Paris, to
stay with Berthe and Rosalie until they don't want her
any more, for Etienne's room will be empty, now that he
has gone with his wife to live at San Remo. Poor Berthe,
she has felt it very much that Camille would not leave
her mother. After all, Berthe is Etienne's mother just
as much, and she has therefore the first right. It is very
hard, every time she wants to see her grandchildren, to
have to make that long journey. Etienne should have
insisted on living in Paris, but he is weak; Camille can
do what she likes with him, just as Amélie does what she
likes with poor Nathan, who will not live long, that is
certain!" The Matriarch sighed deeply. "We will all
have to share the sitting-room, in this house; that is all

the difference. And the big cupboard in your bedroom, Susie, must be for the linen; there is no other."

That evening, Toni came to the rescue. Toni, who had cried passionately for want of her father, suddenly realised that her mother was crying for that, and for something else, too. Toni stopped crying, and listened, while Susan sobbed out all her fear and hatred of Anastasia, all her dread of never getting free of her; of being in her power for always and always; drained by her vitality, swayed by her will, always and always in this nightmare house of foreigners, this house of quarrels, this madhouse. . . .

"All right, all right," said Toni, soothing her. "You needn't worry, Mummy, we'll live by ourselves now, you and I and Gerald. You leave it to me and stop worrying."

But there was not money to live on, by themselves. Bertrand had left none; Anastasia had had the disposal of all that he had made. His wife and children could want nothing, she said, while they were under her roof, eating at her table. And Anastasia had no money, because Paul, her husband, had left her none; she had spent all he had, for Maximilian had promised that his sister should have all that she wanted, always; and Anastasia had spent all that Maximilian had given her; and now Maximilian was dead and had left no money. . . .

"So what are we to live on?" queried Susie, helplessly, clinging to Toni. "Mother has only just enough for herself, but I know she would share that with us, only your grandmother has always been so rude to her—"

"You leave it to me," said Toni again, shouldering her burden, as Louis had shouldered his.

And then she went and fought it out with Anastasia.

Anastasia at first did not even listen. Toni was only a child, only sixteen—though the Matriarch herself had married at seventeen!—and Toni could not possibly know what she was talking about. Anastasia was busy scolding Truda, who was helping her to pack the precious Salviati glasses, lizards and dragons writhing up the stems, crystal powdered with gold. It was Truda who first grasped what Toni was saying, and Truda was horrified. She had herself detested living at home, but it had never occurred to her that there was anything to do but to endure it, and endure it until you got married. For Susie to make a fuss about it now, when everything had been so terrible for " poor Mamma," and then for Toni to dare to lay down the law !—

" Mamma, listen ! " Across the litter of glass and china, and packing-cases and tissue paper, and cotton-wool and wood shavings, the Matriarch and Toni really faced one another for the first time. Toni was very white. Anastasia's eyes were like Medusa's; if she could have glared the child to stone, she would have done it. In the room below the box-room, Susan was still crying in faint exhausted whimpers. . . .

" She's not going to live with you any longer," said Toni. " We are none of us going to live with you. You've tired her out, you and the family. She never had Dad to herself, and it isn't fair."

No young creature ever tirades vehemently against a state of things as they are, without bringing in the phrase " It isn't fair ! " To the young, it seems conclusive. It isn't fair, therefore people must know about it; therefore it cannot be borne; therefore it must be swiftly altered. Later on, an older Toni did not even bother to say " It isn't fair ! " There it was, an accepted commonplace, woven into the very fabric of existence. There it was, without amazement, beyond destruction—unfair.

" We must all show courage, and not give way at once," quoth Truda, sententiously. " It's no worse for your mother, Toni—though you're quite right to try now and be a comfort to her—than for all of us."

" Yes, it is ! She's not a Rakonitz. She *is* brave, but she's not used to the Rakonitz ways, and she can't bear them. They're all bullies, and she's not going to live with a Rakonitz any longer."

" Toni ! " shrieked Truda, aghast, " you *forget* yourself ! "

. . . But she might have truthfully said : " Toni, you forget your *self* ! "

III

Aunt Elsa and Aunt Gustava and Aunt Henrietta and Truda all rallied round the Matriarch, who had suddenly become in their eyes, and by her own description, a poor stricken old woman, cast aside by her own grandchildren, whom she loved. Maximilian was dead, who had upheld her; and all her children were dead, except Ludovic in Nicaragua—

—"You understand, Wanda, that it is *his* room really, so that you will be ready at any moment to leave it, yes? Perhaps you had better only unpack half your things, and keep your trunk in your room."—

Oh, and Truda was not dead, but then Truda had never counted for much, with her. But this defiance from the youngest generation was a menace, the beginning of trouble. Francis Power and Otto Solomonson both vigorously denounced Toni's interference, and counselled Anastasia to take no notice of it whatever. Louis was quite simply very angry with Toni, and never entirely forgave her. It did not matter what were her arguments, nor what were Susie's feelings; surely now, when he had so much to cope with, surely now, in the midst of the wreckage and sorrow, they need not have selfishly added their clamorous note to the clamour that smote and smote on his brain all day and all night?

So, against the tug and drag of united opposition in the family, Toni forced a separation from the Matriarch, forced a dividing line and divided property, won back her mother and her brother from sweeping inclusion among the Matriarch's movable property from one house to another. Toni took three small rooms in one of the back streets off Westbourne Grove, and discovered, with a sinking of sheer terror at the pit of her stomach, that she actually did not know where their income was coming from; for Susie, exhausted and ill with mourning for her husband, relied pitifully on Toni, and asked few questions. And Uncle Louis was coldly furious, and Anastasia was raging, and the whole family condemned and shrilled their condemnation in her ears at all times,

and Toni's father had only been dead such a very little
while—

—And Toni went to the theatre with Danny, to see
" The Count of Luxemberg." She wore a new yellow
evening frock that her mother had made her just before
the crash; and oh, how she enjoyed herself!

The family never knew about that stolen evening. They
would have said, of course, aghast at such a dreadful
proceeding, that Toni was heartless; that she had not
loved her father; that she did not respect their mourning; that she did not care. But Toni had quite suddenly
felt that she could not bear the lowered atmosphere any
longer. All through her life she was to hunger for
pleasure, as a countryman, in town, hungers for the smell
of grass. And that same longing, her heritage from
Vienna and from her laughing Viennese ancestors, had
risen up and protested against a dreary eternity of soaked
handkerchiefs and dim rooms. Toni had adored her
father; she went on missing him, secretly, long after the
first intensity of his mother's grief, and his wife's, had
found solace; yet for one evening, one defiant patch
of colour wrenched out of the black, she forgot him,
completely and joyously. She forgot that Uncle Louis
was angry with her; she forgot that they were appallingly
poor, with a quaking uncertainty about next week's meals.
. . . Oh, it was such a jolly play; the music was so
lilting and intoxicating, especially the waltz; she revelled
in her yellow dress, so filmy and so bright, after the wear
of stuffy and monotonous black; and her feet, in their
silk stockings, felt quick with twinkling dances. They
took a taxi afterwards, and drove on to a restaurant and
had supper; and Danny, who was treating her, though he
would not say from where he had the money, gaily
ordered a bottle of wine. Danny was most charming that
night. He did not bother to understand why Toni simply
had to have this reaction if she were to go on at all.
He just accepted her mood naturally. He liked theatres
too, especially musical comedies; and he liked wine, and
a pretty, amusing, excited girl by his side. If they were
shocking people, ah well, let people be shocked! It was

beastly at home, and Uncle Louis had told Danny that he
could not go to Oxford and become a barrister, now, but
would have to leave school, and go into some business
or bank or insurance office.   It was simply foul luck, this
whole Nong-Khan affair, just when he and Toni were
growing up and wanted a good time!   The old uns had
all had a good time, you bet!—oh well—

> " Shall we try, just we two,
> You and I, I and you? " . . .

. . . The " Staircase Dance ! "   The Count's uniform
reminded him of Vienna and Franz.   He promised Toni,
in a whisper, that they would run away there together
one day.

As it happened, their truancy was never discovered.
Nobody had seen them.   Toni had her one glimpse, her
one sweet glimpse of life as it should be for her, like
running music; and she slept very soundly after it.   And
the next day, and all the other days, were sombre again,
and people cried, and she wore black, and longed for
her father.

CHAPTER X.

I

Of course Toni did not instantly begin to work, and within a few weeks obtain a position with a large salary, and keep all her family, and never let her mother worry again. The business of life is neither so gracious nor so picturesque. She wanted to train for dancing, but for apprenticeship to any good professor of dancing she found she had to pay a premium, which she had not got; and also she ought to have started younger; and also she would have to train for a good many years before she could hope to make any money. So Toni, with a sigh, gave up as impracticable the idea of expressing herself, with her feet, as a lover of pleasure. It was urgent that she should make money quickly, but she still hoped that it might be possible to make money by the creation of something bright and sheeny and frivolous, so she went to St. Luke's Art College to attend the classes for dress designing. Toni had a natural flair for colour and cut, and it was Zillah Korischelski's suggestion that she might study designing, and so turn her gift to profit. Three terms at the College ought to be sufficient to start her.

"But who's going to pay for this?" Zillah asked.

"Grandmère, I suppose." And Toni added, as a silent postscript: "She took all Dad's money and spent it, so I've a right to a little of hers." But she would not say this to Zillah.

"But, my dear, you've quarrelled with your grandmother. She's in an awful rage with you. Besides, she hasn't a penny capital, and is wildly in debt all round. I know, because I asked her for some."

"You did?" Toni's grey eyes widened. They were

127

sitting in Zillah's Eastern Parlour, where she received
her clients, when there were any. A crystal and a little
heap of sand and a black velvet cushion lay on the table,
symbols of divination.

"You needn't stare at me like that, Toni!" Zillah
retorted briskly. "Your grandmother and uncles got me
into this mess; advised and persuaded me. I have a
heavy rent to pay for these premises; and then they
leave me in the lurch. Certainly I asked her. After all,
in a way I was engaged to Max."

Toni said: "I wasn't aware of it," and something
about her cool disdainful inflexion upset Zillah's temper.
She flushed crimson, and her voice rasped like the voice
of a common woman:

"No, you are not aware of it. And your precious
grandmother was not aware of it, either, nor was your
Uncle Louis. That's the way the Rakonitz men treat you.
Make you think that you are all the world to them,
and encourage you in God knows what luxuries, and set
everybody talking; and then, when other men who don't
seem up to much next to them—" Zillah was paying an
unintentional tribute to Maximilian—" give up hope and
go away, and don't ask you again, then, when you don't
expect it, there's a grand bust-up, and the rest of you
raise your eyebrows and say 'I was not aware of it'—
Thank you!—Well, I was! Only I'm not going to split
on him now that he's dead."

"That's kind of you," said Toni gently. "Uncle Max
gave you all these, didn't he?" Her eye caressed the
wonderful embroidered curtains which covered all the
walls, the silky Bokhara carpet, the one precious Satsuma
bowl on its carved ebony pedestal in a corner.

"Ask your grandmother again," sullenly. "She says
they were only lent to me, and tried to take 'em away.
Pretty room this would have been for me, then, to tell
fortunes in, with yellow poppies on red wallpaper. She's
got trunks full of rubbish to sell; better leave my property
alone, she'd better!"

"Is she hard up already?" Toni felt rather pitiful at
this idea of all the things that the Uncles had given their

favourite sister, with already the shadow of barter on them. Were the Rakonitz exchequers really so low? Then it was no use, she could not ask for anything towards her own training. And yet, if she might not dance, and might not draw, and plan soft shimmering textures into beautiful shapes, must she then really do something grim and commercial? Must she lead the sort of dingy humdrum life which would have seemed so incredible while she was still under her " little princess " illusion, long ago, hundreds of years ago, a month ago. It seemed to her as though she were " getting old in chunks," instead of gradually and evenly growing up from fourteen to fifteen, from fifteen to sixteen, from a child to a schoolgirl, from a schoolgirl to a débutante. Why, since she had just been talking to Zillah, she was older; she had never known quite such contempt for anyone before; she wanted to chill Zillah with her contempt, not just rage about it noisily, and this surely was a symptom of the schoolgirl left behind; and so was this : that she understood well that it insulted Zillah far more than mere noise if she just raised her Rakonitz eyebrows, and curled her Rakonitz mouth to a scornful smile, every time she looked at those blue Chinese tapestries. . .

" Hard up? " said Zillah, in reply to Toni's last question. " I should think she is. There is still a lot owing, I believe, to that man Cohen, for Blaise's little affair. That will never get paid off now. She wouldn't like Louis to hear about it. It would have just about finished Max ! "

Blaise's little affair? What could Zillah mean? Something that Uncle Louis must not hear about, that Uncle Max had never known? More trouble? . . . But Toni was too proud to ask Zillah to enlighten her. It would not be good for Zillah, in her present mood. Besides, she had wanted Toni to ask. It was her way of replying to the accusation contained in : " I was not aware of it." Toni understood that Zillah was treating her as an enemy woman of the same age as herself. She understood, too, that Zillah was now an outsider from the family that she, Toni, must protect. Zillah had been an insider too long;

130

too long a participator in the Rakonitz unity. She knew
their secrets; her hands were full of plunder, and her
tongue heavy with tales.

Toni rose to go.

She did not go straight home to Westbourne Grove.
She went to Holland Terrace, where she found her grandmother among snowy plateaux and ranges of clean linen,
sufficient for a king's household. A quarrel with the
Matriarch did not inevitably mean that you most peacefully never saw her again. On the contrary, it was a
very positive, not a negative affair, perpetually fanned
by the winds of variety and recapitulation in case any
of its detail should be forgotten. The Matriarch expected
Toni to come and see her every day; but when she had
had a quarrel with Toni she expected her to come twice
a day, as there was more doing. . . .

"I'm left to pack everything alone," lamented the
Matriarch. "Truda said she has to pack too, though
what packing *she* can have— Besides, she has Maxine
to help her. I have nobody. One would think
that with all my children and grandchildren—One of
these pillow-cases with the old Valenciennes is missing,
and I always had them washed at home because Aunt
Lena gave me the lace, when I was first married, and
she died of a mistake that the doctors made, when a
kidney poultice would have done as well. If I had been
there—! But that makes no difference to you, of course.
You are selfish. You gad about. You do your hair in
two plaits, against my wishes. You go to live with your
mother's people, as though I had not cared for you all
these years—"

There was an atmosphere of classic woe about the
Matriarch, as her complaints swelled in volume. Her
dressing-gown might have been draperies. She tossed
up her arms; the lines in her face were carven deep as
though into stone; her hair hung in wild grey disorder
down her back. Almost Toni expected to hear her
cracked voice crying: "Woe! Woe!" to Jehovah who
had tortured Job and taken from him his riches and his
children. . . .

" Look, when you go home, and see if your mother has the pillow-case," concluded the Matriarch, imperiously.

" I am sure she has not," said Toni. " We haven't taken anything of yours. Grandmère darling, you look tired." She hauled a chair out of the nearest bedroom. " Sit down; I'll finish this. What do you want done with it? "

The Matriarch was not quite sure what she wanted done with it. The linen had all been pulled from its shelves and chests, more for a grand survey than for any definite purpose; and Anastasia, if Toni had let her, would merely have chanted a long cosmic epic on linen, beginning with the missing pillow-case, and linking on with the fine hand-woven fabric from Bohemia, which had been ordered for Truda's wedding, by Uncle Maximilian, through the agency of Rachel, Countess Janoschaza, who lived in Buda-Pesth, which was down the Danube, up which the Rakonitz tribe had moved with all their belongings more than a hundred years ago . . . but certainly it was too good for Truda, who had always preferred Whiteley's, so what harm was done if the Matriarch provided her with an equivalent supply from there? Yet Truda still thought she should have been given the Bohemian linen. . . . It was the Matriarch's grievance that Truda should cherish this grievance.

But Toni was practical. If Grandmère were moving from the house in Holland Terrace in five days' time, as seemed highly improbable, then the linen would have to be sorted, packed, locked up, labelled, and called for by Pickford's van; all except a minor quantity, sufficient to start them all for the first night in the new house in Ealing; for Truda and Benno Silber and their family were occupying the rooms that might have been Susan's and Toni's and Gerald's.

Aunt Elsa, brisker than Anastasia, for all that she was newly plunged into widowhood, was already, with her four girls and Little Klaus, in their flat in Lower Hampstead. Aunt Gustava had moved away from the Powers, to the Czelovars; for Francis Power had lost heavily in the Siamese sapphire smash, and Raoul Czelovar had not.

Val had been recalled from Munich, as her allowance was now an impossible expense. The Solomonsons were going to live in a hotel, henceforth; rather a cheap hotel; almost a boarding-house. And Wanda, shying affrightedly at the mooted idea of living with Anastasia, had been packed off to Paris, to dwell in a state of useful submission to Aunt Berthe.

It was a queer sensation, to anyone who had known the London branch of the family for long, to look for them where they had all been close together, and to find them, eventually, their solidarity splintered, in unfamiliar neighbourhoods.

—"Look here, Grandmère," said Toni. "If there were anything, about Uncle Blaise, for instance, which you didn't want Uncle Louis to know, you wouldn't mind telling me, would you? I mean, if he had been in debt. He could quite easily have paid if he hadn't died, only, of course, it looked rather a lot to tell anyone about, if you wanted them to think nicely of him after he died."

But it was worse than debt.

The Matriarch wept bitterly while she was telling Toni, and besought her never never to let the Uncles know—forgetting for the moment that the Uncles as a trio of magnificence had ceased.

Isaac Cohen had been very kind. He had come in person to see Anastasia; not as the harsh employer of Blaise, but as an old friend of the family. The Matriarch had begged him to say nothing to the Uncles, and she would repay the twelve hundred pounds herself, bit by bit. Her love for Blaise was so powerful that she succeeded, in that one interview, into beating some of her own indulgence towards him into the soul of Mr. Cohen, who had promised her the silence that she asked of him.

"And not a soul in all this world will ever know," cried the Matriarch; "except myself, and you, Toni, now that I trust you with the secret."

"You didn't trust me with it, in the first place. Zillah told me. She knows."

The Matriarch's uplifted hands flopped helplessly into her lap. Yes; yes, she had told Zillah, in a fatal swerve

of confidence. Zillah was treacherous and wicked . . .
and had better, perhaps, be allowed to keep the Chinese
tapestry curtains.

"Grandmère, have we paid back this debt to Mr. Isaac
Cohen?"

"All of it!" cried the Matriarch, dramatically. "By
saving, and living simply, and denying myself, I have
paid back every penny of it."

Anastasia had hypnotised herself into believing that
she had practised the most rigid economy. Her belief
in her own economy was more real, much more real to
her, than her actual spendings, which might almost have
been described as an absent-minded habit.

"I paid him back six hundred pounds."

Toni had to be remorseless. "The debt was for twelve
hundred, wasn't it? Then six hundred are still
owing."

"My poor boy had sworn he would pay back the other
six hundred himself; can I do anything for it, if he died?
I nursed him night and day; I would not let anyone else
come near him. Me you can reproach with nothing,
Toni. When he resigned from Mr. Cohen's staff, I went
to the Uncles and almost knelt to them that they should
take Blaise as a partner in the firm. For a year I gave
them no peace. They said 'no,' at first, because of
Ludovic, but I said 'is it fair that one boy should suffer
for the mistakes of another?' At last they consented.
Now, I said to myself, triumphant, he can pay back that
six hundred pounds. In a month, perhaps, or less. But
le bon Dieu did not consent. In spite of all I could do,
and I spared no expense that he might be saved, he died,
and followed his father to the grave. He was fondest of
me of all my children, and now Bertrand is dead too,
and Ludovic has not written for a great many years.
Three sons—all my boys, such beautiful boys . . ." The
Matriarch's tears streamed lavishly down her cheeks, but
she did not bow her head, nor cover her face in her hands.
"Blaise was such a brilliant witty boy! Blaise would
have done so much for me . . ."

Blaise—or did she say Benjamin?

II

Towards the evening of the same day, Isaac Cohen was just preparing to leave his office, when his clerk announced that Miss Antoinette Rakonitz was waiting to see him.

" Show her in," said Mr. Cohen, rather surprised. He was more surprised still at sight of the thin little schoolgirl with a pale oval face, and a long plait hanging smoothly over each shoulder, who advanced with superb dignity into the room, and gravely offered him her hand.

" You know my grandmother, Mr. Cohen? "

" I have known your grandmother," said Mr. Isaac Cohen, " for a great many years, and your Uncle Dietrich, and your Uncle Felix, and your Uncle Maximilian, and your Uncle Louis—but your Uncle Louis not so well. Rakonitz and Cohen have done much business together. What do you wish to see me about, Miss Antoinette Rakonitz? " He looked with a paternal smile on this child of his own race; she had brave eyes, he decided, and a fastidious voice which pleased him, for it picked up the words as though in dainty selection. Toni smiled back at him, but she knew that in one moment this benevolent atmosphere must be destroyed. In her next words she destroyed it :

' And you knew my Uncle Blaise? " It was flung out at him like a challenge.

" Ach! . . ." Wary as a cat, Isaac Cohen withdrew his full approval of all that Toni was, and all that Toni stood for. Blaise—Blaise Rakonitz; a nervous name in connection with the firm of Cohen. He remembered that Maximilian had been his great friend, but he remembered too that he was twelve hundred pounds out of pocket—no, six hundred now; Madame Rakonitz had paid as well as she was able, but the rest would be a dead loss. A wonderful woman, Anastasia Rakonitz, but a fool about her son. But what could he do? The boy had died, and the payments had been made, though fitfully; and then that gamble in Nong-Khan sapphires was a bad business. Nobody in the City could have foretold the smash. He would like to have helped the stricken family, but—six hundred pounds dead loss was already a great deal, and if he said nothing further about it, was not that helping? His daughter Leah would have been pleased enough with that six hundred pounds, now that her fourth had arrived. Never mind, he had had great respect for the three Rakonitz brothers; he would not be hard now. Four little grandsons, and there would be five and six and seven if Leah were blessed. . . . What did this child want with him, speaking so boldly of her Uncle Blaise? How much did she know? She was wearing black for Uncle Maximilian, he supposed—no, but surely there had been another Rakonitz in the firm? Bertrand Rakonitz . . . too much of an optimist, always believed that his luck would hold, always buying, buying, buying. . . . Isaac Cohen could have warned him. . . . And then that end. Terrible! Whose child was this child who had come about her Uncle Blaise?

" Your father? " he enquired, uneasily. " Your father, does he know that you are here? Did he tell you to come to me? Or perhaps your grandmother? "

Toni turned very white and haughty, as she always did to conceal any rush of sorrowful feeling. She found she could not say quite simply : " My father is dead." . . .

" My grandmother has lost all her sons now," she said instead.

So, so. Then it *was* Bertrand's daughter. Poor little maiden—but why did she come? And then Toni, waving aside the condolences she dreaded hearing, rushed straight in with her errand :

" My uncle, Blaize Rakonitz, owed you twelve hundred pounds, and my grandmother has paid half of it. She will not be able to pay any more, Mr. Cohen. She is not young, and for many good reasons it will be difficult for her to save and pay, as she did before."

The financier began to understand—she had been sent to plead with him to cancel the debt. But he had been ready to do so, they need not have feared. After all, he was no usurer; he had been their friend. They need not have sent this young girl to appeal to his generous sentiment, surely? Could they not trust Isaac Cohen?

With the expression of a few suave gestures, more than by words, he confided in Toni his intention to wipe off the debt, wipe it away, wipe it out of sight. Toni did not stir—but for one startled moment he thought she would have struck him. . . . He shrank back, then realised that the despotic anger was all in her eyes.

"I cannot understand your mistake, Mr. Cohen. Naturally, the debt will be paid. It is impossible to have the name discredited. There can be no question of allowing you to lose by it. Uncle Blaise, if he had not died, would have paid every penny himself. Uncle Maximilian, if he had known, Uncle Louis, if he knew, would pay you up to the last shilling. My grandmother, if the Nong-Khan mine had not failed, would have paid you the last six hundred pounds, as she paid you the first. As it is, I am here myself to arrange about payments."

"My child," said Isaac Cohen quietly, "you are right to be proud."

But of course he did not expect to see his six hundred pounds back; no hope of that. They were "machula," the family; her speeches were only for effect. Or had she some deeper game to play, behind her rhetoric? Might there be capital, after all, of which he knew nothing? Wait, wait, that was the thing to do—she would soon give herself away. He would be glad to have his money back, which he had thought lost.

"How long can you give me?" asked Toni, "and at what percentage of interest?"

Deep down among Isaac Cohen's instincts was heard a pleased chuckle. The Rakonitz child wanted to deal with him, to bargain, to do business with him; to do him, maybe. Good! He liked her spirit. There could be no harm in hearing what she proposed. Perhaps it would be worth his while; you never know, you never know. . .

"They call me a rich man, Miss Rakonitz, but they called your uncle a rich man, the day before he . . . They called Karl Rosenheimer a rich man, and you remember what truth came out when Rosenheimer and

Blauberg were hammered. What percentage do you call fair?"

"What would you be likely to receive if the money were otherwise invested?"

He shrugged his shoulders. "I have investments that bring me in fifty per cent, that bring me in sixty per cent, that bring me in a hundred per cent."

"But that's the highest," quickly from Toni. "You have probably also investments, Mr. Cohen, on which you lose and lose. That six hundred pounds might have been one of those investments."

"Do you take me for a fool, that makes many mistakes, Miss Rakonitz?"

"You are not the richest man in the world, Mr. Cohen. But if all your investments were successful ones at fifty and sixty and a hundred per cent, you would be! In the contract which you are going to draw up presently, between you and me, it would be fair to reckon the interest I'm to pay you according to an average of the returns on your general investments, not on the highest. If you want high percentages you must take a risk; in this case there is no risk; your money is safe."

"Safe!" repeated Isaac Cohen musingly. "A beautiful word, 'safe.' A beautiful word, little Antoinette Rakonitz. So with you my money is safe. And what guarantees are you going to give me that this is so?"

Toni flushed. "How long can you give me?"

"To pay back the capital of six hundred pounds, and the interest at, let us say, eight and a half per cent—"

"More than the bank rate?" murmured Toni.

She pleased him again by knowing the bank rate. "But yes, certainly more than the bank rate. If I did not wish to get more than the bank rate, I should keep all my money in the bank, should I not?"

Eight and a half per cent—the schoolgirl in her suspected him of having made it a fraction on purpose to muddle her, but the magnificent young Rakonitz was complimented that he had not been too generous; and again she repeated: "How long can you give me? For that, after all, is the main point."

"How long would you suggest?" countered Mr. Cohen, as usual handing back the responsibility of suggestion to her. Toni began to understand that this was deliberate wiliness, and that this was how you were successful in business. Business was exhilarating, after all. She had thought it merely dull hitherto, but if you had to watch like this, and wait like this, and know people like this; advance and retire, feign and skirmish, why, you gathered power, you gathered power all the time. But now there was no escape, she had to give him a lightning glimpse of her hand:

" It is not convenient for me to pay you at once, nor even in instalments."

Isaac Cohen, who also loved the game for its own sake, had to conquer sharply an impulse to suggest that in that case it was for him to dictate the greater convenience of twelve per cent. For dealing with Toni Rakonitz echoed other older dealing . . . and when he yielded to the strangely familiar atmosphere, it was a shock to look up and not see Maximilian's faintly ironic eyes. . . . He must remember that all this talk with Toni was not quite real; only emptiness behind it, as far as actual settlement of the loan was concerned. But still—

" Six years? " he began. " How would that suit you? Six years is a long time, but come, it will not hurt me to wait. We learn to wait, we business men. We learn to be patient. Six years; seven and a half per cent interest."

Toni had hoped for twelve years. Even then, it loomed to her as a sufficiently large undertaking to be preposterous, had Isaac Cohen only known the state of things at home. She sat silent for a few moments, wondering how she could contrive to double the period granted, without lowering her banners, without meanly exploiting his sentimentality, as just a silly pleading girl might have done; as she had sworn to herself, beforehand, she would not do.

" Why do you trouble like this for your Uncle Blaise? " demanded Isaac Cohen, suddenly curious for her motives. " Were you, then, so very devoted to him? "

" He was one of the family," Toni replied. Truth to

tell, she had been indifferent to Blaise. " I loved—Uncle Max."

Isaac Cohen nodded, understanding . . . and, reminded of friendship, he leant across the desk which stood between Cohen and Rakonitz while they did business together, and let his tone drop into intimacy :

" Now confess, my child, you will not be able to pay me six hundred pounds, not in one year, nor in six, not at any percentage at all. You are very very young; you do not earn any money; you have no prospects of earning it, not if you are protected as a young girl should be protected, as my daughter Leah was cherished by me, until her husband, who is a good man and a good business man, Leopold Abrahams, took her away to a home of her own. Confess now, you have been playing, talking—well, we all talk a little more than we mean. You could not, alone, expect to take on this responsibility? "

Toni cried, at a climax of indomitable indignation : " Alone, Mr. Cohen? Who told you I was alone? I am speaking also for my cousin Daniel Maitland, and my second cousin Neil Czelovar, and my cousin Derek Felix Silber, and my brother Gerald Sigismund Rakonitz, and my cousins Valentine Power, and Etienne Czelovar, and Mélanie, Freda, Gisela, and Pearl Rakonitz—" She piled the names on to him, scornfully, as though she would bury him by their sheer weight and resonance. Did he, this little shrivelled man, imagine that they, the Rakonitz cousins, would sanction a state of things which let men talk of a Rakonitz who did not pay his debts, who was slipshod in honour? Uncle Blaise was dead, and Grand-mère was old, and Albrecht and Maximilian and Bertrand Rakonitz were dead, but the young generation were nimble and fierce and debonair as any that had gone before, so why should they take favours from Isaac Cohen? . . .

III

It was only half-an-hour later, walking down Holborn in the rain, that Toni remembered, as the merest detail, that she had not yet consulted this same formidable array of cousins. No matter, use them first, ask them afterwards; she was remorseless. Besides, she had carried her point, more or less. Isaac Cohen had given her ten years; he had promised the contract should be duly drawn up, and sent to her. But he had altogether refused interest, either simple or compound, and there he had stood firm and not all Toni's pride nor argument had been able to budge him. There had been half tenderness, half respect in his courteous goodbye—tenderness for the niece of his friend Maximilian Rakonitz, respect for her uncompromising mettle. She had driven the amusement from his eyes, which had been there when she first spoke of business. . . . Toni's excitement gradually subsided and died down, as she stood squeezed among the crowd on the kerb, with her feet in a large puddle and the cool rain driving into her eyes, hoping to clamber on to the next 'bus. The queer wild spirit of eloquence that had possessed her, the spirit that had sprung up when her eyes encountered the sombre eyes of Isaac Cohen; which had accumulated in her from ancestors of trading Jews, back and back, through the ghettos of Hungary and Italy, from the merchants of Lombard, and the sign of the three golden balls of the first Florentine pawnbrokers; back and still further back to the East, and the Song of Solomon . . . that spirit deserted her now, sank away and was merged into the other Toni—the little flapper daughter of Susan Lake, Toni who was sixteen years old, and rather thin and pale for her years, and ought to drink plenty of milk.

"Mummy darling, how are you feeling now?"

Three poky little rooms in a street off Westbourne Grove, and the Goy grandmother on the other side, Susan's side, saying: "Well, Toni, I thought you would never be home; I can't get this fire to light. The landlady's so disobliging, and your mother has a headache." But Toni had bought, on the way home, a little flask of Eau de Cologne for her mother. She could just afford it, half-a-crown—she tipped some on a handkerchief:

"Mummy *darling*! . . . All right, Granny, I'll see to that beastly fire in one sec."

IV

That night, as she lay in bed, and flicked a wink or two at herself over the day's drama, that night her body paid her back. She had forgotten her body. She had thought life was all rich emotion, adroit dealings, high nobility, and laughter from the ironic depths. She had forgotten her body. There would be that to carry, too. Toni lay, and, in a sense, listened to pain, listened to it throbbing down all her limbs, twitching her taut muscles. Her head was now a hundred times too big for her body, now seemingly shrunk and dwindled to one speck of raging fever. . . . Her fingers felt like loose swollen clusters of bananas . . . and her heart played with her as though she were a fish on a line, being lowered down and down through the bed, and through the floor, into a dreadful abyss—and then, suddenly, when she hoped at the bottom to find respite from spinning torment, jerked her back again, and left her brittle and quivering. . . .

An old refrain echoed in her ears; probably among the first coherent words she had ever heard spoken: "You know what Toni is, when she over-excites herself!"

" I must have over-excited myself to-day," reflected Toni, with a little twisted smile of bonhomie at that other Toni, strong as an Amazon, who did not exist, and who never would. This real Toni of God's conception—this small thin Toni of the racked body, of the cough and the eternal sore throat, and the aching head, and the rheumatic pains, this *idiot* of a Toni would be the one that she would have to tug along with her, impatiently, always, whatever she did. . . .

She could not sing, because her mother perforce shared the same room, and might be disturbed; though it was good to sing to yourself, at these moments. Nothing sentimental, no, something gay . . . a waltz . . . the waltz from " The Count of Luxemberg. . . . Danny had taken her there. . . She would go to Danny to-morrow . . . he had understood when she wanted pleasure . . . he would understand again and help her to pay back Isaac Cohen. . . . Another awful jerk at her heart! . . .

If you could dig your hands into your pockets and whistle
. . but when you can't even do this, when your mother's
asleep, and you can't afford a separate bedroom, and you
are frightened to death at what is happening to your
body, and you will have to work hard all your life, whatever you feel like, because you have pledged yourself to
pay six hundred pounds in ten years . . . only you
mustn't be over-excited, whatever happens; you're not
strong. . . . " None of the family are strong, after
Grandmère." . . . Why after Grandmère?   What had
Grandmère done?   Whatever it was, it wasn't fair, not
fair to Toni, who loved strength. . . . " But I'll have my
fun, all the same ! "

v

" Help to pay? " exclaimed Danny.   " *Help* you?   My
dear old Toni, I think you ought to see a doctor and have
a surgical operation to remove those bats from your
belfry; you'll be alright then—perhaps ! "
    " I suppose you can see that we have got to pay this
debt? "   White with anger, Toni confronted him.
    " Why? " said Danny.   " It isn't our debt.   I never
heard of anything so blooming officious in my life, as
going to see that man yesterday.   He *must* have thought
you a little fool ! "
    " He didn't; he thought I was—"
    " A heroine?   Don't you believe it ! "   Danny whistled
an old student-song that he had often heard while with
Franz at Vienna :   " Mädel, kuck kuck kuck in meinen
grünen Augen . . . " and with one obedient but scornful
look straight into his merry impudent eyes, *stupid* eyes,
that could not see what was real to her, unless it happened
also to be real to him, Toni turned on her heel and
marched away.   He called her back.
    " I don't mind being ground into the earth by your
heel," he remarked, in mock humility; " but I should like
to know what it's all about? "
    She made one more effort to cope with his funny
quality of denseness.   " Danny, let's be grown-ups over

this. We're sixteen, and after all, it's not a child's quarrel, it's a matter of responsibility. Uncle Blaise was your Uncle as well as mine."

" Well—he's dead ! "

" Grandmère isn't dead."

" Are you going to tell her you made this damn-fool promise to pay that old fellow six hundred pounds when you've hardly got tuppence to buy an egg with? "

' He's given me ten years. He was awfully generous. He nearly made me cry. Of course, I'm not going to tell Grandmère; not till it's paid; then I'll go to her and tell her."

" All triumphant ! She'll probably be dead by then, too, so what's the use? "

Toni stamped her foot. " Danny, do stop speaking about people being dead, in that voice ! "

" I'm not going to sob every time I say ' dead.' And you're as lofty and offhand about paying off six hundred quid as though we had just got that for pocket-money every week."

" Are you going to be serious, or are you not? "

" I'm being more serious than you, my child. It's not serious to chuck about promises of hundreds of pounds directly after we are all ruined. Just the same sort of thing as the Matriarch would do ! And the sort of way she'd do it, too ! It's very handsome, and you look awfully like Uncle Max tipping a waiter, but—"

" *Do* I? Oh Danny, do I look like Uncle Max? "

" Not a bit ! " shouted Danny. " What I'm trying to tell you, young Toni—" she hated it when he called her ' young Toni "—" is that every bit of money we make by pegging away at some dull job that we loathe, I, at any rate, am going to spend on my own pleasure, not drop it into your lucky-pig money-box. That's serious, if you like."

" Then your self-respect means nothing to you? "

Danny laughed . . . and she imagined that she recognised him for a typical Rakonitz, in the spirit of that laugh. That was the awful part of it. They were nearly all like that—the men of the family. And the Czelovar men, too. Weak and irresponsible and careless, so that their women, loving them for their lordliness and easy good-nature, knew that they must not depend on them; must never depend on them, except in decorous outward appearance of weakness leaning upon strength. Toni thought she saw the well-known streak leaking out in Danny, in Aunt Sophie's son, in the Matriarch's grandson . . . and that, therefore, from the fatalistic point of view, it would save her from weariness to accept without contesting it. Heredity! . . . She went off to interview Neil Czelovar.

Neil's view of the matter was not as light-hearted as Danny's. Neil was a very correct young man of eighteen. He had just left school; he was just going to Oxford. His father, Raoul Czelovar, had not been financially affected by the fall of Rakonitz. Neil was shocked to hear about Blaise's bad debt, and much more shocked to hear that Toni had done anything so unconventional, and, to his mind, in such bad form, as to interview Isaac Cohen on the subject. Neil said he did not want to be "mixed up" in the affair. He was, in fact, almost comically anxious that not even the tips of his fingers should be soiled by it. To contribute to this ridiculous fund for the restoration of the family honour, would be as good as admitting that he was among those responsible for its dishonour.

"If I were you, my dear kid," was his advice to Toni, "I'd forget all about it."

"I'll try," murmured Toni, dangerously meek. "Shall I begin now, or to-morrow morning?"

"You see, if the old man doesn't hear any more about you and your promise, he will just look on your visit as— well—as a sort of schoolgirl joke. Of course, you can rely on me, Toni, not to say anything about it to anyone."

This reminded Toni of something she had forgotten. She returned to Danny.

"Even if you're not going to lend me a hand," she said, "I suppose I can rely on you not to say anything to anybody about this?"

"About what?" queried Danny. He had already for-go̍tten. Toni curtly reminded him. It was necessary. Danny could not keep a secret, and believed he could, which made him more perilous than if he had known he could not.

"Oh! *that*! I expect I shan't want to. It isn't interesting. I'll try and remember to shut about it, if ever I remember enough about it to want to mention it, which I don't expect I will!"

"I say, Gisela," said Toni, approaching her selection from Aunt Elsa's four good girls, "I want to tell you a secret."

Gisela began to look alarmed.

"Do you know that Uncle Blaise—"

"Toni, I don't think we ought to talk about Uncle Blaise!"

"Why? Don't be silly! I haven't even said a word yet."

"I don't think we ought to," persisted Gisela. "After all, it isn't as if he were still—I bean, he's—I bean he isn't—"

Toni restrained an impulse to slap her. "Uncle Blaise owed a man in the City six hundred pounds," purposely making her statement sudden and harsh, for Gisela had to be galvanised. "I went to see him, and promised to pay it back in ten years. Are you going to help me?"

"Are the others?" gasped Gisela.

"I'm asking the others."

"Toni, I don't think we ought to; I don't really. I don't think it's dice to talk about buddy, especially when it's debts."

There was obviously nothing to be done with Gisela, except to pray silently for patience.

Val, on whom Toni had relied most of all, told her frankly that she was a sentimentalist, and that sentimentalists grew into nuisances.

'I don't care," said Toni. "I'll do it alone, if none of you will help me."

"I'm sorry, Toni. I can't follow you up to these heights. I'm too lazy, and the family slightly bores me, though don't publish that abroad on the next relation's seventieth birthday. And I want to paint, and I like my friends better than my cousins, and I can't honestly see that Blaise's debt matters frightfully to any of us. Why can't you leave it to Uncle Louis? Everybody leaves everything to Louis now-a-days. He must be having a glorious time!"

"He doesn't know anything about it. Don't tell him, Val! you musn't. He must never know. Grandmère tried so hard to keep it a secret; and she paid half, you know. I think it was rather splendid of her."

"Do you?" murmured Val. "Good! Well, go and be splendid, too. If ever I've got a few odd hundreds lying about, I'll let you have them for your pet charity, but I'm not going to pledge myself. It's too solemn, and life's too short. What allies have you got so far?"

"None," and Toni's mouth closed firmly.

"Been to Deb Marcus yet?"

"I'm not going; I hate Deb."

"So do I; and Richard is a bit young, isn't he? Though I believe he's going to turn out one of those grave young plodders. Your best chance, to my mind, is with Derek."

"*Derek?*"

Val nodded.

As a matter of fact, she proved perfectly right. Maxine Silber, a merry-eyed sturdy child of fourteen, whose thoughts for the moment were bent mainly upon school popularity and hockey, whose sense of romance was non-existent, and whose sense of family went back only as far as her own mother, refused to combine with her cousin Toni; because, she argued, they were all dreadfully poor, and were going to be much poorer, and none of them was earning anything; and whatever she earned, in about four or five years' time, her mother would probably need. And mother was much more important than either Uncle Blaise or Grandmère—and if she didn't hurry up she would be late in the field; they were playing Notting Hill that afternoon.

Toni was left alone with Derek. By now, opposition had fired her with all the obstinacy of a fanatic; and instinct carried her straight to the spot where Derek was vulnerable : his vanity-spot.

"We must do it between us," she said; "I felt somehow that the others would fail. It means nothing to them to belong to the Rakonitz family; Danny doesn't care and Val doesn't care, and Neil and Gisela and Maxine are just stupid and thick about it. It's you and me, Derek." She paused to give Derek a chance; but the boy was not prepared yet to pledge himself fully and eagerly on her side. He was uneasy; rather wished he had followed Maxine; rather wished he could laugh, like Danny, at Toni and her sublime nonsense; and yet quite unwilling to disturb her idea of him as a soul more fiery, more chivalrous than the rest. That she should have such an idea of him was a lucky accident, and Derek was always willing to profit by lucky accidents. You had only to sit still . . . they lifted you to the height you wanted to reach, so easily! Like his Uncle Blaise, Derek was showy, showy on the surface. A very handsome boy indeed, the best-looking of all that generation of cousins; with sweet full lips, and on his skin the soft powdery bloom which boys have so much oftener than girls, until their voices break to manhood.

"Tell me, Toni, that old chap, the one you went to see about Uncle Blaise, was he a brute about it? I wish you'd told me; you oughtn't to have gone alone; we could have tackled him together."

"Well," said Toni slowly, "you see, he was a business man, and of course one didn't want him to make allowances, and it's not likely that one could let him go on saying . . ." Her manner conveyed, further than her words, a pictorial conception of Isaac Cohen in a beard and gaberdine, with a balance on the desk in front of him, rapacious for his pound of flesh, and mouthing indignities about Rakonitz honour. That was how she had envisioned him, before her visit to his office, all up Holborn, and up the four flights of dull grey stone, and while she stood outside the door marked : "Enquiries." It was not her fault that within five minutes their positions had been reversed, and she had been the bully, and he nervous and troubled and anxious to spare her. Toni had set out to be the young champion of her family, and while the impetus was upon her she would not be stopped. But Derek was a boy, so it seemed likely, from a traditional point of view, that in the future he would make more money than she; besides, he had a father to free his pocket from too much responsibility; while she would be hampered by her mother's piteous cry for independence from the Matriarch, and by the necessity of educating Gerald, five years his sister's junior, and starting him in some career. It would have been more spectacular for Toni to have carried the debt as her lonely burden, without Derek's help; but she honestly did care for the family before herself; did see that it was better that the six hundred pounds should be paid off, than that she should cut a shining figure.

"Come up to the cave," she remarked suddenly. "We can talk there without anyone interrupting us."

VI

The cave was a hollow, walled by great sacks and creaking clothes-baskets, under one of the out-jutting bits of roof in the smallest attic. It was approached by a sort of maze, in and out of the trunks, ducking your head beneath the low sag of the beams. This attic had not yet been disturbed by the Matriarch's packings, for it held more rubbish than treasures. Gaunt broken pieces of furniture were here; the four carved gilt posts of a Louis XVI bed, lopsided and no more in use; an old perambulator and cradle were disconsolate shapes in these recesses of dust and silence; some huge gilt-framed portraits of bygone Czelovars and Bettelheims stood in a stack with their faces to the wall, and over the battered silk shade of the standard lamp which had once helped to illumine the baroque drawing-room, spiders had draped a grey shimmer of cobwebs.

Derek, tiptoeing behind Toni to their cave, was quite certain that there had never been a doubt in his mind,

but that he and she stood for all that was noble and
sacrificial, against a troop of blundering ordinary beings
who heard no clarions and knew no romance. He was
impressionable to atmosphere, and though Toni's Jesuit
creed was as yet far more instinctive than deliberate,
yet she had done well, for the furtherance of her ends,
to have led him up here.   To her ear, there was a
marching rhythm in the tramp past of a great family;
for the moment, the family was menaced, and Derek's
individual self must be subordinate to his uses in averting
that menace.

. . . Toni started to charm him out of his everyday
mood, with a fantastic jumble of stories. She told him
about the old lady who had spilt wine over the tablecloth so that the Hungarian peasants at her dinner-table
should not feel uncomfortable over what they might
spill. She told him how Anastasia had gathered round
her, in the train, all the emigrés fleeing from the siege
of Paris, and had been so witty and contemptuous about
the Prussians who shot at them, that the journey ceased
to be a nightmare. She told him how Maximilian had
been known everywhere as Le Grand Seigneur, because
of his prestige and straight dealing and "mannificence."
Travelling back again, at random, she told him how
their ancestor, Simon Rakonitz, had been the first to
obtain privileges for the Jews in the ghetto at Pressburg; how he had fought for them, not sparing himself,
so that his name was on a tablet in the synagogue wall, and
they praised and revered him. And she told him how their
grandfather, Paul Rakonitz, Anastasia's husband, had
ruined himself by giving his name as security, in a crisis,
to his two great friends, when he knew that their business
might collapse at any moment; as, indeed, it did, in spite
of his loyal support; and Grandpapa had died broken-
hearted because he could not make good again, and could
not bear to live as a burden on the Uncles. . . .

And then, seeing that Derek was growing a little bored
with these records of integrity, Toni suddenly twisted
into the limelight the more beautiful, more picturesque
figures of the family : Great-aunt Simone, who had had

red-gold hair, like Iris's, only more beautiful, and who
might have been an empress; Isidore and Eugène and
Andreas, those slim young dandies with brocaded waist-
coats, whose travellings into far countries to bring back
precious freight, had linked up Rakonitz with Greece
and Spain and Asia Minor, as well as with Hungary and
Austria, France and Turkey. Oh, and Italy—how could
she have forgotten Venice, when so much of what they
daily fingered came from Venice? And Count Jano-
schoza, who had married Rachel, their youngest great-
great-aunt—he was a splendid hero in blue and green
uniform, bound with fur, for he had fought under
Francis I to free the Magyars in Hungary. And so Toni,
forgetting that she was a jongleur solely for Derek's
benefit, thrilled herself, as she always did, whenever she
thought anew of all her ancestors together; letting slip
from her mind when they had been weak; or when they
had been foolish or tyrannous or unjust, but just
gathering the haughty bits, or the warlock bits. . . . It
was the gradual weaving of the different countries into
the pattern, that excited her so; and weaving in all the
different names that marriage had collected; here they
linked up with history, and here again with royalty, and
always and always with merchandise—and Toni loved
merchandise, in bales and in ships, and, smaller and more
precious, sown up in little chamois leather wallets carried
flat to the body.

The same face, the same Rakonitz face, like a haunting
refrain, a fugue in the symphony of the world; you
sought it and found it through albums of photographs;
photographs of funny self-satisfied ladies in bonnets,
which gradually changed into feathered hats; then the
puff sleeve gave place to the leg-of-mutton sleeve, and
high waists to tight-fitting bodices and bustles, resembling
too nearly your own mother's clothes when you were
little, to be interesting.

And wherever the family sat down to feast, there were
more links—the same old dishes from the same old
recipes, Zwetchkenknödel and Apfelstrudel and Zimmtkuchen, delicious homely realities to show that they

all belonged together.   Toni knew, from Truda, that
fifty years ago, when Anastasia and Simone were little
girls, they too, like herself, had had it impressed on
them that no one in the house must lose their temper
during the hours that the cinnamon cake was rising in
the oven, because the banging of a single door was fatal
to its dignified progress towards perfection.   And
wherever they stood up to dance, someone, Anastasia or
Elsa, or Great-great-aunt Rachel, or Franz Rakonitz,
with his elegant long hands, would sit down to the piano
and play the same waltzes, Schubert and Gungl and
Johann Strauss, or sing lively swinging choruses in
Viennese argot out of the opera " Vogelhändler " :

> " Alle mit einander,
> Alle mit einander !
> Alle mit einander—
> Grüss euch Gott ! " . . .

And, closest bond of all, they needed not to be collected,
always on the same estate in the same land, steadfast and
unmoving, like the old families of England, or the clans
of Scotland.   They were a tribe of nomads, and they
settled and moved on again, and were legally granted
other nationalities, and bought other people's houses and
gardens, and left them again, and they spread and spread
without rooting, and scattered and scattered without
rooting; but, invincibly, the face survived.   Just that one
inspiration, by some strength and for some purpose it
survived, and you never could tell where it would break
through, or in whom. . . . And here Toni felt it all
sweeping down and down, here, where she sat, huddled
with Derek in their cave of the attic, in Holland Terrace.
And Holland Terrace, too, was only an incident.   She
was most of all a family patriot when she thought of the
Rakonitz face.   Toni and Derek were quite unlike, yet there,
vividly, was a likeness, as there was a likeness between
Anastasia and old Albrecht, who was dead; and between
Franz Rakonitz in Vienna, and Mélanie, and Etienne, and
Uncle Ludo who had gone to Nicaragua, and Great-great-
aunt Lena.   Toni did not express herself very coher-

ently, nor did she quite understand as yet why the fact of this single tiny strain of blood, indomitable against all the pressure of the world, made her so proud . . . but she had succeeded with Derek; Derek had caught her hot exultation. Derek could be infected, but he could not infect; he had nothing to give of his own. She could do anything with him now. He gave her his solemn promise that as soon as he began to earn, half of whatever he made should be punctually set aside to clear off the debt of six hundred pounds. He assured Toni that he cared more about paying that by the date appointed, than for any personal indulgence. They saw the debt as though it were a small dark stain upon a fair shield. . . . Toni was wretch enough to prophesy that no one in the family would be so admired as Derek, when he had achieved this for them. Derek basked, anticipating the floods of golden limelight—he, the avenger. . . .

CHAPTER XI.

I

" I HAVE settled it all," said the Matriarch.

Toni's other grandmother gave her a look at once shrewd and querulous, over the rims of her spectacles.

" I haven't heard Toni say anything about it. She's got a will, has Toni. You won't find her doing much she doesn't want to do."

Anastasia Rakonitz and Hannah Lake did not, in Toni's words, " play nicely together." They agreed only on the one fact, that the marriage of Susan and Bertrand had been a sad mistake; but as they viewed it as a mistake from widely divergent points of view, this did not help them very much towards amicability. Mrs. Lake thought the Matriarch queer and foreign, and full of rubbishy ideas, unthrifty and unpunctual in her habits; and she never forgave her for her treatment of Susie. But now that for a year Susie and Toni and Gerald had been living with her, Susie helping her to run a small boarding-house, she was placidly willing to ignore the past, as long as that " poor, silly woman didn't come bothering round too often, driving Susie half out of her wits." She was not in the least afraid of the Matriarch, but allowed the latter's personality to sweep by her like a torrent, without attempting to stem it, but without ever being caught in its onward impetus. Anastasia likewise considered Mrs. Lake a " poor, silly woman," who knew nothing of the world outside England, nothing of foreign languages, nothing of art and diplomacy, and precious stones, and only a very insular amount about human nature. It was queer how a single haphazard act of Bertrand Rakonitz should have brought his mother into such close

153

contact with anyone so incongruous as Hannah Lake;
Hannah Lake, who believed that fashion could be found
at Eastbourne or Folkestone. A dowdy little figure with
quizzical eyes, who made up in commonsense what she
lacked in the adventure sense. They would never, never
have met, these two, in the natural course of things,
antagonistic as they were in race, in principles, middle-
class Christian and cosmopolitan Israelite; or had they
met, would never even have stayed for one appraising
look, had their wills been free to choose their company.
Yet here they sat, in Mrs. Lake's stuffy, small and overcrowded parlour; two old ladies, so one would have said;
perhaps, with a stretch of the imagination, two dear old
ladies, chatting happily over the future of a beloved
grandchild. . . .

"You'd far better take off your mantle," said Mrs.
Lake. "It's hot."

The Matriarch kept on her sable cloak, but enquired
courteously after Mrs. Lake's rheumatism.

"I can't say that all these stairs help it much!"

Anastasia told her firmly what she ought to do for her
rheumatism.

"You may be right," said Mrs. Lake. "But it isn't
what *I'd* do. And as for not doing the stairs at all, as
you say I oughtn't, well, who is to, if I don't? I'm not
one of those that can get others to wait on me all day
long, slaving the flesh away from their bones, like some.
We've all got a right to live."

Most mothers would have been content to stop at this
aggressive hint about the Matriarch's treatment of Susie,
but Mrs. Lake, who had a courage which was almost
sublime in its tranquil discontented style, never left
matters at a hint, for fear the other person should miss
it :

"My Susie had a hard time in your house, Mrs.
Rakonitz; never still for a moment, and you never
pleased, from what she tells me, and forever changing
your mind, and always company for meals; so she
deserves a bit of peace now, and I wish things were so
that I could give her more of it. It's a pity, I must say,

that your son didn't leave her better off, though I liked
Bertie. He was always polite to me. Shockingly spoilt
as a child," Mrs. Lake went on, ruminating to her
knitting, " and never taught regular habits. But his heart
was·in the right place, and Susie *would* have him, though
Tom Lawson would have made her a better husband, as
I haven't liked to have said before this. He was an
auctioneer, and there's something I like about auctioneers.
They've always some pleasant joke to tell at the end of
a day's work. He brought in that chiffonier for me,
over there. It's a handsome piece of furniture, though
it takes some dusting. I shouldn't take Toni to Paris if
I was you, Mrs. Rakonitz."

The Matriarch remained silent all this time, not from
having too little to say, but from having too much. Every
stroke of Mrs. Lake's was deadly; and by the time
Anastasia's upswelling indignation was ready to pour
forth on her, came another stroke, in the same dingy,
kind, ironic voice. First that she, Anastasia, could not
even be trusted to give a proper remedy for rheumatism,
she who had indefatigably nursed so many people.
Allowing for the moment the insults to accumulate :
Susie's seventeen years of slavery, the state of poverty in
which Bertrand had left her, Bertrand's over-indulged
childhood, and the fact that an auctioneer, and the same
auctioneer who had bought, on Mrs. Lake's account,
that atrocity of a chiffonier, could have been for one
moment weighed in the balance against a Rakonitz,
Anastasia, with much dignity, concentrated on the final
question of Toni's visit to Paris :

' What I do for Toni, Mrs. Lake, I do for her best,
and I want no arguments. I gave in to this foolish idea
of drawing-classes, and denied myself, to pay for
them, without question, though I told Susie all the
time that in my opinion they would lead nowhere. But
it is not right for my grandchild to be brought up in
a neighbourhood like this, without travel and languages,
without conversation with brilliant people who have
influence, who have savoir-faire, who can make her
future for her. It is not likely that she would meet

anyone here, or at the drawing-school, whom she could possibly marry."

"Marry?" scornfully from Mrs. Lake. "At her age she's a child."

"In the Orient young girls are married long before they are seventeen. When I was Toni's age, I was already engaged."

"Your cousin, wasn't it? First cousin, so Susie told me. That's why all your children but Truda had bad health, I've no doubt. It's a pity you hadn't waited till you were old enough to know better—"

"Mine was a very, very happy marriage!" cried the Matriarch, excitedly. "And if Toni is not strong, it is because of her mother's silly rule of never giving her more than one solid meal a day, and nothing but bread and milk for supper. For years I fought Susie over that. But no, she knew better, and now look at the poor child!"

"Ah!" commented Mrs. Lake. "*You* would have given her goose-liver sausage and cold potato-salad for supper, I don't doubt. Foreign cooking! I hear that they give little children wine, abroad. Sinful, I call it. I never tasted so much as a glassful of wine till I was turned twenty-one. And anyway, what do you want to be taking the child abroad for? Unsettling her, and she was working quite nicely at her drawing when you took her away once before now, and put her into that millinery place with that flighty Society woman, whom she didn't learn much good from, and the establishment sold up in three months, so that she had to go back again to her fashion-drawing, a laughing-stock, and all that term wasted."

Anastasia loved talking about her plans, and could not resist it, even with Mrs. Lake. She became quite genial while setting forth, with many arabesques, her various reasons for taking Toni to Paris. Business!—she had heard of a splendid opening, an opening in a thousand, at a famous corsetière's. She, the Matriarch, had been offered a half share in this great business. She would buy the partnership and present it to Toni. It was in the fashionable quarter; all the great ladies went there . . . the income of the business was already ten thousand pounds a year, at a modest computation . . . and Toni, bringing in her youth and her enthusiasm, together with the patronage of all the Rakonitz family in Paris, all their friends, and their friends' friends, would naturally double this turnover. Then old Madame Laurentine could retire within a year, or say two years, and Toni would be left in entire command. Such a chance was not to be missed for the sake of remaining in an obscure boarding-house in Bayswater. Besides, it was time Toni should marry, as she had said before. . . . Here there was no one to see her. In Paris she should make her formal début. Probably there would be no need for her to become a corsetière at all at twenty thousand a year, because Berthe Czelovar knew of a young Marquis whose parents were seeking a wife for him, and naturally he had only to see Toni, who was very distinguished-looking . . . although rather pale at present, because she had been underdieted, and had all her life only been given bread and milk for her supper. . . . But when Anastasia had taught her to dress, and how to carry herself, and attended to her coiffure. . . . And anyway, Toni must see a famous specialist who lived in Paris; she must see him at once, no one else would do. He was a marvellous man; royalty travelled to see him from all parts of the world; and it was urgent, Toni might die at any moment, she was very, very ill—

—" I have spoken to my brother about it—Antoinette's Uncle Louis—and he quite agrees with me, and is advancing the necessary money, and we start early to-morrow morning. I cannot understand, Mrs. Lake, what you and Susie have been about, not to see that the poor child is ill." And then Anastasia furnished her opponent with a full list of all the people she had, by her experienced nursing, brought back from the brink of the grave.

" Ah ! " said Mrs. Lake, who really and quite definitely hated Anastasia Rakonitz, " but you don't say so much about them you've driven into it." And her knitting-needles clicked happily. . . .

—"Grandmère darling!" exclaimed Toni, who just
then entered, "you're not going without any tea?" for
Anastasia had risen, and was pulling her sables round her.

"I drink no tea in a house where they teach you to hate
your grandmother. But I, I only think of you, plan for
you. I have made all arrangements, Toni. I have settled
it all. There is to be no argument. I have made an
appointment with Monsieur le docteur Colardeau for
Wednesday, at four o'clock, so we must be in Paris by
Wednesday morning."

II

Toni did not oppose the impetuous flight to Paris.
Conscience told her that she should not go, that it would
be deserting her "side," meaning her mother's and her
grandmother Lake's side; conscience and commonsense
told her that no solid benefit would result from either
the corsetière dream or the Marquis idyll, and that she
had far better continue to learn dress-design along the
daily humdrum route. But for the moment she was in
rebellion against conscience, tugged forward by the old
pleasure-magnet. Paris would be new, and Paris would
be fun and pleasure and change, and Grandmère herself
was an exciting and full-flavoured duenna—

And Toni went.

She told Susan, quite truly, that she wanted to see this
great French doctor; there is no mother alive who will
stand between her daughter and an eminent doctor. So:
"Go, my dear," Susie said; "I wish, though, I could have
had more time to get you ready. And mind you attend
to exactly what he tells you, because you know the old
lady makes up things sometimes. I hope she will look
after you properly, that's all."

Mrs. Lake grumbled, under her breath, a few ominous
prophecies relating to the trip. She also told Toni not
to drink the wine abroad, and Susie told her not to drink
the water.

Anastasia was in high glee at having thus recovered her
granddaughter. They went rollicking off together like
boon companions of the same age. Certainly the

Matriarch was the stronger of the two, physically, but Toni could go a long way on nervous energy before she gave in. They could not stay with Berthe Czelovar and her sister Rosalie, because Wanda Rakonitz was already established there, and Etienne and Camille, with their first baby, were on a visit, too, filling the flat; so they went to an expensive little hotel in the Rue Caumartin, and Toni had a room full of mirrors. They missed the appointment with the eminent doctor, through being at the other end of Paris, and forgetting the time, and losing their way on the Metro. But, as it transpired, anyway, that the appointment had never been made, it was not such a disaster as it might have been. And anyhow, Anastasia gave Toni a glorious fortnight, spent lavishly, bought her dresses and hats and shoes, took her to the opera, and to two plays which she had no right to see, offered no objections when Etienne fetched her for long explorations along the quays of the Seine, or up to Montmartre, or through the Bois; and really only made her life a burden to her in two ways—by continual negotiations for the purchase of a partnership of this or that corsetière business, negotiations which always fell to the ground directly it became an actual question of paying the premium, and over the arrangement of Toni's hair.

III

Now this was an ancient battle between old Rakonitz and young Rakonitz, and whole epics might have been written about it. From the early babyhood of Toni and Maxine, Val, Iris, and Pearl, and as soon as they had any hair worth mentioning, the Matriarch and Aunt Elsa, and Aunt Henrietta and Aunt Gustava, would state with firm authority whether it should lie on the forehead or be pulled away from it, whether it should be decorated by comb or slide or clasp or ribbon, whether it were decent for the ears to peep out or for the ears to lie snugly hidden; whether a becoming bow at the nape were too sophisticated, or flowing curls too youthful. . . . While the children were still so young that they could do no more than silently resent all this interference, the war was between the second generation and the third. Susie and Truda and Haidée asserted, but often in vain, their rights over the hairs of their daughters' heads; Val should have it in a loose mane over her shoulders, because it suited her so well; Maxine should have hers plaited, because it was cooler and more convenient for games; and then each time came the cry: " But what *have* you done to the child? But she looks terrible! But why make a fright of her like this? But she looks like an actress's child. But she looks like the washerwoman's child! But she looks indecent! But for Heaven's sake, Truda—" or Susan or Haidée—"let me show you." The victim would be marched off, and the victim's hair would be rolled off her forehead, and pulled away from her ears, and dragged every painful way against nature and habit, and distorted by remorseless hairpins; and the victim, hideous and transformed, would appear, marshalled by a cheerful and complacent aunt, before her mother, and: " Now see," as dubiously the mother eyed her offspring, " see for yourself, isn't that much better? Turn round, child! Much neater! much more comme il faut! Always like that in the future! Never let me see you again with a fringe!"

Val had grown to emancipation; and after terrific skirmishes, mainly with Aunt Elsa, wound her hair into two heavy shells, one clapped over either ear.

Aunt Elsa cried: " But I must say, *awful*! No man will look at you like that!"

" On the contrary, Aunt Elsa," replied Val, " they look at me much too much!"

" Schäm' dich!" exclaimed Aunt Elsa. And tried Freda's hair in shells over her ears.

Maxine had also successfully resisted the family. But then she had a lightning conductor in the shape of her little sister Iris, whose thick red-gold tresses were a matter of special and romantic interest because they were so like poor Simone's. Aunt Gustava, indeed, was personally affronted with Iris's hair, regarding it as a slur on her own position as the late Karl Czelovar's second wife.

There was so much about hair in the family chronicles. The story, for instance, of Anastasia going to the Paris milliner to buy her first bonnet that would cover up her back hair, a bonnet which she was entitled to, as a young wife of eighteen; and how they despaired of finding a bonnet big enough to cover all those rich brown coils, so they unpinned it, and the young Empress Eugénie came in to buy a bonnet at the same time, and her hair, too, was undone because she had so much, and she and Anastasia sat there laughing at each other, with their long thick hair falling down their backs.

Truda's hair had no very special colour, but when she stood up, and she was a tall woman, it touched the ground, and Benno was very proud of it.

And now, in Paris, the epic rolled on, and included Toni in its cantos. Toni's hair was soft and fine, light brown, and without a curl in it. It used to be curly, but to her dismay it had lately lost its vitality, perhaps from worry, perhaps from illness, and it lay in a heavy quaker-like plait over either shoulder. The Matriarch decided that she was now quite old enough to put it up, especially if a husband were to be found for her. She was supported in this opinion by Aunts Gisela and Hermina, who lived in Paris. Both professed themselves horrified at a young girl having any say in this important matter, and furnished instances and photographs of themselves at the ages of fifteen and sixteen, with their hair in loops and ringlets, and invited the Matriarch to copy that style of coiffure on her grandchild. So the Matriarch strove with Toni, but every time she fixed it into some quaint and uncomfortable erection, Toni marched away and pulled it down. She did not want to marry; she wanted only to flirt; and Monsieur le Marquis, she knew, and other monsieurs, found her most attractive, in spite of the two long smooth plaits. . . .

IV

Suddenly, after a talk with Camille about her parents in San Remo, the Matriarch decided that she could not live another day without seeing her dear Amélie. She could not take Toni, she said, because she only had enough of Louis' money left for one person's return fare to the Italian Riviera; Toni must wait at the hotel till she came back for her, and then they would return to London. So Anastasia went gaily off to San Remo, and arrived there, unheralded, by the midnight train which was two hours late, and caused much excitement and great disturbance in the de Yongs' villa. Anastasia was specially enchanted with Amélie's youngest daughter, Jeanne-Marie, aged eleven. She was shocked to find that Jeanne-Marie could speak neither English nor German; in fact, no languages but French and Italian.

"Now I will tell you exactly what we shall do," Anastasia said to Amélie. "I will take the child back with me to London, now, the day after to-morrow, and will settle her with Elsa, and in return, I will send you Freda. A charming girl, charming, I assure you, but without animation. She wants waking up; she needs the Riviera atmosphere; she needs, too, a husband. You, Amélie, will find her one; it will be an occupation for you, now that Camille is married. There must be men here who will enjoy a good plain wife who can make Eiernöckerl, and Freda has learnt that from me better than my own grandchildren. Of course, she has no dowry. None of those girls can have dowries now. If their father had lived, and if Max had lived—" The Matriarch wept, and Amélie wept with her. . . . "Besides," continued Anastasia, five minutes later, "it will do Freda good to learn the language. All girls should know languages; it is a sin on the part of their parents when they do not. Do you know what happened with us at home? My father gave my sister Simone and myself each the choice whether we would learn English or Hungarian. I chose Hungarian, and Simone English, and then, what do you think? Simone never came to England in her life, but went to live at Budapest with her husband; and I settled in London and had to learn to speak English from the very beginning. When I went to the butcher, I put out my tongue to him and said:

'From ox'; or pointed to my shoulder or leg and said:
'From lamb.' And once—I can laugh at it now—I
wanted my room swept and told my maid to take her
belly and put it on the floor!—le balais, you see; I had
lived so long in Paris. Yes, I will certainly take Jeanne-
Marie with me to England. Do not argue, Amélie. She
needs it, she needs cousins of her own age to romp with;
she is too much grown-up, too much a little coquette. You
spoil her; Elsa will not spoil her. Besides, you would
not keep poor Freda from a good husband. You attend
to me, Amélie, and invite that charming Signor Drago
to dinner while Freda is here. He is so spirituel . . .
and see that he knows that Freda made the Eiernockerl."

So Anastasia, whose word was law to most of the
family, swept off Jeanne-Marie to London, and arrived
unheralded, not at her own home, but at Elsa's, at four
o'clock in the morning, demanding that Freda should be
sent, in exchange for Jeanne-Marie, to San Remo the
next morning, as she had arranged that Amélie should
meet her at the station on the arrival of the through
Riviera train from Boulogne, the same train on which
they had just come. And then, taking Elsa aside, she
informed her, with many smiles and nods, that a Signor
Drago, a very rich man who had a castle near San Remo,
had heard of Freda and had made offers for her hand. . .

Elsa let Freda go.

Not unnaturally, Susie, on hearing the Matriarch was
back, rushed round to embrace Toni, and was, in the
Matriarch's eyes, quite unreasonably annoyed to discover
that Toni had been left alone in Paris.

"Has she, at least, plenty of money?" Susie demanded,
frantically.

The Matriarch hoped so. She said that a young girl
should learn to be independent. "And anyway," she
added, "I shall be very angry with Toni if she has not
gone straight round to Berthe and Rosalie and put herself under their care. It would be more than wrong of
her if she had stopped on alone at the hotel without a
chaperone. Young girls now-a-days are too independent."

A subsequent letter from Toni to Uncle Louis revealed

the fact that she had waited, patient as Casabianca, for
the Matriarch's promised return from San Remo; the
days passed and no one came; so she went round to
Berthe and Rosalie, thinking that as Etienne and Camille
were leaving, she could now have the spare bedroom
there. She found that Camille and Etienne had already
left, and that Wanda had just developed scarlatina, which
meant that Berthe and Rosalie and the whole household
were in quarantine, and could neither see Toni, nor
chaperone her. Toni went back to the hotel, and continued to wait. She had no money; only she was too
proud to tell her relations this; it was betraying the
Matriarch. So she told them at the hotel that her grandmère would be returning soon and would settle the
account. And Monsieur le Marquis d'Adhémar had
called on her persistently; his intentions were apparently
not of the most honourable. . . . "Paris is not a very
nice place to be alone in," Toni wrote. And would Uncle
Louis mind sending her the fare home? She wanted to
return urgently, as her mother might be anxious. She
was quite capable of travelling alone, only please, if Uncle
Louis didn't mind, she wanted to return home *quickly*.

Louis wired to Paris, arranging matters. He then
spoke a few quiet words to the Matriarch. The
Matriarch considered that Wanda must have been, as
usual, very careless to have caught scarlatina.

CHAPTER XII.

I

From this period onward, the family began to notice about the Matriarch's eccentricities, which previously had been diffused more or less evenly over the days, a marked ebb and flow, a sort of crazy rhythm, as though the shock of Ludovic's desertion, and then of her darling Blaise's death, and of the final disaster which swept away Maximilian and Bertrand and her safety of fortune, had had the effect of a sharp dividing line between Anastasia mad and Anastasia sane. Anastasia sane was considerably saner than, possibly, she had ever been in her life before; a charming old lady, quiet and kind and sensible, with a dignity of which her grandchildren were very proud; with a serene but not extravagant optimism; with sufficient control over time and space to realise that luncheon at one should not really be later than half-past two; and that she could not walk more than a couple of miles without growing normally weary. Truda and Susan and Louis would sigh, relieved, during these gentle days; and Danny and Toni and Gerald and Derek and Maxine and Iris would say: "Grandmère's all right . . ."

And then— smell of rain in the air; a wind getting up behind the stillness; distant tramp of feet that could be felt rather than heard; a spirit of goblin unease. . . . They found it difficult to describe how they knew a "bad fit" was coming on. She began to talk more, to hint at alarming plans for all their welfare. She disregarded meal-times rather more recklessly. She would say that she could not sleep unless she first took a walk at night. It was working up again, her bad time—her "good time" she would call it—and apprehension could not stop it,

165

nor memory of catastrophic results from the last bad
time. It was working up. The household, the family,
waited breathlessly. . . . Nearer and nearer—yes, here it
was : " Grandmère's bad again !"

What happened? Anything might happen. She became gay and cosmic; she was not hampered by dis-
tances, for she never got tired; she ignored time, juggled
hilariously with the hours of other people's days and
nights. Obstacles went down before the terrible scythe
of her self-confident laughter, and triumphantly she
eliminated drab details of thrift and economy. . . . She
had the money, of course she had ! There was always
plenty of money for Anastasia. . . . The three Rakonitz
brothers . . . rubies . . . Maximilian. . . . Yes, of
course there was plenty of money. Her grandchildren
need not be deprived of anything. She went through
convention as though it were no more than a paper hoop.
Her queer vagabond quality, tough and genial, which had
always been there, exaggerated itself tenfold. She picked
up friends all over the place; odd ribald friends who
sometimes grimaced, scoffingly, behind her back; or else
little quiet, devoted people, fascinated by her glitter.

That stranger on a motor-bicycle, for instance, whom
she hailed at Shepherd's Bush, after the last tram and
'bus had left. The Matriarch saw no incongruity in arriving home in a side-car, at two o'clock in the morning;
and, of course, she invited the young man to come in,
as he had been so polite. . . . It was surly of Truda to
resent being suddenly woken and asked for the key of
the tantalus !

And the Persian carpet-maker—Heaven knows how
she had discovered him; but she herself brought him
home to the house in Ealing, to repair those silky Oriental
rugs which, she insisted, were getting worn; and her
shrill happy voice could be heard through the thin walls,
as she sat by him while he worked, and told him all about
her cousin Marie, " poor Julius Czelovar's eldest child."
. . . Uncle Julius had never been happy with Aunt Gisela,
who was an overbearing woman, as all the Bettelheim's
were—" Except my mother, who was an angel," said the

Matriarch firmly. " You remember my mother? " The
Persian carpet-maker did not. " So, of course, it was the
best thing that Marie could have done; the best thing.
But Aunt Gisela one day came to see me about the whole
affair, when I was in Paris, and she actually brought
along, for my Truda, a corset—' pour lui faire du ventre,'
she said. I must say, it was black satin embroidered in
forget-me-nots, but Truda would never wear it, she said
a ' ventre ' did not appeal to her." Anastasia laughed
heartily, and the Persian carpet-maker laughed too; he
understood French.

" Poor Marie had no dowry; and you know, young
man, girls were not allowed a choice in those days; her
mother's choice fell on August Goldstein, and Marie had
two younger sisters growing up, Henrietta and Laura;
three unmarried grown-up girls were not to be thought
of. She had a boy friend who grew up with her, and
then became a medical student, and they fell in love
with each other. Marie thought if she could not marry
this young Immanuel, she did not care whom she married,
but August Goldstein was no beauty; like a wrinkled
and shrivelled-up old woman, with brown broken teeth
and a high-pitched voice. When my grand-daughter
marries, my Antoinette—And, by the way, tell me, are
you married, yourself? She is half English, you know.
Her mother, my son Bertrand's wife, is English : a Miss
Lake; they have charming complexions, nearly always,
though Antoinette has the Rakonitz eyes and mouth. So
you need not mind that. Aunt Gisela once said to me—
' If only my marriages turned out as well as your Zimmtkuchen '—I said to her ' Mein Zimmtkuchen ist aber mit
Herzen gemacht '—' But my cinnamon-cake is made with
the heart.' . . . Yes, yes, it is so. There was too little
heart in that arrangement with Goldstein. But an honourable friendship continued between Marie and Immanuel,
who became a doctor in Paris, and they had coffee at a
restaurant together daily after lunch, but nothing in it,
you understand; nothing in it that anyone could object
to. There were rumours that Marie and Goldstein,
although sharing the same home, were never really

husband and wife; anyhow, in the end, Goldstein disappeared, and after some years Marie got her divorce for desertion, and married Immanuel. And in spite of Marie's eccentricities—she once dyed half her hair bright green by mistake—they were very happy indeed, and whatever Gisela says, I am glad of it. . . ."

She took the Persian carpet-maker on a holiday to Devonshire, as her guest; and explained gaily to everyone that there need be no gossip; she was an old woman, and he a mere boy of twenty-six. . . .

"No gossip *at all*!" cried the Matriarch.

Impulsively she presented him with a rare enamel and gold snuff-box which Felix had given her; Louis had the utmost difficulty, afterwards, in reclaiming it. And she never lost an opportunity of extolling him to whomever his rich virtues could not possibly concern. Canvassing among all her acquaintances who had Persian rugs which she was quite sure must be worn out, or would be worn out in a few year's time if they did not instantly have them repaired by an expert, she bethought herself of Louis, and went off to see him, and borrowed his umbrella, and remembered it three days later at half-past eleven at night, when she promptly set out on foot from Ealing to return it to him at Regent's Park, because he might want it at any moment. She knocked up the sleeping household, gave back the umbrella, and pointed out that the rugs in his sitting-room had better be instantly replaced by an Eastern carpet, chosen by a connoisseur in Bokharas—"A charming Persian boy whom I know, so sensitive that never, without a proper introduction by me, would he dream of asking you to buy—"

"Good-night," said Louis, irritably, drawing his dressing-gown of sombre wadded silk closer about his lean figure. "Good-night, dear Anastasia. Thank you for bringing back the umbrella. You are not going to walk home, I trust?"

"I walk everywhere," cried the Matriarch, illimitably energetic.

When she was half-way home, it began to rain, and she

returned to Louis and knocked him up again, to reborrow the umbrella.

Gradually this reckless, tireless Anastasia subsided. . . . Little signs proved the crisis over, and the turn set in. She talked less; neglected her protégé of the hour; regained, little by little, consciousness of the clock. Her voice was less shrill, her eyes not so wild and brilliant. From living in a past of abundant material glory, she sank back and back to a quiet present. She acknowledged fatigue if she walked too far. She was able to sleep. . . . " Grandmère is all right again."

II

And Truda, and her husband Benno, and Aunt Elsa, and Aunt Henrietta, and, of course, Uncle Louis, gathered round to pay the bills and estimate the damage that Grandmère had wrought through her era of capricious fantasies; fantasies of which her bewildered sanity seemed to have not the faintest recollection.

III

In 1913, Uncle Otto Solomonson, Henrietta's husband, died of diabetes; and, on general principles, he would have been very annoyed about it. His death deprived the family of their only pictorially comic Jew; an opposition figure to Uncle Louis, who was always the first to be introduced to any Gentile family into which the second or third generation might be marrying, as show specimen of all that was distinguished and cultured; proof that a Jew need not be necessarily plump and greasy, with a flash of diamonds on his shirt-front, beady eyes, curly black hair, and over-worked gesticulation—exactly like Uncle Otto Solomonson, in fact! But Val, who was developing a vein of irony in her character, and usually went contrary to the family tradition, preferred to supply her friends, artists and " Goys," with an introduction to Uncle Otto Solomonson, because she said *he* was the sort

of Jew they could easily understand, and that was why
he and his type had become the popular conception. . . .
Real Israelites were well beyond popular conception. She
had a funny fondness for Uncle Otto Solomonson:

"Dear Uncle Otto! I know he made Aunt Henrietta
suffer, but I am sorry he is dead. We have got no funny
uncles left now; look at Uncle Raoul; look at Uncle
Louis; and none of the boys seem to be growing up
funny; they're all quite normal; you can hardly tell them
from other boys. Of course, they've had a lot of Goy
mixed in, like you and me, Toni. The last generation, and
those before, were purely Israel. But witness our appalling string of flaxen Saxon names: Gerald and Derek;
Iris; my sweet little cousins, Neil and Sylvia and Helen—
how Helen's face serves 'em right! And the Colleens.
Even little Klaus is calling himself Claude nowadays."

Toni agreed, regretfully, that not Gerald nor Richard,
nor Derek, nor Neil, nor Danny, nor Claude were showing any signs of developing into that true specimen of
a maligned race, which Uncle Otto Solomonson had been.
She added to Val's wail and tribute to the dead, her own.
Only these children of the twentieth century wailed as
though they were conscious of their race, and its romance
and its humour, instead of simply being these things, like
their grand-parents and their great-grand-parents; so it
sounded quite different.

Aunt Henrietta went to live with Emma and Leslie
Moss, and her beloved Colleen grandchildren. There
were not many men of the family to be at Uncle Otto
Solomonson's funeral; and, it seemed, always more
women to sit at home with the widow, and weep, and
remember their Rakonitz men who had died.

IV

But the boys were growing up; Neil and Danny, and
Derek and Little Klaus; and after them, Richard and
Gerald. Uncle Louis began to invite them out to lunch
with him. He would have a spurt of enthusiasm for each

one separately; and invited them out to lunch quite often; in the City, usually; perhaps from the unconscious effort to believe that they were already men, Rakonitz men; and they would come home from these luncheons rather puzzled and rather bored, and a little resentful; and report that the food was jolly good, but that Uncle Louis had been " jawing " them; not on what they had done, but a sort of apprehensive " jawing " as to what they might do in the future, because they were Rakonitz men; and the Rakonitz men, it was granted now, were weak and reckless, charming and generous and plausible—and totally unreliable. Neil liked to be seen lunching with Uncle Louis, for appearances' sake; and Danny ate his lunches like a gourmet, and kept his spirit detached from his appetite; and Derek played up a little more than he had need to, and boasted of what he was going to do, and talked rather too fluently, even patronising Uncle Louis somewhat; and Little Klaus, who always said " I'm going at once ' directly he entered a room, anticipating any lack of fervent welcome, was too ready to ingratiate himself by apologetic agreement with everything that Uncle Louis said; and Richard and Gerald, aged four-teen, behaved like awkward schoolboys, and scowled and upset things, and refused to become confidential with their host, and said afterwards that they didn't know what on earth he was talking about, and wished he wouldn't, because they had done nothing. . . . They did not realise—how should they?—that Louis was hunting for his heir; desperately hunting; seeking for the good stuff in one of them, which would enable him, perhaps, to share his burden a little later, to hand on his burden, the burden of the Rakonitz women. Surely one of these boys—they were only boys, but they would grow up soon; Klaus was grown-up already; Neil was twenty, and Danny was nineteen—surely one of them would under-stand that it was pressing too heavily on him? or were they all unstable as water? All with the curse of Reuben on them? of Rakonitz? And sometimes his anxious favouritism would select this one, and sometimes that one; but they were all disappointing; and he did not think, then, of looking among the girls of the third generation. . . . Nobody realised the pathos of Louis' strained exacting interest in the youngsters of the family.

v

Toni had had a mooching indolent year, following her eccentric holiday in Paris. She had a nervous collapse, and the doctors said that she was very anaemic, and that her heart was not all it should be, and she must drink plenty of milk, and have no worry nor excitement, and rest on her back for several hours a day, and not dream of hard work. . . . So the old refrain came up again, the old jingle : " None of the family are strong, after Grandmère," and " You know what Toni is when she gets over-excited." Susan bravely did her best; laboured indefatigably to make the boarding-house pay. Her brisk cheerfulness was stretched too tightly over the ugly void it concealed; it frayed and frayed to tatters, and the void became more and more evident. . . . No money, debts, illness, more debts, no money. . . . And then, quite suddenly, the boarding-house could not be propped up any longer on a fictitious assumption that it paid. The lease ran out, and it would have been obvious madness to renew. Mrs. Lake sold the goodwill—a hearty word, belieing the fretful, greedy, nagging boarding-house atmosphere; and she and Susan and Toni and Gerald moved back into the three rooms off Westbourne Grove, which happened to be empty again. And Susan began a timid registry office; and threw all her energy, and all her self, and most of her health, colour of her hair and pinkness of her cheeks, and the last pretty plumpness of her girlhood, into making the concern pay; and she lost it all within a few months. She was very thin now, and her hair was not silver, but dusty and streaked with grey. The remains of Mrs. Lake's small sum of money, obtained from the goodwill of the boarding-house, were all spent; and Mrs. Lake fell down the dark stairs where the stair rods were always loose and the carpet always

torn, and damaged her knee-cap, and had to have doctors
and massage and X-ray treatment; and even then, never
properly recovered.

And Gerald, quite naturally, demanded football boots.

The most ardent admirers of Toni's heroism would be
bound to admit that it had lapsed rather from its original
magnificent intentions, during the last year. For one
thing, the Matriarch had tried to atone for the Paris
incident, by paying for a consultation of London doctors,
three of them, of whom two were specialists. She had
also stated, firmly, that she would pay for whatever
invalid treatment or food they ordered for Toni. She
would pay for it out of her own income, allowed her by
Uncle Louis, from the sum he held in trust for her benefit
from Uncle Felix, who had willed it from his solid
dividends in Burmese rubies and sapphires; Felix had
died before the Nong-Khan smash; but unfortunately he
had bequeathed his main fortune to Maximilian.

"I can quite well afford anything, anything," cried
the Matriarch, at the end of 1912. "I shall have this
much more, and this much more, next year, than last
year!" And she proceeded to demonstrate how, by
adding her expenses in excess of her income from last
year, on to next year, on the assumption that as it would
not occur again, she was so much to the good; her
optimism being on a bountiful scale.

So Toni, finding that there were few other pleasures
within reach, gave in to the negative pleasure of exempt-
ing herself from responsibility. She became callous about
funds, and asked no questions whence they originated;
her inflexions were a little bit cheeky about the things
she might or might not safely do, and about what
her doctors—in the insolent plural—had said. And
she dispensed a share in her jellies and Sanatogen
and grapes, brought in by various sympathetic aunts,
as a princess might dispense largesse. In fact, she
really managed to forget how poor they were . . .
until one day she came home from tea and dancing
in Val's studio, to find her mother in a dead faint
across the floor; and her grandmother, frantic at not

being able to get out of bed, nor to make anybody hear her, crying out angrily that it was starvation, that Susie had been starving herself. . . . And then, at the dreadful melodrama of such a word brought within the very walls of home, Toni remembered, in that irrelevant sort of way that odd things are found at odd moments in odd chinks of the mind, that she had pledged herself to pay Isaac Cohen six hundred pounds. . . .

"It's about time I did something," reflected Toni, grimly, as she rubbed her mother's wrists, and slapped her face with cold water. "This is no good!" Incidentally, she also remembered that quite a large bill was owing at the chemist's for her medicines, Sanatogen, chicken essence, etc. Somehow, she had thought that Grandmère was paying for it; somehow, Grandmère wasn't. It was during one of her "bad times.' . . .

—"But it's been one of my 'bad times,' too—I'm really no better than Grandmère!" But, with Toni, these sudden and terrible flashes of self-revelation, led to action. And when her own lapses into irresponsible youth were over, she was the most clear-headed and competent person in the family. She went, now, and had a quiet talk with the chemist, and arranged that her mother should assist him for two hours every morning, and three every afternoon, in his dispensing department, and by this means gradually pay off his bill, and at the same time acquire experience for which he might be willing to pay wages, later on. Then she arranged with the landlady's daughter to look after Mrs. Lake, in exchange for Mrs. Lake's help with the mending of their linen, for the old lady was wonderfully skilful with her needle, and had taught Toni not a little in this line.

Next, Toni applied at every important buyer in the West End for a job as a saleswoman of dresses. She had won her experience during that short but hectic period after Grandmère's influence had procured her a post at an expensive modiste in Bond Street, run by a one-time Society leader. There, under a clever French milliner, Toni had learnt the technical details of the trade, and the mysteries of stock-keeping; she had been sent here, there,

and everywhere to match silks and flowers and ribbons.
The Society leader was a wonderful saleswoman, com-
bining psychology with contempt for her customers.
Toni, who was allowed to assist her personally in selling,
learnt the former quality, and eliminated the latter. . . .
" Remember this, child, that women the world over are
open to flattery *providing* it is based on the tiniest bit of
truth. Not otherwise."

Persisting now with her search for work in the West
End, she was, after a couple of disheartening weeks,
taken on as a junior at an exclusive old-fashioned house
in Dover Street, for the princely sum of ten shillings per
week, and excellent food. She was expected to work
from nine-thirty till six-thirty; the closing hour was, however, very elastic, before the Factory Acts had been
passed; and as now occurred the beginning of the
Summer season, Toni often waited till half-past nine at
night to pack Court-trains and dance-frocks for the
dèbutantes who were floating carelessly through their
late teens, as she herself so longed to do.

A couple of months was enough of this, even though
she picked up valuable experience in the workrooms.
Toni spoke confidently to the head designer about the
chances of a rise, and discovered that, as she had paid
no premium, these were very small indeed : "But if you
like to say, Miss Rakonitz, that you want two or three
mornings off for the dentist, and use them to look about
you, well, I'll wink at it . . . and give you a good enough
recommendation, too."

Toni looked about her. She was by this time attracted
by the wholesale, principally to compare the different
business outlook and experience. An advertisement
caught her eye which promised scope for an ambitious
junior sales-woman. She was amused by her novel
reception. Instead of the usual boring question : " How
tall are you? "—and that slim scrap, Toni Rakonitz,
never gave satisfaction with her faltering : " Five foot
four and a half," though to this day she has never
fathomed why height in the costume trade should pre-
suppose brains and subtlety !—she was greeted with :

"Write your name down, child. Show me your hands, take your hat off, smile, and walk across the room!" . . .

Her voice and manner appealed to the owners of the business, man and wife, and by a stroke of luck, really gentle, artistic and delightful people. She appealed to them, not because she was so radiantly beautiful, nor because she suddenly dashed down in front of them her own designs that would make their fortunes; nor even because she wept crystal tears and said, in the old Adelphi style, that Grannie was in bed and Mummy nearly starving, which, though true, was quite too improbably true for belief. But she was cool, and this coolness of Toni's remained always her great asset in business. Her statements were clear, and her understanding quick. At first sight of her, two things were evident : that she would never be pert nor slovenly. That was enough for Mr. and Mrs. Wolfe.

Two days later Toni was informed, when she came back from a matching expedition, that a Madam Raksomething had been visiting the boss, and had talked a lot, and had gone away again. They didn't say: "The same name as yours," because Toni now called herself Toni Lake, which was easier and more convenient. The model girls giggled that day whenever Toni passed in and out. She felt apprehensive, but dared not ask questions; and apprehension chilled into anger at the idea that even here Grandmère could not leave her in peace. And then somehow it all bubbled away again into laughter, when, the next morning, the Matriarch appeared in all her regal sables, bowing and gracious, and carrying, without paper, two immensely long hot rolls of French bread, a present for Mr. Wolfe, who had happened to mention, in the course of their chat about Continental habits, that he could never get in England the bread which he had enjoyed so much abroad.

—" There is a little French baker I have discovered in Ealing," explained the Matriarch volubly, beaming on all the company, including the model girls, Toni, Mr. and Mrs. Wolfe, three of their travellers, and a customer. "Quite by accident I found it one day when I went in to have a button sewn on my boot because I could not walk any further, and I knew they would be obliging. I find people always obliging—" Then she told them quite a lot more about the baker and his wife, who both came from Grenoble, where Otto Solomonson used to buy all the gloves for the family at Christmas, because he had a brother there in the glove business, the one whom Wanda refused to marry—" And now look at her! She does St. Catherine's hair!" cried Anastasia, using the French idiom for " on the shelf."

The Wolfes appreciated her cosmic geniality, which, by the association of one idea with the next, could run a girdle round about the earth in forty minutes, proving everything in matter to be somehow related. Mrs. Wolfe, for instance, bought her gloves through a friend in Grenoble. . . .

CHAPTER XIII.

I

A rumour ran through the family that Ludovic had been heard of, that Ludovic was in New Zealand, that he was doing very well, that he was a rich man, that he was coming home, that he was to be fetched home, that Danny was going out to find him and fetch him home. . . .

II

Toni was too tired at the end of the day's work to do anything except tumble into bed, but on Sunday afternoon she dashed down to Ealing, and met Danny just swinging out of the front gate.

"Hullo! Good! How jolly you look in that pink tammy-affair. Come for a 'bus ride? Don't show yourself in there or they'll grab you. It's all bunged up with the family."

"Why? Is it anybody's birthday I've forgotten?"

"Oh, I don't think so. I haven't seen any presents going about, and the kissing hasn't been specially lush; in fact, I don't think anyone is in except Aunt Elsa and Grandmère, but they make it seem full up. Oh well, I shall be out of it soon. Toni, I'm off to New Zealand!" He grinned down at her as they stood on the kerb waiting for their 'bus; and two things struck Toni in the same second: that Danny was extraordinarily attractive—and that Danny was going away. He was tall and active, but not graceful. She liked the touch of awkwardness in all his movements. She liked his short square nose and rather long upper lip, his impudent mouth and impudent eyes, and all his strong darkness—black hair, brown eyes,

178

swarthy skin. She liked the immense exuberance in his voice; the impatient vitality in all that he said and did; his mischief, and his graceless disregard of all the world, except in those precious moments without reasonable come or go, when you felt that you were his, and your cause his cause, until he chose to drop you again. Danny, perhaps, was one of the very few souls who could live singly, and do exactly as he wanted to do, with a childish certainty that that was the only way to behave; his was never deliberate rudeness; yet for him, other people had no feelings, no sensitive places, no complicated points of view. When he wanted to read in a room full of people, he opened his book, and read, and was utterly swallowed and absorbed. If he were abruptly tired of talking to some one, he did not stay and entertain him, but gave in entirely to his cessation of interest, and got up and went to bed, or out, or into another room. And if he wanted to sing a song, he leant up against the wall, and without prelude or excuse, he sang, in despite of his audience. Because his stride through life was so unembarrassed, and his view-point so unashamed, people more hindered than he, liked to look on at him, and did not call him selfish. He dared, too, to stake his all on the present moment, whatever the present moment happened to be, and to remain loyal only to his present; if necessary to the present, he repudiated his past, he pledged his future, denied anything he might have said, said everything he had no right to say, destroyed confidences, and knocked down the wall of all existing secrets which should have been sacred. His queer code would not allow itself to be bound by tiresome and pettifogging consistencies. If he liked someone last week, he did not in the least see why he should go on liking them at the moment, if it so happened that he did not like them at the moment.

"I hate Maxine; I've always hated her—her eternal games make me sick; she thinks she can dance, but she can't!" Thus Danny to Sylvia, perhaps. And went on piling up the indictment against Maxine, even to the sunny betrayal of what Maxine, in her spiritual occupation of the central couch in his seraglio, had rashly pro-

nounced last week about Sylvia's dancing. Danny did
not mind at all being marched up to confront his
treacheries face to face, indignant Maxine and triumphant Sylvia together; all confidences unravelling from
his initial pull at the thread. He rather enjoyed it; abided
fearlessly by his utterances to Sylvia, without any
attempted evasions or compromise. . . . Now Derek, for
instance, would, by evasion and compromise, have denied
his own denials, betrayed his betrayals! But could a
prophet have thundered in Sylvia's ear: " Let her who
thinketh she standeth, beware lest she fall!" he would
have saved her from her turn of disillusion and bewilderment. . . .

It may have been that below Danny's disconcerting
irresponsibility was a strange stubborn layer of principles.
A man who walks singly, and abides by his present, must
perforce encounter difficulties.   He may try to explain
things away, to fit himself in, to atone and to amend, and
be for the future tolerant and discreet, and respectful
towards human complications.   But Danny would keep
swinging on at the same pace, his own pace, and in his
own chosen direction, exasperatingly, chubbily dense to
all reproaches.

" I can't see what you're in such a stew about," Danny
would say; then those whom he had failed, or those whom
he had betrayed, would laugh in sheer despair, and after
that laugh they liked him; and they usually went on
liking him, whatever he did. . . .

" Do tell me," said Toni, as they sat isolated on the
front seat of the 'bus that would take them to Richmond
Park, " about Uncle Ludovic.   I've simply been shut
away all the week, and not heard a thing.   Isn't Grandmère frightfully excited?   When do you start?   And how
did you hear about him being there?   Did he write?   And
do you know exactly where he is, or are you just going to
hunt for him? "

" I don't know exactly where he is, but I'm not going
to hunt for him, for the jolly good reason that he might
be in Canada or in the South Sea Islands, for all I know.
So it would be a waste of time."

Toni was puzzled. "But *how* did the news come through, then?" she persisted.

"'Tisn't news, it's only a rumour."

"Well, the rumour, then?"

"I started it," said Danny, in tones that congratulated himself heartily on a bright idea.

Toni's eyes became stern. "Without foundation?"

But Danny noticed nothing ominous. . . . He was all sunny contentment: "I knew the old lady would pay the fare out to anywhere, and believe anything, now she's all on the ramp again, so, in imagination, I just dumped down Uncle Ludo where I most wanted to go, and then went and gasped out that I'd seen a chap who was Uncle Ludo's partner out in New Zealand—and please might I go and look for Uncle Ludo and bring him home, in case he thought he wouldn't be welcomed at home, and was staying away because of that. Then Grandmère uprose and blessed me and—"

"You—lying—cad!" There was no mistaking Toni's voice, now.

"Look here!"—Danny flared into quick wrath, because she was being stupid, and spoiling his narrative, and spoiling his pleasure in it, "just damn well don't call me names!"

"Did you expect I should smile and tell you how clever you are?"

Danny *had* expected it; but you never knew, with Toni. For months you could rely on her sheer love of piracy to mingle with yours and to wink at whatever you said or did, and then, quite suddenly, she went back on you like this. Danny was furious; he liked to be able to rely on people; he hated inconsistency; in fact, for the moment, he was thoroughly the injured one of the pair.

"Listen to me for one moment, please, and don't talk till you have listened." He spoke in those insulting accents which, by their slow, clear, biting emphasis, assumed that Toni was a lunatic. "The family have put me to work for the last two years in an office in the City where we burn electric light all day, and even when the sun is shining, because it's too dark inside to see by daylight. It isn't going to take me any further, and it's done nobody any good, and I loathe it. I've been done out of the sort of life I want; done out of it by the family, again; I wanted to go about, and have as much cricket and tennis and winter-sport as I liked, with jolly people, and not endless fuss and yarns over family this and family that—"

. . . Very vividly, Toni could see Danny leading the sort of life for which he longed; Danny in flannels and blazer, on the river at Oxford, with other cheery careless youths in flannels and blazers. Danny, in the same sort of clothes, one of a group on the lawn of a country-house, and a pretty golden-haired young girl beside him, swinging her tennis racquet. Danny in tweeds, tramping over the roots, frowning a little, intent; forgetting, while he took aim, the whole world of golden-haired girls. Danny standing, naked and brown, on a rock, the sun striking his flesh into a glow, just poised to dive, intent again, thinking only of his dive . . . in love with what his big awkward limbs could do; not in the least self-conscious, just happy and careless. Yes, and of carelessness the family had tried to rob him!—before he was twenty.

As usual, Toni could see Danny's point of view; as usual, Danny could not see hers. And, as usual, they were furious with each other, battling, flushed, words with a hurt swinging up behind them; groping for the vulnerable place, he to hit it, she—yes, when it came to it, she would, in chivalry, slant aside and miss. . . .

"I've wanted things, too," jabbered Toni. "And the same sort of things. Music and dancing, and people singing just because they were happy, singing in their baths!—Hundreds of baths; baths in white-tiled rooms, and not skimping the hot water. . . . I simply loathe geysers. I simply loathe routine—start work at a given time each day, and got to do it, and not even able to leave off until another time of the day, and then only finding worry at home. It isn't fair, it isn't fair to me any more than it is to you; but I would never do what you have just done, to get out of it."

"Then you're a fool," said Danny.

" You're indecent," countered Toni. " Grandmère's old, and sometimes she's not quite . . . not quite . . ."

" Sometimes she's mad! Of course she is! She's as mad as a hatter, now. You're afraid to say it."

" Well, and then you go and exploit her—queerness. You, a man, strong, you build up her hopes and tell lies and pretend you've heard about her son, knowing that she loves him enough to pay your passage and expenses, simply because you haven't the endurance we girls have, to go on with a life you don't like. You're a coward, and a liar, and a cad."

" Very well, then!" He suddenly became curiously blank and indifferent, " I'm a coward and a liar and a cad, but I'm *not* an infernal sentimentalist. During Grandmère's ' queer ' time," mockingly he emphasised the word which Toni's kindliness had used as a shield, " during her queer times, she flings money about all over the place, finances all sorts of cranks; her life is one long chuck-away. Why shouldn't I have a bit of it, instead of the next Persian carpet-maker she meets? The money would go, anyhow; she can't keep it. I want to travel; I want to get away; I want a long journey. I want the sea. It's life to me; I'm dead now."

" I want—I want—I want," scoffed Toni. " If you ' want ' to travel so much, why don't you sign on before the mast, and work your passage out somewhere? "

" Like a blooming hero? Why should I, when I can get it paid for me to travel as a first-class passenger? I'm out to enjoy myself, not to work."

" I hope you have a pleasant journey," Toni wished him, politely.

" I'm quite sure I shall," laughed Danny, his good humour completely restored. " And who knows, I might find Uncle Ludo out there; he's just as likely to be there, as anywhere else. If so, I'll bring him home and not grudge the expense."

Toni realised that he had accepted the sudden lull in the storm, and her solicitude for his pleasant journey, at their face value. This was not to be endured. She knew the chink in his armour; and now, maddened by the

plausible cheery way in which he had used his own
family's tragedy for his selfish ends, she pierced through
to it :

" Perhaps, even if you don't find Uncle Ludo, you will
find your own father. He's just as likely to be in New
Zealand as anywhere else, isn't he?"

Danny was silent; his face was turned away from her,
looking over the edge of the 'bus-rail . . . and Toni, who
knew him, and knew that he always went one worse than
she, was obsessed by the horrible certainty that he was
going to fling back with a taunt about *her* father, who
had thrown himself under a train. . . . She just couldn't
wait to hear it. The 'bus was lurching along at full
speed, but she sprang from her seat, plunged for the top
of the stairs and down the stairs, and jumped, with a
spinning sensation in her head, off the foot-board, into
the middle of the road. . . . The traffic was all round
her; she staggered, turned giddy—

Then a hand gripped her arm, and marched her to the
pavement, and down a quiet side road, shaded with trees.

—" Of all the idiots ! " said Danny . . . and he put
his arms round her, and kissed her. He kissed her over
and over again. It might have been in hate, and it might
have been in love; it might have been in amusement, for
his eyes were laughing, though his mouth was hard. The
kisses that Toni gave him back were all passionate love,
drained of laughter and anger, and she managed to
whisper : " Danny " . . . as though she had never known
him before, nor spoken his name before. . . .

III

—" He is my first cousin."

It was a shock to remember. " Cousins ought not to
marry " was not only a formal theory for Toni. It was
because cousins had married, first cousins, that Bertrand,
Toni's father, and her uncles, Blaise and Ludovic, had
lacked stamina, and had died without much resistance,
if indeed Ludovic were dead or in Nicaragua, or—New

Zealand. . . . Which brought Toni's night-thoughts with
a swing round to Danny again. Naturally, now he would
not go; now he would give up his absurd errantry for a
non-existent Ludovic. She could not help wondering how
he would explain away this Uncle Ludo in New Zealand,
to the Matriarch, who was not easily deterred once her
mind had settled on its object. If he could be decent
enough to own up the truth, own up that he had lied. . . .
And there in the darkness, Toni suddenly flushed, hotly,
proudly, that he should make this decent atonement because he loved her; or even—imagination grew richer
and richer!—because he loved her, he might be awake to
the unspeakable hatefulness of his project, and own up
about it, not blindly for her sake, but for his own, to get
square with himself. Would he? Or would he just
weakly pretend to have heard another rumour that
Ludovic was not in New Zealand any more, or that it
had been another man all along? Easier, of course,
much easier, especially with Grandmère in her "bad
time" when she told everybody everything. . . . Danny
would hate Derek, for instance, to know that he had told
a mean lie. Toni could never be quite sure what Danny
was going to do, even though he was of her own blood,
her first cousin. . . .

It was because Anastasia had loved her first cousin,
Paul, and had desired to marry him, and had ruthlessly
pursued her will, that Toni would have to work now, with
her body, and against it, when it was tired, and when her
throat was sore, and when her head ached, instead of
carelessly following music. If Toni married her first
cousin, and if they had children, and the children would
have children, why she, Toni, would be deliberately
handing out to them what Anastasia had already handed
out to her; if not a certainty, at any rate an eighty per
cent risk; four out of five; four of the Matriarch's five
children; Truda was all right. . . .

Toni, in some ways, was too wise for nineteen, too old
and too wise. It had not been empty talk, when she had
played jongleur to Derek, up in the attic, over the deeds
and the stories of Rakonitz. The family was her passion,

her adoration. She was their votary, shot through and
through with romantic fires. Individual members of it
could exasperate her; she could wrangle with them, do
without them, give and take with them in all the commonplace exchanges of everyday, but the family as a whole,
with its past and its future, its rhythm as of marching
feet, and the one face that recurred like a fugue in the
symphony of the world—that was different from just
bickering with Maxine, or contradicting Aunt Elsa. If
she married Danny, her first cousin, she would be betraying the family again, doing it harm, weakening it, leaving
ill legacies; a son, perhaps, who would die early with a
troubled soul and a twelve hundred pound debt on his
conscience; or a grand-daughter who must not be over-
excited!   Toni and Danny; Bertrand's daughter and
Sophie's son; Rakonitz and Rakonitz—*No.* . . . . " There
must be a stop to this ! "

Toni bent her knee before the altar.

Sacrifice was a little too difficult, unless you could be
splendid about it, without anyone knowing, but just to
satisfy your own inner love of splendour. Toni saw that
she would have to renounce Danny. Besides, she had
taken on what Bertrand had left : her mother; her young
brother, her mother's mother, who had spent all her
money on them when they were in straits, and therefore,
in ordinary gratitude, as well as love, would have to be
supported for the rest of her life. Toni's own impetu-
osity had severed them from the Matriarch, and the
Matriarch's house, and the Matriarch's tyranny. She
would have to stick to what she had taken on. She was
quite sure that if she married Danny on the understanding
that they together would have to support Susan and
Gerald and Mrs. Lake, Danny, a week afterwards, would
say : " I don't see why? " whatever he had promised a
week before.

And then again—so Toni argued hotly with herself,
that night, the night of the glamorous day when Danny
and she, in the very fury of a quarrel, had discovered
that they loved each other !—then again, if her man
were Danny, her man would be yet another of the

Rakonitz tribe, irresponsible, weaker than their women. Was there no man for Toni, stronger than Toni? A man of fresh blood? Already she was looking after the wife of Bertrand Rakonitz because, living and dead, he had left her without succour. Gerald?—she did not yet know what Gerald was going to be, but in his looks and in his walk he was the image of Bertrand. . . . Blaise? She was paying—going to pay—Blaise's debt. And Derek?— Toni's lip curled a little scornfully whenever she thought of Derek, his flexibility, his over-quick response to whatever tune she played. And there had been Maximilian; Maximilian the adored, the Grand Seigneur, the most handsome, arrogant, charming of all the Rakonitz men, but he had shot up to riches on his luck, not on his strength or skill; and he had come down with a crash, and they had all crashed down with him. Better for Toni if she had not loved a Rakonitz male, if it had not been Danny. . . .

But it was Danny!

Toni decided to give him up . . . but not yet, not quite yet.

IV

. . . Then, three days after all this, it was again a shock, though of a different kind, when she found that Danny had gone off happily to New Zealand, without seeing her again. Gone to New Zealand to look for Uncle Ludovic!

V

We achieve heroism, when we learn not to be heroic. Toni, after one raging, racked half-hour, had been suddenly able, by a God-sent miracle, to perceive Danny as really very funny indeed; and she herself as funnier still, for having envisioned herself nobly renouncing him.

Her behaviour, after this, may have seemed, on the surface, irrational. . . . She went to the cash-box where she was keeping all that she had been able to save, in three and a half years, towards future payment of the

Rakonitz debt to Isaac Cohen. It amounted to about twelve pounds.

And Toni spent the lot.

She took a couple of tickets for a big subscription dance to be held that night at the Savoy; she rang up a quite irrelevant man whom she knew and liked, and asked him to be her escort; then, at a very reduced cost price, from the Wolfes, she bought a model evening dress which she had been longing for, ever since it came in; a shimmer of pale crocus flame, over deep garnet, so that she looked like fire glowing in the shadows; it curved softly, as of its own volition, into the new harem shape. Finally, lying as recklessly and quite as unscrupulously as Danny himself, Toni took a single room for the night at the Savoy, with a bath-room attached—white cool tiles!—and told them at home that she was spending the night with Mrs. Wolfe.

" Why ever not? " she laughed at the absent Danny, in imitation, part mocking, part complimentary, of his methods. It amused her to know how Danny would certainly have nodded his approval and blessing on that one night's perfection of pleasure and its accessories, at everybody's full expense, including her own and the unconscious Mr. Cohen's. . . .

She appeared sedately and punctually at business, on the morning after the dance, and went sedately and punctually home. Every penny of the twelve pounds was gone. But she had danced. When she was paid her week's salary, she put five shillings of it into the empty box, beginning all over again. . . .

CHAPTER XIV.

I

In the Spring of 1914, Toni began to travel for her firm, being allotted, on probation, the south and south-eastern circuits. It was, really, an instinctive knowledge of the different types of frocks that would suit different types of women, that first gave her this chance. London customers would often 'phone, and ask especially for her. She never wasted time by suggesting that her customers should try on three dozen unsuitable frocks, but shut her eyes, visualized the completed picture, and then insisted that only perhaps four gowns of the whole collection were suitable for Madame's rather uncommon style!

The first tour was a thrilling experience. She had always longed to see more of England, especially of some of the old cathedral towns; and she liked the jaunty independence, the hawker-and-pedlar atmosphere, of travelling for Wolfe and Wolfe. And she liked the novel experience of staying in hotels that might have been lifted out of a page of Charles Dickens' . . . "Family and Commercial,"—how comfortable they nearly always were, and how good the food! She enjoyed sitting at the table, with other roadsmen, after a tiring round of the big shops, comparing their day's luck. The managers of important drapery emporiums (complete with white spats) used to look astonished, sometimes, at their first sight of Toni. For one thing, though travellers, like the grocer's boy, are supposed always to go round to the back door, this pale, thin, beautifully dressed little girl *never* seemed to know of any entrance except the front one. She was a change, certainly, from the usual glib or rubicund commercial traveller, tough with experience.

But they approved of her haughtiness . . . as soon as she let them once glimpse the charming rogue beneath.

She very rarely lost an order, once taken.

In October of 1915, one of Reggie Wolfe's best travellers died, and Toni was given his tour. She went North now, where big business was; and to the Midlands; and to Scotland. It was a strenuous and most tiring life. Sometimes it took perhaps three hours to show a whole collection, as the samples of their stock-in-trade was called; and then followed inevitably another two hours' hard packing over big hampers—" skips." And always, while showing on one tour, her mind had to be picturing and trying to guess the type of dress the public would be wanting to buy next season. Courage was required at the stock-taking season in town, to buy silks and fabrics and model gowns—costing frequently from forty pounds to fifty pounds each—three or four months before they could be worn. The firm learnt to trust Toni's daring, as second only to Mrs. Wolfe's. Occasionally, workroom juniors and model girls used to get dilatory fits, and fits of nerves and hysteria—Toni's habit was to wait as tactfully as might be until the atmosphere was past all bearing, when she would suddenly flame into a rage, row everybody all round, and reduce the entire staff to tears, contrition, and renewed zealous effort. . . . " But once every six months for that effect, no more ! " Toni decided.

But she liked the travelling best; though that, too, had many disappointments. Buyers who promised to see her on her next journey, and then as easily broke the promise. . . . Toni was too keen and too proud to take such failure with a shrug of the shoulders.

On the whole, she was amazingly successful.

II

Toni was on tour in Scotland, in March 1916, when Danny reappeared in England with the first contingent of New Zealanders, on short leave after Gallipoli, before going to France. She gathered, from impatient questioning of Val and Maxine, afterwards, that he had looked exceedingly bronzed and handsome, that the slouched hat had suited him well, and that he regarded the War as a happy adventure devised for his eager interest. The whole question of his search for Uncle Ludovic had naturally been slurred over and dropped into limbo, like everything else of minor importance, after the fourth of August, 1914. He had had barely time to look round him, in New Zealand, before the war had broken out; and, of course, he had joined up at once. No one but Toni knew how he had procured his liberation from the City. Danny himself had certainly ceased to bother about it.

Others of the family were fighting, besides Danny. Neil and Klaus already had their commissions by the time the New Zealand rifleman was swaggering his black buttons and rampant lion's crest, in London. Little Klaus, to everybody's amazement, was promptly mentioned in despatches, for coolness and bravery under fire. Derek was in the Officers Training Corps, talking fluently of what he would do in a year's time, when he was eighteen. Gerald and Richard, who were only fifteen at the outbreak of hostilities, had very little hope that they would have any chance to share in them. Etienne Czelovar was a poet-patriot in the French infantry; and Leslie Moss, the father of the Colleens, got his majority with almost incredible quickness, and after that, a bullet through his head. Away on the borders of Poland, Franz Rakonitz was fighting too, a débonair captain in the 12th Hussars; but the flash of his sword was far enough distant for the family in London to forget that he was on the enemy's side; and anyhow, he was only killing Russians, not English. . . .

About 1917, the news wound a tortuous way through to the Matriarch, that Franz Rakonitz had been killed.

For the last two years of the War, Etienne was a prisoner in Germany; Derek, an airman along the first line of defence on the East Coat, his Headquarters at Shoeburyness; Richard, in the Autumn of 1917, just when he had attained the military age, and was hoping fiercely to be sent to France, was interned for having

been born in Munich, in the house of his grandfather,
old Hermann Marcus; and by some stupid oversight,
never naturalised; little Klaus was invalided home, with
a D.S.O., and a strangely inappropriate reputation for
dash and resourcefulness. Neil, of whom one might
have expected these gallant qualities, was also invalided
home, from Mesopotamia, with nothing more picturesque
than shell-shock and subsequent breakdown.

And Danny Maitland went cheerfully through the War
from beginning to end, with very little leave, and a great
deal of hard fighting in the trenches, and came out as he
had gone in, a rifleman in the New Zealanders, his
slouched hat still pulled forward at a swaggering angle
over his eyes, even more bronzed and more exceedingly
handsome, gloriously fit, and tinged with incredible regret
that the War should be over so soon!

II

Those of the Rakonitz family who remained civilians
in London did not suffer as much from a war against
Germany and Austria as might have been expected. In
a funny sort of way, although they never thought of
themselves as English, they also never thought of themselves as anything but English. Anastasia had now been
forty-four years in England; so had Elsa; and Louis only
a year or two less. They had all been naturalised in the
normal way of business; and those of the second and
third generations who had not been born in England, such
as little Klaus, were also naturalised. It was a stroke
of irony which made Richard, sturdy, stolid specimen of
Winborough school-boy, the only victim of muddle in
this respect—except for Aunt Gustava; and as Aunt Gustava rarely stirred more than a quarter of a mile beyond
her home with Raoul and Constance, the five-mile limit
imposed on her did not actually inconvenience her much,
although the spiritual insult caused her to be thoroughly
offended with England and English officialdom, for the
duration of the War. She never passed a policeman
without sniffing and pouting.

Rakonitz was not an aggressively enemy name, and did not have to be changed; though the younger Silbers turned their " b " into " v," for business purposes, and for the sake of Iris and Derek at school. Little Klaus got his D.S.O. on " Sellabach "; and though he had waveringly been " Claude " whenever anybody could remember it, in pre-War days, he went back again to " Klaus," with an unexpected spurt of pride which pleased his Uncle Louis immensely, even more than the D.S.O. had pleased him. . . . Perhaps, he thought, hopefully, perhaps Klaus, the grandson of Ludovic Rakonitz, was, after all, and despite his surface habits of apology and vacillation, the best and toughest of the family's men-to-be.

But Louis was just beginning to notice the girls. . . .

Val Power, by the time Armistice Day came round, was well-known, as an artist, for her bold poster and decorative work. She had had two one-man exhibitions, and enthusiastic reviews from all the critics who counted. At least two-thirds of her pictures were red-starred : " sold " on the first day. Her posters were splashed about London, too; outside the theatres; on the platforms of the stations on the electric railway; on advertisements, and on book-covers. She was a R.B.A.; and when she went to the type of dinner-party where " Eminent Men and Women " were gathered together, her dresses were afterwards described in the Press. . . . Val was rather touched on discovering that one of these cuttings, headed " Smart Lady Artists," and emphasizing the astounding fact that feminine genius nowadays was both fashionable and well-groomed and did not wipe its oily paint-brushes on its hair, lay secretly folded inside Uncle Louis' pocket-book.

Val had reached this stage of her fame by dint of making sacrifices neither for her family nor for her country, but solely for her work. Aunt Elsa, in a scene of great power and volubility, called her selfish; Val countered gracefully by sending her one of her pictures, signed. Aunt Elsa hung it in the drawing-room, and proudly called everybody's attention to it. . . . Her own three good girls were doing war-work, and secretarial work, and house-work—"Every blooming work under the sun!" quoth Val, disrespectfully. Val wanted to see Mélanie have a good time. Mélanie was a dear; her plain face lit with love of the children she had never had. But she had lately been appointed Matron of a large London hospital for children, and was receiving a high salary, and much praise for her competence. Val impetuously declared her altogether beautiful, seeing her once with the folded white bands of her office about her broad face, with its high cheek-bones and sloe eyes; and would have insisted on painting her, only Mélanie snubbed the intention, saying she had no time. Pearl was willing to be painted, and Pearl was much prettier than Mélanie; but Val could not forget her with fat pink cotton legs and frizzed hair, as the fairy queen of Toni's plays of their childhood; and wickedly immortalised this memory; Toni rocked with joy when she saw it, and begged it as a birthday present from Val.

Freda was still in San Remo, because Amélie's dogged conscience, still abiding by the Matriarch's original orders, refused to yield her up until she could "get her married"; so Jeanne-Marie remained on at Aunt Elsa's, where at any rate, Amélie believed, she would be safer and better fed than in France during war-time. Pearl, the youngest and literally the fairest of the four little Rakonitz nuns, had obtained her B.Sc., and was lecturer and demonstrator at the Alma Lawrence College for Women. Aunt Elsa watched these careers wistfully. She was still hoping that Pearl, at least, might develop some latent sense of coquetry. Aunt Elsa was now nearly seventy, but she was still a roguish, charming little Viennese lady, who knew in every susceptible fibre of her body and soul when a man was approaching, even before he had entered the room. She had upset Sylvia Czelovar, when reluctantly Sylvia had trailed her Guardsman fiancé the dutiful round of the family—"Once is enough, Harry; we need scarcely ever see them again "— by whisking off Harry to a corner of the drawing-room, and there most shamelessly flirting with him, listening

with appreciation to his most lurid Mess stories, stories
which he had never brought within a hundred miles of
Sylvia herself; twinkling at him, twitching his ear;
capping these stories, even, with one of her own, in a
discreet whisper—but Harry's sudden roar of joy shook
the candelabra crystals, and set them reeling in a jocund
dance.

"You're a nottee boy!" cried Aunt Elsa . . . and
Mélanie, Gisela, and Pearl looked up from their crochet-
work, and lidded her exuberance with a gentle chorus of:
"Mother," "Mother," "Mother!" . . . Lieutenant Harry
Thurston said that they *could* stay to dinner, that Sunday
morning, when Sylvia had already said that they could
not. He pronounced the Eiernöckerl splendid, and the
Zvetchkenknödel top-hole; and when he drove Sylvia
round in his little A.C. two-seater to visit the Matriarch,
after that dinner, he told her that Aunt Elsa was a sport,
and "It"! He had not noticed how many daughters
she had—

—"Do you mean all those girls sitting round the table?
I liked the one who kept on passing me things; she had
some sense."

"That was Mélanie." Sylvia wondered, a little apprehensively, in what state they would find Aunt Anastasia.
She did not know for certain that it was one of her
'bad times.' Raoul Czelover and his wife were not in
the very throng and thick of the family.

Val, on the other hand, knew perfectly well that
Anastasia had, the week before, taken all the linen, all
the towels and sheets and pillow-cases and table cloths,
soiled and clean, from Truda's house, saying positively
that they were hers, not Truda's. She had even remembered to empty out the clothes-basket, and to pull off the
bed-linen then in use, and had arrived with her loot,
plus seven additional trunks and cases, at the tiny house
which Toni, by now, had managed to rent in Bedford
Park. Their small rooms were already overcrowded
with Mrs Lake's unwieldy furniture; just as their linen-
cupboard was already profusely stocked from the same
ample mid-Victorian source.

" Grandmére darling, are you *quite* sure that some of this linen isn't Aunt Truda's, after all? Hadn't it better go back to her?"

Anastasia, in a state of magnificent indignation at the implied doubt, had the cab loaded up again, and drove off to a very questionable boarding-house in Bloomsbury, where she was now—well, Val called it : " Queen of the Bloomsbury Brothel."

. . . Val had been happy in obliging her cousin Sylvia with the address, without mentioning that the Matriarch was not quite as well and decorous as she had been when Sylvia had last seen her, a year before.

Sylvia was a great deal more Wyatt than Czelovar; more in the style of Canterbury and the Dean, than European baroque. She was exquisite, demure, and still childishly in subjection to Good Form. Her mother had treated her always as though she had been something rare and breakable ; the school to which she had been sent had been so exclusive as almost to exclude everyone except Sylvia herself; the type of school where you had riding lessons three times a week, and dressed every night for dinner. When her brother Neil first took her to dances, they had very often danced the whole evening together, languidly refusing introductions to " rabbits," in a way which their small sister Helen described as : " sheer thwank ! " Helen was a great trial to Sylvia, who could not understand why her father showed such curious, ironic partiality for the little Yiddisher changeling. Harry Thurston had looked startled when he had first seen Helen. . . . Sylvia hastily arranged for him to lunch with Uncle Louis.

Sylvia had kept aloof from her father's family, but had not dared ignore them altogether. Uncle Louis would have been furious if she had not formally taken her fiancé to call upon the Matriarch; it was due to the Matriarch's position as head of the tribe. So that Sunday afternoon they tootled up in his car; and were admitted into an atmosphere that was a medley of the tawdry and the sinister; a slightly hysterical atmosphere to boot. . . . An enormously plump Belgian was crying and rocking himself to and fro in the drawing-room; and the proprietress was a foreigner, too, and had brilliant metallic hair, and gave Harry an artificial rose—" Puisque vous êtes mon allié. . . ."

" Madam Rackernitz says will you please both to come up to her bed-room." The slut-of-all-work breathlessly delivered her message, and gazed with admiration at Sylvia's flower face in its great ruff of skunk.

" Did you tell her," queried Sylvia, " that Mr Thurston was here with me? "

" Yes, miss. That's all right—She said will you both go up? She ain't in her own room, she's in somebody else's, number fourteen, 'cos of the 'pendicitis."

Sylvia and Harry went up to number fourteen, which was not the Matriarch's room, but somebody else's. Sylvia never knew what she had been spared, for in the Matriarch's own room were a row of Bücklinge with bright and fishy odours, drying on the window sill; whereas in somebody else's room were only seven Belgians in various states of fear and collapse, clinging round the Matriarch's dressing-gown, and begging her for reassurance about Carolina, their darling Carolina, who had just been removed to the hospital for an operation. . . .

" I arranged myself this morning," cried the Matriarch to Sylvia, " that she should have a bed with only four other beds in the ward. It's a shame, when her brother has died for our country, the same as this young man might do! " genially beaming at Harry. " I am very, very pleased to see you. You have a treasure there, I can tell you, in this little Sylvia of ours. I have forgotten your name, but I have told the girl to get lunch for us as soon as I have put up the rest of my hair. They give you very good pot-au-feu here. . . . Mon cher Monsieur, you must be patient; we have now done all we can! "—this was to the fat gentleman of downstairs, who had just come into his room, and who was apparently the father of Carolina. " For the rest, you must pray to le bon Dieu, not to me, but—" turning again to Sylvia —" it was a good thing that I had my hot-water bottle with me, in the night. They called me as soon as the attack started, and I came in as you see me now. But tell me again, what is your fiancé's name? Harry? Of course I shall call him Harry; is he not going to be one of the family? And now, my dear Harry, I will tell you exactly what you are going to do. You are going to my room, number twenty-one, just along the passage, and you will get my purse, which you will find on the bed, perhaps, or in the pocket of my mauve moiré dress hanging on the door; and you will take it, and run out, and buy a bottle of wine for our lunch, to celebrate this occasion, because they have no licence here. . . . Yes, you see I am already treating you as though you belonged to us, sans cérémonie; that is right, isn't it? And Sylvia shall tell me all about you, while I dress myself. I tell you, I have quite forgotten the time and everything; it might be past mid-day, for all I know—all night nursing that poor, poor girl! "—The Belgian family broke into fresh lamentations. The Guardsman, rather dazed, but on the whole taking it better than might have been expected, went obediently to fetch the Matriarch's purse and to make awed acquaintance with the Bücklinge on the window-sill; and Sylvia, when he had gone on his errand, tried in vain to explain to the old lady's abundant hospitality, that the time was just after half-past four, and that they had already dined with Aunt Elsa.

III

Benno Silver was killed in the air-raid of September 8th, 1915, while walking home, in the pure moonlight, from a very satisfying dinner of the Worshipful Company to which he belonged; and absently trolling : " Die Wacht am Rhein." . . . Benno could not have had a more amiable death than swift oblivion on top of this blend of food, music and sentiment, beloved of his South German soul.

Most of his invested capital had " gone West," as people were beginning to express it, in the Nong-Khan " salted " mine; for he had had implicit faith in Maximilian. Since then, his earned yearly income had been barely more than enough for the needs of his family. Now that, too, had "gone West"; and Maxine's prophecy was realised, that whatever money she earned would be needed to supplement the two or three hundred a year which was all that her father had been able to leave Truda, rather than go into Toni's fund for repaying Isaac Cohen.

Maxine was eighteen when Truda was thus widowed, and had just finished a complete secretarial training. The head of her college thought enough of her intelligence to recommend her for the best job then at her disposal. Maxine went into the City, as confidential secretary to a firm of foreign bankers. Even more than Toni, she promptly discovered that she had a gift for business, and that it thrilled her beyond any more womanly occupation; she did not see business, as Toni did, for a romantic thing. Maxine was sturdily unromantic in all she thought and said, and she was perfectly at home with the hard heads, hard facts and hard figures that now came her way. She liked interviewing men who were on the make, and getting the better of them; bulls and bears were dear to her; a sudden boom on the foreign market was more her meat than costume drama at the Haymarket. She could deal with enormous mails without ever getting muddled or contradictory. Her employer soon learnt that she had initiative and sound judgment, and raised her salary; and when he was away or ill, left things in her hands to a degree which amazed Uncle Louis, when he heard about it from other City men, old cronies of his. Maxine of home life was rather a hoyden, especially in her manner with men. Danny once assured her, earnestly, of her total lack of charm; this statement had had a deep effect on Maxine, who quite naturally behaved henceforth with even less charm than before. She was handsome, in the style of those big, dark, amber-skinned maidens, with slow dreamy eyes, who can still be seen by the hundred in Zion, carrying pitchers of water upon their heads. But Maxine's temperament, in startling contrast, was essentially that of the modern girl, ardently fond of games, bored with psychology, but carrying banner-high the courage of her own opinions, whether right or wrong; satisfactorily without moods and graces, to those who desired an honest comrade; adoring her mother and Iris, irritated by her grandmother, exasperated by her brother Derek. Derek and Maxine were a living contradiction of the traditionally devoted twins. A favourite pastime of both of them was imagining how pleasant life would be without the other. Maxine was too downright for Derek; he resented her success at business, which made him feel that he ought to admire her!—and admiring Maxine was not part of a manly man's programme. Also she was undoubtedly head of the house, and that did not suit Derek either. Maxine was woven of tougher, rougher stuff than he. Her one weakness inherited from the Rakonitz side was generosity that amounted to reckless idiocy. However hard up, Maxine could not control her impulse to scatter presents; jolly, royal, expensive presents; she could not bear not to stand treat; she did not wait for " occasions " to give flowers and fruit and sweets, but flung about a trail of them right and left, wherever she went, certainly wherever she loved. Maxine shopping, might almost have been Grandmère . . . just as Toni, arriving an hour behind punctuality at an appointment, laughing and unconscious of her sins, might again almost have been Grandmère. . . . But they both touched sense at the fundamentals; and by the end of the War, when Grandmère was " bad again," it was on Toni and Maxine that the after-burden fell, as a matter of course, to adjust and to clear up. They had begun to shoulder the responsibility in 1917, when Louis fell ill.

IV

Louis' collapse, when it came, was so complete as to give the semblance of death, and then re-birth. It was really a form of delayed shell-shock; but the shock, for him, had already been in 1910, when the Nong-Khan mine collapsed. Before then, he had amounted to scarcely more than legend in the family, a legend slightly subservient to the Maximilian legend, but told in the same style of elegant prose. He cared less for racing and gambling, more for the arts. He hated business. He had retired from business early, so that he could live a spacious, epicurean sort of life, free from dinginess and responsibility. He had not married because he liked the loneliness that could choose its own companions, and not have them settled on him. He had always lived like a tolerably wealthy man; had belonged to two celebrated clubs; had travelled first-class, Pullman and litsalon; his rather dandified clothes were kept in perfect order by a well-trained valet. He had his box at the opera. He was a modern Maecenas, generous but querulous in his patronage of young artists, buying from them any work of art which happened to please his discrimination. When he went abroad, which was often, he went, not to the most ostentatious, but to what was distinctly the best hotel of cosmospolis; the maître d'hôtel knew all his private tastes in wines and sauces; the head waiters remembered that he tipped lavishly, but that unless they were careful in their attendance, they would be exposing themselves to his suave irascibility.

This was Louis' life, as a matter of course.

This had been Louis' life.

Then came the shock and the smash . . . and a most unpleasant future to be faced—or not faced! Louis' precious loneliness was broken into as many pieces as a costly bowl fallen from a tall pedestal. He had to see a great deal of the family. The family fussed and swarmed round him, and brought him their troubles; therefore, he had to see less of his own friends, because it was bourgeois, and thus distasteful to him, to trail a family about, and impose them on a circle who had hitherto thought of him as a solitary and distinguished figure, with charming cultured manners, and no grievances.

And he had not been able to escape listening to a great deal that was bitter about Rakonitz, and the firm of Rakonitz.

Maximilian was dead. The men of the family went on dying; even the caprices of accident, illness and fate, fixed on the men for their victims, not on the women. Louis stood alone, actually and spiritually and morally, trustee for all those remaining. No one was any help. He had always thought of himself as a weak character; but for seven years he had perforce to behave like a strong man, a grim hard man of unwearying nerves. His habitual air of pessimism, which in the era of their sleek fortunes, he had worn like a sombre, elegant cloak, now merged into genuine melancholy. He could never get away from the strain of reducing his daily hourly life, by petty economies, to a very much meaner scale . . . a small house in Regent's Park—his aestheticism could not contemplate flats !—no valet . . . only one club . . . then no club at all. Hospitality dwindling—Louis, lavish like all the Rakonitz tribe, had liked to play the host, scornful of price. He went to fewer good concerts . . . hardly travelled at all. Then he had to cope with the Matriarch's dip and sway of eccentricity . . . it grew worse . . . and then came the War . . . and that got on his nerves. . . . What would happen to them all, to all this family of women, if England went to bits, and the last of the capital he held in trust for them, went to bits? He was frantic with the responsibility—he saw all young Rakonitz that was left, going out to fight, going out to be killed, those whom he had desperately hoped would relieve guard later on . . . soon . . . very soon . . . he could not go on much longer . . . could not go on at all . . . sometimes we die from living against the grain.

They called it a nervous breakdown. It actually dated from that evening in 1917 when he had heard Franz Rakonitz had been killed. He and Franz had met sometimes, in their gay and dandified bachelordom, and, for all their disparity of years, had had good times, in Vienna, and Paris and Budapest. Now Franz was dead and out of all the fuss; a death which sounded like the gay ring of a coin. . . . But he owed that to being twelve years Louis' junior, and pretending to be younger still, for fighting's sake. And he had no convolvulus choke around his liberty. With the exception of Dietrich in Rome, and that boy—Bertrand's boy—Gerald, and Louis himself, Franz had been the only male Rakonitz left. And now he was dead—like Maximilian. . . . Louis, on hearing the bad news, fainted down the stairs of his house, and hit his head . . . and went to bed for a year. He nearly died that year—his heart and his nerves, the doctors said. Always thin, he became thin as a skeleton; always melancholy, his flame was all but quenched in melancholy. He dared not get well, for fear of what was accumulating for him, when he should get up again. He hardly ate, and he hardly slept; and his nurses, who adored him, nevertheless reported him "very difficult indeed."

The women of the family, recognising that Louis was ill, behaved beautifully—and nearly drove him over the sheer edge of distraction. In shoals they came to sit with him, to cheer him up, to assure him over and over again that he need not worry in the least, that all was well with them, with their money affairs, with their children . . . till his mind was a humming swarm of suspicion as to what disasters could lie beneath their parade of jovial contentment. The sight of Louis, very much the well-beloved of the family since Maximilian's death, lying there a gaunt outline of bones, great hollow mournful eyes, and helpless twitching fingers, roused all their most bosomly qualities. They brought their own warmth and vitality to him in chunks, hoping that he might be able to assimilate some of it. Sometimes, when two or three of them happened to meet at the bedside, they would forget Louis' actual presence, and chatter and gossip to each other in shrill quarrelsome oblivion of any need for a peaceful atmosphere.

"The great thing," cried Anastasia, overwhelming the nurse's attempted authority, "is not to treat him as an invalid. Let him think he is quite well, and going to get up tomorrow. I know; I have nursed—" and forthwith came the list.

At just about the crisis of Louis' illness, Anastasia was

204

in great form. She had bought a house, so she said, a
fine large house, which would divide into four flats.
These she would furnish. She already had some furniture of her own, including what she could take from
Truda; and Louis could let her have some of his—yes?
His small house in Regent's Park could only have used
up half of his previous possessions; the rest, no doubt,
was stored—

"And they are all thieves and robbers," cried the
Matriarch, "these storing people. I know them. They
are spoiling your furniture, chopping it to bits. Yes, yes,
don't contradict me, Elsa, it's probably out in the damp,
every bit of it. Sometimes they use it themselves, or
hire it out; I know them. Now, with me, it will be quite
safe, and you will save money, and these are all good
things, isn't it so? You see now, already I have enough
furniture for my four flats, and all the linen, too, because
all Truda's is mine. I bought it for her at the time of
her wedding, at Whiteley's. . . . I told her it was only a
loan, but she has forgotten; Truda is very obstinate,
sometimes. Bien! I will have paid for the house already,
in two years, with these four furnished flats, and still the
house will be mine to leave to my grandchildren, and I
need not worry any longer what is to become of them.
Nor need you, Louis. And I daresay I could live in it,
meanwhile, myself, in the basement. Yes, yes, I tell you I
mind no sacrifices."

Louis groaned.

"But you are speaking rubbish, I tell you, great
rubbish!" Aunt Elsa expostulated. "If the house is not
four flats, it has to be made into four flats, and that
requires money, a good deal more money than you dream
of, 'Stasia. You are no business woman."

"What! I no business woman? But me you can
teach nothing! And all poor Max's friends used to come
to me for advice when I gave those dinner-parties, and
you and Albrecht, poor Albrecht, were glad enough to be
invited, Elsa, though you may forget that now. . . . Yes,
yes, and I remember when you gave a party yourself, a
week after the one at which I entertained Wilmenski

himself—you remember him, Louis. But yes, of course
you must—the man who made his million in South
African diamonds. And you borrowed all poor Truda's
silver, so that you need not use your own, and yet your
dinner-party was a failure, Elsa, because at the last
moment you would not go to the expense of fresh goose-
livers. Always these little economies at the wrong
moment; and you call me no business woman! I tell
you, it's *big* business to know when to spend!"

Louis groaned again.

But, nothing daunted, Elsa and Anastasia swung gaily
along into the very scrum of a quarrel, and, metaphorically, had each other in shreds upon the floor . . . before
they arose, and put on their furs, and reassuringly patted
Louis' hand, and promised to come and sit with him again
quite soon—

"And let me see some plumpness next time, or I shall
be very, very angry," cried Aunt Elsa, shaking a playful
finger. They met Aunt Gustava in the doorway. Aunt
Gustava had come to sit with poor Louis for a little
while. If the others under-estimated his feeble state,
Gustava was prone to exaggerate it. She walked on
tiptoe, and she whispered, and she rustled to the window
and drew down the blinds, for fear the light would
hurt his eyes; and then, suddenly thinking he might
imagine himself dead already, tactfully drew them up
again half-way. . . .

"Now," she whispered, tiptoeing back to her chair
beside his bed, and using mostly monosyllables that were
nice and easy to understand, "I am going to tell you a
little joke, just a tiny joke. It will make you smile, but
it will not upset you, because it is only a small one. I kept
it for you. Now, are you ready? Listen! . . ."

On the whole, Louis preferred Val's visits. He told
Val some of what he felt about the older generation, and
they became friends on it. The only subject on which
they differed was the Matriarch herself. Even now,
Louis would speak no ill of her, own no flaw in her. Val
was a frank young iconoclast in her opinion of the
Matriarch and matriarchal conduct, but Louis shook an

obstinate head, and grew feverish and angry in defence
of the half-sister whom he so admired.

Nobody ever knew what decided Louis to turn back
from becoming that comfortable thing, a male Rakonitz
who had died and left his burdens to someone else. Perhaps some hint drifted down to his consciousness,
through Val, that the girls of the third generation had
taken on what he had let fall; and that if he recovered,
it need not be to cope with lonely responsibility. . . . A
queer new Louis was born out of the shell of the old.
A Louis with rather a mischievous twist to him. A
young Louis, with a quest for adventure in his soul;
and a joy at finding that he was alive and not dead, and
could do live things—ride on the tops of 'buses to stimulating and exciting out-of-the-way spots, like Greenwich
or Peckham Rye, or the shadier off-streets of Tottenham
Court Road; funny little eating-houses, Louis discovered
in his pioneerings; unsuspected bits of garden and
square; small but fascinating museums and picture-
galleries, that he had not known were in existence. And
furthermore, he discovered street musicians, and shops
that were not West End shops, and the interest of prow-
ling over empty suburban houses, and around Hampton
Court and the Tower and Soho. He and Val knocked
about a lot together, now. She felt amused and tender,
both, at Louis' renaissance; at his comical equivalent for
foreign travel. He was popular with Val's friends, the
unmoral and inconsequent youth of the twentieth century, with its hardness and its cubist angles. He argued
with them, and teased them; if they were feminine, flirted
with them in his courteous semi-deferential, semi-ironic
style; and told them anecdotes of when he kept a pack
of greyhounds; or of when, in the past, he bought a
labourer's hut for ten pounds, and, as the mood took him,
roughed it—the roughing was possibly one of Louis'
delusions!—possibly the hut was complete with every
luxury for roughing it. . . .

Val invited him down to stay in a little cottage which
she had rented for the summer of 1918, on the moors in
Cornwall.   Louis arrived with a trunk whose weight

would have tested the resources of nine porters; and a large case of mineral waters which he steadily refused to touch because he said he did not like the taste. Val, unpacking for him, discovered seven graduated changes of underwear, from the eventualities of arctic to tropical weather; a trousseau of the most expensive and perfect material and cut, the newest suiting dating from pre-War tailors, and most of them, he boasted, pre-Boer War. He also brought ten pounds of dried prunes for stewing, in case there were no dried prunes to be procured in Cornwall; his own eider-down, and all his own sheets and pillow-slips. In conclusion, Val unpacked what she described as Uncle Louis' ointments and unguents, pigments, myrrh and frankincense, that must have made his toilet-table the most distinguished in Cornwall.

Louis, in this renaissance period of fresh young enthusiasms, contrasted with the mellow yet sardonic flavour of his personality, was an unforgettable figure. He still occasionally lapsed into melancholy; and Val discovered that if she wanted him cheery, the best way was to mope herself, when he would immediately prove to her, being constitutionally perverse, that nothing was as bad as it looked. It used to amuse Val to find words that would exactly define and describe him; this aquiline, monocled " swell"; punctilious, pernickity, opinionated; this mid-Victorian Don Quixote; this strong man who was so weak; this weak failure who was so unexpectedly loyal and proud and strong; this Rakonitz who so heartily and healthily hated his family, but who lived for his family, and resented the slightest insult to it; this economist who would now rarely take a taxi, but who never gave less than a half-crown tip, usually more; this Israelite who had not the least sense of business, nor the least wiliness in the furtherance of his own interests; this—tragedy with a sense of humour.

. . . One glimpse of Louis, lunching with a friend at London's most supercilious hotel. The manager, who had known the three Rakonitz brothers well, of old, came, bowing and beaming, to welcome Mr. Louis Rakonitz

to his dining-room after such a long absence; very anxious
to hear what Mr. Louis Rakonitz thought of their new
scheme of decoration :—" We only re-opened this room
last night."

Louis screwed in his monocle, gave one critical look
round, and turned to that very sophisticated edition of
a tapioca pudding which he always specially ordered for
himself, fancying that he liked plain food. His friend,
a well-known member of Parliament, burst forth into
enthusiastic praise of the new scheme of decoration; but
the manager's eyes were still fixed on Louis. . . .

" I find it very depressing," said Mr. Louis Rakonitz.
" Very depressing indeed. It could not be more depressing."

The manager was broken-hearted. He immediately,
and to the amazement of the other diners, caused all the
blinds to be lowered, the curtains to be drawn, and the
lights to be switched on, so that Mr. Louis Rakonitz
could judge of the colour-scheme by artificial light. . . .

" Very depressing indeed," repeated Louis. " Worse,
if anything," and he let his monocle fall again.

v

The War was over. And—" Grandmère's all right
again ! " said the family, with a long breath of relief.

vi

For the first time, the younger ones of the tribe were
gathered together in Truda's drawing-room, settling up,
going through the smudged and crumpled bills; finding
out just what irremediable mischief had been done; what
could still be put right; what could be paid now, and
what, in instalments, later on; what jewels had been sold
or pawned. . . . Anastasia had previously tried to hurl
the pawn-tickets into the gas-fire, crying out that possessions were a curse !—but Maxine had rescued them.

For the first time on these weary occasions, Uncle
Louis was not present. The younger ones had decided

not to bother him, so soon after his recovery from a
serious illness. Truda was not in the room, either; like
all housewives at this period, she was going through a
difficult time with servants; and Maxine, the best
daughter in the world, wished to spare her mother's
nerves all the friction she could. Nor was Susan at the
council; her own mother, Hannah Lake, was ailing,
and needed continual nursing. Besides, Toni thought
Susan might be given a rest from the effects of matriarchal irresponsibility. . . .

The younger ones decided that neither Aunt Elsa's
presence nor Aunt Henrietta's were required.

. . . Toni, Maxine, Gerald, and little Klaus. Derek
had promised to be there, but failed at the last moment.
Danny lounged in about half-way through the discussion,
but sat silent, with his brilliant mocking eyes fixed on
Toni. Iris followed him in, unperceived; too much of a
child for official admission. Yet she was eighteen—and
Anastasia herself had married at seventeen; and at sixteen, Toni had defied the Matriarch, and had interviewed
Mr. Isaac Cohen.

They sat round a table, and went steadily ahead with
the tiresome, stubborn, and often humiliating business
in hand. . . . " Did she actually sign a contract for the
conversion-into-flats business?" " Yes, but it's missing."
"Who's the builder? Conway and Thomson? I'll see
them tomorrow, on my way home." . . . Their level
tones were competent and unexcited; Toni did not often
over-excite herself nowadays. She had learnt better.
She had learnt, too, not to plead with—whom?—that " it
isn't fair!" Futile to say: " It isn't fair!" as she used
to say it. Futile for Maxine to rage hotly against the
Matriarch as a personal factor causing all this upheaval
and sacrifice. Waste of breath. Enough, for the
moment, to go through with an unpleasant job. . . . Toni
and Maxine knew beforehand that reality would very
likely be worse than their worst anticipations. For,
.inally, they had learnt not to be optimists, these grandchildren of Rakonitz.

Two hours . . . three hours. . . . And then the Matriarch opened the door, and glanced with affectionate concern at the ring of tired faces under the glaring incandescent light :

"What—none of you dancing? " she cried gaily.

—And forthwith went to the piano, and threw back the lid, and began to play a Viennese waltz; and looked back, over her shoulder, with encouraging nods and smiles. . . . For it was not right, no, certainly it was not right for these young people to be so serious. Pale lips, and shadows under the eyes?—her grandchildren ought to have rosy cheeks ! . . . Her body swayed and jogged a little to the infectious rhythm.

They held back, grimly . . . at first. Presently the buoyant lilt seized hold of them. . . . Presently the Matriarch's will had its way, its triumphant irresistible way. . . . Presently they were all waltzing, modern steps perhaps, the " hesitation " and the " twinkle "—but otherwise not so very differently from how they had danced, as children, to her playing of the " Blue Danube."

At the corners of Danny's mouth lurked a small ironic smile. . . .

CHAPTER XV.

I

Richard Marcus called to the two horses, one grey, one roan, at the end of his furrow, swung the traces as they turned, scattering the clods with their great hooves. Then he began a new furrow, shearing through the stubble, turning back the earth in chocolate loamy slices. He did this again and again, patiently, not stopping to rest nor to look round, nor to listen to the exultant bird-chorus that went swinging up to the soft showery sky. Richard loved all these things of England; showers and bird-song, and the harsh pungent smell of roots and manure from the field, next to the one he was breaking up for the autumn sowing; but he absorbed them without constant pause from his work, to meditate and be conscious of his well-being; he knew they were there, and his, inevitably, and that was enough; his, for as long as he lived and worked on the farm.

It was not yet his own farm, this piece of Exmoor; but his father had promised him that if he stuck to it for a couple of years, and learnt his job, and was still of the same mind, preferring no other career, he would buy him a partnership with Mr. Brace, who was now the owner of the two hundred acres called "Six Acres." Ferdie Marcus could not but be aware that he owed Richard some good compensation for those twenty months in an internment camp. Richard's eighteenth birthday had been in the Autumn of 1917. He had wanted to fight, more than he had wanted anything else in the world. Of all the branches of the Rakonitz family, he was least a foreigner. . . . Yet he had been born in Munich. His great-grandmother was Rachel Rakonitz,

the youngest of Simon and Babette's ten children. She
had married Count Janoshaza, a Hungarian nobleman,
and they had lived at Budapest. Their only daughter,
Dorotéa, married very young; Bela Ladislov was a Czech,
whom Janoshaza used to bring home to the castle, after
boar-hunting. Bela and Dorotéa were a marvellously
happy couple; their sole fear had been that their one child,
also a Dorotéa, should marry away from Hungary. Perhaps their very fear, perversely, caused this sorrow of
sorrows to befall them. Dorotéa was only eighteen when
she met Ferdie Marcus on one of his gay student holidays
in the Tyrol, and fell in love with him, and he with her.
When his military service was over, his father, without
consulting him, sent him to England, into the business of
a friend over there; but Ferdie, in defiance of the typically
Teutonic bully, first journeyed down to Budapest.
. . . When he went to England, it was with a wife, a
slim, dark-haired girl, with wide eyes, and the sweetest
mouth in the world—so Ferdie said. Theirs, too, was a
very happy marriage. Deb, their little daughter, was
seven before old Hermann Marcus decided to interfere
with it by an imperious message that he was on his death-
bed, and naturally desired to make it up with his son, at
a time most inconvenient both to Ferdie and Dorotéa.
The habits of filial obedience were still very strong in this
generation; so back they went to Bavaria, and made a
long stay in Munich, encompassed by Hermann's despotism, for old Marcus did not die, and had no intention
of dying. Instead of that, he failed in business, and a
stroke deprived him of the use of one leg and one arm,
just after Richard was born.

Dorotéa died at Richard's birth. . . .

A little later, Ferdie Marcus returned to England with
old Hermann, whom it was now his disagreeable duty to
look after; and with Stella, his sister, who would be
guardian of his household, and of Deb and Richard. In
spite of his father and his sister and his two children, he
was very lonely. His round, rosy, good-humoured face
was not of the kind that betrays a secret sorrow, and
most people thought that Ferdie had too quickly forgotten

Dorotea. Richard grew up sturdy and broad-shouldered, a very complete type of gruff British school-boy, despising rhapsody, keen on games, outwardly stolid and unemotional. . . . Nothing much happened to disturb his careless, take-it-for-granted acceptance of his English birthright nor his inarticulate pride in it, until the outbreak of war between England and Germany proved, to his utterly dazed understanding, that he was an enemy alien. He was fifteen then. Until he was eighteen, the military age, he had to wait about, and do nothing—except watch his old school-fellows preparing for the front, presently to face the dangers that were forbidden to Richard himself. It was during those tormented years of waiting for internment that Richard learnt how he loved England, the England for which he might not fire a single shot; learnt to love fiercely, and as an outlaw might love his home, the soil of England, the traditions of England, the very heart and meaning of England. Doggedly he determined that in spite of rejection, he would still dig himself into this obstinate, indifferent country of his choice. . . . When internment was over, and war was over, as it must be some day, he would become a land-owner, having longed in vain to be a soldier. He would earn the right to call a fragment of English earth his own; it should return him passion for passion; out of its sweet, damp huskiness, he would grow wheat. . . . There were more ways than the way of battle to be a patriot, even for one of the children of no-man's-land. He would marry an English girl, and they would have English children, and never go abroad . . . never, never! —for Richard, by dint of suffering, had become a fanatic.

Now, in the March of 1919, when the woods were muddy and drifted with last year's leaves, yet hinted a first smattering of primroses; when the streams ran down clear and cold from the upper hills; and Exmoor humped into quiet greens and fawns and duns that were yet as romantic as its later purple, now the dream was beginning to take shape, at last.

. . . He stopped ploughing for a spell, to light his pipe, and to scrape away some of the caked earth from off his

boots and corduroy breeches.   He was bare-headed; his
dark hair clung in close damp rings to his forehead; his
eyes were light blue and set deeply under frowning
ridges.   There was power in his broad build and out-
thrust underlip, and yet a queer sensation of helplessness,
too. . . . Looking at Richard standing there, where
brown fields sloped up to meet the grey sky's downward
slant, you felt that somehow things would go against
him; that his would be a defiant, not a lissom life.   Others
might slip through, easily and gracefully, into sunshiny
green pleasure-lawns. . . . Not Richard.   Not Ishmael.

The old postman came limping along the road, paused
at sight of Richard, and signalled him, over the low
hedge, to come and fetch his letters.   Without much
enthusiasm, Richard tramped across.   One letter from
Deb—but this would be full of Naomi news—her baby
daughter was still a wonderful new toy.   A letter that
could wait.   Another from Molly Dunne—Richard smiled
over this.   He liked Molly's letters; jolly little schoolgirl!—but she was eighteen now, though her handwriting
still sprawled like a puppy's legs.   Molly hated lessons;
she liked animals and hunting.   No hurry . . . no hurry
for anything. . . . He had kissed her, once upon a time,
in that orchard of plum-trees down in Kent.   He remembered how her lips had been stained with the over-ripe
fruit.   And he had damn well shaken her, too—rude,
ignorant kid!   She had called him a Hun, and a white
feather, and had chucked a plum in his face!   Of course
he had shaken her. . . . But how could she be expected
to understand?   He was half mad at the time, just before
his eighteenth birthday. . . . Oh well, all over now!   His
children and Molly's would be English. . . .

He thrust her letter down into his pocket, and opened
the third of the batch.

" Infernal nuisance ! " he growled.   It was from Aunt
Elsa, who wanted to come down to Exmoor, with her
three good girls and Jeanne-Marie, for an Easter holiday.
She suggested that Richard should find rooms, perhaps on
the same farm where he was working, perhaps in the
village.   But they must be cheap rooms, and clean, and

they would like it better on the farm—" Because then my
girls can help you." Richard grinned—and then swore.
He didn't fancy the idea of being " helped " by Mélanie,
Gisela, Pearl and Jeanne-Marie. Just at the lambing
season, too, when all his time would be taken up. What
did Aunt Elsa imagine her girls could do? Walk behind
him carrying his tools in a golf-bag? " You will feel the
beds, yes? . . ." and she wanted him to get in their dinner
for the first night. A plump fowl from the farm—Aunt
Elsa had no doubt he could get it for them very cheap, if
not as a gift; or did he sometimes shoot birds?—" Oh,
rather ! " said Richard, sardonically, to the landscape.
" Partridge and grouse, always, at Easter. I'd better
make 'em a rook pie, I think." In Heaven's name, what
did they want to plague him for? Aunts were bad enough
when you had to go to London; but when they elected
to come to Exmoor . . . He sighed; then, being without
sentiment, crammed this letter down into the same pocket
that Molly's letter was in, and started the horses again.

II

May the fifteenth—Anastasia's eighty-fourth birthday.
. . . And one of Grandmère's good times. Back again
with Truda and all the grandchildren in the house at
Ealing. Like a river of milk and honey, the days flowed
tranquilly by. . . .
—" And I'll make plenty of Crême-Düten, as usual,
Mamma. We don't know how many of the family may
be coming, this afternoon."
Not very many. Not as many as in the exuberant days
of the Rakonitz unity and glory. There were gaps . . .
there had been a war . . . some had forgotten, or were
careless even when reminded : " It's Aunt Anastasia's
birthday tomorrow." " Oh, Mother, I needn't bother,
need I? Birthdays don't really matter ! "—thus the new
generation, the half-Goy generation. Some of the youngsters hardly knew each other when they met, family
festivals occurred now so rarely. . . . " The Uncles are
here ! Send for the children ! " and an expectant stir

and rustle. . . . Long ago. The Uncles?—well, yes, Louis, perhaps.

Other changes !—queer to see Danny and Neil, Gerald and Little Klaus, all lounging about the rooms, while the girls—the girls could only arrive late because they were in business, because they were the wage-earners—" Toni and Maxine have promised to get off an hour or two earlier . . . Mélanie will come as soon as she can . . . and Pearl . . ." The new era . . . and the boys had not yet settled down to jobs, after the War. . . .

The Matriarch, over by the fire, reading a letter to a sympathetic group, Henrietta and Haidée and Gustava— " Elsa not here yet?" " Not yet; Elsa will be coming with Amélie, who has brought Freda back from San Remo at last, and is fetching her own Jeanne-Marie." . . . And then, weeping a little over the letter : " That dear Aunt Gisela, a hundred and four last January the thirteenth, and she never forgets a birthday; what a wonderful memory !—But she writes to tell me Aunt Hermina has died. . . . Yes, yes, she was the younger, that is what makes it so sad ! " And, indeed, when the Matriarch put it that way, it sounded a premature death, an early-snowdrop sort of death, for Aunt Hermina Bettelheim, aged one hundred and three. " They never even let me know she was ill, that is what hurts me so much—" The tears rolled down Anastasia's cheeks, lingered in the deep furrows, splashed on to the letter ! " I used to be told everything, first . . ."

—" Many happy returns of the day, Auntie." " Many happy returns, Aunt 'Stasia, darling . . . Mother sends these, and hopes you won't mind her not coming . . ."

—Gaps—ghost-gaps in the circle. "Elsa not here *yet*?" " You want Truda? She is in the kitchen, watching the Crême-Düten; they have to be watched so carefully ! " " Yes, Toni will be here directly she can get away.—Such a dear, dear girl—she works too hard ! " " Many, *many* congratulations, dear Anastasia !" " I am so pleased, so *pleased* to see all of you—such beautiful flowers—" But she was quiet, quieter than usual. A little depressed. Better after tea, perhaps, when all the grandchildren

would be collected. Good—here were Louis and Val:
"Now we will have tea!" But even a depleted family
could not all squeeze into the rather cramped dining-
room, at the same time; tea would have to be in two
relays. The younger ones must wait in the drawing-
room, divided from the dining-room by a curtain, now
drawn aside.

—"Hullo! here's Maxine!" . . . Danny, Val,
Maxine, and Gisela, Gerald and Little Klaus, in rather a
bored group over by the window—"D'you remember
Grandmère's birthdays, when we were children?" "Mrs.
Ischel used to give the large cake with the red sugar-rose
on it—it was always kept for Iris." "Look at Iris now!"
Three self-possessed flappers, Iris and Helen Czelovar
and Moya Moss, the latter two with bobbed hair, laughing together on the sofa a little way off. "Not as silent
and respectful as we were, are they?" . . .

Val leant back with half-closed eyes. . . . It seemed as
though she were only watching the swirl of smoke from
her cigarette, but really she was seeing again the baroque
drawing-room in the house in Holland Terrace . . . the
wraith of Uncle Max was there, and the wraith of Uncle
Felix; Bertrand and Ludovic and Blaise, the Matriarch's
three loose-limbed sons, swung in and out in lordly
fashion, bantering Susan and Truda, flirting with Haidée.
. . . And funny little Uncle Otto Solomonson strutted
about, tapping furniture and pompously appraising the
marks on the Sèvres and Dresden, for all the world as
though he were a pawnbroker. . . . And old Albrecht
Rakonitz had added solemnity to the feast, as representa-
tive of a generation even older than the Matriarch's, the
same generation as Great-aunt Hermina, who had just
died. . . . Sometimes relations from abroad had entered
with messages, like ambassadors, and with gifts that had
lain about in costly heaps. The Matriarch's birthday—no
one had dared forget!

"I feel old and sentimental," Val confessed. "Where's
all the gusto and the barbaric splendour? Where are
the drums and cymbals, the dancing-girls and Mrs.
Ischel? Why is everyone so uncannily mild and amiable

and quiet? I wish they would get up and trample on us, like they used to. . . . Once upon a time," she chanted, "Rakonitz women were playthings, and Rakonitz children were nuisances, and the older generation snubbed the younger generation, and ordered their marriages and their style of hairdressing, and all was as it should have been. . . . I don't see much of my family, God knows; but when I do, I love them dearly and desire them to treat me as dirt, in the good old way ! "

" You got cheeked by Moya Moss," Danny reminded her; " what more d'you want? "

" I know what she meant." Little Klaus had sidled into the conversation in his hesitating manner—Toni called it his " D.S.O. manner." " I think I know what she meant. This party—it's like dancing that goes on after the music has stopped. . . . Iris went into the kitchen just now; I think I will go in—I mean, Aunt Truda might want some help, mightn't she? Would she consider it cheeky? I'm so sorry ! " Still apologising, Little Klaus meandered away again.

" So he loves Iris, now," Gerald commented drily. " It was all Toni, when he first came back, and then it was all Maxine. I must say, he does keep it in the family. It's rather a compliment to his cousins, in a way. Only, of course, it's rotten for cousins to marry . . ." he did not see Danny's frown. " Is that Toni? " A ring at the bell was heard, and voices on the door-step. " Someone's with her—who is it? Aunt Elsa?" But though Aunt Elsa's voice had distinctly sounded in the hall, only Toni came in at the dining-room door, warmly embraced her grandmother, bestowed a few festive kisses on the other aunts, and—" Yes, Grandmère, she did come in with me, but she went straight through to see Aunt Truda, in the kitchen."

" But how odd ! Why? Why should she? Didn't she bring Amélie and Nathan with her? Or is Amélie following."

" Aunt Elsa is alone," Toni replied evasively, and slipped through into the further room, and over to the group by the window. " Hello, Val! Hello, Danny !

. . : I say, I believe something is up. I met Aunt Elsa getting off the 'bus at the corner; she was almost crying, and frightfully agitated, with her toque a bit on one side —and not even her best one, even though it is Grand-mère's birthday."

"Toni, don't tell me that you know all the graduations of Aunt Elsa's toques? It's uncanny!"

"I do! I've known them for years. This was the one given her by 'that good girl Gisela'—Sorry, Gisela, I didn't see you. . . . It's a ripping toque. Well, but you know, she snapped and barked at me the whole way up the road. Told me that I was late, and that I had a green face, and what did I want to ask questions for? That's not a bit like Aunt Elsa, lately. *Something's up.*"

"Elsa!" The Matriarch called out through the open door of the dining-room. "But Elsa! Where are you?"

"One moment, Mamma!" came Truda's voice, also agitated, from the kitchen at the end of the passage.

"There is something wrong," declared the Matriarch positively. "Louis, there is something wrong, I can feel it. Why do they talk in there? Why hasn't Amélie come?"

"It's all right, 'Stasia, what can be wrong? You sit down." Aunt Henrietta rose and pushed back her chair; she was going into the kitchen to find out for herself.

"It's Toni! She is dead!" cried Anastasia, forgetting that a moment ago Toni's arms had been round her.

"I'm all right, Grandmère," Toni sang out, from the inner room. "So's Gerald; he's here; so's Danny; so are Maxine and Iris."

Truda and Aunt Henrietta came into the dining-room, and Aunt Elsa, looking very flushed.

"Mamma," said Truda, in a quick low voice. "Come over here, come into the hall, bring Uncle Louis. I told Elsa you had better be consulted. Amélie said not, because it was your birthday—"

"It was *I* said no, not Amélie!" cried Aunt Elsa. "The poor Amélie is far too upset. I hurried away as soon as Mélanie came home to look after her."

They were all away from the dining-room table by now,

except Aunt Gustava, whose claims to be consulted had unfortunately been overlooked; and Haidée, with whom Aunt Gustava was not on speaking terms. Silently these two offered each other Krem-Düten.

Iris ran through the dining-room, and into the drawing-room. Her elder cousins called her over.

"Iris, what's up? You were in the kitchen just now. What are they all whispering about?"

"It's something about Jeanne-Marie," said Iris. "I don't know what, because of course Mummy said ' Remember the child,' directly Aunt Elsa started. And then they spoke German, so I could only hear the names; Aunt Amélie came into it a lot, and Jeanne-Marie and Richard."

"*Richard*? Richard Marcus?"

Iris nodded. She was breathless, and very pleased at being dramatically the first to disclose the name. Little Klaus followed her in.

"He'll know, if he was in the kitchen—he understands German."

Danny hailed him across the room, but just as Klaus turned irresolutely in their direction, he was also called by the Matriarch:

"Klaus, you are to go straight out, yes? And round to the tobacconist's, where there is a telephone, and ring up the boarding-house where the Marcuses are staying. I can't remember its name, but they will know, and ask your Uncle Ferdinand to come round here at once. Say it's important. Say he is not to bring his sister Stella; Stella is not serious."

"*Who* will know?" asked Klaus, a bit dazed, for all that he had been in the Intelligence during part of the War. "The tobacconist?"

Maxine called out: "You'll find the number under ' Montague Hall Hotel,' Klaus. It's ' Kensington, three-five-something'; but they've closed down the 'phone at the tobacconist. You'll have to go to the station. By the time you get through, it will be just as quick to go round to Uncle Ferdie yourself."

"Who told you to interfere?" cried Aunt Elsa. "Now,

Klaus, what are you waiting for?" And she gave him three pennies.

Maxine shrugged her shoulders, looked at Val, who looked at Danny, who looked at Toni and Gerald. . . . Something queer was happening among their elders. The limpness that Val had complained of had stiffened to a quality that was horror—but not entirely horror. . . . It was as though they had been given food, some of their old food, to bite on, which had once made them lusty and arrogant and despotic. There was more body in their voices, more sparkle in their eyes; there were stronger lines in their faces. A new energy possessed them. Yes, it was very sad, what had happened!—oh, terribly sad! Most agitating—a shocking, dreadful thing!—but at least it had revived matriarchy. . . .

They were standing close together now, a little knot of them, talking in rapid low tones, with many gestures. They had remembered to admit Aunt Gustava into the secret cause of tumult; and more reluctantly, after a pause, Haidée Power. Haidée was one of the younger ones, but still, she was of the same generation as Truda, and as Truda knew . . . but let it be recognised that both Truda and Haidée were privileged, and did not come in on any rights, only because they were married; a good thing " the girls " were not here yet : Wanda and Mélanie the unmarried maids, the unmarried Israelite maidens . . . as much out of it in the present hubbub, as " the children " —so the boys who had fought in the War, and the girls who were now the chief wage-earners of the family, were swept back into nursery submission; swept back to where they had been fifteen and twenty years ago.

" It's nothing to do with money," Toni hazarded. " If it were—" she was silent, but the cousins knew what she meant. If it had been anything to do with money, they would not have dared shut out the third generation.

But here was something that was not proper for " the children " to know. . . . A faint tang of lewdness hung in the air. . . . Once or twice Aunt Elsa's voice got beyond control :

" But I *tell* you, Gustava—you are so blitz-dumm!

How can they marry while he is still down there, and it is only to-day she tells us?"

"Sh! . . ."

"He ought to be whipped! A nice girl like that, and one of his own cousins!" Truda spoke indignantly.

"Nice girl? *Nice* girl? Since when do nice girls . . .?"

"Sh! . . ." again.

"I've had enough of this," Toni declared, and walked straight up to her grandmother. "Do you mind telling me what's happened, Grandmère? We all want to know."

"Nothing at all has happened," replied Anastasia, crushingly.

"You mind your own business, isn't it?" cried Aunt Elsa.

Aunt Henrietta said: "The children have not had any tea, yet. They must be hungry. Come, Toni, we have finished. Won't you all come in and have a good tea now? And we can go into the other room."

"There is half a cinnamon cake left, and plenty of Crême-Düten," said Truda; "And the water should be boiling for fresh tea."

Obediently "the children" flocked in; obediently they seated themselves round the tea table. The elder contingent rustled into the drawing-room.

. . . "Danny," said Maxine, in a meek thin little voice, "will you have the red sugar-rose, or shall I?"—And then they all burst out laughing. The situation, as far as they were concerned, was really quite comic—" But I'm worried about Richard, all the same," remarked Val. "I like Richard, although he can't stand me at any price. He thinks I'm not solid. But it would be idle to pretend, at my present state of sophistication, that I can't put a few twos together. . . . Gisela, you were all staying down at Exmoor for Easter, weren't you? Was there anything up between Richard and Jeanne-Marie? She's wild enough."

Gisela turned purple. "I dote thik you ought to ask be, Val. Of *course* I didn't dotice adythig; eved if there had beed . . . and besides . . ." and she looked hard at

Val, trailing her look meaningly on towards Moya Moss and Helen Czelovar, who were under sixteen. . . .

"Children," said Toni, half in burlesque, and half in earnest, because she really wanted to speak freely in this matter of Richard and Jeanne-Marie, "wouldn't you like to go and finish your nice tea in the hall?"

Another ring at the bell saved Toni from a volley of school-girl indignation. It was Little Klaus and Ferdie Marcus, whom he had after all fetched in person, because the line was broken down. Ferdie's good-humoured face was worried and perplexed. He was, sooth to say, a bit afraid of the family, although he had no idea what his present errand portended. The Matriarch came forward, looking rather more stately than usual. "I'm very glad to see you, Ferdinand, and yet, to-day, very sorry."

"I mustn't forget to wish you many happy returns, Anastasia," he faltered.

Gravely she thanked him. He became aware of Aunt Elsa, Aunt Henrietta, Aunt Gustava, and Truda and Haidée behind them; a reproachful force of women. Then Uncle Louis' voice cut incisively into the silence.

"Come out with me, Ferdinand. I must speak a few words with you. 'Stasia, we will meet you round at Elsa's presently, and arrange this matter, once and for all. Tell Amélie; but for God's sake tell her not to cry, I know what her crying is like, when she begins," he finished irritably. "Like yours, Elsa!" And he departed with Ferdie Marcus. Even Uncle Louis had turned suddenly adult, though, perhaps, he was not . . . enjoying himself as much as his contemporaries. They were gathering strength with every moment. . . .

Aunt Elsa and Aunt Henrietta went upstairs with the Matriarch, while she put on her toque and mantle. They were all three going to Aunt Elsa's at once. Aunt Gustava wanted to go, but they would not let her. So furious was she at this slight, that she actually complained to Haidée about it, forgetting that she was not on speaking terms with her. Gustava supposed it was because she was only poor Karl's *second* wife, that she was deliberately not invited to share in their troubles, their important troubles. . . . She wouldn't have minded being left out of the minor and less delectable ones.

"Dunnee!" called out Aunt Elsa, from the top of the stairs, "Dunnee! you are to go at once and call a taxi, yes?"

—Wanda arrived, with Emma Moss, both carrying flowers for the Matriarch's birthday, just as Anastasia and Elsa and Henrietta were stepping into the taxi. Wanda and Emma were a little disconcerted at their reception. . . .

"Not now," cried the Matriarch, waving them away. "I have no time now. Give them to Truda; she will give you tea. I have no time. I must go to poor Amélie . . ."

The taxi drove away.

III

It was decided, after much bustle and many conclaves, that Richard and Jeanne-Marie should get married at once, and that they were to live in San Remo. San Remo need only know that there had been an affection between the cousins, of many years' growth; that on the arrival of the parents from Italy, the parents from England had called on them, and thus the arrangement was happily consummated. That was all that San Remo need know. So Richard must give up his idea of farming; fortunately, as yet, no money had been sunk in it; and Nathan de Yong, his future father-in-law, would take him into his bank in San Remo, and they could all live together in the de Yong's villa, where Camille and Etienne were already resident with their little son. Happily it was a large villa.

So the family decided.

They talked over Ferdie Marcus, making him realise that *the least* Richard could do, after the unspeakable sin he had committed, was to fall in, absolutely and without protest, with any plans that should be made for the righting of the unspeakable sin . . . and so on. Ferdie had to hear it a great many times. And the salt tears

that Amélie wept, during the agitated week following
the scene on the Matriarch's birthday, would have been
enough, had they been collected, to drown the whole of
the Rakonitz family, and most of the Czelovars and
Bettelheims, to boot.   Between-whiles of weeping,
Amélie showed herself the material of which most Latin
mothers are made; with a sense of injury as firmly set as
her own rigidly corsetted bosom; a passion like that of
a consuming tigress, both for and against her erring
daughter; and a shrewd eye over business, and the
furtherance of the de Yong interests, without the slightest
consideration for anybody else's.   An awkward woman
to deal with, Amélie de Yong.   Etienne Czelovar, her
first son-in-law, was used to the type, from experience
of his own mother, Berthe.

But it would go hard with Richard.

Against him in the matter, as well as the de Yongs,
were his grandfather, Hermann Marcus; the Matriarch,
and Aunt Elsa, and Aunt Gustava, and, certainly, Uncle
Louis—Uncle Louis was coldly furious!—Also Francis
Power, bringing in all the British mid-Victorian era to
back him; Truda, who could not get out of her head that
Maxine might have been in Jeanne-Marie's place; and,
queerly enough, Richard's own sister Deb, married to
Samson Phillips.

—" Deb ! " ejaculated Val scornfully.   " Deb-in-the-
manger ! She *would* disapprove of freebooting, naturally;
she tried, and hadn't the pluck . . ."

It was lucky that no one heard Val, except her mother;
Haidée Power only laughed, her usual ironic tinkling
laugh that meant so little mirth.

IV

And Jeanne-Marie herself?

Nobody quite knew. She was a wild creature, Jeanne-
Marie, but seemingly she had constructed her own trap.
It was she, on the moors of Exmoor, who had provoked
Richard to sudden frenzy, and had then taunted his last
control over this frenzy. . . . It was she who had run,

and laughed, and run again, her short thick golden hair blown straight back from the white, haughty little face, and gay almond eyes that could be as hard as green ice. A queer elf, this Jeanne-Marie. Why had she behaved like this? Did she love Richard? Hard toil in the sun and in the wind and rain had made a fine man of him, tanned and stalwart and muscular. He had little grace and no graces; and he did not laugh readily, just sometimes an ironic twist to his lip, a glint of amusement under the grim ridge of his brows. A knotted, craggy sort of man, Richard. Jeanne-Marie may have been sick of the nimble Latin. . . . She had been still a child when the Matriarch had fetched her away to England; but a Riviera child; a child of the palms and the Casinos, with a chic flop of the broad-rimmed hats she wore. And there had been a long visit home, since then, during the last year of the War. Amélie had let her return to Aunt Elsa's to finish her schooling, as she had begun it over there, so Jeanne-Marie had re-appeared among the three good girls, the three little Rakonitz nuns, with the habit of painting her mouth a vivid scarlet. And she not yet eighteen! Imagine the horror of Aunt Elsa! But Jeanne-Marie went on using lip-salve, nevertheless. She carried a stick of it about with her. When she played games, as un-selfconscious as any English tomboy, when she climbed trees and let her long slim legs dangle, or tray-tobogganed down steep and bumpy grass slopes, shouting lustily, her short skirt ripped into tatters!—at these times it was odd to notice the artificial carmine of her clear-cut little mouth.

Jeanne-Marie had vowed to Richard that she would not be treated like a French nor an Italian girl; she would not be absurdly chaperoned, nor drilled into marriage; she was modern; she would not be ruled by the jeune-fille traditions of etiquette; she would make her own arrangements; she would make no arrangements at all; live as she liked; live free; snap her fingers at the out-of-date solemnities of dowry, and parents who "approached" each other. She was like an English girl; she had lived in England.

And next : " Richard, are you afraid? You are not afraid, are you? I'll show them that I'm not. I'll show them that I'm English and free. Richard, they are going to fetch me back in May, Mamma and Papa. If I've done nothing before then, to show them, they will catch me, they won't understand. . . . I'm not a bit like Camille, I'm more like—like—" She stopped. Richard only learnt later, on whom she was modelling her madness.

Spring on Exmoor, and everywhere that sudden movement of the sap. . . .

" Oh, Richard, *slow* Richard, take things lightly ! Run ! Can't you run? . . . Can't you do something to-day that you will forget tomorrow? Oh, Richard, you make me laugh so ! You make me love you so—just for to-day."

And once again : " If I prove to them that I'm me, and not Camille, they will see then that it's no good preaching and bothering me . . . me, me ! . . . I'm not a bit afraid of being me ! Look, Richard ! This is Gisela, when I tell her sometimes how I mean to live—' Oh, I do think it's awful to talk like that ; I bead, suppose subwud should thig you beant it? I wish you wouldn't, Jeanne-Marie. Supposig a *ban* heard you? I'b sure Richard would thig you leart it frob us ! "—The imitation was delicious.

Yes, Jeanne-Marie had been wild as a young faun, that Spring on Exmoor ; and lawless as a gipsy. She would steal and rob and plunder if she liked—she would do as she liked—she would be free ! . . . She ran as Atalanta ran, before the golden apple was dropped at her feet ; and then, quoth Atalanta—or Jeanne-Marie, eyes slanted defiantly sideways—" If I like the apple better than the race, I will have the apple ! " A bad child, a mad child. . . . And not, like the traditional princess of caprice, as true as steel beneath, but disloyal to her own badness and madness ; a backslider ; a feather in the wind. . . .

For suddenly she took fright. Suddenly she rushed to her mother, as a million old-fashioned heroines might have done, sobbing out all the sad story of her remorse, of her half-crazed fear of what might happen . . . clinging to her mother, begging for protection,

begging to be saved from consequences. . . . Suddenly the whole old-fashioned paraphernalia of chivalry
which she, pretty little wanton, had burlesqued so
often, was called into movement again. . . . Richard
had wronged her, Richard would have to marry her, or
her parents would know the reason why—

"It will be all right, Mamma? He will, won't he?
You will make him, won't you? He can't say no, now?"
—It was reaction. Jeanne-Marie was not quite the
modern girl, yet. As through a gap where the dykes
had seemed impenetrable, the family law rushed in, the
family will, the family pressure, surging back again where
it had lately been kept out; Mamma and Papa and the
aunts and uncles, and the "in-laws," and the great-aunts,
and the elderly cousins; councils, whisperings and excitement and horror. . . . No help for Richard!—Jeanne-
Marie had let it all in again on the third generation. She
was a traitor . . . and she and Richard were to be
married from Aunt Elsa's house on June the first; after
that, they and the deYongs would go back to San Remo,
together.

CHAPTER XVI.

I

BECAUSE they were departing for San Remo on the same afternoon as the wedding, Aunt Elsa gave a party the evening before. There was a suffocated note of apology in the celebration, for really it was not quite as it should have been, this wedding. . . . Amélie and Elsa and Anastasia had agreed that the more it had the outward semblance of being like all the other family weddings, the better for Jeanne-Marie. And outwardly it seemed a gay enough party, for the older ones; who were, in fact, exhilarated to the verge of hysteria. Everybody talked shrilly and loudly, and ate and drank a great deal. The family in San Remo drank the health of the family in London, and the family in London returned the compliment and the speeches. And they united to drink the health of the family in Paris and Vienna, and the few stragglers still in Budapest, Constantinople, and somewhere in Spain. . . . They drank to Aunt Elsa, as their hostess; and to the health of Camille and Etienne and their little son; and even, as a hurried after-thought, to Hermann Marcus, Richard's grandfather, who could not be present because of his paralysis. And they drank Richard's health, of course, and Jeanne-Marie's. . . . Jeanne-Marie kept very close to her mother all the evening; her eyes were demurely downcast, as was seemly in a jeune fille and a young bride-to-be—except when she glinted defiantly, an oblique sparkle of green ice, at the bridegroom.

Val was in a quarrelsome mood. She quarrelled with Deb Phillips most of the evening; she snapped at Gisela; and practically turned her back on her usual friend and

229

ally, Uncle Louis. She got up to go early, with the
nearly audible remark that all the fuss made her
sick. . . .

"Come back to my studio, any of you, for half an
hour, before you go home? I'll make some coffee."

"I don't mind if I do," Danny responded, shaking off
Aunt Gustava's attentions, as a spaniel shakes off water;
"You make jolly good coffee, Val."

When they got outside, after all the goodbyes, and the
hectic allusions to next day's festivities, they found that
Richard was with them. He walked with them almost in
silence as far as the studio, with a gruff: " May I come in,
too, Val?" while she was looking for her key.

"Shall we be sentimental, and give Richard bacon and
eggs for supper?" Val suggested, a few minutes later,
when her two cousins had dumped themselves comfortably on to divans and cushions. "He's not likely to get
them for some years, you know."

Danny said: "Yes, I'd quite like some bacon and eggs.
There was too much to eat at Aunt Elsa's, I simply
couldn't get started. Two eggs, if you please, Val; and
—let me see, four slices of bacon will be enough, I think.
Got any kidneys?"

"And a kipper or two?" Val asked, busy over the
stove behind a screen. "Modest little Danny, how did
you manage at caffé-latte, abroad? Have you ever been
on the Continent, Richard? I forget. Or is this your
first time?"

"Oh, I was born there," Richard replied, with a wry
smile. "I'm a foreigner, you know."

"Then you won't be dismayed when Etienne comes up
to you, embraces you on both cheeks, and says to you:
'Me, my sensibilities are of the first rank.'"

Danny chuckled reminiscently. "When I was first
introduced to Etienne, he spoke as follows: 'Let me
pray you, my dear cousin, while welcoming you to San
Remo, that you will not judge me by what I am this
afternoon; for without my dear mother, who is more than
half of me, and a much better half, as you say in England,
where I had so happy a time on my last visit, thanks to

the family, to whom I beg you to make my compliments when you write, I am indeed less than half a man.' "

" What did you answer to that? "

" I? Oh, I said 'How-d'you-do!' I was stunned."

" He'll be flowering to Richard, all day long, as they'll be living in the same house; you might send us a few of Etienne's choicest blossoms sometimes, Richard. I rather envy you, living with him."

" Do you? "

" I rather envy him altogether," remarked Danny. " I'd give anything to get away again, only I suppose I'm stuck down for life now, in this foul town of yours, or until I think of replanting Uncle Ludo somewhere nice and spicy," he added, in audacious challenge to an absent Toni.

" What d'you mean, Danny? "

Quite shamelessly, he told them. Toni had had a lot of trouble, for several years, in guarding the secret of the New Zealand venture.

Val and Richard looked at each other ! " Is he a cad? " the former queried, " or just our dear little Cousin Danny? "

" If you're going to take it like Toni, I'm off," Danny said, thoroughly injured at the reiteration of the word " cad " as applied to his blameless conduct.

" Hm . . . Toni knows, does she? "

" Rather ! How funny of her never to tell you."

" Perhaps you asked her not to."

Danny grinned. " Fancy letting *that* stop her ! "

" Danny, you're hopeless."

" I say straight out what other people think, that's all; and I do straight out what other people want to do, and so I'm always being slanged ! Still, if I want to use the Uncle Ludo camouflage again, soon, it may be just as well that she hasn't spread it about the family. The Bahamas would be a good place, next time, I think. . . . Who was it telling me that they had seen a tall man with the Rakonitz lip, hanging about the quays of Nassau and looking as though he longed to be fetched home? Lord ! " impatiently drumming his feet against the divan, "here we are at the end of May and it's not once been hot yet. Give me the sun!"

Val gave him eggs and bacon instead. "Don't be so Ibsenish, Danny. 'Give me the sun, Mother, give me the sun!' was what that man in 'Ghosts' said, when he got softening of the brain."

"I shall get stiffening of the brain if I go on being cold much longer. Do you remember, Val, how the sun used to blaze down, day after day, on the Corniche Road, fierce, baking showers of it, that stung your back?"

Richard thought moodily: "I hate the sun, I loathe its monotonous grin and monotonous glare, always the same. I'll never get away from it now." . . . And he thought of cool green lanes, and cool brown earth hissing softly as it drank up the rain; and the peace and the rightness of it all, down in the country in England, where the houses were not eternally white, and the sky not eternally blue, and the road not dusty.

Val and Danny were chattering again, a sort of rhapsody of Italy and the Riviera. Richard just caught fragments, against which he built up in contrast his England, his English world. "Do you remember?" they were saying, over and over again; and "Do you remember?" eagerly cutting off the other's words, to push in their own. They had loved the Continent, these two. . . .

"Funny little mountain villages, on peaks in the Maritime Alps . . . white and pink and purple and lemon houses, all of them swarming up and up, in a pyramid towards their own campanile . . . ripping shape, they were! . . . and a couple of cypresses sticking into the sky . . . black cones against sharp bright blue . . . and the terraces of olives . . . miles and miles of terraces . . . hundreds of terraces, and hundreds of years old . . . glorious honey-coloured, no-coloured walls . . . they weren't mortared, you know, and yet they held; the stones were simply poised, all sizes and all shapes and all colours . . . chinks and crevices—the dry quick lizards darting in and out—the men of the country had the knack of building walls like that . . ."

. . . Richard thought of mellow autumn-tinted walls which were of brick, not of stone; dull reds and browns of low-lying farms and their barns and granaries; and walls that shut in the parks of those great country-houses where the lawns were like rich green moss, so that you longed to run on them barefoot, knowing that they would never hurt your soles as the dusty roads did, or those steep, stony mule-tracks that Danny had just mentioned. . . .

"And if you're going up, and a donkey is coming down, there's just room to stand aside and politely let him pass, because, of course, it's his track, and not yours; he passes you with his baskets of logs swaying on each side of him. Sometimes it isn't olive-wood, but those great wicker flasks—demi-johns—'dummi-junni,' they call them there! filled with the wine of the country. He's nearly always driven by an old woman who has obligingly twisted a blue or an orange handkerchief round her head, because she knows we like local colour. She's bent quite double, so that her nose touches the ground as she walks—"

"Shut up, Danny, you're exaggerating! Well do I know that old hag. . . . She wishes you: ''cé sera.' And you compliment her on her donkey, and she deprecates her donkey but compliments you on your looks, your youth, and your Italian accent. 'My poor beast makes but an ugly figure beside yours,' she will say, with that delightful Italian courtesy which, like the full-flavoured Italian dishonesty, you can never hope to meet anywhere else!"

. . . Richard thought of the Somerset rustics who had tramped past him on the wet field-paths, with their gruff comfortable voices: "Evenin', Zur! Good weather fur crops, zur." He got on well with these men, always. They seemed to recognise that he was of their own human clay, and no alien. . . . "Enemy alien—enemy alien." God! how the phrase had stung him during the War! And now he was going to live among them—aliens —and to him, enemies; now, when he was just beginning to cover the desolation and the sore; beginning to dig himself in—

"I fell awfully in love with a donkey, once," Val confessed. "He had the sweetest face, soft tender pinks and greys, and eyes like the inside velvety part of a bean-flower. I was so smitten that I fell straight back into a cactus, yea, I buried my face in a prickly-pear, and I wept because I wasn't an alluring lady-donkey. Don't say 'You are!' Danny, or I'll slay you."

"I was drinking again, from your lips, the sound of 'luxurious tropical vegetation': cactus and prickly-pear; the olive, the vine, the laurel, the wild fig, and the cypress; it makes the classics come alive, rather! . . . I can see the happy young Ligurians in goat-skins leaping and rolling about on the violets, and singing in the sun."

"As a matter of fact, I was rather astonished I didn't hear much singing in Italy, except at the stations: 'Pane-vino-*frrrutt* . . . à!'" Val carolled in imitation. "And then their voices aren't picturesquely liquid, as they're always supposed to be, but high and harsh and mono-tonous, with pain grating under the jingle."

"You forget the song of the violet-man along the front, when the Riviera spring begins: 'O ché belle viole! Sono speziale, le mie viole'—Oh, and I'll tell you when I heard them singing—the soldiers, about four o'clock in the morning under my windows, swinging along between the palms and the sea, and then up into the mountains for manœuvres; they sang ripping choruses, all about 'passione.' They really made passion sound quite a cheery rollicking business; it's so lugubrious over here in England."

Richard thought: . . . Over here in England, where the trees were not grey and spiky, with sinister fleshy leaves, nor else black spears against a blue sky; but trees as God made them, and damn the pagan gods!—Trees that were called oak and elm and beech; and they did not live odd unnatural winter lives, but of God's grace, when they were weary of their summer, turned yellow and red and brown, and withered, and died, and were born again. . . . He knew he would think of the light flame-green of beeches in April, when he was down there, outlawed among the olive, the cypress, and the prickly-pear. Songs, too . . . Danny was singing again—" D'you remember their eternal tune, ' Nostalgia,' Val? "—

. . . but blending with it, beating it under and drowning it, Richard heard another song, as he knew he would hear it echoing, down there, where he did not want to go—

" Drink, puppy, drink, and let every puppy drink
  That's old enough to lap and to swallow;
  For he'll grow into a hound . . ."

—a hunting song, after a windy run with the Devon and Somerset; after cold boiled beef, pickles and ale. He remembered how the hounds had looked, suddenly streaming up Dunkery, tiny patches of white and brown on the grass—

" For he'll grow into a hound . . ."

. . . Poor devil, poor little pup! So much happier, lolloping about in the stables, on crooked legs that were first too short and then too long, its body too big for its head, and its fat little belly too much for its legs. . . . He remembered a litter of them on the farm at Six Acres—not hounds, of course; wire-haired terriers. He had been going to have one. . . . But then Jeanne-Marie appeared . . .

" Drink, puppy, drink . . ."

the refrain hummed itself disconsolately away. . . .

" Do they have any sport out there? " he asked abruptly, trying to kill, with his own voice, visions running parallel with all that Val and Danny were saying about the Riviera.

236

" If you call it sport ! They'll love you, if you do. The
darlings go out with terrific pomp and pageantry and
fancy dress, keepers and guns galore, and ' sport-dogs '
leaping all over them, and their wives bidding them
emotional good-byes at the villa gates—and they come
back with two finches and a tomtit that they limed on a
tree before they shot 'em. They've got a terrific sense
of the theatre, though, in Italy. They adore ceremonial,
and what they call ' beautiful occasions.' They make
processions out of everything; if you go for a walk, they
wish you ' Buon' passeggiata.' "—

Danny chimed in : " And if you go for a bath, a very
rare felicity unless you're in a hotel, they wish you ' Buon'
bagno,' and if you sit down to tie spaghetti round your
neck, they wish you ' Buon' appetito,' and if you go to
open a window in a public restaurant— "

—" They wish you Hell and Hades," Val laughed.
" There's a Great War that's always going on in Europe,
and for which there is no armistice, and that's the War
of the Windows. I look forward to it, when I go abroad.
The English party opens them, and the French or Italian
or German party bangs them down again. . . . Of
course, *they* breathe concentrated essence of garlic
instead of air."

Richard grunted. He liked to be able to move about,
without having good wishes festooned round his arms
and legs. He detested theatricality, he abhorred cere-
mony, and pageantry made him miserable. . . . Would
Val and Danny never stop gossiping and comparing?
Now they were talking about the way the local priest
comes to bless the house you live in; every year, in full
robes, he sprinkles the walls and carpets with holy water;
his acolyte following with a basket in which you can
unostentatiously drop your eggs and cheeses of thankfulness. But Richard liked his religion decently in a church
on Sunday morning, not carted about the streets. . . .
And now they were describing the comic carabinieri, who
went about in twos as though they were stuck on a tin
stand, and who met every train, nobody knows why, and
hurried home to their lodgings, between every train, to

wash their white cotton gloves; and were seen emerging again, pulling them on, still damp. . . . "It's terribly important to wear white cotton gloves when you are meeting a train," quoth Val.

Richard thought of that great son of Ajax, in his stolid reliable dark blue, the English policeman, whom nothing could fluster. . . . You knew just where you were with him. But no arm of the law down there; only arms of the law, flapping in agitation—down there, where he did not want to go. . . .

"The four winds," said Danny, "do you remember their names? Gorgeous sonorous names: Scirroco, il Greco, Maestrale and la Tramontana!"

. . . Beastly, pompous, boring names that meant nothing!—Talk about an honest "sou' westerly," and you knew it would bring showers that drew up the crops; or the north wind, and you put more coal on the fire, and sent it in a stiff roar up the open chimney. . . . Damnation! that would be another thing that he would miss—a fire that you could control with a stout poker. . . . Was he mad, letting himself be taken captive into a country that was not his own? . . .

II

"Richard is looking bored!"—Val's voice struck across his bitter musings. "What's up, Richard?"

He lingered on, until she had got rid of Danny. Val seemed to understand, after her one look at Richard, that he had to be alone with someone that evening, the evening before his wedding. He had to tell someone. . . . He told Val. It all burst out of him, pent-up dread of what he was going to, his pent-up love-song for what he was leaving behind; it burst from him, with the rare and dreadful eloquence of a man who is usually inarticulate.

"So you don't love Jeanne-Marie?" she mused, when he had finished. "Then—Richard, how could it have happened? You might tell me that, too."

He got up, paced the length of the studio two or three times.

"She—she's very pretty, Val, and you know I hadn't had much . . . I was interned for two years, you know." She heard the shudder still in the word, when he used it. "And afterwards I went straight down to the farm. I'd been there ever since; doing nothing but outdoor work makes a fellow fit. I was fit, and I'd been alone a lot, and—she was awfully pretty, Val."

"Go on," said Val, softly. "You wouldn't have given in for just those things, Richard."

"No, I wouldn't. Of course not. I know what's . . . decent, I suppose. But Val, she said that girls nowadays were different, that they didn't expect . . . I mean . . . She wouldn't *let* me behave decently about it. I wouldn't have touched her at all . . . because I didn't want to marry her; she's not my sort, and not the other sort either. But she wanted to show her parents . . . she said love ought to be taken lightly, not all formal and full of for-evers, and . . . Oh, she seemed to think I was infernally slow, and a prig. Once we were in the orchard. There was a new moon, and I had hauled her out so as not to see it through glass. The orchard grass was very long, and drenching wet, so I carried her; she looked at me as though she loved me—oh, hell! as though she were mad about me . . . looked and looked. . . . I felt as if I were swimming—And then, quite suddenly, she snapped off, and laughed and said, with her funny clear bit of an accent mixed into the slang : 'I can do that until the cows come home with any man, whenever I like!' and she begged me, if anything happened between us, not immediately to turn familyish and make her offers of marriage. . . . She called it 'all that oppressive rot!' You can't be chivalrous to a girl who laughs at it, and thinks it funny. She made me promise . . ." he stopped.

"That's all very well," said Val. "Promise what?"

"She was like a wild creature, sometimes," Richard swerved off again from being explicit. "She used to get frightened of me, and seemed to delight in being frightened, and make herself more and more frightened on purpose, so that she should be hurling against it all the time—I can't quite explain, Val; it was her way of giving herself thrills, she said. Only I couldn't stand too much . . ." And he finished again with a lame: " She was awfully pretty, you know."

" Well, and to put it crudely, she made you promise that love between you should be light, and a quick thing, and quickly over; and that you would not let her down by asking her to marry you afterwards. Is that it?"

" Yes," he muttered reluctantly. " That's it."

" *She* let you down, the little beast!" stormed Val. " Turned round on you and demanded just what she'd made you promise not to give, demanded it as a right, played on the old weaker-sex string. . . . Something upset her pose, I imagine! . . . Is she going to have a baby?"

The man went a dull red. " She thought she was. She isn't. It was enough, though, to make her tell her mother."

" And the family did the rest. You've been trapped, Richard. I'm sorry to sound so melodramatic. But if she was out for free love, and even if the corollary had been true, and not a false alarm, it was up to her to stand the racket. Modern girl, indeed! I *knew* there was something wrong. . . . I knew it all the evening at Aunt Elsa's while they were fussing about wedding-cakes and wedding-dresses. —Richard, you fool, why didn't you tell someone before?"

" There was no one to tell. I couldn't go about telling those sort of things. She's only a kid; she's only eighteen. And it isn't all off her own bat, either . . ."

Val spoke a shade more tolerantly: " Then all this idiocy of free love and light love and love for an hour— pagans up-to-date—isn't her own inspiration. She's been reading too much, silly little goose." She dismissed Jeanne-Marie with a contemptuous shrug.

" She adores you," Richard blurted out. "She would do anything for you, Val. She would do anything—by you."

" What do you mean, ' by ' me?"

Her cousin fronted her steadily. " I mean, because you had done it first."

It was Val's turn to flush scarlet. " Because I had done it first," she repeated, under her breath. Then, frankly, but in her usual lazy half-humorous manner : " Yes, but look here, Richard, my life is my own affair; you can't say, any of you, that I go about unloading it on to other people, and damaging them and their illusions. Even if Jeanne-Marie had a rave on me, I'm not responsible for what she has done to you."

" Oh, well, what does it matter? All the same in a hundred years ! "—Richard's attempt to sound jovial was like the drag of a cart uphill over the stones. " What *does* it matter? I daresay I shall forget what I wanted, and settle down."

" Oh, come along," cried Val impatiently. " Let's chuck reticence; let's be reckless and romantic while we're about it. I've given you a glimpse of ' my secret life,' Richard, let's hear all about yours, and then decently, we'll bury it for ever and ever. . . . ' Who'll sew its shroud? I, said the beetle, with my thread and needle ' —or should it be ' neetle?' Go on, Richard . . . what *do* you want? Go on; I'm feeling rather flesh-and-bloodish to-night."

" I wanted a son," said Richard, in his most matter-of-fact tones. " Not a beastly little foreign brat who has its hair cut wrong and sits up till ten o'clock every night and drinks wine at table and knows everything it oughtn't to know, even how to pay compliments. . . . I want a real son, Val. Freckled and snub-nosed as you like, but—oh, English ! not full of rotten ideas; a kid that's got some pluck, and won't show when he grazes his knees; and a kid that speaks my language without a foreign accent. Lord ! " he groaned, " fancy having a son that speaks English with an accent. I don't think I could bear it."

" You'll have to bear it," said Val, steadily, " if you mean to stand by Jeanne-Marie." She said " if " . . . and there was a glint of mischief in her eyes, of more than mischief. . . . She was not letting it all come through, yet. But, after all, it was not too late to save this cousin of hers who had so wanted to fight for

England in the War, and who had not been able to fight, and who wanted to be English and to live in England and to have English children.

Richard was telling on, more vividly than he knew, of the children he had meant to have, and the wife he had meant to have. . . . Molly Dunne . . . good old Molly. . . .

"She rides like a perfect young demon, Val; you ought to see her. We have had no end of good times together. And she's not always leaping off the deep-end, expecting you to do hysterical runs and jumps and climbs for idiotic reasons : to impress her, for instance, and because they are dangerous." . . . He was harking back, scornfully, to that green elf-circle into which the tall Riviera girl had lured him. "If Molly and I do that sort of thing, it's simply because we happen to come across 'em. Oh, Molly's all right. She's been adopted by the most topping aunt; my pal, Greville Dunne's mother. Molly's father was a sea captain; got drowned. They're all seafaring men, the Dunnes, the whole lot of them. Of course, Mrs. Dunne would never want to live with us, or interfere or anything, or poke her nose where she's not wanted. . . . I say, Aunt Amélie's pretty awful, isn't she?" Under the schoolboy phrasing, was horror; horror that intensified Val's fierce longing for battle on his behalf.

"My son," said Richard, as though he were saying good-bye to someone very real and sturdy and full of health . . . "My son would have been—instead of me, you see, Val. It's no good kidding myself that I'm English, even to the extent of being Jewish and English. I'm not. It was a damned shame, but I was born in Bavaria, and so I have had to put up with it, being interned and all that, and not being able to give anything. I would rather have gloried in an arm or a leg off, I believe, or both, or my eyes," grimly. "That sounds like swank, but it's not swank. It would have proved how much I meant it. But my son and Molly's, born in England and perhaps inheriting a bit of land that I had worked for him in England, *that* would have been nearer

242

to it. And *his* son would have been right in. By that
time, if there's another war, it wouldn't have mattered
that his grandfather had been an alien. He could fight
on the English side. That's what I meant by : ' instead
of me.' Val, one gets fed up with men who go round
spouting patriotism, scribbling it all over the wall . . .
but you asked me to talk, and I've told you."

Val wished herself sufficient power to say what she was
going to say strongly enough to break up the harm that
was binding him. . . .

" You can't marry Jeanne-Marie."

" Got to," said Richard.

She let herself go : " Sentimental heroics ! I've no use
for them, Richard. The same sort of silly sacrifice that
you find in books and plays, where one man bears the
crime of another man and never, never tells—as though
that were any good to the other person ! It just messes up
everything and makes everyone miserable, for nothing.
—Oh, tramp up and down, if you like, and call yourself
a swine and a cad, and rant the usual old weak clap-
trap about a girl's good name, and making an honest
woman of her—she's making a dishonest man of you !
It's dishonest to give up the task you've set yourself, instead of sticking to it like death. Bearing the burden for
other people?—You've got to bear the burden of your
own sins and mistakes, and surely that's enough to go
on with? If Jeanne-Marie hasn't that much courage,
well, she's no good. Why should you chuck up Molly's
happiness, your son, your land, the things you want, the
things that have your soul's choice in them? Your son
and your son's son and all your life? They'll be some
good to England, feeling about them the way you do;
but you'd be done for, as Jeanne-Marie's husband; a
rotten, sham, conventional, bloodless marriage, just to
please the family. She wanted to be a modern girl?
Then damnation, let her have it, let her *be* a modern
girl ! Why should I put up with these cheap and gaudy
imitations of me—and a semi-imitation at that?—D'you
think that *I* would hurl myself into my mother's arms,
and yelp for a man to come along and be chivalrous?

But Jeanne-Marie's a foreigner and a Rakonitz, and she
has reverted to type. She *enjoys* the old drama of scurry
and scenes and fuss and shocked aunts. She enjoys this
forced marriage and the feeling of protection surging up
round her, building barricades of cottonwool for her—
maidenhood."

"Stop that, Val!" savagely.

"Oh God!" said Val, collapsing into the deep armchair. . . . Soon she began to laugh. "I can't help it,
Richard; I'm sorry. The spectacle of the strong, silent
man always makes me shout, especially when he's walking
up and down my studio; the wicked squire and the
maiden in distress—Boo-hoo! . . . let's ring the church
bell—synagogue bells. . . . And then you have the con-
founded cheek to tell me that she's copying me!"

"I never liked you, Val," said Richard, and he gripped
her by the shoulders, smiling down at her rather
pleasantly.

"Dear, dear Richard, I am quite sure of that. . . . As
Etienne would say, my sensibilities are of the first rank!
—Oh, tell the family to go to hell, boy; you can't live
abroad; don't be silly. Honestly, I don't see any need for
you to be interned twice."

"There's one thing you have left out," he argued,
desperately, against himself. "A man feels a worse
wicked-squire when he gets one of his own people into
trouble."

"And doesn't a girl feel worse, when she gets one of
her own people into trouble? That small son of yours—
Tim or Bill, or whatever you're going to call him, is for
England. You can make up your mind to that. If you
give in to the family, it will take us years, us younger
ones, to break them down again. They're in close for-
mation, now. We shall have to fight despotism all over
again, Toni and Danny and Gerald and Maxine and the
rest of us. It's only their usual arrogance to assume that
Jeanne-Marie should be specially privileged because she's
one of the family. She can't eat her maidenhood, and
have it. Oh, curse the little blackleg! She's lost ground
that it's taken us years to win . . . all this prominence

and celebration and wedding . . . human sacrifice at the
altar, and blood all down the steps . . . you dare to
throw them in, your son and your dream—sacrifice to the
insatiable family. The same old sour sick story of ready-
made conduct, and no one has the imagination to think
of the consequences. Which of them, Aunt Elsa and
Aunt Amélie and Aunt Anastasia, which of them has
really had the slightest vision of what your life with
Jeanne-Marie will be like? Or what your children will
be? They planned their own lives without bothering
about consequences—look at Aunt Anastasia and her
marriage!—and now Toni's got the brunt of it. It's *not*
all the same a hundred years hence. . . . I shouldn't
like to be that shadowy grandchild of yours, Richard,
if you marry Jeanne-Marie tomorrow. No, we may not
be so moral as they are, but we're fifty times decenter.
Oh, smash 'em, Richard, smash 'em! For all our sakes.
At the eleventh hour, now, to-night, go and tell them
you're not going to marry her, and stick to it, and then
go back to Exmoor and drive your plough again."

She stopped, breathless. Richard still said nothing.
But her intuition knew this cousin of hers. He would not
slowly yield. He would remain stubborn until quite
suddenly he broke to her view. And now Val knew, too,
how you felt when you were saving someone from death;
working their arms when they have been near drowning,
or battling through a crisis of an illness. She knew the
defiance that you put into it, the challenge, the last ounce
of strength; how you used every scrap of eloquence
which you possessed, and even some that you were not
aware that you possessed; how you would do everybody
else in and everybody else down; snap every promise;
say all the things that are better not said; fling decorum
away, and, last of all, your superfluous better self; and
wrestle, naked and unscrupulous. . . . Reward enough to
win. Richard!—If she had been Richard's mother, that
night, she could not have felt for him more tenderness,
more fierce protection. She *was* his mother, that night. . .

"Shut your eyes, Richard. I want you to see England,
as you'll see her when you have lived in San Remo for

a few years. After you have lived a few years with all
your in-laws, boxed up in the same white villa, with the
windows shut, and the chauffage going strong except in
the very heat and stuffiness of summer, and all of them
talking, jabbering, quarrelling, so that you can't get away
from it all; voluble over their petty domestic affairs and
yours, eternally. And they'll get older and older, and
they won't die; and the older they get, the more they'll
have to be consulted and respected, because for some
obscure reason, age has to be consulted or it gets offended.
. . . And there will be hard white hotels with green
shutters, and a hard blue sky and sea, and spiky palms,
and people who dress up and promenade slowly up and
down, all talking at the tops of their voices—that's what
they call animation and vivacity. It's in the blood,
abroad; you'll get tons of it, Richard. Everybody says
everything five times; they say : ' Si, si, si, si, si,' instead
of ' Yes '; and they kiss you on two cheeks, instead of
one. It's over-emphasized, life abroad; you don't get
down to the bare bones of it, much; but it's animated,
of course. Plenty of gaiety and confetti and fancy dress
and music and temperament, and men who are openly
glad to see you, and who can't talk with their hands in
their pockets, and still think ' Oskar Villder ' our greatest
writer, and sound as though they were having a row
when they are only discussing last night's dinner. And
there will be ' La Patrie,' and ' Fascisti '; and the gavott-
ings of endless compliment, and— now, Richard, *now* . . .
you are there, in the thick of it, permanently, so that you
can't get away, there in the heat and dust and the glare
and the noise ; see it and smell it, I tell you . . . and *now*,
if you can bear it, think of England . . ."

"I'm not going to stand it," said Richard, suddenly,
in queer thick tones, as of a man who has been drinking
heavily. He did not say good-bye to Val, but went
straight out of the studio.

She had no doubts about what he was going to do.

CHAPTER XVII

I

" ICHABOD ! " said Danny. . . . " The glory is departed !
Do you think she will ever—"

No, never again. . . . Toni shook her head. She
was looking very white and weary.

" The shock was too much for her. If it hadn't struck
at her like that, just an hour or two before the wedding.
. . . She had been so excited and pleased that it was
all going to be all right—I do think Aunt Elsa might have
sent round the same evening. If only I hadn't already
gone home, before Richard came back—" Her voice
was full of indignant regret. She could have managed
it, somehow, so that Grandmère should not have woken
up so piteously gleeful and triumphant on the morning
of the wedding of Richard and Jeanne-Marie. " She
was already half dressed in her new brocaded plum and
black, and some of her hair done," Toni added mourn-
fully. " Imagine ! Grandmère ! I actually believe she
would have been in time."

Danny laughed. He was taking the Matriarch's tragedy
more lightly than any of the other grand-children. " So
you think Richard ought to have stuck to it, so that
Grandmère might, for once in her life, have been
punctual? What an autocrat you are, young Toni !
But your own notions of time are a bit hazy, you know.
It was just midnight when I left Richard in Val's studio ;
so it must have been about two o'clock in the morning
when he turned up at Aunt Elsa's. Lord ! I wish I'd
been there ! " His eyes sparkled, imagining the scene.. . .

" I wish I had, too," breathed Toni. They were resting
in a couple of deck-chairs under the rather sooty lilac
bushes in the little back garden of Susan's house. On

either side of them, were rows of other little sooty
gardens, lovingly tended for the sake of what they might
bring of the country to this suburb of London. But it
was evening now, beginning to grow dark, and the darkness bloomed and blurred the dividing walls, enchanting
away the ugly marks and symbols of property, so that
Danny and Toni might have been lying out in a wide-
spread single garden.

Toni was glad of the freshness and the quiet; she
had been all day at business; and from six o'clock
onwards, down at Ealing, helping Aunt Truda to nurse
the Matriarch, ordaining what was to be done, how much
could be paid for, for whom they were to send, and who
was to be kept out.   Grandmère gently smiled, and
whispered " thank you," and gave no trouble.

This nightmare of Grandmère giving no trouble had
been going on for over a week, ever since Anastasia had
been laid low with a stroke.

Danny remarked : " You know, Toni, I think it might
buck you up, in a way, if you just remembered that she
was working up, anyhow, for another of her bad times,
and that you've been spared that. I'm quite sure she was.
Whenever she gets over-excited. . . ."

Toni's smile was half sad, half mocking. . . . " Yes,
whenever she gets over-excited ! " Then she flamed out :
" Don't you think I would a thousand times rather have
her in the worst of her ' bad times ' than—like this ? "

" She was much funnier, certainly, the other way,"
agreed Danny. Toni could never make out if Danny
were wilfully and deliberately dense over anything con-
cerning the Matriarch; or if he really, in some queer
way, lacked that subtle understanding, with which, even
against his sympathies, kinship should have gifted him.
" Ever so much funnier. Do you remember, Toni, last
time, when she picked up that stray mongrel, in the
middle of the night, when she was looking for a boarding-
house, and lugged it into a strange hotel and asked for
the proprietress, and insisted on having a room, and
enquired if there was a doctor staying in the house, and
if so, she must see him at once. It didn't matter a bit

that he had malaria, and that he was asleep, and that it was one o'clock in the morning. She dragged the mongrel into the poor fellow's room, and woke him up, and informed him that he must perform a surgical operation at once on the dog's tail, and dock it, and then it would be a beautiful dog, but that its tail was really much too long . . ." Danny threw back his head and roared with laughter at the recollection. " Still, you know, in the long run, she was much more expensive and more of a general nuisance when she went mad than now, when she's quite quiet and good, and not ordering people about. And she was about due for a fine old ramp, wasn't she? She had had nearly a year's good time."

" Maxine and I hoped it would go on."

" Oh, you and Maxine bother too much about everything; 'specially you, Toni. She deserved it."

" Oh . . ."

" She did. Why should it have mattered so much to her whether Richard married Jeanne-Marie, or whether he didn't? They're not even her children nor her grandchildren."

" They are in the family."

" Oh, the *family*!" He groaned. Then reflected, more cheerfully : " At anyrate, there's not much more of it left, now." But he kept this to himself. There were some moments when even he was afraid of being scorched by Toni's flaming Rakonitz devotion.

" I think," she was still vainly regretting the catastrophe, " that if she had only been *there* when Richard broke off the wedding, she might have escaped this stroke. She could have *done* something, then, raved and cursed. . . . But just simply to hear that what she had arranged, and what she felt to be right and inevitable to keep the family in grace, just to hear that it was all over, and that Richard had gone back to Exmoor, and Jeanne-Marie to San Remo, and Aunt Amélie and Uncle Nathan too; and no one had said good-bye, and Aunt Elsa was in bed; it was feeling that matriarchy had been defied successfully, and all tradition and decorum violated; and that it was all over and that she had not even been there, and there was nothing more to be done about it, nothing more she could do or say . . ."

—Dimly but surely, Toni realised that this was what had brought on the final defeat of the flesh. And she, who had suffered from matriarchy, had the greatness to mourn it as impersonally as she might have mourned the fall of a dynasty. "Richard's responsible, and Val, too; Val was behind him; she told me so."

"I bet she was; good old Val! good old Richard! good luck to 'em both! Long live freedom! I say, what'll become of her, do you think?"

"Who? Val? —Oh, Jeanne-Marie. Oh, that's easy to prophecy; she'll be very demure and sedate for about a month, and then she'll begin to feel better, and Aunt Amélie will buy her a lot of lovely clothes, and some eligible vicomte will pass that way, or a marchese—"

"And Richard will plough up fields, steadily, for ten years, and then he'll marry, and plough up more fields, until his sons are old enough to help him plough up fields. . . . Queer chap, Richard! He wants to go deep, but not wide. Never seems keen on roaming. . . . He must have had fun, though, that night, swinging in with his: 'I won't!' and 'I'm damn well not going to!' and 'Go to Hell!'"

"Great fun . . . but I'm never going to forgive him."

"Good Lord!—was there ever such an infernal little idiot!—Why not?"

"It's not such great fun for me, is it, to have Grandmére helpless on my hands for the next twenty years or so?"

He was momentarily sobered, acknowledging her right. "Do you think she'll live as long as that?"

"All the Bettelheim women live till they are over a hundred; and her mother was a Bettelheim. Besides, do you imagine that I *want* her to die?"

"Yes," replied Danny. "Of course you do. Don't be dishonest, Toni."

"Don't be callous! If you loved her—"

" I don't. I never pretended that I did. I can't help
it if she is my grandmother; and it's no good looking
at me as though I were a sort of reptile, Toni, that you
couldn't pick up without screaming. . . . I don't love
people like you do. And the more I'm reminded that
they belong to me, the less I seem to feel about them."

" That's because you only feel about yourself."

"—and you," he said, in his most matter-of-fact tone.
" But you are wrong, Toni, when you accuse me of
selfishness because I don't love people. I'm unselfish. I
give them much less bother by going through life and not
loving them. Love's a burden; it raises all sort of obli-
gations and fuss and torment. I should think people
would be grateful, at times, for someone who isn't always
shoving love down their throats. If others love you,
you feel you ought to love them back again, and you are
upset because you can't, or you love somebody else more,
or you feel you ought to be showing them all the time
that you do, or doing things for them, or letting them
do things for you. The world is all cluttered up with
sentiment and martyrs, and you are the biggest sentimentalist of the lot, young Toni. You don't know what
freedom is, in this family. But now the glory has departed. . . . Ichabod! Ichabod!" he chanted again,
finding some perverse pleasure and reassurance in the
sound of the word. . . .

" Oh, it has, it has, Danny! That's just it. It was a
bigger smash-up than just this one blow over the
wedding. Do you remember Grandmère and Aunt Elsa
and all of them, at Grandmère's last birthday? They
were forming up again, they were ordering us about
again, for the first time for years. Jeanne-Marie's
wedding was *their* wedding, arranged by them. . . . They
were holding disgrace away from the family. The
young ones were as unimportant as if they had not been
there at all. It was almost like it had been when we were
children, and the Uncles were still called in, and the
family was colossal, and nobody ever missed a birthday. . . . It was almost like that again, for a little while;
and I thought it might remain like it for always. . . . I

was frightened, Danny, but I couldn't help being a bit
glad, too . . . like when a great cruel animal, which
you think is down and out, begins to stretch itself, and to
eat and to lick its wounds and lap up the blood and
grow strong, and its muscles ripple under the flesh. . . .
You can't help being glad, because it had been such a
strong animal. . . . And you can't help being sorry when
you see it after a death blow. It's I, and not you or the
others, who have been with Grandmère this last week."

"Oh, they'll never form up in a phalanx again," comfortably. "There seem to be less of them, somehow;
don't know how it is; nobody has died, but there seem
to be less of them, now, than even at Grandmère's birthday, and on the eve of Jeanne-Marie's wedding. They're
a bit scattered and subdued, and some of them have
gone to bed, and some have gone back to San Remo;
and, of course, Grandmère was about nine people all by
herself. . . . Well, Toni, it's a damn good job. Now
there's nothing to prevent us getting married and going
away!" He got up, and came and stood behind her,
leaning over her chair. She felt his cheek warm against
hers; she felt his kisses on her neck. . . . "Darling . . ."

Yes, she had known he would not spare her to-night,
because she was tired, and without much resistance.
That was the worst of a lover like unchivalrous
Danny. . . .

"Now there's nothing to prevent me," repeated Toni.
"*Now* . . . with Grandmère ill and helpless, and Granny
ill and helpless, and Mother to look after, and Gerald,
and the house, and business, and everything to pay, and
the family, and so much to do that my head swims when
I wonder what I'm going to do first, or how on earth I'm
going to fit it all in. . . . *Now* there is nothing to prevent
me! Danny, you are a miracle!"

"I've been a patient man," said Danny. "How long is
this going on? What do your blooming grandmothers
and things matter? *Grandmothers*! Good God! When
a man wants a girl, and she's always shoving her grandmothers under his nose! Aren't you young any more,
Toni? Do you want to miss it all, you dearest fool?

Toni, I love you, come along!—I've had enough of waiting. . . . Come along to-night—to-morrow! You'll
never go to those places on the little maps unless you cut
and run for it, now. The family won't form up again and
stop it—you said so yourself. They are done. Now's
your time—or haven't you got Richard's pluck? After
all, he went first and smashed a way for you."

The places on the little maps. . . . Danny's had been
a fascinating wooing, in his own way. Even when he
was seeing her often, she had had letters from him two
or three or ten times a week, telling her about the places
where they were going together. Islands in the Pacific,
strange ports. . . . He had drawn, for her captivation,
odd little maps beside his descriptions in the letters; and
written little calling songs. Now it was a map of Celebes,
and now of the town of Samarkand, with Wigan next to
it, for the sake of contrast. Now the windings of the
river Irrawady, in Burma. Now Lake Titicaca; and
Tiflis in the unknown Caucasus; and the towers of
Arles. . . .

"I've had so little fun for years," wailed Toni, suddenly and desperately sorry for herself. She had danced
—yes, but she had had to fight for her dances; she had
been to the theatre, and heard music, and gone to parties,
and laughed with friends . . . but all this had been
wedged in among dull, everyday things, family, and
business, and heavy weather; and long dreary journeys
for the firm; bills to pay, and bills to pay, and Grandmère's "bad times," and Granny's asthma, and Susie's
worried, wistful little face; the plod of daily life—rent,
and repairs to the house, and chimneys that smoked, and
replacing breakages, and servants, and bad years of
business, irritating work-girls, and delays in deliveries,
and bullying, and Gerald's education that seemed to go on
interminably. —Oh, never a clear, light, careless time,
without check; sun and colour, swift travel, laughing
boys and girls. . . . That weak body of hers, that persistent nagging of heart and lungs and nerves—always
letting her down; no, it had not beaten her yet, but she
had had to snatch her fun in spite of it; defiantly, inch by

inch . . . sometimes saying "I *am* enjoying this!" when tiredness made the game unbearable. . . .

"I heard from the landlord to-day," she said at last, slowly. "Our lease of this house expires at Michaelmas. If we want to keep it on, we must buy it. I could arrange a mortgage, I think."

"*Buy* it? *Buy* a house? Buy a house in the suburbs? God, why not break your leg, while you're about it, and if you're bent on crippling yourself to one and the same spot for ever. What do you want to buy a *house* for?"

"To live in," Toni suggested.

"To keep your grandmother in!" rudely—and then he began to laugh. "I suppose it amounts to that; it *is* to keep your grandmother in?"

"And Mummy. Mummy has really grown fond of this house, you know. We've been in it nearly three years now; and Mummy is a sort of home person. It was jolly, right up against Grandmère and the family, to have been able to give her the house she had always longed for, even without Father in it. . . . Besides, I've grown quite fond of it, too; we're on terms of pleasant intimacy, this house and I!"

"It beats me how anyone can ever be fond of their— box. Don't buy a house, Toni. Haven't you got enough mess and belongings already? You want to cut burdens away, not add 'em on. Buy a sailing-ship, if you want to, if you have got the money handy! It would suit me much better."

"You may or may not believe this most extraordinary thing," said Toni, "but I wasn't thinking about you." Then, impulsively: "You're right, I *don't* really want this house, Danny. But quite apart from Mummy and Gerald, we can't drag Granny about all over the place, with her rheumatism and asthma; I honestly don't imagine a sailing-ship would suit her."

Danny apostrophised the lilac-bush: "Did ever another man, in his courtship, hear the word 'grandmother' quite so often, I wonder? Granny and grandmère and grandmother! —After all, Toni, you have a brother. How old is he? Twenty-two? Twenty-one? Anyway,

it's about time he began to look after his family. I
shouldn't wonder," seriously, " if young Gerald weren't
a bit irresponsible."

Toni thought about Gerald. He was still an unknown
quantity in a great many ways. A queer philosophic lad;
an industrious worker, with an indolent personality. His
quizzical eyes viewed the world as a spectacle for dry
observation. He was especially nice to his mother, and
very fond of Toni; but she had yet to learn whether he
was a very hero of unselfishness. . . . He did not betray
many of his future intentions; and he looked most dis-
concertingly like Bertrand Rakonitz; and he walked with
Bertrand's loose gait; and above all, he had inherited
Bertrand's gift, which amounted to genius, of not being
present during a row. . . .

" It's not that he means not to be there, or tries not to
be there," Toni explained. " He just *isn't* there. He
might be in Lancashire, or in Wales, or round the corner
posting a letter, but he's not *there*. . . . He doesn't like
rows ! "

" He's a sensible fellow, then. Why don't you do the
same? You don't like rows, or do you? What rows are
there, anyway?"

" I can't give you a list, Danny. You know what rows
are; they just happen, and grow, and spread about. Some
of the worst are with Granny's family. She's got a
married brother, and some nephews and nieces, Bella and
Irene and Alfred. They don't do a thing for her, but they
come and see her sometimes, and complain about the
carpet in her room . . . they say it isn't thick enough.
I flared up over that last time that they came; told them
to go out and buy her another and bring it home in a
taxi and not mind the expense ! " Danny chuckled.
" Then they informed me that I was wanting in respect,
and that I had no right to upset Granny, at her age;
Granny had a bad night on top of it all, and Mummy
looked three times more worried than before, and I felt
like a beast. . . . Sweetheart Gerald was playing tennis,
that Sunday afternoon ! Besides all that, he's rather a
dear. In four or five years' time, when he's earning

well, and if he isn't married, I may be able to hand over to him."

"Then in four or five years' time," he mocked duration, "I may hope for the pleasure—"

"No, Danny. You'd be just as much my first cousin then, as you are now."

He scowled into the darkness. He could argue with this attractive and exasperating Toni whom he loved, over the question of leaving the weak to fend for themselves, or to go to the wall, but he could not do much against this first-cousin business. It was queer how he never felt as though Toni were a near relation . . . nothing so tedious; and if he forgot, could he not make her forget? "It isn't as though there were anyone else whom she cared for," he argued, half aloud.

"Are you quite sure of that?" she murmured.

Danny sat up. The dreaminess went from his voice. "I say, was there, Toni?" Silence. "Toni!"

"Yes. One. I expect I loved you all the time, really, Danny," she teased him. "It was only a small circle shut up inside your big one."

"Go on, tell me. It amuses me, Toni. I shan't mind." He was minding already. "Do tell me. I don't go in for jealousy, you know. Why didn't you marry him?"

"I might have," Toni replied coolly, "if it hadn't been for Grandmère. . . . Oh, don't laugh, Danny."

"The leitmotif of all your love-affairs, my Toni! —So Grandmère didn't approve of him, and quite soberly and excellently, you gave him up?"

"No, not a bit like that. Grandmère approved of him most highly. That was just it. Only she didn't know the subtle but off-hand way that we do things, nowadays. Look you, Danny—here was a handsome and eligible young man, of good family; a Goy, certainly, but that can be overlooked; and here was I, an eldest granddaughter, and a maiden of Israel. Here were things just in that promising stage when good intention should solidify; when, in short, the young man should be 'approached.' . . . I'm giving you Grandmère's point of view, Danny. As a matter of fact, things were just in

that promising stage when one walks about in a muzzy
dream of paradise, and a wrong word spoils it all, a word
drags down the whole castle. . . . He knew hardly anything about the family; I had kept him well outside it—
Oh, I'm not such a damned fool as you think me, and I
was going to have this, family or no family! I wasn't
in the mood for sacrifice. Well, Grandmère heard hints
here and there; you can't help hints getting through, and
she formally sent for this man of mine. She granted
him an interview! He was a bit astonished. . . . It was
the time when she was staying in the Bloomsbury Brothel,
you know, and her room was full of dried fish and sables,
and the old family lace, and the mongrel dog, and some
very expensive flowers, and pâté de foie gras, and the
big paintings of Simon and Babette Rakonitz, in their
gold frames, and an improvised clothes-line. And she
brought out the bronzes and the Sèvres. . . . I'm not
sure if she was dressed, or not; I never found out. Probably she was wearing that lovely stiff black taffeta, with
the spreading skirt, but hadn't quite finished doing her
hair. She asked my man his intentions; she asked him
what he was going to settle on me; she made enquiries
about his honourable family, and told him a great deal
more than was necessary about our honourable family.
. . . I gather that she was quite regal and magnificent,
with about seven generations of Rakonitz forming up
behind her, and the ghosts of the Uncles looming about
the room. . . . She told him he was winning a treasure;
she told him how carefully (she imagined) I had been
brought up; she told him how many had already sought
my hand in marriage; and then, lest he should lose heart,
she encouraged him by saying that I loved him. In short,
she bestowed my hand on him in marriage—he was
terrified out of his wits, and never came near me again!
That was all, Danny."

"I'm glad she has had a stroke," growled Danny.
"She shan't spoil things for you again—interfering old
tyrant, arrogant old beast, I hate her! How dare she
spoil things for you?" He did not condemn the rival who
had been frightened off by too much pressure at the

wrong moment. . . . Danny knew how he must have felt about it. For the moment, he was gallantly and selflessly incensed on Toni's behalf.

"It's all right, Danny, don't get worked up; I've got over it. A year or two later, you came back. I'm sorry to damage your pretty view of the steadfast little girl at home, while you fought to keep the Huns from her. You, of course, never wavered in your faith?"

"About seven times," replied Danny, nonchalantly. "I remember how I had to keep four going at once; two in New Zealand, one in England, and one who had got off the ship at Cape Town, on my voyage out. I got so sick of writing love-letters to them, that I put a piece of carbon-paper in between the four sheets, leaving a blank for the name, after 'dearest'!"

Toni shook with joyous laughter. "Did I get one of the carbon-sheeted letters, ever?" she enquired, tenderly.

"Perhaps. I don't know. No, you didn't; you were different. But you don't like me a bit, Toni; I wonder why you love me?"

"You went away to New Zealand to look for Uncle Ludo without seeing me again after . . . Without saying good-bye, didn't you?"

"My dear old Toni, I discovered the next day that if I didn't take the 'Rotorua' I should have to wait over a week, and meanwhile Grandmère would have forgotten about it, and spent the money she meant for my fare, on three furnished flats and a bowl of goldfish. You know what she is! I simply had to make a dash for it."

"You loved your trip to New Zealand better than me." She was being exasperating again.

"Look here, Toni. You can't say that a trip to New Zealand can compare with you; or the other way round. One is one thing, and the other is another. It's like asking a fellow whether he prefers asparagus or the-day-after-tomorrow. I loved you better than any other woman, *and* I wanted to go to New Zealand. *And* I went. You're so illogical."

"You don't like me a bit, Danny; I wonder why you love me?"

He stood considering her in the faint light which still came from the western sky behind the railway line; a train shrieked past, half a mile away. . . .

"You're small and delicate and white and big-eyed, with no strength in your substance at all; you're not a bit robust, and you mustn't be over-excited. In fact, you are so like a scrap of paper that a man thinks he can tear you into bits—until he comes to try it, and then it's that queer strong Japanesey stuff that doesn't tear, that won't tear. But I still don't know how I love you, Toni, you funny fragment of elegance and fashion; your dresses are always perfect, and your shoes and stockings, and one never knows why your hair and your shape are mysteriously a day ahead of the whole West End—"

"That's my job," said Toni.

"And I like it. It's artificial and exquisite and quite unreal, and no earthly use; and, of course, completely ridiculous—because I know that if it came to it, you would be neither a fashion-girl nor a scrap of thin paper, but a sailor and a sport, and a very demon for pleasure. We'd have a glorious time, Toni. We'd fight like hell, you and I, as we always do, but we'd have a glorious time. Toni . . . come along. Dear—please don't make me wait any longer!"

. . . She was rather near to yielding, then. . . . If she had not remembered, with her absurd trick of remembering at the exact moment to spoil happiness for herself, that this was June of 1919, and that, by her promise to Mr. Isaac Cohen, she was due to pay him, in seven months, six hundred pounds.

II

Really, he loved her best when they were fighting. Most of their attraction for each other lay in the fight, and his knowledge of her style of fighting, her parry and counter-thrust, the half laughing, half eager spirit in which they met, and, passing lightly and swiftly over the quietness and agreeing, suddenly clashed again, sprang back for their weapons, faced each other. . . . It was a stimulating pastime, and it went deeper than pastime. Danny easily got tired of love that was all gold and glamour and kisses. He did not get tired of goading Toni, challenging her, daring her by every means in his power. She said things to him that risked losing him for ever, but he admired her for taking the risk. The very exasperation that he felt for her outlook, her insistence on the Rakonitz family, and decent behaviour, even this exasperation was somehow or other bound up with—with the *fun* of wooing Toni. She was like a princess immured in a high castle, who played the somewhat startling part of herself hurling rocks and pouring hot oil on the gallant rescuer below.

III

Toni had accumulated four hundred and nineteen pounds of the six hundred owing to Isaac Cohen. It had been a slow business and a difficult business, heaping this together. Often she had had more, and then it had gone again, been spent during those strained times when she or Susan or Granny had been ill, when business was so bad that no commissions were coming in at all; two or three times more than Toni could afford, had been spent at the end of Grandmère's bad times, helping Maxine settle up; it was not fair to let Maxine do it all. Twice, Toni herself had spent some of this money on pleasure, wildly, in those moments when she could not bear to do without, whatever the cost; when she rebelliously decided that she need not do without. So the four hundred odd, had been gathered together, and dwindled again, and swelled, and shrank, almost every week a different total. Now she was within seven months of having to pay it— and was a hundred and eighty-one pounds short.

For over a year now, she had been wanting to start in business on her own. Mr and Mrs Wolfe were going to retire. Toni knew she could do well. She was known in the world of modes; her judgment was respected, her taste acknowledged. She had that rare blend of character which would take risks with a cool head. If only,

someone believed in her sufficiently to finance her. There
had been two or three tentative offers among Mr Wolfe's
richer business friends—nothing definite as yet. This
was 1919, and it was already foreseen that the abnormal
post-war boom would last perhaps a year, and then sub-
side again into post-war depression. You think solidly
before you offer a couple of thousand pounds capital to
a girl of twenty-six. Toni was phenomenally young for
the position she had won. She and Maxine were earning
about equally—they both had the sort of shoulders on to
which their seniors quite happily unloaded responsibilities.
Maxine had an advantage in the actual realm of figures;
but Toni was an artist, too; she could manage subordi-
nates in a way that made them love her, though they
realised it was useless to ask for favours or favouritism
from this stern young manageress. Toni's ambition
longed to go forward without check. Her home handi-
caps were heavier than Maxine's; even Grandmère,
though living in the same house as Maxine—or probably
for that reason!—pressed nearer Toni's heart. Grandmère's fall was more to Toni than an old woman ill; she
visualized it as the reverse side of romance. Then Benno
Silver had left his wife with a small income, at least;
Bertrand Rakonitz had left his wife nothing. Toni's
imagination urged her to go forward. She would start in
business on her own; she would buy the house for her
mother; she would pay off the Rakonitz debt, clear away
dishonour from the Rakonitz name; think forward for
children and grandchildren, so that if there were to be
any, they could be over-excited with impunity; she would
look after the family. . . . But Toni's was a dual personality; that gay little sister to the sterner Toni, still wanted
to throw off burdens, instead of picking them up; to kick
the house into one corner, and the business into another,
and the family into a third—and then to dance away with
Danny, with a snap of the fingers for the past and a careless laugh for the future. . . .

Another hundred and eighty-one pounds!

IV

It was Danny who unwittingly gave her the clue, and
the reminder where to get it.

" Young Derek's by way of becoming a millionaire,"
he told Toni, meeting her at Charing Cross one evening,
as he so often did, to take her home; for the trains were
crowded at that hour and she was usually dead tired.

" Derek? "—and now she knew from where that extra
lump of cash could be scooped. She had seen so little
of Derek lately. He lived a rather knowing life apart
from the family; but Derek had been the only cousin who
promised her help with payment of this debt of six
hundred pounds. She had not called on him for help yet;
before the War, and during the War, until the last two
years of it, he had been still a boy, and then he had been
in the Air Force; and since then, though he had hinted
mysteriously at dabblings, buyings and sellings, and the
possibility of various scoops, she had believed that in his
usual way he was swaggering.

" Why, what's Derek doing? " she asked Danny,
casually.

" He lunched me to-day in terrific style; out to impress
me. I played my part rather well : the loafer, the failure
of the family, the poor devil who would never do anything. Derek had a glorious time." Danny grinned
happily. " You should have seen him with the wine list;
what Derek doesn't know about wines ! . . . He knows
the waiters by name, too ! And his new suit came from a
West End tailor ! What a nut ! You know, Toni, we
ought to be proud to have young Derek in the family ! I
was absolutely cowed by all the splendour. . . . I tried to
eat my fish with the asparagus-holders, not knowing no
better ! " His twinkling gaze met Toni's, and she laughed
outright.

" Is there anything behind it, do you think? "

" Well, yes, I'm afraid there is. He has been in a
theatrical set lately, and speculating in all this sub-sub-
sub-sub-letting of theatres. He explained it all to me, but
I'm an amateur, and a bit dull, and couldn't quite grasp

the jargon, only I gathered it is possible, if you are in that set, to buy the fourth lesseeship of one of the smaller theatres, in the morning; and re-let it at a much larger rental to a fifth proprietor, the same evening, making about a couple of hundred pounds on the deal. That's what young Derek has done, or is going to do. What a good-looking fellow he is—I wonder you're not in love with him, Toni."

"With Derek? With my horrid little Cousin Derek?"

"He's a much smarter man than your horrid little Cousin Danny. And he was an officer during the War. But anyway, there's no hope for you, Toni; he told me all about it over the cheese. . . . She's a married woman, and very beautiful. Oh, a regular stunner! The whole affair is most wicked and highly flavoured. You never saw such a hero as Derek is going to be, when he abducts her from her cruel husband. I forget if she's an actress or not—or perhaps the cruel husband is an actor; I was so dazzled, by that time, with all the good wine and food, what I'm not accustomed to, and the high-class knives and forks and spoons flashing into my eyes, and Derek's waistcoat buttons and general sophistication, that I didn't take it in quite as clearly as I should. Besides, apparently it's such a secret that he could only tell me in code and by symbols, and with awful ellipses at every critical point in the story. I have had to swear by all the gods that I won't tell a soul."

"Is that why you are telling me and the rest of the railway carriage?" murmured Toni.

"Oh, I forgot. Perhaps he meant me not to. Oh, well, he's sure to tell you himself for swank's sake. Pretend you don't know, won't you, Toni?"

"No," said Toni, "I won't."

"Look here," Danny dropped buffoonery and was serious, "you've got to promise to pretend not to know, when he tells you, or you'll get me into trouble for telling you—because I've only told you in confidence."

"Dear me! But I betray confidences. I betray them like anything."

"Then you have no right to," growled Danny. "Hang

it all, Toni, I was his guest at that lunch ! " He began to be extremely masculine in his code.

" Yes, that makes it worse," Toni agreed cheerfully. " I'm going over to Ealing to-morrow night; I'll see Derek then. I want to see him, anyway."

" What about? "

" Business." Her lips shut firmly; nor could all Danny's persuasion, and he was most persuasive when he chose, open them again on that subject.

So Derek had made—or was going to make—two hundred pounds? He would have nearly twenty pounds of that left for his tailor, when Toni had paid off the Rakonitz debt.

CHAPTER XVIII

I

"Oh, that debt—yes, of course I remember, Toni; I'd never forgotten. It's not likely that I. . . . Well, Toni dear, just wait two or three years, and I'll pay off the lot, twice over if you like."

Toni said, to her horrid little Cousin Derek—how handsome he was, by the way!—"It's got to be paid in two months, not in three or four years."

"I said two or three years," injured at her lack of accuracy.

"I said two months."

"Toni dear, I've struck oil—in a sort of way. I can't tell you more, now. I'm pledged not to. Besides, you wouldn't understand—"

"Business?" Toni queried, innocently. "Oh, but I might, if you explained it to me, rather slowly and clearly, you know."

Derek was too conceited ever to grasp irony at his expense. "Theatrical business, my dear girl. Very different from the A.B.C. stuff of commercial travelling. You have to be in the know—"

"Yes, of course. And, of course, I didn't think it possible that you could be making anything like a scoop—well, say anything like a hundred pounds, *yet*. . . . When one's a beginner—Oh, it isn't that I don't believe in you, Derek; I do. But when one's a beginner, unless one has a *very* out-of-the-way sort of flair, a gold-diviner's flair—"

To the end of his days, Derek was never to appreciate quite how much of a minx was his Cousin Antoinette. On he came, now, with the rush of a conceited young mackerel, hoodwinked by the glitter of the silver spoon she trailed for him:

264

"A hundred pounds?" he swaggered. "Suppose I were to tell you that I'd made more like two hundred, a few days ago, between lunch and supper. What would you say to that?"

Toni sighed. She never enjoyed an easy victory: "I should say you'd better hand it over to me at once, for your share in paying off our debt to Isaac Cohen," coldly. This exposure of iron beneath her velvet cajolery, was deliberate. . . . It was not good for one's self-respect to exploit Derek a second longer than was necessary.

"Toni dear,"—Derek put on an air of complete frankness, but beneath it he was kicking himself for a too-talkative idiot, "I can't tell you more now, but that two hundred pounds—I know I can trust you, Toni—well, it's pledged. As a man of honour. . . .'

"Yes. It *is* pledged."

"Don't be an obstinate little fool, Toni. I tell you—there's a woman, and mind you, not an ordinary woman at all, to whom I've made a sort of promise mixed up with this two hundred pounds."

"Yes," Toni was acquiescent again. "Every word you say is so true, darling Derek. Even that little bit about my being no ordinary woman. . . ."

Derek swore, in a very manly fashion. . . .

"Toni dear," starting the air-of-sudden-frankness all over again from the beginning—a super sudden-frankness, this time. "Children's games and children's talk—all very well, you know! And I'm not going to let you down, either. I've told you—in two or three years—a couple of hundred quid won't make much difference to me, then. Double it, triple it, if you like. I'll be responsible for the whole show . . . and you can keep whatever you may have saved, for a trousseau, or a fur coat. . . ."

"Very handsome of you," murmured Toni.

"But I'm going to talk to you now," sinking his voice to a deeper throbbier note, "in the way a man talks to a girl who enjoys his confidence, and whom he can absolutely trust. . . . I mean, as much as though she were another fellow."

Toni reflected that she certainly *did* enjoy Derek's

confidences . . . in a way. And as far as absolute trust
went—she foresaw that he was going to trust her as
absolutely as he had trusted that other fellow over the
restaurant lunch and the asparagus-holders. . . .

"She's unhappy in her marriage," Derek spilt the
precious liquid of his secret, drop by drop. "Toni, she's
the loveliest—Oh, my God, you should see her in a
certain evening-dress of hers—infernally expensive—she
told me its name : ' Tulips-in-my-garden '—"

"Three shades of pink, mauve and blackish-red. . . .
Yes, we had the offer of it," put in Toni, profes-
sionally.

"She's horribly unhappy—my God, I can't bear to
think of it. Nobody else knows. . . . The man's twenty
years older than herself, and plays juveniles still. And
plays the swine at home. You'd know his name at
once. . . . I mustn't even give you a hint. I'm the only
person who understands—the only person whom she's
honoured with a chance to understand. If I could tell
you. . . . Well, of course, I can't. Still, you're no fool,
Toni. You know by now that when a woman in trouble
appeals to you to help her out of it—And I can't help
knowing she cares. Well, of course, one can't help
knowing. She's got one evening-dress—my God! You
should see her in it—"

Toni began to wonder whether she were to be made
free of all the lady's wardrobe. She also wished that
Derek would exclaim "Holy Moses !" for a change. . . .

"My God! . . . and it's called ' The Eleventh Hour.'
Next time she wears it. . . . I'm to know . . . a sign that
she can't bear her life any longer—that we're not to wait
any longer. Well, Toni dear, I've got to have some cash,
to start on, when that happens, haven't I? I mean, when
a goddess stoops. . . . And mind you, she's used to the
best. She says she'll rough it with me, but it's not fair
to ask a delicate, hyper-sensitive woman to rough it, or to
worry about a thing like money. That's the way I look
at it."

"Hurrah !" cried Toni, letting her voice swing out into
sheer levity.

He stared at her, offended: "What d'you mean: hurrah?"

She relapsed again into the demure confidant: "I believe in chivalry. And it's so rare. All you say about not letting a woman worry about money because she's delicate. . . . It's rather beautiful, Derek!"

Derek's suspicions were easily lulled. Besides, what was there to be suspicious about? It *was* rather beautiful to feel like that about women (not cousins, of course! not sisters?—but *women*. . . .)

"My God! . . . if you could see her in a hot-stuff brocade cloak thing of hers—'Après moi le déluge,' it's called."

"Water-proof?"

"Brocade, Toni! Opal brocade. Whoever heard of brocade being waterproof!"

"How lovely! I shall call her 'The Opal-Brocade Lady.'" Toni was apparently musing aloud, oblivious of Derek. He smiled tolerantly—she had always been a romantic kid! And naturally, his story had excited her.

. . . "It's meant a great deal to me, being able to talk to you openly like this, Toni. I won't say 'Thank you' . . . but I've told you, now, what I've told no other living person. . . ."

II

"Except me," chuckled Danny to Toni, a few days later. "To each of us is given one person who calls forth our uttermost swank—it's usually the person who annoys us most! And I'm that person, to Derek. However much he's swanking, he swanks more to me. So he took me to see 'The Opal-Brocade Lady'; couldn't resist it. You are a young devil, Toni! pulling his leg like that. It's Ruthven Latimer's wife, Hebe."

"What's she like?" casually.

"Her dress? Oh, it was a sort of shot gauzy affair, draped over an embroidered something else which shimmered in the opposite direction from the shot. Quite attractive. . . . 'Peacocks will dream to-night,' I think it was called!"

"Ass!" laughed Toni. "Tell me about the woman, instead. I shall be christening dresses, myself, all day long, if I can get the capital put up."

"Any hope?"

"Yes. Lots of hope. No cash, as yet."

"What do you suppose I'm going to do, if you set up in business, on your own? You'll be absorbed—swallowed. I know you."

"Get some work," suggested Toni.

"How strenuous all the world is! 'Get some work'— it's a parrot-cry, an obsession. No one ever says 'Get some play,' or 'Laugh and love,' or 'Go to Buenos Ayres —hurry up—you've never been there'! . . . No: Get some work. I'll work with my hands, especially if I can work at different things in different places; but you don't suppose I'm going back into the City, again, do you? Now? After the good old War? I'd rather starve."

Toni did not retort: "Because you know you won't." . . . She was amazed, sometimes, how one sacrifices utterance, however apt, however true, to popularity.

"Go to Buenos Ayres, then!" she said instead, but already missing him and aching for his presence beside her. . . .

He shrugged his shoulders. "It's you who keep me loafing here. . . . One has to be free-hearted, to loaf round the world and enjoy it. I'd always be wondering if you'd changed your mind, if I'd capture you by rushing back. No good. I'm tied by you, and you're tied by the family —I say, Toni," Danny had a sudden disconcerting trick of memory, when she least expected it, " d'you remember, before the War, just about the time of the crash, how you went to some old Jew-fellow and promised to pay him about five hundred quid that someone in the family had let him down?"

"Uncle Blaise. Six hundred pounds."

"Have you ever thought of it, since? What a funny kid you were; haughty as a swan and prickly as a hedgehog, about anything to do with the family. You wanted *me* to help you pay. . . ." Danny's head went back, and Danny's infectious laugh rang down the garden.

Toni cried triumphantly: "The whole six hundred pounds will be paid on the date it's due: January 31st, 1920!"—and brought his laugh to an end. He stared at her, angry, yet admiring. . . . Toni had her moments of beauty, rapt luminous moments . . . and this was one of them.

"You've got it?"

"Most of it."

"How? Who gave it to you?"

"No one."

"You . . . didn't save it? All that ? Alone?"

"Oh—" impatiently, "saved it and spent it and saved it again. . . . What do you think I'm made of? I said I would!"

"You—splendid—idiot!" ejaculated Danny Maitland, from the depths of his heart.

Toni was not sure whether or not to be pleased at his tribute. She supposed it was the best that Danny could supply!

—"Six hundred pounds! All that cash lying about loose and nothing much to spend it on. . . . Look here, Toni, let's do a bunk on it, you and I? What about it? Tampico and the West Indies—Cuba and Jamaica . . . then round by Cape Horn, touching all the ports east and west of South America—up along the Californian coast— and we can get on a tramp steamer from San Francisco to the Pacific Islands. Why—four hundred pounds would do it, easily, and we can leave a couple of hundred to see your mother through, and prevent you from worrying, Toni—" Danny was quite pathetically proud of himself for having improved so much as to think of Susan, and the probability of Toni worrying about Susan. Perhaps, he added, being generous, it would even be possible for Toni and himself to manage their Pacific Island trip on a little less than four hundred pounds. For he was fond of Aunt Susan, and so did not mind economising for her sake. . . .

"Oh Danny! Danny!" Toni's wail toppled over the sheer edge of desperation, into laughter. "Oh well—on the next six hundred pounds I save. Any contributions,

Danny?" She held out her hand. He looked down at its empty hollow, sobered by some thought she could not fathom . . . then lifted it and laid it against his cheek.

"Selfish beasts we all are! D'you mean to say not one of them helped you to collect this—this Fund for Encouraging Rakonitz Lunatics? Not Maxine nor Val? Klaus? Derek?—"

"Oh, Derek will have to pay up. *He* promised. . . . I worked on his vanity until he promised. The others were too stiff for my moulding." An unrepentant Jesuit still, she coolly made no secret of her unprincipled conquest of the weakest of her cousins. . . . "As a matter of fact, I'm still about a hundred and eighty pounds short of the full sum. That's why I was so glad when you told me that two hundred pounds had just tumbled into Derek's pocket."

"You won't get any of that, Toni. Not a hope. Derek means to run away with this Hebe woman, and he'll want every sou of his two hundred, for her. He's infatuated."

"Then he'll just have to get uninfatuated. Or at anyrate, not get infatuated on *my* money. I won't have it."

"*Your* money? And *you* won't have it?" Danny looked at her, his mouth whimsically awry, and the latent tenderness dying from his eyes. "That's going a bit too far, young Toni. Robbing Derek to pay Blaise. . . . After all, it's Derek's family too, if it's family you're so keen on."

"So are you, if it comes to that."

"I can look after myself. I'm not sure that poor Derek can—when you're on the war-path."

"Poor Derek!" echoed Toni, her voice at a white heat of scorn. ". . . It *is* my money, Danny. He promised it to me . . . on his honour."

"Don't rant."

"Nobody can talk about honour without ranting. . . . What does it matter?"

"It matters this," squarely facing her, his hands in his pockets, "that when a man makes some money, never mind how, and is keen on a woman, never mind who, he has a right to do as he likes about it, without interference."

Then the fierce storm broke on him: "Do as he likes? Have *I* done as I like? Do I want him to buy me a pretty box of chocolates with his money? Am I cadging to Derek? . . . But I've saved and stinted and sweated and denied myself soft warm things, beautiful things, all these years—and I'm not going to lose now, at the last moment, lose the complete thing that will give my mind its rest, because Derek—Derek—Derek must have his toy, his petty love-affairs. Let that stand in my way? Why, he'll have thousands of love-affairs. If he's too mean and small to stand by his word willingly, with fire in his heart, then he's got to go under, whining. He's got to be used. . . . What do I care? I gain no loot by it! It isn't self-indulgence that's turning me into a beggar. . . . It's a cause. And a losing cause . . ."

—"But not Derek's cause," said Danny, unmoved. "Yours. That makes all the difference, Toni."

"So you're on his side?"

Danny twinkled at her: "The side of the oppressed people," he quoted, "'the side of Belgium—of the little nations . . .' Oh, the posters haven't been torn down so long, Toni. The lesson is impressed upon my soul, which is also the soul of British chivalry! . . . Who's for freedom? . . .'We will not lightly sheathe the sword—'"

"Derek can be managed." . . . Toni was smiling now, that stubborn mischievous smile of belief in her own powers, always most provocative of Danny's wrath. He went quickly down the garden whistling on a defiant note: "'An' they're hangin' Danny Deever in the mornin'!'" . . .

She understood that he had officially declared himself on Derek's side.

III

But they were glad of the excuse to fight again, those two, Danny and Toni, those two lovers. The strain had been too much . . . and both felt that something was bound to give way soon, and to break. Derek was only an excuse, a solid object over which to battle, where before had only been a tumbled confusion of ideals and counter-ideals. There they stood, Toni for family life, Danny for freedom, things that were old as the mountains and big as the world, eternal things. . . . But they believed they were fighting as to whether or not Derek Silver should be allowed to spend his two hundred pounds on a love-affair pleasurable to himself, or on a promise weakly given, repented and forgotten. Derek did not matter, nor his promise, nor his lady. But they provided sufficient excuse for the exultant combatants. Danny and Toni loved each other too passionately to be idle about it, to wait, to argue and to hope. And neither was of the quality that gives way. Facts were stubborn. Toni would not marry her first cousin. And Toni had her responsibilities, her mother, her grandmothers; she could not leave Maxine to shoulder the burden alone. She loved Danny. And he was a Rakonitz male. If you are decent, you think of consequences. Grandmère had not thought of them. First cousins. And here, always, since the War, was Danny, urging her, tempting her, pleading. . . . Facts are stubborn. What was Toni to do? Fight him . . . much better to fight, much more fun. Something to do, at anyrate. Something to break the strain. Stickiness—their lives had got stuck. When facts shifted, they only shifted to a more unendurable, more bewildering pattern than before. Grandmère pulled low with a stroke . . . and then the date drawing nearer for this debt to be paid. Toni would not give in, yet. If she and Danny could not safely love each other— then active shining joyous hate, blesséd hate, the test of weapon ringing hard upon weapon. . . . A younger pastime than stagnation! Toni laughed. . . . So Danny imagined he could victoriously oppose her, where *Derek* was concerned? She, who had "managed" Derek from the time when he was a pretty clinging baby with dark curls and a perpetually quivering underlip? In for it! If Derek's love-affair must be wrecked, to divert that two hundred pounds into Isaac Cohen's pocket, whither it was so fantastically pledged—then wreck it! And be as unscrupulous as you please.

—But Danny, equally or more unscrupulous, was yet no Jesuit. His methods of warfare were so open and easy, so cherubic, that they became surprisingly difficult. He kept to no rules. If, to further his ends, he betrayed to Derek all that had ever been told to him, in pre-battle days, by Toni, he also passed on to Toni, the enemy, in a lazy amused fashion, all that Derek had replied in confidence to him, about Toni, about his intentions, about Hebe Latimer, and the two hundred pounds. So that Toni was never in the dark. It is disconcerting to fight strategically, if you are never in the dark; to plot against the plotting foe, directly after their general has strolled into your tent with a complete map of their plan of campaign. . . .

Derek was plastic. He was like a tube of tooth-paste left about for either Danny or Toni, whichever was the last to pick it up, to twist into yet a different shape. Derek believed fervently in the permanence of whichever shape he happened to be in for the moment; but both Danny and Toni knew otherwise, and were bitterly humorous in their exchange of experiences.

Danny made Derek see that Toni was out of all sympathy with any knight-errantry on Hebe's behalf, because she meant to have that two hundred pounds for Isaac Cohen.

Toni made Derek see that Hebe could not fail to be impressed by a man, and to adore him, who came to her, head up and with stern-set lips, a white-faced young paladin, saying: "Dear one, I have a debt of honour to pay. My family name must be cleared, and only I can do it. I won't selfishly put myself first, or even you. . . . 'I could not love thee, dear, so much'"—the rest was pure Lovelace.

Danny made Derek see that this was all bunkum, and that Toni was cleverly influencing him for her own ends —as indeed she had boasted having done before, when she had coaxed that fatal promise out of him. " And the less you tell Hebe about our rotten old family, and the lowness of its exchequers, and the less you jaw to her about your responsibilities, the better for you—as far as she's concerned ! "

Toni made Derek see that a man of the world, a man of experience, a gay philanderer, albeit mellow with sophistication, knowing women, you understand, not a mere clumsy callow youth stuttering excitedly over his first love-affair . . .well, such a man, even such a man as Derek himself, for instance, knows better than to kill romance and pledge his independent swaggering radiant future, by eloping with a married woman who happens to be temperamentally incompatible with her husband—" He'd divorce her, and you'd have to marry her, and sweat like anything to keep her for ever in humdrum rooms, and be worried to death. . . . Women can't see ahead in these things. They always want certainty at once, and Hebe in the frying-pan is happier than she'll ever be in the fire. She's got her luxuries ; she's got you. And you've got your freedom. It's lucky that you're too wise to be a fool, Derek ! " . . .

. . . And then, with her usual collapse of luck, Toni got influenza. She knew that in whatever shape she had left Derek, it was in the process of being altered out of all recognition, by a gaily grinning Danny, who would not hesitate to take advantage of the illness which was putting her out of action.

When she was well enough to take command of her side again, she realized that the war had reached a stage where further manœuvres were too indecisive, and that a more drastic blow must be struck, if she were to have that six hundred ready for Isaac Cohen on the date appointed.

Between Toni's indomitable will, Danny's truly devastating lack of reticence, and the impressionable substance
of which Derek was formed, the struggle had not been
unworthy of celebration in epic verse, another Iliad.
Behind the three combatants, dim figures might have
been discerned, unconscious, even, of their participation,
yet intimately concerned. Ruthven Latimer, for instance,
who played juvenile leads and was a swine to his wife;
or, if you prefer it, and by way of contrast, Isaac Cohen,
the kind old Jew who had not wanted Antoinette
Rakonitz to pay him back her Uncle Blaise's debt of
honour. Or—here is yet another figure, stepping forward
for a few minutes out of the background; a tall thin
man of about fifty-seven, with thick white hair, and
quizzical black eyes; an air of the gentleman adventurer
about him, though it would be difficult to fix this down
on to any special point of his appearance, clothes or
voice; he had a pleasant voice. We first meet him leaning
up against the bar of " Niki's " night-club, explaining to
the bar-tender the ingredients of a certain drink popular
in South America.

And this was where Danny first met him, too.

" You know South America, then? " He could never
refrain from dropping into casual talk with any stranger
who had crossed the Equator.

" Lived there for nearly twenty years, and may be
going back again. England's a poor place on the whole.
No drinking after ten—and it's a quarter to, now. Here
—have one with me? . . . I wish I could get fresh limes.
You don't get the proper flavour of a ' Lima Lifter,'
using this bottled stuff. Not bad, though!" He nodded
qualified praise at the man in white linen behind the
counter, who looked relieved.

After a couple of drinks each, the two men strolled
back into the dance-room, and sat down together at one
of the small tables, at the far end from the band. . . .
Jazz was in its noisiest stages, in the early Autumn
of 1919.

"If you care to come round to see me, any evening, at my studio," said the older man, attracted by Danny's vitality, as most people were, whom he did not shock at first hearing by his irreverences. "I could show you some things I've picked up, that might interest you. My name's Maitland."

"So's mine . . ." and Danny added lazily: "You're probably my traditional long-lost uncle!" —Then he thought of Ludovic Rakonitz, and laughed aloud.

"We might possibly be related—we're not unlike. Is your father alive? What was his other name?"

"Oliver." Danny did not reply to the question as to whether his father were alive or not; he was still rather ashamed of his ignorance on that score.

A flash of scrutiny. . . . "I can't quite place you," said Oliver Maitland. "Let me see—you look about twenty-eight—"

"Twenty-five. Am I your son, by any chance? I don't want to be tactless, and I promise not to be melo-dramatic . . . but it would be interesting to know," quoth modern youth, conforming, in its own queer fashion, to its own queer standard of decent behaviour.

"I'm not sure. . . . Your mother—?"

"Sophie Rakonitz."

"Ah! . . ."

'You *are* my son," said Maitland, after a moment's pause. Then his shoulders began to shake at a whimsical recollection which even after so broad a span of time, still had the power to amuse him mightily.

"Good. Let's have another drink on it."

"After time, sir. Very sorry, sir," said the waiter, on being summoned and given an order.

"Yes, but look here—"

The waiter moved away, with a gesture that depre-cated the law, but obeyed it.

"Shall we tell him the sensational truth, and ask 'em to make an exception for us? Damn it, it's not every night that parent and child meet for the first time—"

"*Almost* the first time," chuckled Oliver Maitland.

" I've met you before, you know! Once. Did the Rakonitz lot do you pretty well?"

" No, they didn't. Sorry to complain, but they went bust when I was a kid of fifteen."

" Hard luck!" sympathetically. " They were rolling when I knew 'em."

" You'd have worried about me, if you'd known, wouldn't you?" Danny thrust with deliberate malice at this casual father of his—whom, as a matter of fact, he found amazingly to his liking. He need not have dreaded a scene; without apparent effort, both men, the old and the young, treated the situation from an angle of light-hearted semi-ironic good-fellowship.

" I never worry," Maitland confessed, producing his cigar-case, and offering it. " I should, of course. But it pays better not to. I'd have done you no good, fussing round. Is the old lady still alive? Old Anastasia Rakonitz? I suppose not."

" Yes, she is, but my mother—" Danny hesitated. Stopped. " You knew, I suppose? She—she died ages ago, when I was a kid, down at Cotsford."—But need he bother to break it gently? . . . Oliver Maitland could not have cared for his wife, or he would not have so nakedly deserted her.

" Your mother?—Oh, you mean Sophie, Sophie Rakonitz. Yes, I heard. But she wasn't your mother, my boy."

Silence for a few moments. Danny's heart was thumping wildly. Yet he resolved, whatever happened, not to give way to any sort of emotional exhibition before this pleasant grinning devil, this charming, travelled, sophisticated gentleman, who spoke of all things as though they were equally trivial, and mattered less than the flavour of a " Lima Lifter." All his life long, Danny had tried to inculcate this type of philosophy into Toni, believing in it and believing it to be his own. He would play up now. After all, this conversation was really funny. . . .

When he did speak, his voice was on the same casual note as Maitland's; his pose was as indolent; his eyes mocked equally at the whirling jigging couples that passed their table, at their glasses, empty by compulsion, and at their own drama of disclosed relationship. They were very alike, these two men; irresistibly, comically alike. . .

"Sophie Rakonitz wasn't my mother?" repeated Danny. "How extremely—diverting. Then I'm not related to any of the—the family?"

"The Rakonitz family? No. Poor Sophie!—she couldn't have a child. But she was crazy about 'em. So she adopted you and said nothing about it. . . . Women are queer. It was just her pride, you see," mused Sophie's husband, "couldn't bear her people to know that she was barren. So when you were dumped in her arms, a few weeks old, she made me swear I'd not tell a soul that you weren't her own. Well—I was off, anyhow. Sick of the domestic business. She wasn't the type that could hold a man—I've yet to meet one who could, by the way. And the wanderlust had got me again —Ah, you know something about that, do you? It made no difference to me, in Mexico, whether you passed as Sophie's son or not; in fact, it was better that you should, because the Rakonitz family were rich, then, and I could be sure they'd keep you. It wasn't likely that they'd leave their money to a—"

"Bastard," Danny furnished, tranquilly.

Apologetic, but unrepentant, Maitland hastened to say: "If you're squeamish over words—?"

"Not in the least. It used to be a proud title, at one time of mediaeval history. Philip the Bastard!—that was in 'King John.' I often wondered what bastardy felt like. Curse you, Father!"

"Not at all, not at all." Maitland waved aside the compliment diffidently. "People are sometimes prejudiced, but not much, and the War's made a hell of a difference. Did you fight, by the way?"

"Yes. Don't change the subject, yet, though; I'm just getting enthralled. Then I've no legal right to call myself Maitland at all? I'm Daniel Rak— No, *she* wasn't my mother. Would you have any sentimental objection, Daddy dear, to telling me my mother's name?"

Oliver Maitland had no sentimental objections to any-thing. It was not in his nature. But by no effort could he now remember the name of the heroine of the slight but charming incident in his career, which resulted in Danny, sitting now at a table with him at " Niki's."

", Alice? . . . No. Bee? or Chloe? . . . *Was* it Chloe Carmichael? "

" Oh, I hope so," murmured his son, entranced. " To wake up one morning and find oneself a Carmichael—"

" Anyhow, *her* real name was Carrie Mills . . . but that tour never touched Plymouth, I know. Plymouth. . . . *Got* it! It was Nell. Of course it was. Nell—Nell—"

" Nell—?"

Maitland leant back in his chair, hopelessly, and gave it up. "Sorry, my boy. It's simply slipped my memory altogether. Twenty-six years, you know—and I've led a full life."

Danny's eyes twinkled: " Am I far from being your only child, sir? "

" There's a levity and a want of respect about your manner towards me, Daniel—"

" Confound it! You can't ask me to respect a father who doesn't remember my mother's name! "

" Nell—Nell . . ." Oliver Maitland was genuinely distressed that he could not furnish a reply to what he felt was an eminently reasonable demand on the part of his newly-found son—" Look here, er—Dan, I honestly can't call that name to mind, but do go on calling yourself Maitland, if you like. No difference to me, you know! And if a cheque for a couple of hundred quid is any good to you—"

"—Instead?" Suddenly Danny broke into an uncon-trollable shout of laughter. What man had ever before been offered a cheque for two hundred pounds, in lieu of his mother's name? . . . A girl in yellow whom he had often seen before at this dance-club, and admired for her supple boneless dancing, paused by his table, attracted by his merriment; she smiled an invitation. . . .

" Come on! " cried Danny. He sprang up, slipped his

arm round her, and they fox-trotted down the room to the sinister strains of "The Vamp."

—When he returned alone : "Thanks very much," he said to his father. "Yes, rather, two hundred will do me very well. I can get away on that."

"Where d'you want to get to?"

"Anywhere—far enough," flung back Maitland to Maitland.

"You're in luck; I'm not often in funds like this. My bank account is usually well on the debit side; but a man to whom I did a good turn once, put me in the way of a really good investment—this boom, you know! Pity not to profit by it. I made five hundred a few weeks ago, and managed to keep back a couple of hundred to pay a debt of three or four hundred which falls due next month. So there's your cheque, and nobody'll miss it. Come home with me, now, and I'll write it out for you, and give you a decent drink into the bargain."

"—' and show you some things I've picked up, that might interest you,'" quoted Danny, from the beginning of their rather eventful conversation. "A few family photos, for instance?" as they strolled out of "Niki's," side by side, two gentlemen in evening-dress with light overcoats, who, one would have said, had become pleasantly acquainted in there, chatting over a "Lima Lifter."

It struck Danny, with a pang of wry distaste, how any member of the Rakonitz family would have fussed, over a discovery akin to the one that he and his father had just made. . . . This kinsman of his suited him so well— his turn of humour, his vagabond carelessness over the heavy side of life, his style of financial reckoning, his refusal of sentiment—Oh, damn! Why couldn't a fellow have been brought up with this sort of thing all around him? To have suddenly been jerked face to face with any other type of parent but Oliver would have been intolerable. Oliver was a scoundrel, but he was all right. . . . Danny would probably never see him again; nevertheless, he was heartily glad to know that he came of a stock and quality that suited him—even though . . . a

love-child. *Love*-child!—his mouth twisted sardonically
. . . oh, well!

And it struck Oliver Maitland, like a sharp knife
thrust down through his profligacy and selfishness, that
the boy was accepting his position rather gallantly. After
all, gloss it over as you will with airy persiflage, to be
deserted in babyhood, left to be devoured or abandoned
by a family only your own by a lie, and then to be coolly
informed that your mother . . .

He liked Danny. Unquestionably, he liked him. Not
that he was going to let himself be bothered with the
responsibilities of parenthood or any such ponderous
nonsense foreign to his nature— Indeed, he did not
imagine, from a cursory view, that Danny was the type
either to require or to put up with it. They would possibly never meet again, after to-night. Still, for a few
hours, and at the expense of two hundred pounds. . . .
A good thing he had set aside that two hundred for old
Miles Porter!—in a way, one might almost call this
encounter with Danny, the reward of honesty. . . .

CHAPTER XIX.

I

. . Danny was dazed that night. He went home, and slept heavily. The next day was Sunday.

He woke up to the sound of Rakonitz voices . . . voluble excited voices. . . . The Matriarch felt better, and wanted rusks for breakfast; there were no rusks— "Mamma, you know how difficult it is with the servants—" "Rusks!" said the Matriarch.

Derek had not been home for two days, and Truda could not control her anxiety: "It's not as though I did not allow my son all the liberty he can want, but he *must tell me* when he's going to stay with friends for a night. . . . He knows how I worry. Iris, did he tell you, I wonder—?"

"No, Mother, he didn't. He never does. He knows I'd tell Maxine. . . . Mother, *need* I take in Grandmère's breakfast? I'm doing my hair."

"I wish you to take it in to her, darling, and you are so long over your hair. You know how she talks to Gwenny about the family, and about poor Uncle Max and the sapphires and how I keep her short of Bücklinge because I still owe her a grudge over the linen. . . . And it's hard enough to keep a servant nowadays, even as lazy as Gwenny—"

Then, a few minutes later: "Mother, I wish I could have *my* breakfast in bed on Sunday mornings, like Grandmère and Derek and Maxine and everyone but you."

"Iris, you know quite well that I *don't* allow Derek to have his breakfast in bed. . . . At anyrate, I don't think it's right; but I always hope," continued poor Truda, "that it may make him more devoted to his home, if I

282

sometimes allow him little treats. And Maxine is the wage-earner—"

"Hear! hear!" drowsily, through the open door of Maxine's bedroom.

"But Danny is *not* to have his breakfast in bed. Tell him to get up at once, Iris. In this home, it's the girls, and not always the boys and the boys and the boys who are to be considered first . . ."

Truda was one of those rare beings whom injustice made just; and she could never quite forget what she and Sophie had suffered, long ago, from Anastasia's overwhelming partiality for her sons.

"Rusks!" cried the Matriarch, shrilly.

"Danny, Mother says you're to get up at once." Iris thumped once or twice on his door; then ran away; he heard her clattering up with the Matriarch's tray presently. . . .

These people!

. . . And Danny realised, in a sudden flash, that, after all, they were not his people. He did not belong to them. They need never concern him again. He was not related to Rakonitz.

It was a stupendous moment.

Jubilation! Oh—hallelujah! Glory! . . . Why, he had hated them—always hated them. They had exasperated him to a frenzy. Questions and interference, and calling him "Dunnee!" and fuss and fuss, and too much love and affection lying about—the clannishness of the tribe—Grandmère's birthday, and all the other birthdays and feastings and funerals . . . all the family locked and clamped and wedged together in an interdependent mass. . . . But he could not *feel* it! He could feel none of it. Of course not—they were not his flesh and blood; not his kin and his kind. The puzzle was solved, now. They were Rakonitz and Czelovar and Bettelheim— Danny, nameless and uncharted, was free of them. They —they were all wrong. . . . Israelites—cosmopolitans. "Free of them, I tell you!" —Yes, he had to tell someone. He had to tell Toni, at once, of this glorious thundering thing that had happened to him. Danny leapt

out of bed and began to dress. Toni . . . she had always
thought him an utter beast, a callous beast, because he
would not, could not, be proud of Rakonitz tradition, and
share their responsibilities, and adore the Matriarch.
Selfish old hag! He was confoundedly glad she was *not*
his grandmother. . . . But Toni would understand now,
when he told her. —He rushed out of the house at
Ealing, without waiting for breakfast; and within an
hour of waking up, was already at Bedford Park, already
with Toni, who was, fortunately, alone in the sitting-
room.

Breathlessly, exultantly, he poured out an account of
his meeting with his father at " Niki's," and of Oliver
Maitland's revelation.

—" So you see, I'm not one of the family at all, Toni.
I don't belong to the family; I'm not even related to
them—"

A lovely glowing pink poured suddenly into Toni's
pale face. She had been bewildered, at first, by Danny's
gladness over his isolation. . . . But soon, very soon,
came her radiant enlightenment:

" Then—if we're not related, you and I, if we're not
first cousins—Oh, Danny . . ."

II

—Danny stood still—stared at her. He asked himself
if he could possibly have failed to realise this most
brilliant of the changes which had happened to him since
last night. Need he betray to Toni that he *had* failed
to realise it? Why . . . no, it would hurt her too much.
Besides . . . he had rushed off here at once and without
hesitation, to share his ecstasy with her; that might have
been, *must* have been, because softly, sub-consciously,
he already knew that now the vital barrier to their
marriage was down—down.—Not first cousins! Not
even related! . . .

" Toni—" his brown eyes glowed down on her . . .
she slipped into his arms with a little sigh of rest—relief
. . he could not quite say which. But he was just a

trifle provoked, still, that she should have had to fashion
and present to him the real reason for his new-born
happiness.

"Toni—" lifting it away from her, and re-presenting
it in his own warm charming plausible way—"Toni dear,
that's just it! Don't you see—we can marry now. Why
not? as I'm not a Rakonitz at all. You'll be marrying
a stranger."

"You're an odd sort of creature, Danny," Toni remarked presently, her voice a little tremulous still . . .
but she looked quite a young girl now, and not, as she
usually did, a tired-out child or a worn-out woman; quite
a young girl, with wet happy blue eyes, flushed cheeks
as soft as Southern fruit, and lips with that eager glorious
curve of a wave that is just going to break in the sun.
The Matriarch would have nodded approvingly: "That
is how my grandchild ought to look!" . . .

"—But you *are* odd, Danny. What other man in the
world would have been so pleased at finding out that he
belonged nowhere, after he had been sure all his life of
just where he did belong."

"It suits me," said Danny. He paused—then went on,
enamoured of his new loneliness as though he had always
pursued an enchanting gipsy, and had caught her at last.
. . . "That explains it, and I can't explain it any other
way. It suits me to belong nowhere, and to have no
claims on any family. It's thrilling and a bit dangerous,
and above all, it means freedom. . . . Oh, don't you see?
—I believe I'm now the free-est man alive. I don't know
who my mother was, nor her name, nor anything about
her. And I can't find out. I may be of any race and
any ancestors—I may have met them—or her; I might
sail in my uncle's ship to-morrow, or talk with the keeper
on my grandfather's estate—or buy bootlaces in my
sister's shop. . . . I shall never know. I'm cut off from
knowing; stripped for living my own life. All that I
inherit is mysterious, and my temper is mysterious, and
my desires. Except what comes from my father—and
he's only been in my life for a circle of three hours, perhaps. I shan't see him again, I know. Oh, he got on

with me all right—but he's like I am, he doesn't want
to be bothered. . . . It's all right, Toni—" for she had
suddenly clenched her hand over his fingers, crushing
them, in fierce sympathy. "Yes, it *does* hurt—but I
don't mind being hurt in that sharp hard sort of way.
It's mess and fuss that make me sick. I'm damned proud
of being an outcast, and of standing alone, answerable
to no one. And as for not knowing my own name—
Good Lord! It's *fun*, not to know one's own name and
never to know it. I can't imagine a better or a more
ridiculous joke—can you? Unbranded—I'm a maverick
in the tame herd. I might call myself Danny Maverick!"

"And what will you call me?" put in Toni. She had
been swung along with his mood, and for sheer love of
him, into those up-in-the-air and delicately drunken
realms where, indeed, nothing matters except to laugh;
where relations and illness and houses and debts suddenly
became light as balloons and as tossable; where it was the
most fantastically funny thing in the world to be nameless, or to be called Maverick or Smith or Konstantino-
politalienischedoodlesackpfeiffegeselle (which Uncle Otto
Solomonson had long ago told her was the largest word in
any language!). . . . And again how absurd, how
grotesque, that Danny should have been living all these
years with a grandmother who wasn't his grandmother!
She felt that she could laugh and laugh and never stop
laughing, over that—"Shall I be Toni Maverick,
Danny?"

"Then you *will*—you will marry me, now? The other
things—about looking after people and earning money at
business and all that—you're not going to let them
count?"

"I'll manage them all, somehow. Oh, it'll be easy—"
For what was not easy, when you felt so powerful, and at
the same time so buoyant? . . . You just touched difficulties and they shot away and out of sight.

"Danny . . . Danny . . ."

. . . This feeling . . . like carnival-time in a little
town by the sea . . . you felt slender and slippery and
moonshiny . . . a round yellow ball of a moon, and

snowflakes tumbling in light showers. . . . Yes, that was unreal, but then it was unreal and topsy-turvy to know that Danny was not, after all, what you had known so well he must be—Cousin!—cousin! . . . snowflakes and moonshine—and now Toni's carnival time had come . . . dance in the white streets, and whirl into small lit spaces and out again. . . . " Danny! . . . Danny! Danny! "
—Little Toni was over-excited.

Rushing swift and steady like a golden river, below all this toss and glitter, was the good knowledge, now, that all this time she had been wrong about Danny; he was not just another of those terrible Rakonitz males, weak and fascinating and irresponsible. She was linking herself to a man with different blood in him. . . . How she had dreaded an inevitable recognition, in the future, of the old tiresome familiar traits, one by one. No more fear of that. Danny was not stupid, not dense nor callous. He was quite simply not a Rakonitz; that answered all questions. He did not love Grandmère and did not care when she was ill—because he was not a Rakonitz. He would not help her to pay Blaise's debt, caring nothing for the family honour—because he was not a Rakonitz. He had chafed against restraint and family ties and business, even to the extent of inventing that Uncle-Ludovic-in-New-Zealand lie—well, perhaps that could not be quite excused even from one of alien blood. But it was not still the same sin and betrayal it would have been from a man with the rhythm of the family in his blood, the " must," the loyalty, the— patriotism, for want of a better word. Your country has a thousand faults, it may have ruined you, but you fight for it. . . . But Danny, the cuckoo, was not to blame. She loved him, and she could marry him. She loved him more for being proud of what many might have considered shame; for being cheerful and ordinary about it, scorning sentiment; for being brave about it, instead of afraid . . . afraid as a fox might be, without an earth to run to; with never an earth, now. There was strong stuff in Danny . . . from his mother, maybe; from " Nell" who had not wanted him, any more than

288

Oliver Maitland wanted him. Laughing and unwanted,
that was Danny. . . . Toni gave another little sigh, and
rubbed her face caressingly against his shoulder. . . .

"When, Toni? Soon? To-day's Sunday. Tomorrow,
sweetheart?"

She yielded, deliberately enjoying the sliding sensation
of letting herself go, headlong down a man's impetuous
will. "Tomorrow," she acquiesced—and he heard her
luscious gurgle of contentment, as he bent down his head
over hers.

Danny took a risk, as he always would; at his own peril,
he tested her: "I've got the money for a special license.
But what about your mother and Gerald? What will the
family say? Oughtn't we to ask Uncle Louis? How will
it affect Grandmère's illness? Is it fair to Maxine?"

"Let 'em rip!" cried Toni, still in rebellion. And
again: "I'll manage them all, somehow." One stroke of
luck had made of her an optimist. Like a true child of
Vienna, she reacted swiftly from old unhappiness. Wine
in her veins, and wine—no, wings on her head . . . she
could soar, she could leave the arid levels—"I've been
good for *years*!" cried Toni, hotly indignant. . . . How
dared they postpone her release so long?

Danny pushed on—pushed too far: "And your debt
to Isaac Cohen? Ought you to chuck that?" He spoke
solemnly, confident now that Toni, his Toni, was no more
an ass and an idiot.

"Oh, I needn't. I've got that, ready to deliver."

"I thought you were about two hundred pounds
short?" Danny remembered the two hundred pounds in
his own pocket. Amusing, how that sum recurred! He
supposed some sentimentalists would immediately have
given it to Toni, with a lavish gesture. Not he. Toni was
going to be taken away from duty and honour and all
that morbid rot, now. Toni was to enjoy herself. . . .

"Derek gave it to me, yesterday."

"*What?*"

"I told you I'd settle his affair for him," laughed
Toni.

"How?"

" I went straight to Hebe Latimer, and told her that
my cousin Derek Silver had no money of his own and was
earning nothing—he'd been boasting, of course—and that
whatever little he might have for some time was owing
on account of a bad family debt which he had undertaken
to clear off. The simplest method is the quickest, sometimes. It was enough for the ' Opal-Brocade-Lady.' . . .
I'd guessed she was extravagant, from his description of
her clothes : 'Eleventh Hour,' and the rest of it ! She
threw him over. And with one despairing gesture, Derek
paid his debt to me, and dashed off—to the dogs, I suppose. He'll be all right, in a week or two. But I won,
Danny ; grant me that I won—" She threw back her
head, in that old manner of " my-imperial-sway " that
had always so aggravated Danny, while she was still a
child with long thick curls.

He stood staring at her. . . . Then :
. . . " You—*you Matriarch* ! " he said, slowly.

III

. . . Something was pulsing between them, like mad
Toni thought it was a heart. What had happened? . .
" Danny—why—why do you call me that? "

Get away from the family? Free of the family? But
—if he married Toni, he'd never be free of the family !
He would be sucked back, back into the vortex. For
Toni, who could do the sort of things she had just done to
Derek, remorseless autocratic interfering things, Toni
was the Matriarch over again. And he had nearly
married her, not seeing it—no, forgetting it . . . because
he *had* seen it, two or three times in the olden days.

—Just as he had exulted in being free of them. God !
what an escape. . . . Danny sighed deeply, like a man
who has stepped back from the very edge of death.

" Danny ! " cried Toni, in a panic . . . seeing him
recede and still receding. . . .

One wrench—and then he'd be away, eternally safe
from Rakonitz. Danny was jealous for his new and
shining gift of freedom—but he would have to defend

it, now, by every brutality he possessed . . . or Rakonitz
would have it. Rakonitz fed on human freedom, and
grew strong on it.

"It's no good, Toni," said Danny, harshly. "I'm off.
I can't stand it." He avoided her eyes, all the blue dying
from them. . . .

"I haven't done anything," whispered Toni, forlornly.

"Yes, you have. What you did about Derek—it's
typical. You're the Matriarch over again. You're her
grandchild and just like her."

"I'm not. I'm not." Oh, but he was cruel; he was
scattering her short carnival-time with every word he
spoke. "I'm *not* like Grandmère. Danny, don't let them
say it—" In a panic she appealed to that other Danny
who had loved her ten minutes ago : "I'm not, am I?
Why, I'm quite different in everything. I—I—know all
about Grandmère. I put things right again, after her—
her bad times. I'm—clever at business. It's because I
wouldn't be like Grandmère, that I wouldn't marry you
while I thought you were my first cousin." Confidence
surged back, and with it, anger at his accusation. "I'm
not like Grandmère, Danny. How dare you say I am?"

But the remorseless voice of Danny went on: a
passionate indictment of all the world who had suffered
from Rakonitz, piling up against Rakonitz at last :

"It's because you are so exactly like her, and know it,
that you've been afraid to behave like she behaved. You
try and think you're cool and logical and modern—but
all that passes away, and you'll be more and more the
Matriarch, as you grow older. You'll be the bully of
the family, and yet they'll all come to you, as head of
the family, for advice and help . . . because you care
about them most. And you'll glory in it. If any one of
them does something you don't approve of, that you don't
think is good for them, or that isn't just as you'd already
planned it—*Smash*! You'll smash it, as you smashed
Derek's trumpery little affair. You're proud and arrogant—Worse still, you're officious. You're the Matriarch.
There'll always be a Matriarch, in this family—"

"I won't be—I'm not—I'd be miserable. I'm going

to marry you and get away from it—enjoy myself—you said so—"

"If I let myself marry you, it isn't you who'd get away from the family; it's I who'd get dragged back into it. Stuck here, fast, in the morass . . . your husband. Haven't I felt your will, and their power? Why, I wouldn't have a gleam of a chance. Poor fish—I'd be done! All the old fuss and swarm and clatter—funerals and birthdays, sentimental responsibilities—Thank God, I've seen it in time to save myself. Only just, though. I don't belong any more! I'm not a Rakonitz, not related. . . . I'm going to put myself out of danger, Toni!"

"There *is* no danger, oh, please, please, there's no danger. I'm not a bit like Grandmère; not a Rakonitz at all. My mother was English, Susan Lake, and Hannah Lake, and George Lake, my grandfather. I'm like them —I'm a Lake—I'm not like anybody. . . . You can't prove it—" Toni, poor little Toni, terrified, plunging at random. . . . A losing cause, now, that was too much even for her gallantry. Her own cause.

"Exactly like the Matriarch—let me go, Toni—I *will* go—d'you think it doesn't hurt like the very devil, when I love you . . ." —Danny was trampling on and through with it, more boisterously, more vehemently and wildly than ever, now, because it seemed as though he were deafening himself to a future reverberate with longing for Toni, and empty with need of Toni. . . . "But I can remember dozens of little things—Yes, and *you* get your 'good times' and your 'bad times,' too— you throw about money in your bad times, after you've saved it carefully. You suddenly get gay and optimistic —and you chuck up things—go to Paris—'The Count of Luxemburg' after your father died—you were willing enough to come away with me tomorrow, just now, leaving to chance the lease of the house, and starting in business on your own—"

"You tried to make me. Oh—beast, Danny, *beast*! To try and make me, and then hurl it at me for one of the things that prove it—"

"But you *would* have," he insisted. "You flicker so
—you're all over the place—'Toni mustn't be over-
excited' . . . and then for years you're calm and controlled again, and unselfish, and work hard, and get
everything in order; and people say what a wonderful
head you've got for so young a girl, and how you carry
everybody's burdens—And you do, too, in your 'good
times'—you . . . Matriarch!"

"But that's me—it's me—not Grandmère!" sobbed the
girl, bewildered, racked, yet still defiant. Oh, he might,
he might leave her alone now. Even if it were true—
and it was not true, too awful to be true. . . . Surely,
even then, she need not know it?

"Let me look at you, then—" Danny gripped her by
the shoulders, stared at her face—laughed—pushed her
away again—"It's all there—every line of it. The way
her eyebrows go, and the corners of her mouth, and that
long obstinate chin. Her voice and her walk and the
strength of her hair. . . . And I expect she was as—
bewitching, when she was young. I'm not going to be
bewitched back again into the family. They've had me
for nearly twenty years—"

"—They've *kept* you for twenty-five years." She tried
to push back again some of the blows he had dealt her,
so that they should hurt him.

"Kept me. Yes. I'm not grateful. Let me *go*,
Toni!" . . . but she had not touched him, lately. It was
he who suddenly took her in his arms again and kissed her
and kissed her, pressed her backwards with his hard
merciless kisses. . . . "I'm not—I'm not." "You are
and you can't get away from it—you can't throw away
your skin, and turn back your blood to flow another
way." "I'm not—I won't lose you, for the family. . . .
Danny!" "I hate the Matriarch. She's wicked. I
should hate you, however much I loved you. I should
stop loving you. I have stopped" . . . but his kisses
bruised her . . . quenched her and drowned her, his
closeness darkened the world. . . . Only his voice beat
through, saying things that were untrue—that were
devilishly true . . . things she would remember whenever

she started awake at night—" If you were not—the Matriarch . . ."

Defeated—but here was still a rag of pride that could be lifted as a banner : " If I *am* like her . . . if it's true. . . . .Very well—yes, it is true—I'm glad. I want to be. I'm Toni Rakonitz—" For if you have a name of your own, there are penalties. If you *have* a name of your own—Toni Rakonitz bit down her teeth upon her under-lip! she would not say this to Danny. . . . Anyone can be chivalrous to a fallen enemy, but perhaps it takes Toni Rakonitz, prone and beaten, to be chivalrous to a victorious enemy.

Exhausted, she did not try to hold him any more. He never stopped pounding her with words, with threats, with his own rage at losing her and his greater terror of being caught back. . . . His last kisses . . . like a shower of sparks, whirling away backwards. . . . He was gone now . . . would that tearing insistent bell never hush its clamour?—how long—how long had it been ringing?

IV

. . . . It had to be stopped, somehow. Toni walked quietly to the table, and took the receiver off its hook. Perhaps that was how dead people walked? . . .

" Hullo ! "

A loud whirring in her ear—then a babble of excited voices—one of them sounded like Maxine's—cut off in the middle of a sentence. The girl at the Exchange said "What number please?" . . . Then more whirring. "Are you 0341 Bedford West?" "Yes." "Trunk wants you—here you are." Then an angry discussion : "Look here, I'd just got through—don't cut me off." —"I was on to this number first—and it's important!" —Yes, that was Maxine. And utter complete silence. . .

" Hello? " repeated Toni, wearily.

" Hello, is that Miss Rakonitz? "

" Speaking."

It was a business acquaintance, and a great friend of Mr. Wolfe; apparently he was staying with the Wolfes

for the week-end at their country cottage. Mr. Wolfe
had spoken to him several times about Toni's desire to
start as a costumier, on her own. Toni had a considerable
reputation in the trade; she could sell her goods; she had
the "flair." Now, after final discussion, Mr. Caley was
prepared to put up the necessary capital, and had rung up
to tell her so.

"But, Mr. Caley, I can give you no guarantees, and
no security—"

"Your name's good enough. . . . Look here, we must
fix an appointment. Would Thursday—"

And then, sharply, mysteriously, he was cut off. Toni
waited, listening. . . .

"Is that you, Toni? I've been trying to get through for
ages. Some man was on the line. Look here—you've
got to come down at once and tell Grandmère . . ."
Maxine was agitated.

"Tell Grandmère?" —About Danny? Did they all
know, already, about Danny? Not that it mattered. . . .

"Val rang me up just now—she's all to bits . . . you
know how Val adored him! I must hurry and get down
there . . . the usual arrangements—it isn't as though
there were a man in the family—"

"There's Uncle Louis?" suggested Toni, mechani-
cally.

"Uncle Louis is dead. You must come over at once,
and tell Grandmère."

v

—The old Matriarch, and the new. Anastasia smiled
up at Toni, a very sweet welcoming smile. She was so
glad to see her. . . . "You are looking well," she
whispered. "That hat—the scarlet cock-feathers— Yes,
yes, it is chic—it suits you when you wear it pulled
forward like that."

She could not break the news that Louis was dead;
not for a few moments. . . .

"Grandmère, darling, I have something really nice to
tell you—I'm actually going to be able to start 'Toni's'

at last; a friend of Mr. Wolfe has promised to finance me . . ."

And he had said : " If you were not the Matriarch—" . . . No, no, that was Danny. Business and the City and the world of commerce had said : " Your name is good enough."

EPILOGUE.

WHEN Naomi Phillips first uncrumpled what she had found at the back of her mother's old toy-cupboard, she wondered what it could possibly be. A chart of buried treasure, perhaps? No—too much writing and too few islands about it. Naomi, aged eight, laid it flatly on the floor, and lay prone almost on top of it, puzzling it out . . . for she could not always be expected to play with her cousin Jimmy, even though he and Tom and Uncle Richard and Aunt Molly had come all the way from Exmoor to stay with them. Jimmy was only three.

"The Rakonitz Family Tree" was printed on top. That meant nothing. If it was a drawing of a tree— well, it was a very bad one. The names "Deb" and "Richard" on the far right of this torn and yellowing sheet of paper, first enlightened Naomi. It was— it was a sort of map of the family, and "most inter*ust*ing!" Why, Deb was her own mother. And . . . following backwards—here was Grandfather next to someone whom Naomi did not know; someone called Dorotéa with a little d. against it.

Queerly thrilled, now, by these branching intricacies, this strangeness that suddenly parted to reveal familiar names, Naomi began to explore. . . .

—*Two* Dorotéas.

And two more people with the same name, one on top and one further down : Ludovic. Were there any more? Yes—she pounced on Maximilian and Maxine. Not quite the same. Almost. She knew Aunt Maxine, of course . . . she was a sport! And along the same line, neither higher nor lower, were the Uncles : Uncle Gerald, Uncle Derek and Uncle Klaus. She and Betty always called them "The Uncles."

Two Klauses! Naomi chuckled—this was good fun,

like a game. And two Giselas. . . . *What* names ! They
only began to get easy like one's own name, ever so much
further down. Why did somebody called " Czelovar "
keep on happening, over and over again?

Naomi clambered up and clambered down, more fascinated every moment by her discoveries. Most of the
higher-up names, so clearly and finely printed by Truda
for Toni, long ago, were relations of whom Deb's little
daughter had never heard. But—suddenly she recognised her nice twinkling old Aunt Elsa, whom she knew
as well as anything, *miles* away from her mother; wedged
almost into the top line where the dates began to be
" historical." And Aunt Pearl, who seemed fairly young,
as young as most people, anyway, lived pretty near the
summit, too. Or was the tree standing on its head, with
the roots, the sturdy old roots, where Simon Rakonitz
had married · Babette Weinberg in 1806, a year after
Trafalgar? " What lots of children they had ! " Naomi
counted them. Ten. Ten brothers and sisters. She
would have liked a brother or two, herself.

" Anastasia m. Paul Rakonitz "—and, in a different
part of the paper, " Paul m. Anastasia Rakonitz." . . .
This, for some reason, amused Naomi. She began to
laugh. . . .

" What's the joke?" asked Richard Marcus, coming
into the nursery in search of his eldest son, who was
standing solemnly burrowing a hole in the plaster wall
with his feet. " By Jove ! that's a genealogical table, isn't
it? " looking over his niece's shoulder.

" No," replied Naomi. " It's the Rakonitz Family
Tree. Uncle Richard, why aren't Jimmy and Tom in it?"

He pulled a pencil from his pocket, wrote " m. Molly
Dunne " beside his own name. . . . " Jimmy " and
" Tom " were added, with a semi-humorous pride that
Richard would not for worlds have let anybody suspect.
Jolly nice kids, both of 'em. *English* kids.

" Tom's the youngest of the youngest of the youngest
of the youngest of the youngest, isn't he? . . . Oh ! "
Naomi suddenly grew very red. For now " Naomi,"
too had her place in the family tree. She could not

explain why she so much liked looking at this, and looking at it. . . .

"I think Betty would like to be in, too, if you don't mind, Uncle Richard. She's only four, of course, but I think she'll kick up trouble if she's left out. Betty has lots of character for her age."

Richard grunted. . . . He could not find, for a moment, the right place for Toni's daughter—

"Here—look, right on the other side. Under Aunt Toni, it would be, wouldn't it? *Ripping* Aunt Toni! . . . she's the most important and the favouritest of all."

So Toni was popular with the young generation? —"the most important"—yes, Richard supposed she was. "She's the Matriarch all over again, in a way!" —And Richard, whose wits moved slowly, thought he had made a discovery. . . .

"'Toni m. Maurice Goddard.' Offspring, three—so far: 'Babette. Paul. Antony.'"

. . . But a benevolent matriarchy. The children loved her much more, he believed, than he and his contemporaries had loved Anastasia, who had died when she was eighty-nine. . . .

"Uncle Richard, who's *this*, next to Aunt Iris?" Naomi's finger pointed to the name "Danny."

Richard's deep-set gaze considered the problem for a moment, half frowning . . . smiling a little, too. Then he drew a line heavily through "Danny," scoring it out.

"Oh! Why do you do that?"

"He ought never to have been there, my dear."

THE END.

The first Virago Modern Classic was published in London in 1978, launching a list dedicated to the celebration of women writers and to the rediscovery and reprinting of their works. While the series is called ''Modern Classics'' it is not true that these works of fiction are universally and equally considered ''great,'' although that is often the case. Published with new critical and biographical introductions, books appear in the series for different reasons: sometimes for their importance in literary history; sometimes because they illuminate particular aspects of women's lives, both personal and public. They may be classics of comedy or storytelling; their interest can be historical, feminist, political, or literary. In any case, in their variety and richness they promise to confuse forever the question of what women's fiction is about, while at the same time affirming a true female tradition in literature.

Initially, the Virago Modern Classics concentrated on English novels and short stories published in the early decades of the century. As the series has grown, it has broadened to include works of fiction from different centuries and from different countries, cultures, and literary traditions; there are books written by black women, by Catholic and Jewish women, by women of almost every English-speaking country, and there are several relevant novels by men.

Nearly 200 Virago Modern Classics will have been published in England by the end of 1985. During that same year, Penguin Books began to publish Virago Modern Classics in the United States, with the expectation of having some 40 titles from the series available by the end of 1986. Some of the earlier books in the series were published in the United States by The Dial Press.